J. P. Carter is the pseudonym of a bestselling author who has also written sixteen books under the names Ja~ ~~d James Raven. Before becoming a full-time writer, he spent a career in journalism as a newspaper reporter and television producer. He was, for a number of years, director of a major UK news division and co-owned a TV production company. He now splits his time between homes in Hampshire and Spain with his wife.

Also by J. P. Carter:

In Safe Hands (DCI Anna Tate book one)
At Your Door (DCI Anna Tate book two)

LITTLE
BOY
LOST

J. P. CARTER

Published by AVON
A division of HarperCollins*Publishers* Ltd
1 London Bridge Street
London SE1 9GF

www.harpercollins.co.uk

A Paperback Original 2020
1

First published in Great Britain by HarperCollins*Publishers* 2020

Copyright © J. P. Carter 2020

ISBN: 978-0-00-831333-3

Typeset in Minion Pro by Palimpsest Book Production Limited,
Falkirk, Stirlingshire
Printed and bound in UK by CPI Group (UK) Ltd, Croydon CR0 4YY

This one is dedicated to little Oliver Proctor, the latest addition to the family.

'The whole country has been shocked by the most appalling scenes of people looting, vandalising and thieving. It is criminality pure and simple. And there is absolutely no excuse for it. We will not put up with this in our country. We will not allow a culture of fear to exist on our streets. And we will do whatever it takes to restore law and order and to rebuild our communities.'

Prime Minister David Cameron speaking in Parliament during the London riots, which shook the capital in August 2011.

PROLOGUE

The tension was mounting in the back of the armed response van as it sped towards its destination.

Officer Barry Noble's mouth had gone dry and his heart was thumping against his ribcage. He didn't doubt that the other members of the seven-strong team were just as nervous as he was. But then they had every reason to be as they prepared to confront members of one of London's most notorious gangs. They were taking part in a series of coordinated pre-dawn raids across the capital, targeting a major drug-dealing network. More than a hundred officers were descending on fifteen addresses south of the River Thames, and Noble knew that they could never tell just how much resistance they'd encounter.

This was the second operation in just over a week that he had taken part in. The first raid, on a flat in Lewisham, had been hugely successful. No shots were fired and three significant arrests were made. The team also recovered a large haul of Class A drugs and an arsenal of weapons, including a sawn-off shotgun, two Beretta pistols and a Kalashnikov assault rifle.

This morning's target was a house in Balham that had been under surveillance for several days. An Afro-Caribbean man named Warren Fuller was renting it. He was one of the gang leaders responsible for the huge rise in violent crime across London during the past year, which included over a hundred and forty murders.

Officer Noble was all too familiar with the grim statistics. He was reminded of them every day at Scotland Yard briefings and when he read the papers or tuned in to TV news programmes. It was a sad state of affairs all right, and there was no sign of the situation ending any time soon.

As a Londoner it filled him with sadness. And as the father of two children it scared him shitless. The streets were no longer safe; youths as young as twelve were carrying knives and running drugs, and some inner-city council estates were fast becoming no-go areas.

'We're approaching the property,' the team leader announced suddenly. 'So brace yourselves and be ready to expect the unexpected.'

Noble felt an instant jolt of adrenalin. He sucked in a silent breath and tightened his grip on the assault rifle he was carrying.

Less than a minute later they turned into a quiet residential street that was lined on both sides with parked cars.

The van came to a stop in the middle of the road about thirty metres short of the mid-terrace Edwardian house, and three support vehicles pulled up behind it.

Warren Fuller and several other people were known to occupy the property. The surveillance team weren't sure exactly how many there were because a number of men and women had been seen coming and going. At least one had been identified as a guy who was wanted for questioning in connection with the murder of a rival gang member. For that reason the team had been warned to expect fierce resistance.

Noble and six other officers exited the van and with cool professionalism moved onto the pavement and jogged towards the house. The sun had yet to rise so their dark, padded vests and visored helmets were like shadows against the low walls and hedges.

There were no lights on in the house, which Officer Noble hoped meant that the occupants were still in bed and would therefore be less alert and responsive.

As they moved through the small front garden, Noble noticed it was paved over and held only a selection of wheelie bins. The team had been instructed to force open the front door with a battering ram and charge right in and, as he watched from the relatively safe distance of a few men back, he saw they wasted no time getting on with it.

Within seconds the door was off its hinges and they were piling inside. The three officers at the front moved along the narrow hallway to check the ground-floor rooms, while Noble and three others started up the stairs.

Noble was the first to reach the landing, and just as he did so a door to the right was wrenched open. A man wearing boxer shorts and a startled expression stood there. Noble recognised him instantly as Warren Fuller.

'Don't move,' Noble screamed as he pointed the rifle at him. 'Just stay there and put your hands behind your head.'

But Fuller ignored him and quickly stepped back into the darkened room, pushing the door shut behind him.

Noble rushed forward, twisted the door handle, and pushed it back open. As he entered the room, Fuller charged at him and grabbed the barrel of his assault rifle, which he tried to rip from his hands.

Noble's finger was poised on the trigger, and the sudden movement caused him to squeeze it unintentionally. The gun exploded and a split second later a cry rang out as the bullet claimed a victim.

But the victim wasn't Warren Fuller.

CHAPTER ONE

Three days later

The images on the television screen filled Detective Chief Inspector Anna Tate with a deep sense of despair. They showed police officers under attack, buildings and cars on fire, shops being looted, and other acts of mindless, wanton vandalism.

It would have been shocking enough if it had been happening in some far-flung, lawless country. But these appalling scenes were being captured by news cameras right here in her beloved London. What's more, most of the action was taking place south of the River Thames, where Anna lived and worked. When she turned down the volume on the TV she could hear the urgent chorus of sirens outside.

According to the news, the neighbourhoods worst hit were Brixton, Peckham, New Cross, Rotherhithe and Clapham, all within a short distance of her terraced house in Vauxhall. It was why she'd changed her plans and decided not to take her daughter out for dinner at the local McDonald's. Far too risky.

Civil unrest had descended on the capital three nights ago following a police raid on the home of a known drug dealer named Warren Fuller. During the raid his twenty-seven-year-old wife Grace was shot and killed by a firearms officer who claimed it was a tragic accident. She was in a bedroom with her husband when the officer entered. The gun apparently went off during a struggle between the two men, and Mrs Fuller, who was cowering in a corner, was hit in the chest, the shot killing her instantly.

Within hours of the news getting out there was a backlash, with Grace Fuller being described as the latest victim of brutal police tactics. Her family called for the officer who fired the shot to be charged with murder.

It didn't matter that she was the wife of a dangerous gang member. What mattered was that as well as being unarmed, she had also been four months pregnant with her first child.

The situation quickly spiralled out of control as people took to the streets to protest against what they were calling the murder of an innocent bystander. They were even claiming that the killing had been racially motivated because the victim was black.

Anna, who had spent the last month off work, had already contacted the office and offered to report for duty. She'd been told to stand by and wait for a call back.

Meanwhile, she had heeded the warnings to stay indoors and so had watched the drama unfold from the comfort of her living room sofa.

She had expected the riots to be short-lived, but instead they'd spread like wildfire and had become increasingly more violent. Disbelief had given way to anger as her city was being torn apart before her very eyes.

'We're now hearing that Scotland Yard is calling for re-inforcements from forces around the country,' the newsreader was saying over footage of a pitched battle between hooded rioters and police. 'So far two hundred arrests have been made and fifty people have been injured, including ten police officers. This afternoon the Prime Minister convened another meeting of the Government's emergency response committee to discuss the growing crisis, which is being likened to the riots that engulfed London in 2011.'

Anna was a detective inspector back then, and she could well remember how bad it was. The unrest lasted for five days and nights and spread to other parts of the country. Five people died and damage to property topped two hundred million pounds.

Those riots started after an undercover police officer shot dead a man of mixed race who was suspected of being armed and a threat. Since then the seeds of disorder had again been taking root, and what was happening now had been widely predicted. In fact, Anna had been surprised when she heard the Metropolitan Police Commissioner himself describe London as a powder keg. The comment came during a speech in which he criticised the latest round of spending cuts that were being imposed on the force at a time when the city was in the grip of an epidemic of knife and gun crime. In the previous year the number of murders in the capital had reached a ten-year high.

As a senior officer with the Major Investigation Team based in Wandsworth, Anna had seen first-hand how dangerous London had become in recent years.

It was due to a combination of factors – the sheer number of ruthless gangs, a growing sense of alienation felt by ethnic groups and those living in deprived areas, and a significant reduction in police numbers. Plus the skyrocketing cost of living that was pricing many Londoners out of their own city. A culture of grievance and blame had been allowed to take hold and now the city was suffering the consequences.

Anna's eyes remained anchored to the TV screen as she sipped lukewarm coffee from a mug. The newsreader had linked to live coverage from Brixton where a double decker bus was completely engulfed in flames. A reporter at the scene explained that the youths responsible had been chased off by police in riot gear, and went on to remind viewers that the district had also experienced mass rioting back in 1995, sparked by the death of a black man in police custody.

Next came pre-recorded footage of a supermarket being looted in Clapham. The looters were making so much noise that Anna almost didn't hear her phone ringing. She had to rush into the kitchen where she'd left it on the table.

The caller ID told her it was her boss, Detective Chief Superintendent Bill Nash.

'I've been expecting you to ring, guv,' she said. 'I'm surprised it's taken you so long.'

'Well I was hoping I wouldn't have to,' he replied. 'But as I'm sure you've seen for yourself, things have got much worse out there today and I'm afraid your compassionate leave is over. I want you back at work immediately.'

'Is it for general support or something specific?'

'Specific. We've got an unusual case, and I need someone on it I can trust to do a good job. It's like a war zone out there and we're stretched to breaking point.'

'So what is it?'

'Four hours ago rioters set fire to a derelict pub in Camberwell,' Nash said. 'The brigade were on the scene pretty quickly and put the blaze out before it destroyed the building.

But there was a fatality. A boy no older than ten or eleven was found inside and it seems he died from smoke inhalation.'

'Do we know who he is and what he was doing in a derelict boozer?' Anna asked.

After a beat, Nash said, 'He hasn't been identified yet, but we know why he couldn't escape the fire. He was chained to a wall in the cellar.'

CHAPTER TWO

Even after seventeen years on the force, Anna still found it hard to believe some of the things that people did to one another. The thought of a small boy dying while chained in a cellar like an animal caused the blood to stiffen in her veins.

'Forensics haven't yet processed the scene but it's believed he's been there since before the riots began,' Nash said. 'If so, then whoever put him there probably wouldn't have known the building was going to be set on fire.'

'Has anyone been dispatched to the scene?' Anna asked.

'DI Walker is there but I want you on this as senior investigating officer. And bear in mind that we've been drained of resources. Some of your team are helping out elsewhere and things are going from bad to worse so who knows how the hell we're going to cope . . .'

'Should I arrange for a squad car to pick me up?'

'No point. You'll need to make your own way. Virtually every vehicle in the Met is being deployed as we speak.'

'OK. What's the address of this pub?'

'I'll text it to you. It was known as The Falconer's Arms before it was abandoned four years ago.'

'I'll get there as soon as I can.'

'Thanks, Anna. There *is* something else you need to know. You're probably aware that the rioters have been targeting police cars, ambulances and fire appliances—'

'That really doesn't surprise me, guv. It's what they always do.'

'I know, but the homes of about half a dozen police officers have also come under attack. And some addresses are even being circulated on social media.'

'Jesus.'

'I'm telling you because I assume you won't want to leave your daughter alone in the house. Once it gets dark, we're expecting another night of complete mayhem as many more nutters take to the streets.'

Anna checked her watch. It was four-thirty p.m. Only a couple of hours of daylight left.

'I'll call Tom and get him to come over,' she said. 'I'm sure it won't be a problem.'

'Good. Sorry, I should have asked . . . how are things working out between you and Chloe? It's been a couple of weeks since we last spoke.'

'It's not been easy to be honest, especially for Chloe. She's still struggling to come to terms with what's happened. And who can blame her? She's been to hell and back.'

'But she's back where she belongs now, Anna. And you'll both get there in the end, of that I'm sure.'

A wedge of anxiety lodged in Anna's chest when she hung up the phone. She had spent every day of the past month with her daughter and she didn't feel ready to leave her now and return to work. But in the circumstances, she really had no choice.

It had been a tough four weeks for both of them, not least because they'd been the focus of frenzied media attention, which was understandable given the level of interest in their story.

Anna had reluctantly agreed to take part in several press conferences and to give interviews to a number of journalists. After all, the papers and TV news organisations had played a vital part in helping to reunite her with her daughter, and she felt indebted to them.

The story was still considered to be newsworthy even though there had already been blanket coverage. The latest edition of a popular magazine, which had been delivered that morning, carried one of the interviews Anna had given, and the feature was spread over no fewer than four pages.

But naturally Chloe had hated being thrust into the limelight, and not only because she was a mere twelve years old. Her life had been turned upside down and she was trying to deal with a tsunami of emotions from grief to the shock of learning that she wasn't the person she thought she was. For most of the time she suffered in silence, but the tears flowed whenever she was asked about her father and the woman named Sophie who had helped to raise her. The pain and sense of loss was there in her eyes for all to see, and it broke Anna's heart.

She had done her best to shield her daughter from the glare of publicity and to make her feel safe, comfortable and loved. But the poor girl had been so traumatised by events that it had proved to be a real challenge. It was only in the past week that Chloe had started to open up and engage with the mother she'd been told had died ten years ago.

Anna had been granted two months' compassionate leave and she'd been hopeful that by the end of it they would have formed a much-belated bond. But now she feared that these bloody riots might set them back and shove a dirty great spanner in the works.

CHAPTER THREE

As usual Chloe had spent most of the afternoon closeted in her room. It wasn't the room she had occupied when she'd last lived in the house – up until the age of two. Anna continued to use that room as her study, and the walls were still covered with photos taken before Chloe's father abducted her. Anna had wanted to leave it be so that Chloe could see that her real mother had never stopped thinking about her . . . Or given up searching for her.

This bedroom was a work in progress, and Chloe had yet to put her own stamp on it. Many of the belongings she'd brought from her previous home were still in boxes, including books and posters and some of her clothes.

The door was ajar so Anna knocked lightly and then eased it open and stepped inside. Chloe was sitting on her bed with her back against the wall. Her knees were up and her precious photo album was resting against them. Anna had laid eyes on the album for the first time a month ago, and it had been a moving experience. It was her daughter's link to the past, filled with ten years of memories that Anna hadn't shared with her. And for Anna it was a painful reminder of what she had missed. All those Christmases and birthdays that made a child's formative years such a joy. They were all there in the photos, but Anna found it hard to look at them without choking up.

'Are you all right, sweetheart?'

Chloe looked up and smiled. It was a half-hearted smile, but Anna was used to that. She knew her daughter needed more time to embrace her new life. Things could only get better.

Anna crossed the room and sat on the edge of the bed. The fact that Chloe no longer flinched when she got close was the clearest sign yet that they had made significant progress in the short time they'd had together.

'I'm afraid I have to go out to work,' Anna said. 'I know it's sooner than expected but it can't be helped.'

Chloe frowned. She seemed curious rather than alarmed. 'Is it because of all the rioting?' she asked.

Anna chose not to tell her about the boy in the cellar. It would only play on her mind and stir up painful memories of her own kidnap ordeal at the hands of a brutal villain.

'It's connected to the riots, yes,' she said. 'There's been a serious crime and they need me to take charge of the investigation. But I'm going to call Tom to get him to come and stay with you.'

'He doesn't need to. I'll be OK by myself.'

There was an edge to her voice, but there always was when the conversation turned to Anna's boyfriend, Tom Bannerman. Chloe had convinced herself he wasn't happy that she had entered their lives because it made it less likely that he would be allowed to move into the house in the near future.

For her part, Anna wasn't sure what to believe, although it was undoubtedly true that it had placed a strain on their relationship. Tom had only stayed overnight on two occasions during the past month and in that time they hadn't had sex or gone on a date.

'There's no way I'm leaving you here by yourself,' Anna said. 'A lot of bad things are going on out there and I want to be sure you're safe.'

Chloe responded with a shrug, so Anna reached out and placed a hand on her knee.

'I love you so much, sweetheart. You know that don't you?'

Chloe hesitated, and for a fleeting moment Anna thought she was going to say that she loved her back for the first time. But instead, Chloe nodded and said, 'I know you do, Mum.'

Anna was disappointed, but took comfort in the fact that at least her daughter was now calling her Mum. It was something Chloe had struggled with in the beginning. That was because the only mother she had ever really known had plunged to her death from a warehouse roof only four weeks ago.

'I'll get Tom to make you some dinner and I promise to come home as soon as I can,' Anna said.

As Chloe shifted her gaze back to the photo album, Anna's breath caught in her throat. She still found it hard to look at her daughter without feeling the swell of emotion. They'd been apart for so long and there had been times over the years when she thought she would never see Chloe again. There was still so much they didn't know about each other, so many unresolved issues.

One of those issues was that her daughter did not like to be called Chloe. After her father ran off with her, he changed her name to Alice. Alice Miller. She said she preferred that name, which was why Anna referred to her as sweetheart most of the time. She didn't want to make a big deal of it at this early stage because it was one less thing for her daughter to have to wrap her young mind around.

Anna knew she had to be patient. Indeed, the child counsellor appointed by social services had warned her that it would be a long, mentally challenging process. Not only was Chloe still shell-shocked from what had happened to her, she was also only weeks away from her thirteenth birthday, so hormones were flooding her developing body and she was facing a storm of social, physical and emotional pressures.

Not for the first time Anna found herself staring intently at Chloe's face, mesmerised by the button nose, dimpled chin and bright blue eyes. She had retained most of her baby features and it was amazing how accurate the age progression image of her had turned out to be. Anna had commissioned it on the tenth anniversary of her disappearance and it had been instrumental in bringing her home. The only difference was her hair, which her adoptive mother had recently allowed her to have cut short and dyed blonde.

'You're doing it again,' Chloe said, without moving her eyes from the album. 'I told you I don't like it when you stare at me.'

Anna laughed. 'I know and I'm sorry. I just can't get over the fact that I've got you back. And I'm terrified of losing you again.'

Chloe turned to face her. 'I don't want to lose you either,' she said. 'You're all I've got.'

Anna stood up quickly to stop herself crying. Tears came easily these days, usually triggered by something Chloe said or did, or just because she was finding it increasingly difficult to control her feelings.

'I'll go and ring Tom and then get ready,' she said. 'Is there anything you want?'

'No, thank you.'

Anna leaned over and kissed her daughter on the forehead.

'I'm going to take good care of you, sweetheart,' she said. 'You're my world now, and I promise I won't let any more harm come to you.'

As she stepped back out of the room, Chloe was still turning the pages of her album, no doubt reliving some of the memories it contained of the times she'd spent with her father and the woman who'd brought her up from the age of two.

CHAPTER FOUR

Tom was a social worker who always stayed in his office on Fridays to deal with the paperwork he had accumulated during the week. In the seventeen months they'd been dating he had often skived off early to meet Anna for a drink or to come to the house to cook her dinner, and she was pretty confident that she could rely on him to help her out even though it was such short notice.

'No problem,' he said after she explained the situation over the phone. 'I'll have to pop home first but I can probably be there in under an hour.'

His flat was just over a mile away in Nine Elms, so Anna could live with that. Tom was Mr Reliable, after all. She had never known him to let her down or disappoint her. It was one of the reasons she had fallen in love with him – he was the exact opposite of her ex-husband.

Matthew had been selfish, short-tempered, egotistical and controlling. Tom, on the other hand, was kind, calm and generous.

The pair were also miles apart physically. Tom was a six-foot hunky black man with tight curly hair and the most amazing come-to-bed eyes. At forty-seven he was four years older than she was.

Matthew had been five foot six and pale-skinned, with severely receding fair hair. If he hadn't been murdered three years ago he would now be forty-four.

'Are you sure Chloe won't mind me babysitting?' Tom asked. 'I always get the impression she doesn't like having me around.'

'It's your imagination, Tom. I've told you that. She's just finding it hard to relate to anyone right now, including me.'

'Well I hope you're right. For both our sakes I need her to like me.'

'I can assure you she does. We have to give her time to settle in to her new life. It's all so overwhelming for her. And scary.'

'I can appreciate that, Anna. And I have to say that I think she's coping really well, considering she's only twelve. She's a remarkable girl . . . You must be so proud of her.'

'I am. I only wish I could wave a magic wand and take away all the pain that's still eating her up inside.'

'You will,' Tom said. 'It's early days, and it's clear you're doing a good job. It's such a shame your compassionate leave is being cut short.'

Anna sighed. 'I know, but it can't be helped. It's really kicking off out there, and no way can I just sit back and watch it on the telly.'

She told him then what Nash had said about the homes of some police officers coming under attack.

'Well don't you worry about Chloe,' he said. 'If anyone comes to your house to cause trouble I'll make sure they regret it.'

Anna was comforted by his words, and as she started to get herself ready, she reflected once again on how lucky she was to have him in her life. But an unwelcome thought had crept into her mind: *Would he stick around?*

Even before Chloe came back into her life, Tom had begun to feel insecure. He had wanted to move in with her, but she had resisted, telling him, truthfully, that she wasn't ready. She was content with the arrangement they had because it gave her a degree of independence. It meant she'd been able to spend much of her spare time searching for clues to Chloe's whereabouts, mainly through social media appeals, the FindChloe Facebook page she'd set up, and interviews with newspapers and magazines.

She took the view that cohabiting would not only have made things more difficult, but that it wouldn't have been fair on Tom either.

However, in recent months she had begun to fear that unless she agreed to move their relationship forward, there was a chance Tom would get fed up waiting and end it. In fact she had almost reached the point where she was going to invite him to move in.

But as soon as she got Chloe back she knew she couldn't do it. At least not yet.

Her daughter took priority over everything else. Including the love of her life.

*

It didn't take Anna long to get ready. She kept the make-up to a minimum and changed into a black polo sweater and navy trousers. She dragged her long dark hair back into a ponytail and put on her three-quarter-length overcoat. October had arrived with a vengeance and she wanted to be prepared for what was almost certainly going to be a long, cold night.

She went back into the living room to pick up her shoulder bag, and caught the tail-end of an interview with Gary Trimble, London's Police Commissioner, who was appealing for calm.

'The death of Grace Fuller was an unfortunate accident,' he was saying. 'It in no way justifies this mindless criminality. I would urge those responsible to think what they're doing to this great city and to community relations.'

Anna was in no doubt that his words would fall on deaf ears. The blue touch-paper had been lit and the riots were not going to end any time soon.

She knew she had to try to view them as a distraction and to focus on the boy who had died in the pub cellar, but it wasn't going to be easy – that much was obvious.

She was on her way out the front door, having told Chloe that Tom was on his way over, when her phone rang. She smiled when she noted the caller ID: it was DI Max Walker, her most trusted wingman, who was already at the crime scene.

'Hello, guv,' he said. 'The boss told me he'd called you in. I'm sorry you're having to cut short your leave.'

'Can't be helped. I'm just leaving the house. Should be there within fifteen minutes, traffic and rioters permitting.'

'OK. I'm just ringing to let you know that we're pretty sure who the boy is.'

'That was quick.'

'Well it wasn't difficult because I recognised him from the photographs that were plastered all over the papers on

Tuesday morning. I reckon he'd still be front-page news if it wasn't for the riots.'

Anna felt a pang of dread. 'You're not talking about Jacob Rossi? Son of Mark Rossi?'

'I am.'

'Oh shit. I was hoping that story would have a happy bloody ending.'

CHAPTER FIVE

Anna checked with central control before setting off. Camberwell was only about two miles away, but she wanted advice on the safest route to take.

She felt a shiver grab hold of her spine when she was told that rioting had broken out around Vauxhall tube station and along South Lambeth Road, both within walking distance of the house.

She sent this information to Tom in a text and urged him to take care. He responded instantly:

I won't bother going home. Will go straight there xx

Anna let out a breath. She didn't want Chloe to be alone in the house for too long. That wouldn't be fair, or sensible bearing in mind what Nash had said.

Control's advice was to approach Camberwell from the north, but to nevertheless expect some trouble along the way.

She drove with the radio on and listened to continuous

news coverage. But at times it was a struggle to hear what was being said because of the urgent screams of police sirens and the roar of helicopters circling overhead.

The rush hour was already well underway and the roads were busy. It seemed incongruous to Anna that life carried on as normal in those parts of the city that hadn't so far been affected by the rioting.

The impression she got from the news was that some neighbourhoods were effectively lawless. There were reports of several buildings being razed to the ground in Peckham, police officers being attacked in Deptford, and a Sainsbury's supermarket being looted in Clapham. And a mob of masked youths was now gathering outside MIT headquarters in Wandsworth where Anna and her team were based. The unrest had also reignited racial tensions in the city with white and black gangs fighting each other, and a black shopkeeper had been beaten up in Lewisham in what was being described as a racist attack.

The more Anna heard the more her heart rate increased and her breathing deepened. Something in her gut told her that these riots were going to be more widespread and destructive than those of 2011. There weren't enough police officers to cope, and social media would almost certainly play a more effective role in fanning the flames of anarchy.

Only one death had so far been confirmed – the boy in the cellar. But Anna found it impossible to believe there wouldn't be more over the coming hours and days. The media hadn't yet been told about this first fatality, but the news would soon be out there, and Anna would have to do her best to hold back the details until the parents had been informed.

If DI Walker was right about the identity of the lad – and she had no reason to doubt him – then they would later be heading over to Bromley and the home of Mark Rossi and his wife. Anna had never met Rossi, but like millions of other people she knew quite a lot about him from his appearances on the television.

The man was a Celebrity with a capital C, one of the most popular and versatile TV presenters in the UK. He'd hosted game shows, a travel series and a number of one-off light entertainment programmes on various channels. His last screen appearance had been on Tuesday morning when Anna had watched him make an emotional appeal on BBC news for information on the whereabouts of his ten-year-old son, Jacob.

The boy had disappeared on the Monday while walking home from school. It was feared he'd been abducted because his mobile phone had been switched off and he had never given his parents cause for concern before.

Anna would have to talk to the team who were on the case to find out how far they'd got. But she strongly suspected that the investigation would have been hampered by the riots. After all, there was only so much the Met could cope with at any one time.

The closer Anna got to Camberwell the more uncomfortable the journey became. She saw groups of hooded youths who were clearly roaming around looking for trouble. Roads and pavements were littered with rocks, broken glass, shopping trolleys and wheelie bins, and she counted no less than four fire-damaged cars, one of which was still smouldering.

She got her first glimpse of actual rioting as she passed through Kennington. Traffic came to a sudden standstill because a building was ablaze up ahead, flames and smoke billowing into the sky.

Two squad cars were blocking the road and vehicles were being directed down a side street. As Anna followed the traffic she looked to her left and saw a mob clashing with police in front of the burning building. The officers, who looked to be greatly outnumbered, were using their shields to protect themselves against a barrage of missiles.

Anna got the impression that the rioters were relishing the thrill while at the same time showing a breathtaking sense of impunity. It was scary to think that such havoc was being unleashed all over the capital. On the radio they were now saying that it had spread across the river into East and North London. Shops were being ransacked in Tottenham, which was where the riots of 2011 began.

Anna suppressed a shudder and told herself that however bad it got on the streets she must not lose sight of the fact that she had been given a specific task: to find the bastard – or bastards – who had imprisoned a young boy in a derelict pub cellar where he met a cruel death.

CHAPTER SIX

Five minutes after her mother had left the house, Chloe was still lying on the bed looking through her photographs.

It was something she never got tired of doing. Some of the photos made her smile while others made her want to cry. As usual she flicked to her favourites, including the one that showed her taking her first paddle in the sea, and the one where she was sitting on her father's shoulders and pulling at his hair. She touched his face with her finger and a ball of sadness grew in her chest. Despite what he had done she still missed him. A part of her wished she had never found out the truth. At least the memories of her years in Spain would not have been so bittersweet.

As always it was like a trip down memory lane, each picture a precious moment from her previous life as Alice Miller.

She now knew that her father gave her that name when she was two years old. He changed his own name as well from Matthew to James so that when he ran away with her nobody would ever be able to find them.

She didn't discover the truth until just over a month ago. That was when everything changed and she learned that she wasn't – and never had been – the person she thought she was.

She had always believed what her dad had told her – that her biological mother had died of cancer shortly after her second birthday. But it was a lie that carried on for ten years. And now she had to live with that. To put the past behind her and move on. A new name. A new mum. A new home.

It was proving difficult, though, and there'd been times when she had wanted to run away from everything. From the pain, the memories, the lingering grief, the pressure to adapt to this new life.

There were so many questions, so much that she didn't know about her past, so much that scared her about the future.

For one thing she didn't want to have to go to a new school in a few weeks, but she didn't have any choice. She wanted to go back to the school in Shoreditch where she'd spent the past three years. Most of her friends were there, including Rhona, Charlotte and Sue. But her mum had told her it was on the other side of London so it would take too long to get there and back every day.

It wasn't her mum's fault. She knew that. Her mum only wanted what was best for her and she couldn't blame her for what had happened. Her dad should never have done what he did. It was wrong and cruel, and she wished that he was still alive so that she could tell him so.

His face stared up at her now from the album and she felt the swell of tears in her eyes. It was one of the many photos taken during those seven years they lived in Spain. He was standing in front of the bar he ran, squinting against the bright Spanish sunshine. Chloe knew it would have been Sophie who took the picture – she was always snapping shots on her phone and then had the best ones printed so that they could go into the album.

Chloe turned the page and there was Sophie, the woman who became her adoptive mother. Black hair; kind face; wide, familiar smile. This one was taken just over three years ago during the last day they all spent on the beach together. They'd had a picnic, swum in the sea, and played ball games.

It was a few days before Dad brought them to England, and just several weeks before he was killed.

Her mobile phone rang, jarring her out of her reverie. It came as no surprise to see that it was her mum. Who else could it be?

She wanted to check that Chloe was all right and to reassure her that Tom would soon be there.

'I'm still fine,' Chloe said off the back of an audible sigh. 'You've only been gone about ten minutes.'

'I know, but I'm almost where I need to be, and once I'm there it'll be more difficult for me to ring you.'

'There's no need to worry. I was just about to go downstairs and make myself a cup of tea.'

'Well I bought you a packet of your favourite chocolate biscuits. They're in the jar.'

'I know. I had some this morning.'

'Of course you did. I forgot. Well enjoy your evening and please be nice to Tom. He really does think the world of you.'

Chloe wasn't so sure about that. Tom seemed nice enough, but she sensed that he wished it was still just the pair of them.

Him and her mum. Two grown-ups without any kids around to spoil their fun.

She had overheard them speaking in the kitchen just a week after she came to live here. Her mum was telling him that he wouldn't be able to move in because she wanted her daughter to settle in first. He said he understood, but it had sounded to Chloe like he wasn't too happy about it.

She returned her attention to the album. The last photo on the last page. It was one of her at the age of nine. She was standing in front of the marina in Puerto de Mazarron and she was eating an ice cream.

Minutes after it was taken, the man she now had nightmares about turned up. After that nothing was ever the same again.

Chloe put the album back on the bedside table because she didn't want to upset herself if Tom was going to turn up at any minute.

She got off the bed, checked her reflection in the wardrobe mirror, and decided that she didn't need to change her clothes. She was wearing faded dungarees over a tight, red sweater, one of the outfits that she was convinced made her look a couple of years older than she was.

The noises outside were getting louder, and it wasn't just the sirens she could hear. There was shouting too now and it sounded close by.

She peered through the window. Her room was at the front of the house with a view of the road. She could see some of the neighbours huddled outside their homes talking amongst themselves – they all seemed to be looking up the street at something that Chloe couldn't see.

She wondered if the vandals who had been causing all the trouble across London had turned up here. She hoped not.

She'd seen them on the telly doing damage to shops and throwing things at the police who were trying to calm them down. It was truly frightening.

She gathered it was happening because a woman had been shot and this had made a lot of people very angry. But it didn't justify what they were doing. That was what her mum had said and she agreed. Innocent people were bound to get hurt and that wasn't fair.

She knew that she'd be safe so long as she stayed in the house. Even so she couldn't help feeling a bit nervous. She swallowed down the butterflies that rose in her tummy. She'd learned from bitter experience that if bad men were determined to get at you then it was hard to stop them.

She consoled herself with the thought that she wouldn't be alone much longer. Despite her reservations about Tom she knew he wouldn't let any harm come to her. Her mum would never forgive him.

Downstairs in the kitchen she put the kettle on. It was the first time she'd had the house to herself and it felt really strange. It still didn't feel like home and she wondered if it ever would.

When the kettle boiled, she poured the hot water over a tea bag and carried the mug into the living room. Her mum hadn't switched the TV off and on the screen there was a car on fire and lots of hooded men standing around it cheering.

But Chloe was more interested in the glossy magazine she spotted lying on the coffee table. It was one she hadn't seen before and she guessed it had been delivered with the shopping that morning.

There was a photo of her and her mum on the cover below a headline that read:

REUNITED AT LAST
THE FULL STORY BEHIND A MOTHER'S
TEN-YEAR NIGHTMARE

Chloe picked up the magazine and sat on the sofa to read it. Soon she was oblivious to the sounds out of the street that were growing louder by the minute.

CHAPTER SEVEN

By the time Anna reached Camberwell the neighbourhood was relatively quiet. The rioters had either moved on to other areas of South London or were lying in wait somewhere until darkness descended.

They had left a trail of destruction in their wake. Rows of shops had been damaged and looted, walls had been daubed with slogans, and bins had been emptied across roads and pavements.

Some people had begun to clean up while others stood around in groups looking shocked and bemused.

Anna was relieved to finally arrive at her destination – a street close to Camberwell bus station that was mostly residential.

Two police patrol cars and a forensics van were parked in front of the derelict building that used to be The Falconer's Arms pub. It was set back from the road with a large forecourt that was littered with ash and puddles left by the firefighters.

Three uniformed officers in hi-vis jackets were standing

beyond the crime scene tape that was stretched across the entrance.

Anna pulled up behind one of the patrol cars and climbed out of her Toyota. At once her nostrils were assaulted by the acrid smell of smoke and noxious fumes.

She paused on the pavement to look up at the building and assess the damage that had been done to it. The two-storey structure had clearly never been an architectural landmark. It was square and bland, with a painted brick facade and a pitched tiled roof that had been partly destroyed by the fire. The front double doors had been forced open, no doubt to allow the firefighters to get inside.

Anna was no stranger to Camberwell and she had a vague recollection of having visited the pub some years ago before it closed down. It was unlikely to have been a social visit, so she had probably come here on police business back when the area was a crime hot spot. It still was to some extent, with drug dealing a serious problem along with knife attacks. But in that respect it was no worse than most other parts of London.

She showed her warrant card to the uniforms and one of them went to get her a paper suit and shoe covers from the forensics van. As she slipped them on she was told that two detectives were already inside the pub along with crime scene investigators and the pathologist.

Anna ducked under the tape and trudged across the forecourt. As she approached the building, two figures wearing pale blue forensic suits stepped out through the doorway. She didn't recognise them until they removed their face masks and lowered their hoods. Detective Inspector Max Walker and Detective Constable Megan Sweeny.

'We saw you arrive, guv,' Walker said. 'Welcome back to duty. Did you have much trouble getting here?'

Anna shook her head. 'There was a pitched battle going on in Kennington, but I managed to avoid it.'

'You were lucky then. And so were we. Soon after we left headquarters a mob of rioters turned up outside and I just heard that it's getting nasty there.'

'Well I was expecting things to be a lot worse here,' Anna said.

A muscle flexed in Walker's jaw as he wiped a hand across the fine film of sweat that had gathered on his bald head.

'They've moved on to Peckham,' he said. 'A few hours ago it was pretty bad here apparently. A group of about a hundred crazies tore along Camberwell New Road and spread out into neighbouring streets to cause havoc. Some stopped off at this place and a petrol bomb was lobbed through an upstairs window. So far we haven't found any witnesses who saw who actually did it, and I'm not sure we're going to. It took only minutes for the fire to spread, but most of the damage was to the roof and first floor. The brigade was quick off the mark and got here before the whole lot collapsed into the cellar. By then the rioters had cleared off.'

'If it had there's a good chance the boy's body would never have been found,' Sweeny added.

Anna could tell from the pained look on the detective's face that she'd been affected by what she had encountered inside the building. But having joined MIT just over three months ago, at the age of thirty-five, Sweeny still sometimes struggled to cope with the harsh realities of the job. Anna was the first to admit that it did take some getting used to.

'I gather the pathologist is here already,' she said.

Walker nodded. 'It's Gayle Western. She arrived about half an hour ago. She's already made arrangements for the body to be removed after you've seen it in situ.'

'Then let's get to it. Are you sure it's Jacob Rossi?'

'One hundred per cent. He's wearing the school uniform Jacob had on when he disappeared on Monday. And there's a name tag sewn into the inside of his blazer.'

DC Sweeny stayed outside so that she could make some calls, and Walker led the way into the building, warning Anna to tread carefully because it was structurally unsafe. 'Just so you know we've had to ignore the advice from the fire brigade, which was not to come in here until they've carried out a full risk assessment,' Walker said. 'They've got so much on their plate with the riots that it could be days or even weeks before they get around to it.'

'We'll just have to do what has to be done as quickly as we can,' Anna said.

The interior was a total mess, with wet, charred rubble everywhere. Part of the ceiling had collapsed and above it light shone through the damaged roof, revealing clouds of ash and smoke swirling in the air.

Walker stopped in the middle of what would have been one of the pub's bars. He pointed to a crime scene investigator who was examining an open door at the rear of the building that hadn't been touched by the fire.

'There are two doors and five ground-floor windows that look out onto a small car park round the back,' he said. 'They're all still intact because the fire didn't reach them. So we're able to see that the lock on one of the doors is broken and the boarding has been removed from two of the windows, along with the glass. It's my guess that whoever brought the boy here gained access through one of them.'

'So why wasn't the building more secure?' Anna asked.

Walker shrugged. 'That's a question for the estate agents who've got a for-sale sign out front. They're bound to say that they thought they'd done enough to keep people out. But you and I both know that vandals and homeless people are breaking into derelict buildings all over London every day.'

'That's true,' Anna said. 'So where is the cellar?'

'We're standing on top of it.' Walker gestured towards an interior door to their left that stood open. 'That leads to the stairs. It was closed when the brigade entered the building after they'd put the blaze out. But there's extensive damage to the floorboards next to it and the cellar was filled with smoke. The fire officers who went down there reckon it was so thick they didn't spot the boy's body until one of them almost tripped over it.'

Anna could feel the blood pounding in her ears as she followed Walker down the rickety stairs into the cellar. It was much larger than she'd expected it to be, stretching almost the entire length of the building. There was no electricity, but natural light came from above through the damaged ceiling.

A lead weight formed in Anna's chest as she took in the scene. At one end of the room the parts of the ceiling that had come down were piled up on the soaked floor. There were no windows and the bare brick walls were festooned with fixtures that had once been attached to beer kegs.

Four forensic officers were present, and one of them was the pathologist, Gayle Western. She was crouched down next to a grey, inflatable mattress on which lay the body of the dead boy.

Anna experienced a cold shiver as she stepped forward and confronted a scene that she knew would haunt her forever.

CHAPTER EIGHT

Chloe loved reading, so she had no problem wading through the magazine article that ran to four whole pages.

It mostly repeated what had already appeared in newspapers and on the television during the past month. But there were more details and more photographs. She found it odd the way the writer kept switching between the names Alice and Chloe, and she wondered if readers would find it confusing.

The photos were all in colour and each of them provoked a different reaction. There was only one that she hadn't seen before and it was of Sophie on her wedding day. The man she married was standing next to her with a wide grin on his face.

Bruno Perez looked very different back then. He was slim, handsome and smartly dressed in a grey suit with a yellow flower in one lapel. Nothing like the brutal monster who Chloe saw for the first time eleven years later when he turned up at her father's bar in Spain.

He was the man they were running from when they fled to England, the man who went on to murder her dad and then force Sophie to take her own life. The man her mother and everyone else described as a violent psychopath.

Chloe's eyes settled on another photo and this one caused the breath to freeze in her throat. It was of a tall, ugly building and below it were the words:

It was from the roof of this warehouse in Deptford, South London, that Sophie Cameron and her estranged husband, Bruno Perez, fell to their deaths as Detective Anna Tate and her daughter Chloe looked on.

Four weeks had passed since that night, but to Chloe it still seemed like only yesterday. Every time she closed her eyes, she recalled every horrific second of what happened on that roof as well as the events that led up to it.

It began that morning when she and Sophie were getting ready to go on holiday to Spain, the first time they'd been back there since leaving three years ago.

Chloe didn't know at the time that Sophie planned for them to stay and never to return, fearing that Bruno had found out where they lived in Shoreditch and was planning to do them harm.

After Chloe had packed her suitcase, she pleaded with Sophie to let her go and see one of her friends who lived close by, just a brief visit before they were due to leave for the airport. Against her better judgement, Sophie allowed her to go. But it proved to be a costly mistake because Perez was waiting outside in a van.

He snatched Chloe off the street and then phoned Sophie to tell her what he'd done. Chloe was in the room when he made the call and she could still hear his violent words, as though it had happened only hours ago:

'You should know that before I arrived at your place today my intention was to abduct you and then make you wish you had never been born. But catching hold of Alice allows me to take your punishment to a whole new level and to make sure your suffering is not short-lived . . . Alice will be my guest for a couple of days and I'm going to have some fun with her. I even plan to share her with a couple of the guys who work for me . . . I'll send you photos and maybe even a video.'

Perez then threatened to kill Chloe if Sophie went to the police. Sophie knew she couldn't take the risk so she did the next best thing – which was to enlist the help of the woman she had only just discovered was Chloe's real mother – Detective Anna Tate.

Before describing what happened next, the article took readers back ten years to when it all began, and Chloe read it with tears streaming down her cheeks . . .

Anna had only recently divorced her husband Matthew following an affair he had. They shared custody of two-year-old Chloe, although the girl resided with her mother.

Matthew started begging Anna to take him back and when she refused he abducted their daughter after sending Anna a note that read:

You won't let us be a family again because I made a stupid mistake. So I'm starting my life afresh with my lovely daughter . . . Don't bother trying to find us because you never will.

41

Matthew acquired fake passports in the names of James and Alice Miller and moved to Spain where within weeks he met an English ex-pat named Sophie Cameron, who was working in a restaurant. He told her he was a widower and that his wife, Alice's mother, had died of cancer.

But Sophie also lied to him by saying that she was single when in fact she was married to a man who was in prison for a vicious assault on another man. His name was Bruno Perez.

Sophie and the man she knew as James fell in love and spent the next seven years together, during which they did not find out the truth about each other.

Sophie acted as Alice's adoptive mother even though she and James never married. The three of them were a happy family in all but name.

Then three years ago Bruno Perez was released from prison and the life they'd created for themselves came to an abrupt end.

Perez, who was part of a crime family operating in Spain and the UK, set out to punish Sophie because she had refused to provide him with an alibi that would have kept him out of prison. Instead, she saw his conviction as a way to escape an abusive relationship at the hands of a violent control freak.

With the help of his family and various contacts inside the Spanish police, Perez tracked Sophie down to Puerto de Mazarron on Spain's Costa Calida, where she, James and Alice were living. He turned up there and made threats against Sophie, forcing her to confess to James that she hadn't been honest about her past.

James forgave her and they decided it would be too

dangerous to stay in Spain, so they fled to England and rented a house in Southampton.

However, Perez traced them again after only a few weeks. James was returning home from the town centre when he spotted Perez following him. He decided to confront the man, but first he phoned Sophie and told her to flee the house with Alice and wait for him to call her.

But he never did call because he was stabbed to death in a park. Sophie chose not to tell the police that Perez was the killer because she knew they would never be able to prove it. She also didn't want to take the chance of losing Alice after the authorities discovered that Sophie wasn't her real mother.

So she moved with Alice to London, rented a flat in Shoreditch, and worked as a cleaner for three years.

Meanwhile, Anna knew nothing about any of this until just over a month ago when she found out purely by chance that her ex-husband was dead and that their daughter was last seen three years earlier leaving a house in Southampton with a mystery woman . . .

Chloe paused to wipe the tears from her face with a tissue. Her heart started beating rapidly as though it was about to explode in her chest. She blew her nose into a fresh tissue and turned to the fourth and final page of the article.

The top half contained two photographs – one was of her as a two-year-old and the other was the age progression image that was supposed to show what she looked like now. Even Chloe had to admit that the forensic artist had done a good job. The resemblance was striking.

Underneath the photos the story continued:

It was a twist of fate that ended Detective Anna Tate's ten-year-long search for her daughter.

She was heading up the investigation into the abduction of nine children from a nursery school in South London and the murder of one of their teachers.

Anna appeared on television news bulletins and among those who saw her was a man named Paul Russell, who was dying of cancer in a hospice.

He got in touch with her just days before he passed away and told her that he used to be a master forger and he had produced the fake passports for Anna's ex-husband that enabled him to take their daughter to Spain. He also revealed that the pair had moved back to the UK three years ago. He knew because he had been approached to provide them with more fake documents.

Anna hired a private detective who picked up the thread and the mystery started to unravel. Police in Southampton confirmed that a man named James Miller had been murdered in a city centre park three years ago and that he'd been living with a child and a woman who disappeared after he was killed.

Anna then told this story to the Evening Standard newspaper, which ran it over two nights.

Sophie Cameron happened to read it, and that was when she discovered that the man she had known as James Miller had been living a lie and that his ex-wife was still alive.

A heartbroken Sophie realised that the net was closing in and made arrangements to flee the country with Chloe. But Bruno Perez suddenly appeared on the scene again and kidnapped the girl. He took her to one of the *warehouses owned by his family, and Anna's police colleagues traced him there.*

Before they could arrest him he took Chloe to the roof and held her hostage while demanding that Sophie come to him.

In an interview with this magazine, Anna described what happened – how Perez held on to Chloe and threatened to jump off with her unless Sophie took her place.

Chloe's adoptive mother agreed to do so without a moment's hesitation. She then told Chloe that Perez was the man who had murdered her father and that Detective Anna Tate was her birth mother.

Sophie Cameron then took matters into her own hands. Rather than wait for Perez to pull her over the edge, she pushed him backwards and they both plunged to their deaths.

Chloe broke down then and sobs racked her body as that awful scene was replayed in her head. Tears flowed and she felt the muscles knotting painfully in her stomach.

It was a full minute before she got a grip and managed to stop crying. She inhaled a deep breath and decided to go and clean herself up before Tom arrived.

But as she rose from the sofa a noise outside seized her attention.

She stepped over to the front window and pulled back the curtain. To her horror she saw a group of young men with their faces covered marching along the middle of the road. Some were punching the air with their fists while others were holding up placards. On one of them, Chloe saw the words: *Kill all cops.*

45

CHAPTER NINE

The boy was lying on his back on the inflatable mattress with his head resting on a single pillow. His eyes were closed, his mouth open, and his lips were red and badly cracked.

He was chained to the brick wall, his wrists shackled by a pair of leather manacles with mini padlocks attached.

There was no way he could have done anything to escape the fire since the chain was only about five feet long.

Gayle Western, the forensic pathologist, stood up and turned to Anna. She spoke through her forensic face mask, her voice tense and clipped.

'This is beyond barbaric,' she said. 'The poor lad didn't stand a chance.'

'How long has he been dead?' Anna asked.

'Only a matter of hours. And it seems obvious to me that death was due to smoke inhalation and carbon monoxide poisoning. Tell-tale signs include the colour of his skin and the state of his lips. During the post-mortem I expect to find damage to his upper airways and respiratory tract.'

The boy was wearing a blue shirt drenched in water, and grey trousers. Next to him on the floor was an uncovered quilt and a pair of black scuffed shoes, along with several empty plastic water bottles and food wrappings.

Walker drew Anna's attention to a small polyester holdall between the mattress and the wall.

'It's filled with sweets, sandwiches and various drinks,' he said. 'It suggests to me that whoever abducted him had planned to keep him here for a while.'

Walker then pointed to something else that Anna hadn't yet noticed. It was a portable camping toilet with a steel frame and a plastic seat over a disposable bag.

'Seems like his captor – or captors – thought of everything,' he said. 'The bag's half-filled with urine.'

'So if the boy has been here since Monday it must have been emptied on a fairly regular basis,' Anna said. 'It means that the perp or perps might have been caught on nearby CCTV cameras.'

Walker nodded. 'We've thought of that and I've already asked for a trawl to be carried out. But we shouldn't expect results soon. Most local uniforms are dealing with trouble elsewhere.'

'Of course they are,' Anna said.

'In any case, there aren't many cameras in the immediate area and some have been vandalised by the rioters.'

Surveillance cameras had proved enormously effective during the 2011 riots and were instrumental in bringing many offenders to justice. It stood to reason that they'd become prime targets during subsequent periods of civil unrest.

Anna knew that it was just one of a number of problems that would in all likelihood hinder her investigation. The sheer scale of what was happening on the streets would swamp the Met's resource structure, slow down communication lines, and make it difficult for officers to move freely, and safely, across the capital.

'The boy's blazer was hanging from a nail over there,' Walker said, with a flick of his head towards the opposite wall. 'It's already been bagged up. There were no personal belongings in the pockets, but his parents have said that he was carrying a mobile phone and a wallet when he went missing. There's no sign of them or his school rucksack.'

'Do we know what kind of wallet it is?'

'Just one of those folded Velcro types that kids like, and it had his name on it. He supposedly carried his front door key around in it along with loose change and some sweets.'

Anna stepped closer to the body and crouched down beside it. As she did so she felt tears push hard against her eyes. She had attended a great many ghastly crime scenes since joining the force, but this was one of the most unusual. An icy chill slid down her back as she took in the marks on his wrists where he'd try to free himself from the cuffs. The sight of his emaciated, tear-stained face caused the heat to rise in her chest.

A wave of fury rattled through her at the thought of how much the lad would have suffered. And not just when the smoke drifted down into the cellar and started robbing him of oxygen.

There seemed little doubt that he had been here since Monday when he disappeared, chained up for four days and nights and terrified beyond belief. The questions surged through Anna's mind.

Had he spent the nights in total darkness?

Had he been physically or sexually assaulted?

Was this the work of one evil monster or several?

What was the motive?

Was he a victim of human trafficking or had the intention been to seek a ransom from his parents?

Anna stood up and said to Gayle, 'Can you tell if he's sustained any injuries to his body?'

Gayle shook her head. 'His face and hands are unharmed as you can see. I've checked beneath his shirt and there are no cuts or bruises on his torso, but I haven't removed his trousers. I won't know for sure what he went through until he's in the lab.'

Anna dragged her eyes back to the boy and tried to bring to mind the photo of Jacob Rossi that she'd seen on the news. But when that failed, she took out her phone and googled his name. In the picture his family had shared with the media Jacob was in his school uniform and grinning at the camera. He had short, dark hair and a thin face with high cheekbones. It struck Anna that he was the image of his famous father.

'Before we break the news to his parents, I want to talk to whoever has been leading the investigation into his disappearance,' she said.

'It's a DI Joe Benning who's based over in Bromley,' Walker told her. 'Control have already been in touch with him and he's on his way here now.'

'Good. In the meantime, we mustn't allow the press to get wind of the fact that it's a small boy who died here.'

'One of the calls DC Sweeny is now making is to the media liaison department,' Walker said. 'She's briefing them on what we've found and asking them to ensure the fire brigade keep schtum.'

Anna asked Gayle how quickly she'd be able to perform the post-mortem.

Gayle shrugged. 'I really can't say for certain. Everything is up in the air because of the riots. I have no idea how many bodies we'll have on our hands by tomorrow morning. But I promise I will try and prioritise this one.'

Anna knew that she could depend on Gayle to do her best. The pair had worked cases together for some years, and had become firm friends as well as colleagues. They knew they could count on each other to pull out all the stops when it mattered.

Anna cast her eyes around the cellar and asked Walker how much more work the forensics team needed to carry out.

'Unfortunately most trace evidence will have been destroyed by the water,' he said. 'Everything down here is soaking wet, and they're concerned that the ceiling is unstable. So the aim is to haul stuff out as quickly as possible after the body has been removed.'

Anna nodded. 'Then we'd better leave them to it. We need to crack on and inform the parents. After that we have to try to pull together a team and I fear that's not going to be easy.'

Anna started towards the stairs just as another suited-up figure came hurrying down them. She saw at once that it was a man because he wasn't wearing a mask or hood.

He was somewhere in his forties with closely cropped brown hair and a pale, gaunt face that was tight with tension.

'DI Benning,' he announced to no one in particular as he held up his ID card. 'I got here as quickly as I could.'

Anna pulled down her mask and introduced herself, but instead of making eye contact with her, Benning stared beyond her at the boy's body.

'Please tell me that's not Jacob Rossi,' he said.

'I'm afraid there's almost no doubt it's him,' Anna said. 'It's our guess he's been here since he went missing on Monday.'

Benning got near enough to see for himself that it wasn't a mistake and his body went rigid.

'Oh my God this wasn't supposed to happen,' he said. 'I promised his parents that I would bring him home to them.'

Anna's heart went out to the detective, who was clearly devastated. He had obviously put everything into finding the boy and in doing so had no doubt got close enough to the family to feel their pain.

'His name tag is on his blazer, which has already been bagged up,' Anna said. 'But so far there's no sign of his phone or wallet.'

Benning shook his head. 'My gut was telling me all along that I'd find him alive.'

'And he still would be if a petrol bomb hadn't been hurled into the building.'

Benning turned away from the body and looked at Anna. Tears had welled up in his eyes and he spoke through gritted teeth.

'What the fuck am I going to say to his parents? I made them believe that there was hope.'

'You won't have to say anything to them,' Anna said. 'That will be my job. This is now an MIT investigation.'

Benning shook his head again. 'I need to stay with it, ma'am. I can't just step back. Not now. And I'm guessing that with things the way they are you're going to need all the help you can get.'

Anna nodded. 'You're absolutely right on that score, DI Benning. It makes sense for you to be part of the

51

team considering what you already know. I'll make a call and get it sorted. It shouldn't be a problem.'

'Thank you.'

Anna reached out and touched his arm. 'And rest assured that we'll do everything we can to find the bastard or bastards who put him here. As far as I'm concerned whoever was responsible might not have meant for him to die, but they still deserve to spend the rest of their lives behind bars.'

CHAPTER TEN

Chloe was now back upstairs at the bedroom window and her heart was in her mouth.

Youths wearing hoods and masks were still trooping past the house and she could see now that they were heading towards the council estate at the end of the road where a large mob was gathering. There was lots of shouting and chanting, and in the distance the sound of police sirens.

Not all the youths were on the move. Four of them were standing outside the house across the road where an elderly man was yelling at them over his fence because his wheelie bin had been pushed over and rubbish was strewn across the pavement.

Chloe couldn't hear what was being said, but she could tell that the youths were laughing at him and making abusive gestures with their fingers.

Suddenly one of them pushed open his gate and charged at him. The old man turned to rush back into his house but he wasn't quick enough. The youth, who was wearing a grey shell suit and a black scarf around the bottom half of his face, caught up with him before he reached his front door.

He grabbed hold of the old man's jumper, pulling him to the ground effortlessly, and kicked him several times in the chest and stomach before raising his arms like footballers do when they score a goal.

Chloe swallowed hard and fought the urge to be sick. Her whole body started to shake involuntarily.

She watched the youth walk back onto the pavement and high-five one of his mates, while the old man struggled to get up from the ground.

It was all too much for Chloe and she was about to turn away from the window when something else caught her eye. It was a car and it was pulling up at the kerb in front of the house. She recognised it immediately as Tom's white Honda and it sent a wave of relief flooding through her.

She hurried down the stairs and got to the front door just as the bell rang. Tom was standing there when she opened it, phone in hand and smartly dressed in dark trousers and a brown leather jacket over a white shirt and tie. He looked as relieved to see her as she was to see him.

As she stood to one side to let him in, he shook his head, and said, 'We're not staying here, Chloe. Get your shoes and coat on. I've just sent a text to your mum to tell her I'm taking you to my place.'

Chloe was shocked and a frown tugged her eyebrows together.

'It's too dangerous here,' Tom said by way of explanation. 'The area is filling up with rioters who are bound to cause a lot of damage. It's best I get you somewhere safe. It'll be dark soon and Christ only knows what it will be like then.'

Chloe had no problem with that. She was scared now. Terrified in fact.

Her black puffer jacket was hanging up in the hallway and her trainers were under the stairs. It took her less than thirty seconds to slip them on.

'Leave everything else,' Tom told her. 'We need to move.'

Tom took the keys from inside the door and locked up as they left the house.

He held Chloe's hand and pulled her along the short pathway towards his car. She had to trot to keep up and his grip was so tight it hurt.

'Don't be afraid,' he said. 'We'll soon be away from here.'

But Chloe was afraid, more so now that she was outside and able to see along both sides of the street. To her right smoke was rising above the heads of the crowd in front of the estate, which was about a hundred yards away. The shouting and screaming had got louder and she could also hear windows being smashed.

To her left more rioters were heading in their direction towards the flats, and some were pouring out of the grocery shop on the corner, grasping bags and boxes of goods that they had no doubt stolen.

To Chloe it was like a scene from one of those end-of-the world movies where society breaks down and there's no law and order. It just didn't make sense to her that so many people could behave so badly.

'In you get,' Tom said to her as he let go of her hand and wrenched open the front passenger door of his car. 'Quick as you can.'

Chloe felt numb with shock as she sat down and Tom slammed the door shut behind her. Her hands were shaking so much that she couldn't put the seat belt on. She was still fumbling with it as Tom got in behind the wheel.

But before he had even switched on the engine there was an almighty crash and the windscreen shattered into what looked to Chloe like a thousand pieces. Another crash followed and caused the glass to cave in, showering both of them with sharp fragments.

Chloe screamed and Tom swore out loud. In the same instant, Tom's door was jerked open and hands reached in to seize his right arm. He hadn't buckled his belt so there was nothing to stop him being pulled from the car.

Chloe carried on screaming and only realised that the door on her side had also been opened when she felt herself being dragged out.

'She's just a kid,' a male voice yelled. 'Leave her be and let's give the black cunt a kicking.'

Chloe was dropped onto the pavement where she landed on her right side with a painful thud. She'd stopped screaming, but now she was struggling to breathe as the terror took hold.

Tears impaired her vision, but that didn't stop her from bearing witness to what was happening. The car was now surrounded by a group of rioters and Tom was involved in a scuffle with three of them in the middle of the road. They surrounded him while throwing punches and insults.

Chloe scrambled to her feet and called out his name. He snapped his head towards her and shouted, 'Go back into the house, Chloe. Now.'

But as soon as the words were out of his mouth, the men closed in and started to pound him with their fists and boots.

Chloe couldn't just stand there and do nothing while the man her mother loved was badly beaten. So without thinking she ran into the road and screamed at them to leave him alone. But by then others had gathered round and were cheering the attackers on.

No one paid her any attention so she rushed right up to them and tried to pull them off Tom. Surely they wouldn't hurt a twelve-year-old girl, she told herself.

But she didn't get far before someone shoved her in the back and she fell face down on the ground. As she lay there her head spun and her senses were battered by all the noise and commotion. She managed after a few seconds to haul herself up but saw straight away that there was nothing she could do to help Tom. Through the chaos of bodies around her she watched as the three men who had beaten him picked him up. They threw him onto the bonnet of his own car and forced his legs through the broken windscreen. That was when Chloe saw that someone was in the driver's seat.

A moment later the car lurched forward and roared off down the road towards the estate, with Tom lying face down on the bonnet. Dozens of jubilant rioters followed.

Chloe stared after it, scarcely able to breathe, her mind paralysed by fear and dread. Her thoughts were in disarray and despair clawed at her insides.

She decided to ring her mum to tell her what was happening. But when she reached in her pocket, she discovered her phone wasn't there because she hadn't brought it with her. It was still in her bedroom.

She stood there frozen to the spot for what seemed like ages. Then her mind suddenly seized on what Tom had told her:

'Go back into the house, Chloe. Now.'

She forced herself to move and turned back towards the

house. But that was when she realised that she wouldn't be able to get back inside for two reasons.

The first was that Tom had put the keys into his pocket after locking up.

And the second was the fact that two men were standing in their tiny front garden. One was peeing up the wall while the other was daubing something on the front door with bright red spray paint.

As the dauber stepped back to admire his work, Chloe saw what he had written.

POLICE BITCH LIVES HERE

She couldn't think what else to do now other than to give in to the panic that was spiralling through her.

So she sucked in a breath to stifle the scream that was bursting to get out. Then she started to run, with absolutely no sense of where she was going.

CHAPTER ELEVEN

Presenter: *'This is the BBC news at six o'clock. Police are preparing for another night of extreme violence across London as the rioting continues. A number of buildings have been set on fire and shops and stores are being looted.*

'A police officer in Deptford has been rushed to hospital after a man he was trying to arrest attacked him. Since Tuesday a total of ten officers have been treated for injuries sustained during confrontations with rioters.

'The main trouble spots right now are Clapham, Peckham, Vauxhall and Tottenham, where mobs of youths are on the rampage. Clashes between rival gangs and different ethnic groups are also being reported. The Metropolitan Police Commissioner, Gary Trimble, has announced that officers are being drafted into London from other constabularies.'

Commissioner: *'The situation we're facing in the*

capital is a serious one, and I urge the public to steer clear of areas where violence has broken out.

'More than fifty people have been hurt so far and the number of arrests is into the hundreds. I want to impress on those taking part in the rioting that they will not escape justice.'

Presenter: 'But as the Commissioner was issuing that statement angry mobs were congregating outside several police stations in South London. Missiles have been thrown at windows and police patrol cars. I'll pass over to Brian Cohen for a detailed roundup of what's been happening . . .'

CHAPTER TWELVE

The first thing the detectives did when they stepped out of the building was to take off their forensic suits.

Anna then fished a pack of cigarettes from her pocket and offered them round. Walker took one but Benning said he wasn't a smoker and popped a mint in his mouth instead.

It was almost dark now and the temperature had dropped significantly. The street in front of the pub was quiet, but sirens continued to scream across the city.

Anna dragged on the fag and tried to push the image of the boy in the cellar out of her mind. But it was impossible.

She needed to focus on the mystery of why he'd been put there and by whom. Solving it presented a significant challenge, though, because the crime scene had been seriously contaminated, and it was becoming clear that she would be working with fewer people than usual.

'I was about to drop in on Jacob's parents and update them on progress – or rather the lack of it – when central control contacted me,' Benning said, his voice laden with emotion. 'All the way here I prayed that it wouldn't be him. I still can't believe it.'

'How have they been coping?' Anna asked.

'With difficulty, as I'm sure you can appreciate. Jacob is – or was – an only child. The couple doted on him.'

'Did they have any idea what might have happened to him?'

'None at all. He was a good kid by all accounts. He'd never been in trouble or gone missing before.'

Anna looked at her watch. It was after six already.

'I'll head to Bromley now to break the news,' she said. 'Any chance that you can come too so that you can brief me on the way?'

'Of course.' Benning pointed towards the road. 'I got a lift here from a colleague. She's waiting outside. We can go in her car or yours.'

'We'll go in mine. I don't want to leave it here.'

The three of them crossed the pub forecourt to the entrance where DC Sweeny was waiting. Beyond it a few of the neighbours had gathered to see what was going on, while another group had started cleaning up the debris on the street left by the rioters.

Anna introduced Benning to Sweeny and the DC told them what she'd been doing.

'I've talked to media liaison and they've agreed not to release details until we give the go-ahead,' she said. 'I've also contacted the estate agents who are responsible for the building. The manager, a Mr Bob Turner, said they sent someone to inspect it two weeks ago. The back doors were all locked and the windows boarded up apparently. They were due to revisit in another week. I've asked him to provide us with a list of all the people who have access to the place.'

'And who owns it?' Walker asked.

'A property developer bought it off the brewery eighteen months ago,' Sweeny said. 'But they haven't been able to shift it, partly because of problems with planning permission. It was last viewed by a potential buyer three months ago.'

'It's probably safe to assume that whoever abducted Jacob had already made plans to bring him here,' Anna said. 'They would have known the building was empty and must have come here before Monday to check it out. A pub cellar was the perfect place to hide him. I suspect he was warned not to make a noise, but even if he'd screamed and shouted I doubt very much that he would have been heard.'

'So the perp could be someone who lives or works around here,' Walker said. 'Someone who's familiar with the building and was able to slip in and out unnoticed. I reckon the inflatable mattress and provisions were placed in the cellar before the boy arrived.'

'That's why we need to secure CCTV footage and carry out a door-to-door,' Anna said. 'Surely something will turn up.'

She took out her phone to call DCS Nash so that she could arrange for DI Benning to be seconded to the investigation. As the screen lit up she saw that she had a text message from Tom, which had been sent about ten minutes ago.

FYI I've picked Chloe up and am taking her to my place. It's all kicking off in Vauxhall so I want to make sure that she's out of harm's way.

Anna immediately speed-dialled Tom's number, but when there was no answer, she tapped out a reply to his message.

Bless you, hon. I knew I could count on you to watch out for her. Keep her safe for me. We'll talk later.

'Is there a problem?' Walker asked her.

'Thankfully, no,' she said. 'Tom just let me know that because of the disturbances in Vauxhall he's taken my daughter to his flat in Nine Elms. It means I won't have to worry about her if I'm working through the night, which I assume I will be.'

Anna then phoned Nash and updated him. He agreed with her that it would be a good idea to keep Benning on board and said he would sort it.

The boss had already been told that the dead boy had been identified as the son of celebrity Mark Rossi and he pointed out, unnecessarily, that it would spark a media frenzy even if the riots continued to dominate the headlines.

'So what's the situation with my team?' she asked him. 'How many officers will be working with me on this?'

'You'll have to make do with just a handful to start with, Anna. You've got Walker and Sweeny, and at least four other detectives are still here at headquarters waiting for instructions, along with a few admin staff. The rest have been assigned elsewhere. We're currently dealing with a shooting in Lewisham, a stabbing in Bermondsey, a hostage situation in Mitcham, and lootings galore. Plus, we're trying to disperse a mob of about a hundred lunatics who are gathered in front of our building slagging off the police.'

'I've been told there's trouble in Vauxhall as well,' Anna said.

'That's correct. The Marwell Estate, which I know is close to where you live. There are clashes between black and white youths. Two rival gangs are using the riots as an excuse to tear into each other.'

The Marwell Estate had once been a smart and respectable place to live. But in recent years it had been tainted by drug dealing, prostitution and racial tensions.

Anna told Nash that she was now planning to go and see Jacob Rossi's parents at their home in Bromley.

'While I do that DI Walker and DC Sweeny will stay here in Camberwell and see what they can dig up from neighbours and CCTV,' she said. 'They'll also feed through some tasks to the lads back at base. I'll aim to get everyone together for a team briefing later.'

'What about forensics?' Nash asked.

'The team are in the building as we speak and the stuff they recover will be rushed back to the lab. But it's pretty messy down in the cellar so I'm not sure they'll come up with much that's useful.'

'And the boy's body?'

'Gayle Western is on hand and will arrange for it to be transported to the mortuary,' Anna said.

'Well at least you're on top of things. That's good.'

'Will you be hanging around, sir?'

'The Commissioner has just summoned me to a crisis meeting of senior officers at the Yard,' Nash said. 'But call me if you need to and be careful out there. We're all bracing ourselves for a hellish night.'

The others had heard what Anna said to Nash so there

was no need for her to repeat it. She told Walker and Sweeny to do the best they could.

'And before it gets dark can one of you take photos of the outside of the building and the surrounding properties?' she said. 'I haven't got time to look around so it will be useful to have some snaps for the evidence board.'

'Consider it done,' Walker said. 'We should also put this place under surveillance since those responsible for taking the boy might be planning to come back.'

Anna nodded. 'That's a good point, Max. After forensics have finished up it'll be deserted again. Can you sort that out as well? Someone sitting in a car or watching from one of those houses across the street should do the trick.'

Anna then turned to DI Benning, who was staring back at the pub with his jaw tightly clenched and his eyes intent under a jutting brow.

She could tell that he was in a state of complete shock, and she briefly considered telling him to go home. But she thought better of it, knowing she needed him to pass on everything he had learned about Jacob Rossi and his family since the boy's disappearance.

'It's time for you and me to go to Bromley,' she said, and her words seemed to snap the man out of his reverie. 'I don't want the news to leak before we've spoken to Jacob's mum and dad.'

CHAPTER THIRTEEN

Sheer terror compelled Chloe to keep on moving. She was walking now because she physically couldn't run any more; she'd already fallen over twice, her breath was coming in ragged gasps and there was a sharp burning sensation in her chest. At the same time her head was filled with strident voices that were screaming at her to do different things.

Find a police officer and tell him or her what has happened to Tom.

Knock on someone's door and get whoever answers to phone your mum.

Don't forget what you've been told so many times – which is never to stop and speak to a stranger in the street because they can't be trusted and they might hurt you.

And the streets were swarming with strangers, mostly angry young men who were making a lot of noise and causing a lot of damage.

She'd searched desperately for Tom as she'd walked past the estate where the crowd of faceless rioters were brawling with each other. But there had been no sign of him or his car.

It didn't mean that he wasn't still alive, she kept telling herself. They could have driven him down one of the side streets, or onto the estate itself. Or perhaps he'd regained consciousness and had managed to run away from the men who had taken him. Oh God, she hoped so.

The estate was behind her now and she was on a street lined on both sides with small shops. Some of them were being targeted by the rioters who were smashing windows and kicking at doors. A clothing store was on fire and a shop selling electrical goods was being looted. Burglar alarms were going off and there was smoke everywhere. The noise was deafening, and there were no police around to restore order.

Chloe wished she'd remembered her phone because she was lost without it. It meant she couldn't call her mum to ask her what she should do. As it was, she had no idea how to respond to what was happening. It was far worse than the nightmares she'd been having in which that horrible man, Bruno Perez, had risen from the dead so that he could kidnap her again. At least those weren't real and she always woke to find that she was safely tucked up in her bed.

But this wasn't a nightmare. It was real and she was scared and helpless and lost.

She didn't know her way around this part of London. Nothing was familiar to her and everything was strange and threatening. There were so many people, but no friendly faces amongst them, no one around who looked as if they might be able to help her. She was alone, confused, gripped by a raging panic that had seized control of her legs and was propelling her forward. But to where?

She had no idea where she was going. She needed someone

to tell her, someone to grasp her by the hand and assure her that everything was going to be all right before leading her to a place of safety.

She needed her mum.

The flashing blue lights of a police car appeared as if out of nowhere, stopping Chloe dead in her tracks.

The vehicle screeched to a halt in the middle of the road junction that was just up ahead. The sight of it lifted her spirits, but only for a fraction of a second because that was how long it took for the rioters to turn their attention to it.

The police car was bombarded with missiles, including bottles that smashed against the shiny bodywork. It started to back up but collided with a van that had stopped behind it.

As the rioters rushed forward, two police officers leapt out of the car and sprinted towards what looked like a small park beyond the shops.

Chloe decided that her best option was to follow them, but as she stepped off the kerb into the road she failed to check if it was safe to do so.

It wasn't.

A motorcyclist tore past at that very moment and she heard him scream at her to get out of the way. At the same time there was a loud squeal of tyres on the tarmac as the rider swerved dramatically in a bid to avoid hitting her. But Chloe didn't react quickly enough.

The nearside saddlebag struck the side of her body and the impact sent her flying back onto the pavement.

Her head struck the concrete first and an explosion of pain pulsed through her entire body.

It was the last thing she was aware of before a huge black hole opened up and she was sucked into it.

CHAPTER FOURTEEN

On a normal day the eight-mile journey from Camberwell to Bromley would have been fairly straightforward, even in rush hour. But this day was anything but normal and the riots were causing traffic chaos.

Diversions were in place, main roads blocked, and warnings were being issued over the radio to avoid certain areas.

Anna and Benning got stuck in a jam on Denmark Hill within minutes of leaving the crime scene.

'This shit has been brewing for ages,' Benning said. 'We should have been prepared for it. There were enough bloody warning signs. The gangs, the stabbings, the growing contempt for the law among young people. But no. The powers-that-be thought it would be a good idea to cut police numbers and take a softy softly approach to criminals. Utter madness.'

They were the first words he'd spoken to her since getting into the car, having been on the phone to his superior officer. Anna couldn't help but agree with him. It was hard to believe that the capital, and indeed the whole country, had been so ill-prepared for public unrest on this scale, given what had been happening in other parts of Europe, including France with the costly Yellow Vest protests.

'It's already obvious that these riots are much worse than those of 2011,' he said. 'And they're still gathering momentum. Last night they were more widespread and violent than the night before, and I guarantee that tonight will be even worse.'

Anna's thoughts turned to Chloe and she wondered how she and Tom were getting on. Her daughter had never been to Tom's flat so the whole experience of being taken there for her own safety must surely have unsettled her.

But Anna was confident that Chloe was being well looked after, and she was so grateful to her boyfriend for seizing control of the situation. Not having to worry about Chloe meant she could concentrate on the job in hand. A job that was going to be difficult, demanding and emotionally challenging.

'We can't allow the riots to sidetrack us, DI Benning,' Anna said. 'We have to focus on the case. So I'd like you to start telling me what you've unearthed during your missing person's investigation.'

Anna took her eyes off the road for a second to look at him. Sweat beaded his top lip and she could tell that the guilt would be eating away at his insides. He'd had four days and nights to find Jacob Rossi and he'd failed, even though the boy had been alive the whole time. That was a lot for any detective to handle.

'You can't blame yourself for what's happened,' she told him. 'You did your best. But as we now know this is an unusual case. Not a run-of-the-mill abduction. There's something more than a little strange about it.'

He nodded. 'That's what the skipper just said. But it doesn't make me feel any better. And the rest of the team are going to be just as devastated when they find out.'

'How many officers have you had working on it?'

'Well on Monday night and Tuesday there were twenty of us, including uniforms and the liaison officer assigned to the family. But then it fell back to five on Wednesday because of the riots. It's been a struggle since then.'

Anna felt a chill flush through her body. It was awful to think that the rioting that had resulted in Jacob Rossi's death had also had such a serious impact on the investigation into his abduction.

'So start from the beginning,' Anna said. 'I was on leave until a couple of hours ago so all I know about the case is what I saw on the news. And that includes the appeal made by Jacob's father.'

'OK,' Benning said, and Anna felt his eyes on her. 'But let me say at the outset that I'm aware of your own personal story, ma'am, as is everyone else in the Met. So I know that you can appreciate more than most what the boy's parents have been going through, and that will be a great help.'

Anna bit down on the inside of her cheek and felt her stomach tighten.

'That's true up to a point,' she said. 'But I was lucky in that I eventually got my daughter back. The Rossis will never see their son again.'

Benning explained that Mark Rossi made the 999 call to report his son missing at six p.m. on Monday. It was passed on to Bromley CID and prompted an immediate response.

'I was the only one in the office at the time so the case fell to me,' Benning said. 'I believe the boy was abducted shortly after he left his school – the local private prep school – to walk

72

home at about three-thirty. At three-fifty his mobile phone stopped transmitting a signal. There was a delay in raising the alarm because both his parents were out when he was due to arrive home, and they only realised something was wrong when they discovered he wasn't there and that his phone was switched off. They spoke to the school and several of his friends and there was nothing to suggest he hadn't headed straight home.'

'Did he usually walk home alone?' Anna asked.

Benning nodded. 'Since he turned ten a few months ago. His parents are now cursing themselves for letting him.'

Anna was well aware that there was no legal age for when a child could walk to and from school alone. In fact she'd read somewhere that ten was the average age at which most British parents felt it safe for their offspring to do so.

'And how often did the boy let himself into the house?' she said.

'A couple of times a week apparently. His dad works all kinds of hours on his programmes and his mum is a solicitor who's based in the town centre. The school is only half a mile from their house so it didn't take Jacob long to walk there and back, but only during daylight. He wasn't allowed to do it in the dark – then, he would either be picked up by one of his parents or get a lift from a friend's mum or dad. Unfortunately the route he usually took includes a short stretch with fields on one side and woods on the other. And the whole area is a bit of a CCTV black spot, so vehicles can pass through it without being picked up at either end. Consequently, we had no joy with vehicle identification.'

'So the abductor was probably aware of the situation with cameras.'

'That's the assumption. It comes back to the whole thing

being carefully planned from the snatch to the choice of the pub cellar as a sort of holding cell. We're looking for someone who put a great deal of thought into this.'

'And you've found nothing to suggest what the motive could be?'

He shrugged. 'There are the obvious conclusions to draw. He was the victim of a sexual predator or a psycho who wanted to kill him. Or it was someone who intended to ask for a ransom from his well-off family. But so far there's been no contact or demand.'

'It could also be someone who has a serious grudge against the parents and wants them to suffer.'

'That occurred to me too. Mark Rossi might well be a popular TV entertainer with the viewing public, but the nature of his job as an entertainer means that there are plenty of people out there who aren't so fond of him. He's the target of a fair amount of online abuse. Plus, he's made a few enemies of people who used to work with him at a production company that went bust.'

'That sounds interesting.'

'It was run by his stepfather, Isaac Rossi, and employed twelve permanent staff. Most of them have struggled to find work since while Mark Rossi's career has continued to blossom.'

'Have you talked to them?'

'Only one of them. He's a former producer named Gavin Pope, who lives in Richmond. He recently confronted Rossi in front of everyone at a TV industry event and accused him of not doing enough to help his former colleagues.'

'Is he in the frame?'

Benning shrugged. 'He claims he knows nothing about the abduction but doesn't have a cast-iron alibi. He says he spent all Monday afternoon at home by himself and was joined in the evening by his wife.'

'Is he the only suspect?'

'There's one other,' Benning said. 'A bloke named Neville Quinlan who was seen hanging around outside the school three days before the abduction. He's on the sex offenders' register having abused two boys some years ago. He lives a few streets away from the school but he claims he was out walking on Monday afternoon and didn't go past the school. He reckons he can't recall which route he took, which sounds dodgy to say the least.'

'We'll need to interview both of them again,' Anna said.

'That goes without saying.'

Anna sucked on her lower lip in concentration for a few beats, her mind racing with questions. 'Well it's clear we have two strands to this investigation and two perpetrators. The first is the kidnapping and whoever carried it out. The second is the fire and whoever started it.'

She paused there to listen to a newsflash on the radio. There were two breaking stories relating to the riots.

A security guard had been stabbed while confronting a gang of youths who were looting a store in Brixton. And three children under ten were in hospital with serious burns after flames tore through a parade of shops in Lewisham, trapping families in the flats above.

'It's not even seven o'clock yet,' Anna said. 'I hate to think what the death and injury toll will be before this night is over.'

The thought made her catch her breath and it continued to play on her mind as they headed towards Bromley to deliver the news that no parent should ever have to hear to Mr and Mrs Rossi.

CHAPTER FIFTEEN

In her dream, Chloe was reliving one of the saddest occasions of her young life – the funeral two weeks ago of her adoptive mother, Sophie Cameron.

It had been the first time Chloe had gone inside a crematorium and it all proved too much for her. Half way through the short service she became so tearful that Anna had to take her outside.

It was her own fault for insisting on going despite the advice of the child counsellor who had told her it would be best if she stayed away.

But she'd had to go because she'd needed to say goodbye to the woman who had nurtured her from the age of two.

The woman who had changed her nappies and potty-trained her.

The woman who had picked her up at the end of her first day at school.

The woman who had taught her how to read.

The woman who had made the ultimate sacrifice in order to save her life by jumping from the roof of that warehouse.

In the crematorium garden Anna held her in her arms and tried to console her. It felt strange but comforting.

Eventually she stopped crying and when the service was over the only other two people who had attended joined them – Sophie's closest friend Lisa, and Jane, the sister Sophie hadn't seen in years.

They both spoke fondly of Sophie and said how much she had loved Chloe. And they both made a point of saying that Chloe should be thankful that her birth mother, Anna, had never given up searching for her.

There were more tears when Sophie's ashes were scattered over one of the flower beds in the garden. And Chloe was awestruck when the clouds above parted suddenly and a shaft of sunlight spread warmth over her adoptive mother's remains.

*

A noise wrenched her back to consciousness. One moment she was surrounded by the serenity of the crematorium garden, the next her senses were being pummelled by a harsh mix of thunderous sounds.

When she opened her eyes, she was staring up at a face she didn't recognise. It belonged to a young black woman wearing a hooded parka and a thick woollen scarf around her neck.

The woman was leaning over her, and when she saw that Chloe was awake, she smiled and turned her head towards someone who was standing to one side of her.

'Christ almighty, I thought she was dead,' the woman shouted. 'But she's alive.'

'Well now you know she's all right we should get going,' replied a male voice.

'But we can't leave her here. She's just a kid.'

'Makes no difference. She's not our problem. We need to stick with the others. If we don't, we'll end up like her or get ourselves arrested.'

The woman turned back to Chloe and said, 'Where are your parents, love?'

Chloe opened her mouth to speak, but the words stuck in her throat and she started to sob instead.

The woman stroked her cheek with a gloved hand and leaned closer to make herself heard above the racket around them.

'I would call for an ambulance but it'd be a waste of time because it won't turn up,' she said. 'I can phone your mum and dad for you, though. Have you got their number?'

Chloe shook her head, but it was so painful it made her cry out.

'You've got a nasty bump on your forehead,' the woman told her. 'I saw what happened with the motorbike so I reckon you're lucky you weren't more seriously hurt. The bastard rode off without stopping.'

Chloe took a deep breath and managed to find her voice, which was weak and barely discernible even to her own ears.

'How long have I been . . .'

'Only about a minute. We were close by when it happened. I came straight over.'

'I'm lost and I don't know where my mum is,' Chloe said.

'You poor thing. What's your name?'

'Alice.'

'Well mine is—'

Before she could finish the sentence the man who was with the woman suddenly grabbed her arm and pulled her roughly to her feet.

'Stop pissing about, babe,' he snapped. 'You either come with me now or I'm leaving you here.'

The woman looked down at Chloe with a pitying expression on her face, and said, 'You'll be OK. Just get to your feet and move away from this street to a safer place. Then find someone who can help you. I would if I could, but I have to go. I'm really sorry. Good luck, Alice. And take care of yourself.'

The woman disappeared, leaving Chloe lying on the pavement, her lungs clutching for air, her head spinning.

She made herself ignore the pain in her head and struggled to get up. As she did so her muscles burned with the effort and tears streamed down her cheeks.

As soon as she was on her feet, she felt giddy and sick, and her eyes drifted in and out of focus. But once she regained her equilibrium, she was able to start to take in what was going on around her.

And it was enough to cause the fear to swell up inside her like a big inflated balloon.

There seemed to be even more angry people on the street, and many of them were standing around the abandoned police car that was now on fire. Others were smashing their way into shops to steal things and anyone who tried to stop them was being threatened or attacked.

Chloe felt invisible because nobody was paying her any attention. They were all too busy running riot to even notice her. Or if they did see her, they didn't care that she was so obviously in desperate need of help.

It meant she would have to look after herself, first by getting away from the violence and then by trying to contact her mum.

As she started walking again, she realised that lights were coming on because it was getting dark. It made her heart pound even faster and ignited a fire in her belly. She was sure now that she was going to die out here. What was happening was more scary than any story she had ever heard and any film she had ever seen. And it was just as frightening as that day when she left the flat and Bruno Perez grabbed her and pulled her into his van.

She passed a man who was smashing the windows of a bus shelter. Then two other men who were openly brandishing long, lethal-looking knives.

Further on she came across a homeless man lying in a doorway, his face and blanket splattered with blood.

Then a woman rushed past her pushing a shopping trolley with a large TV in it.

Chloe did not see any more police – it was as though the area had been left to the mercy of the rioters. She'd seen the violence on the television over the past couple of days, but it hadn't seemed so bad then. She'd been detached from it. Watching from a distance. Secure in the knowledge that it was happening to other people and not to her. But now she was caught up in it and she was petrified beyond belief.

She came to a corner where looters were ransacking a convenience store. Through the broken windows she saw young men and women feverishly clearing the shelves.

The street to the right looked to be deserted, but it led nowhere. There was a large open car park on one side of the road and several low, windowless buildings on the other. They looked similar to the factories that were situated close to the flat she used to share with Sophie in Shoreditch. At the far end of the street was a high wall in front of a partially demolished building.

Chloe turned into the street without hesitation and headed for the car park, which was empty and had very little lighting. She thought it would be a fairly safe place to hide while she worked out what to do next.

But before entering the car park, she glanced back over her shoulder – and was just in time to spot something that caused her heart to lurch in her chest. Two men wearing hooded jackets were now standing on the pavement outside the convenience store on the corner.

As Chloe watched, one of them lifted a finger and pointed directly at her. She saw his lips move, but wasn't close enough to make out what he was saying. But her stomach flipped when she saw his companion break out in a slow, leering grin.

CHAPTER SIXTEEN

It turned out to be a relatively uneventful journey to Bromley for Anna and DI Benning. They drove south through Dulwich, Forest Hill and Beckenham. Thankfully the riots hadn't yet spread to those areas. But traffic remained heavy and it took them close on an hour to get there.

Benning had phoned ahead to let the family liaison officer know that they were coming. He told her only that they had an update, not that Jacob's body had been found.

Mark and Clare Rossi lived in a large detached house close to a park. They'd moved in only ten months ago, which was when Jacob had been enrolled in the private prep school nearby.

Anna felt weighed down by dread as she drew the car to a halt on the driveway. No matter how many times she delivered news of a loved one's death, it never got any easier.

The FLO answered the door to them. She was a tall, thin woman and she introduced herself to Anna as Phillipa Moore.

'Jacob's parents are waiting for you in the living room,' she said. 'You should know that they're fearing the worst because I haven't been able to tell them what you've got to say.'

'Well it's not good news, I'm afraid,' Anna said.

Moore nodded. 'That's what I thought.'

On the inside the house was modern and spacious, with light-coloured walls and carpets. One of the first things to catch Anna's eye was a framed photo of Jacob on a table in the hallway. He was wearing a football kit and giving a thumbs-up to the camera.

His parents were sitting next to each other on a long white sofa in the living room. They were facing a wall-mounted TV that had been muted while tuned to a news programme showing footage of the riots. Another white sofa was positioned at an angle to it and behind that patio doors provided access to the rear garden.

Mark Rossi stood up as Anna and Benning entered the room. He was wearing an open-necked shirt and jeans, and his face was pale and unshaven. He seemed a shadow of the man she had seen so many times on the television. Anna knew he was in his mid-forties but he looked much older here in front of her, which was understandable in the circumstances.

He switched his gaze between the two detectives and panic flashed across his features.

'So what's happened?' he said, anxiety rattling in his voice. 'Have you got news about Jacob?'

'Can I suggest that you sit back down, Mr Rossi, and I'll explain everything?' Anna said. 'I'm Detective Chief Inspector Tate and I'm now leading this investigation.'

Rossi opened his mouth to reply but his wife beat him to it.

'Does it mean you've found our boy?' she said, her voice wavering with emotion. 'Is that it?'

Mrs Rossi spoke while remaining seated, her back ramrod stiff, her hands tightly balled together in her lap.

She was a slight woman about the same age as her husband, with short curly blonde hair and a narrow face. Her eyes were glassy with shock and exhaustion, and Anna wondered how much sleep, if any, she'd had since Monday night.

After an awkward pause, Anna cleared her throat and bit down on her bottom lip. There was no easy way to say what she needed to say so she decided just to come right out with it.

'I'm really sorry to have to tell you both that your son is no longer alive. His body was found a few hours ago. We got here as quickly as we could to inform you.'

Clare let out a shrill cry of anguish and dropped her face into her hands. Her husband screwed up his face and said, 'Are you sure it's him? Please tell me it could be a mistake.'

Anna shook her head. 'You'll be asked to make a formal identification, Mr Rossi, but I can assure you that it isn't a mistake. If there was any doubt I would tell you. The boy who's been found is definitely your son. A blazer with his name in it was near to his body.'

Rossi started crying then, great wet sobs racking his body. He dropped back onto the sofa and put an arm around his wife.

Their suffering was palpable, and Anna knew it would intensify after she told them how and where Jacob had died.

The FLO hurriedly left the room, saying she was going to put the kettle on, and Anna was certain she saw tears in the woman's eyes.

It didn't surprise her, though, because she felt like crying herself, and if she'd been alone she probably would have.

Instead, she sat down on the other sofa and Benning sat next to her. His breath sounded laboured suddenly and his hands shook. It was as though the guilt he felt had reared up to consume him. Anna had seen it before with other detectives who believed they had badly let down victims of crime. One thing they all had in common was that they always found it hard, or in some cases impossible, to forgive themselves.

It took Rossi almost a full minute to regain control of his emotions. As his wife continued to sob into her hands, he wiped his tears with his sleeve and looked at Anna. Red veins laced the whites of his eyes and the lines across his forehead were more pronounced.

'We need to know what happened,' he said. 'Was Jacob in an accident? Did someone hurt him?'

An image of their son chained up by his wrists in the cellar resurfaced in Anna's mind, sending an icy flush through her veins.

She swallowed back the lump in her throat, and said, 'It saddens me to have to tell you this, Mr Rossi, but your son died this afternoon from smoke inhalation while trapped inside a derelict building that was set on fire by rioters. Whoever was responsible for the fire almost certainly wouldn't have known he was inside.'

Clare Rossi's head shot up and the shock was evident in her expression.

'Are you saying that our son was alive all this time?' she sobbed.

Anna nodded. 'He was indeed, Mrs Rossi.'

The woman turned her gaze on Benning and her features hardened.

'So why the hell didn't you find him? You told us that you would. You promised.'

'There's a reason that DI Benning's team were unable to locate Jacob,' Anna said. 'The person or persons who abducted your son went to great lengths to ensure he wouldn't be found.'

Clare frowned. 'What do you mean? Where has he been since Monday?'

There were times when Anna wished she hadn't followed in her late father's footsteps and become a copper. And this was one of them.

She pushed back her shoulders, drew in a breath, and said, 'The building Jacob was found in is in Camberwell and it used to be a pub. It's been derelict for some years. It appears that Jacob was taken straight there after he was abducted on his way home from school. And he remained there until today. If it wasn't for the riots he would probably still be alive.'

'But who would do such a thing?' Rossi said. 'And why didn't anyone know he was there? Surely someone would have seen or heard him crying out.'

'We have no idea at this stage why he was taken there,' Anna told them. 'However, we do know why nobody came across him and why he couldn't escape. But you really need to brace yourselves for what I'm about to . . .'

'Oh, just get on with it, Detective,' Rossi cut in. 'I'm sure there's nothing else you can say that will make us feel any worse than we do already.'

Anna knew that he was wrong on that score, but she also knew that they had a right to know the full story. And better they heard it from her before it was in the public domain.

She left it a beat and then spoke in a low, sympathetic voice. 'I'm afraid your son was being held in the pub cellar. And he was chained to a wall. When the building went up in flames the smoke deprived him of oxygen. His body was discovered by fire officers after they put the blaze out and went into the building.'

The couple reacted in different ways to the gruesome revelation. Rossi lifted his head, squeezed his eyes shut, and screamed something unintelligible at the ceiling.

But his wife made not the slightest sound as her eyes rolled upwards in their sockets and she slumped forward onto the floor where she promptly passed out.

CHAPTER SEVENTEEN

The car park was enclosed by a brick wall about six feet high. There was a strip of grass with trees and bushes in front of it, and this was beyond the reach of what little lighting there was.

Chloe was hiding behind one of the bushes that lay directly opposite the entrance, which also served as the exit. It was from there that she was watching through the branches as the two men in hooded coats stood talking to each other beneath one of the lampposts.

Instinct told her they were up to no good. Why else would they have followed her onto an empty car park?

She'd had a bad feeling about the pair since spotting them outside the convenience store on the corner. It was creepy the way one of them had pointed at her, which had prompted the other one to grin.

They were close enough for her to see their faces. Both were white, and one of them had a beard. She always found it hard to judge a person's age, but she reckoned they were at least twice as old as she was, which put them in their twenties.

The one with the beard was tall, with wide shoulders. His mate was shorter and fatter, and wearing glasses.

Chloe's bottom lip quivered as the fear spiralled through her. Just because she was only twelve it didn't mean she was naïve. She knew how easy it was for a girl to fall prey to rapists and perverts. It was something her friends at school had talked about a lot and there were always horrible stories on the news and the internet.

She'd already had her own close shave with Bruno Perez, who had threatened to harm her. But it turned out that he'd never actually intended to and had kidnapped her only to get to Sophie. Chloe feared that if these two men got their hands on her she wouldn't be so lucky.

She could see them looking around, peering into the shadows while exchanging words. Suddenly the tall one pulled down his hood, cupped his hands around his mouth, and shouted, 'There's no need to be scared, little lady. We saw you come in here so we're worried that you might be lost and all this violence is freaking you out. Let us help you. Come out from wherever you're hiding and we'll make sure you get home safely.'

There was a moment, just a moment, when she was tempted to believe him. It would have been so easy to do so. But one thing she had learned in the past few months was never to trust anybody, not even those closest to you.

The problem was she was trapped. To get out of the car park she would have to break cover and run towards the road. And there was a good chance they would catch her.

It was also highly likely they would spot her if she stayed

put. The bushes and trees were spread out and not very thick. If she moved, even a short distance, she'd be sure to draw their attention.

She knew that screaming for help would be a waste of time. Nobody except the two men would hear her. There was so much noise still: burglar alarms were going off in nearby streets, sirens were blaring, dogs were barking, and it seemed as though thousands of people were yelling at the same time.

Silent tears drained from her eyes and acid burned in her stomach. The swelling on her forehead was throbbing so much it was forcing her eyes into narrow slits. She felt as though some invisible being had grabbed hold of her body and was shaking it.

As warm liquid ran down her legs, Chloe realised she'd wet herself. It seemed like her bladder was shedding gallons of pee. She had never lost control like that before and it served to heighten her sense of helplessness.

She started mouthing a silent prayer, begging God to come to her rescue. But it was cut short when the bearded man shouted again, and this time the tone of his voice was nasty rather than nice.

'Listen to me, little lady. We're only trying to help so we don't appreciate being fucked around. If you don't want our help then come out from behind whichever tree or bush you're hiding behind and tell us. Otherwise you're really gonna piss us off and that won't be good for you.'

So she'd been right to trust her instincts. These men did not have good intentions. While other people were taking advantage of the riots to steal things and cause damage, these two wanted to seize the opportunity to commit a different type of crime, with her as the victim.

The icy fear was now flooding her entire body and making her flesh tingle. She held her breath and closed her eyes as she pleaded again for God's help. She felt desperation crashing over her like waves and struggled to control her thoughts. When she opened her eyes again, she was shocked to see that the car park was now empty. And there was no sign of her two stalkers.

Chloe couldn't believe it. God had answered her prayers, and while her eyes were closed had made the men go away. It was nothing short of a miracle.

She breathed a huge sigh of relief and slowly stood up behind the bush to get a better view of the car park.

The pair were nowhere to be seen. They must have dashed out through the exit and were probably already stalking another victim.

Her thoughts turned to what she should do now. It no longer seemed like such a good idea to stay hidden behind the bush. She was a safe distance from the violence all right, but she couldn't be sure that the two men wouldn't come back. Plus, the cold was already penetrating her body, and if she didn't keep moving it would soon become unbearable.

She looked out beyond the car park. The road was empty, but in the distance she could see flames reaching into the sky from a burning building. And there was no let-up in the level of noise. The sound of sirens persisted and she could hear what she took to be the thumping of a helicopter flying above the city.

She made up her mind to leave the car park and go in search of someone who could help her, preferably a police officer who'd be able to contact her mum either by phone or police radio.

She wondered if her mum was even aware that she wasn't at Tom's house, and that Tom had been beaten up and might well be dead. Or did she think they were both safe because what took place outside the house hadn't been reported to the police?

The vision of how Tom was bundled onto the bonnet of his car and driven away raged in Chloe's mind. It wouldn't have happened if he hadn't come over to take care of her. For that reason she felt partly responsible, and also guilty for having harboured negative feelings about him during the past month. She told herself she would be nice to him from now on, assuming they both got through this.

She put thoughts of Tom and her mum on hold and stepped out from behind the bush. She felt physically weak and drained of energy, but she wasn't going to let that stop her moving as quickly as she could, and she broke into a sprint across the car park.

But just as she was approaching the road, the two men appeared again. They burst out from behind trees on either side of the exit and came running towards her.

Chloe stopped dead and screamed, her body going stiff with shock.

The pair were on her before she could get away. The tall one caught her left wrist and pulled her roughly towards him, then wrapped an arm around her chest. She tried to scream but he pressed a hand over her mouth.

'Don't bother to struggle you stupid little bitch,' he snarled. 'You're going nowhere.'

The other man, the shorter one, stood in front of her and shook his head.

'I'm surprised you fell for our little ruse,' he said. 'Did you actually believe we were going to pass up the chance to have some fun with a horny little mite like you?'

His lips curled into a thin smile, and Chloe saw that one of his front teeth was missing.

'How fucking old are you, anyway?' he said.

The other man removed his hand from her mouth and she told them that she was twelve in the hope that they would think she was too young to harm. But the man in front of her licked his lips and his grin widened.

'It's our lucky night then,' he said. 'You must be a virgin so it'll be a first for both of us. And a first for you too when we take you back into the bushes and you get to feel our cocks inside you.'

Chloe tried to break free but the man holding her tightened his grip and she found she couldn't move. Her heart drummed frantically and her knees started to shake.

As they began to drag her over towards the trees, she carried on screaming. And they didn't bother to stop her because they knew that no one could hear.

But Chloe was determined to put up a fight as long as she was able to and managed to yank her arm free of the shorter man's grip. Then she threw herself onto the ground, causing the taller man to stumble and almost fall on top of her. She rolled onto her side, expecting to be wrenched back onto her feet.

But instead something extraordinary happened. The sky appeared to open up and a bright shaft of light poured down on her.

'It's a copper chopper,' the bearded man yelled. 'I don't fucking believe it.'

Chloe did not need his words to be translated. It was a police helicopter directly above them, probably the same one she'd heard hovering nearby. And all three of them were caught in the beam of its powerful searchlight.

It was so bright that Chloe had to cover her eyes as she heard someone say something through a loudspeaker. She couldn't make out the words, but they prompted her two attackers to lose interest in her immediately and run away as though their lives depended on it.

Chloe thought the helicopter would follow them, but instead it moved away from her and started to descend towards the ground on the far side of the car park.

Her heart leapt into her mouth because she knew that it meant she was about to be rescued. God hadn't abandoned her, after all. She didn't believe for one second that it was through sheer luck that the helicopter crew had spotted her being attacked. God must have made sure they would fly over the car park so the wicked men would be scared off.

She started to walk towards it while waving her arms so the crew would see her. But she stopped after taking only a few steps when she saw that the helicopter had started going back up again.

The reason became clear when Chloe heard voices behind her. She spun round to see a large mob of rioters pouring onto the car park. Some were already throwing objects at the helicopter even though they were too far away to reach it. The closer they got the further the helicopter rose into the sky, and as it did Chloe's hopes of being rescued faded.

Soon the car park was filled with a crowd of people jostling and jeering and sounding really pleased with themselves.

Once again Chloe found herself in the middle of the madness. And despite the fact she was obviously the only child there, nobody seemed to notice her.

CHAPTER EIGHTEEN

Clare Rossi had been unconscious for barely thirty seconds. She was now back on the sofa, sobbing into a handkerchief as she struggled to control her anguish.

Her husband wanted to call a doctor, but she was adamant that she didn't need one.

'I fainted, Mark,' she said. 'I don't need a doctor to tell me why. It was because I'd just learned that my darling little boy is lost to me forever. He died while chained to a wall underneath a fucking derelict pub.'

Anna gave an involuntary shudder and fought to keep her own emotions in check. The couple's suffering must have been off the scale since Monday when Jacob went missing, but at least they'd had a smidgen of hope to cling to. It was hope that had kept Anna going during her ten-year search for Chloe. Without it she would not have wanted to go on living.

So she could appreciate the sheer intensity of the pain they were now feeling. And how the news she had just delivered was going to tear into shreds any plans they might have made for the future.

'I want to see our boy,' Rossi said, with tears gleaming in his eyes.

Anna took a breath and held it for a couple of seconds before speaking. 'I completely understand,' she said. 'I'll make arrangements for that to happen before the post-mortem takes place, which I'm hoping will be tomorrow.'

Anna felt a dull beat thudding in her chest. She invariably found it difficult to ask and answer questions at times like this. There was always the risk of coming across as detached or insensitive, which was a sure way to alienate the victim's next of kin.

At least in this case DI Benning's team would already have obtained much of the information she needed. Information such as the names of Jacob's closest friends, whether or not he'd had a presence on social media, and other details about his life up to this point. But there were a number of specific questions that now arose in the wake of the strange circumstances surrounding his death.

'You need to know that whoever abducted Jacob went to some effort to make him comfortable in the cellar,' Anna said. 'An inflatable mattress and blanket were provided for him, and he was given food and drink. He even had access to a portable loo. It raises the question as to why he was kept alive in that cellar for so long.'

Rossi's eyes narrowed. 'There's been a lot of speculation that he might have been taken by child sex traffickers, or by a paedophile who was going to . . .'

Instead of completing the sentence, he pressed his lips tightly together and shook his head. He simply couldn't go there.

'I can tell you that it doesn't appear as though Jacob suffered any physical harm before the fire,' Anna said. 'He was fully clothed when he was found and no cuts or bruises were visible on his body.'

'So can you say for certain that he wasn't abused while he was in the cellar?' Rossi asked, his voice high and trembling.

Anna chose not to respond directly to the question for obvious reasons, and instead said, 'I know that DI Benning will have discussed with you the possible motives behind your son's abduction. But in view of this tragic development we'll have to give it more consideration. One of the most challenging aspects of this case is going to be determining whether the person responsible is known to you, assuming for now that there's just one perpetrator.

'You see, one of the lines of inquiry we're considering is that Jacob was taken in order to punish you for a perceived wrongdoing, in which case it could be that he would have been released at some point. So I need to ask you a question that I know you've already been asked. Can either of you think of anyone who might have done this? Someone you've upset, or even someone who's made threats against you for whatever reason? And not just in the recent past. People can hold grudges for years before something provokes them into committing an act of revenge.'

Rossi said that he had been threatened and abused online by anonymous trolls and Benning confirmed that his team were still going through his social media history, including his Twitter, Facebook and Instagram accounts.

'The only person to have threatened me to my face is a former colleague named Gavin Pope,' he said. 'I've given the detective here his details. It happened about eight weeks ago when he approached me at a television awards dinner. He was drunk and he called me a bastard in front of my wife and our table guests. Then he told me that he and others who felt like he did would one day get their own back.'

'What was your reaction?'

'I just told him to leave me alone and eventually the security guards ushered him out of the venue. But, look, I can't in all honesty believe he would go so far as to kidnap our son to get his own back. He never struck me as a psycho . . . just someone who is angry, jealous and mixed up.'

'And I gather this relates to your stepfather's TV production business that folded several years ago.'

'That's correct. It went under just before my stepfather died and there was no money in the pot to meet redundancy payments and pensions so the staff were not happy. Several of them, including Pope, resented the fact that my career went from strength to strength afterwards while they struggled to find work in the industry. And Pope claimed I should have done more to help them. I know for a fact that he wound the others up. Two years ago they demanded that I take responsibility for my stepfather's debts and when I refused they threatened legal action. Nothing came of it, though, and since then Pope is the only one who hasn't let it drop. I've had nasty calls and emails from him, and on one occasion he turned up here to accuse me of blackening his name in the TV industry, which wasn't true.'

'And is there anyone else you believe we should talk to?' Anna said.

It was his wife who answered, directing her words at Benning.

'We asked you two days ago about the man who was seen outside Jacob's school,' she said. 'It's rumoured that he's a convicted sex offender. You assured us he would be spoken to.'

'And he was, Mrs Rossi,' Benning said. 'He told us he was nowhere near the school on Monday.'

'And you believe him?'

'At this stage there's no evidence to suggest he's lying to us.'

From then on the couple struggled to respond to questions as their shock gave way to the first wave of grief. Clare insisted on going upstairs to lie on Jacob's bed. The FLO took her while Rossi tried his best to concentrate on what Anna was saying.

He told her that he was sure his son had not befriended any strangers or been lured into a trap by someone online.

'He had a phone and a tablet,' Rossi said. 'But because he was only ten we were strict about how he used them. We monitored his calls and installed parental control apps on the devices. And we didn't allow him to have Facebook and Twitter accounts. We also made sure . . .'

Rossi suddenly choked up mid-sentence as the emotions surged through him. He lost his train of thought and started shaking his head.

'I'm sorry but this is too difficult,' he said. 'I need to go and be with my wife.'

'That's not a problem, Mr Rossi,' Anna said.

He stared at her, tears fringing his eyelashes. 'I also intend to phone my mother and get her to come back over. She went home this afternoon, but I want to be the one to tell her what's happened to her only grandson.'

'Does she live far?'

He shook his head again. 'Two streets away. She can be here in minutes.'

Benning's team had already checked out Jacob's bedroom and belongings, so there was no need to repeat the exercise now.

Anna got to her feet and offered her condolences. She then dropped one of her cards on the coffee table and told him to call her at any time, day or night.

Before leaving the room, she said, 'I want to assure you, Mr Rossi, that we will work around the clock to find the creature who abducted your son, along with whoever set fire to the building while he was inside it.'

*

Officer Moore, the FLO, joined Anna and Benning outside on the driveway. Her expression was strained, her eyes mournful.

'I'm struggling to get my head around this myself,' she said. 'It's such a terrible shock.'

'Are you OK to stay here?' Benning asked her.

'Of course, sir. I wouldn't have it any other way. They've got to know me, and I'll do whatever I can to help them through this.'

'Once news of this gets out the press and TV outfits will turn up here in droves,' Anna said. 'You need to be prepared for that.'

'I will be. A bunch of reporters and photographers were here all day on Tuesday, but they disappeared after the riots started.'

Anna turned to Benning. 'Is there any chance you can station a patrol car outside?'

He shrugged. 'I can ask, but I very much doubt it. Last I heard almost every available officer had been drafted into areas hit by the riots. Those still here are on standby.'

'I feared as much,' Anna said. 'Stretched resources are going to be a problem throughout this investigation.'

It was something they would all have to bear in mind. At

any other time the Jacob Rossi case would have been a priority. But the Met was under pressure like never before. In addition to the widespread looting and vandalism, a police officer had been stabbed and three small children had fallen victim to arsonists. Anna didn't want to speculate on how many more atrocities would be committed during the hours ahead.

'So what's the next step?' Benning asked her.

'We need to get the team together for a briefing,' she said. 'It means going to Wandsworth. I'll call first to check on the situation there. On the way I'll drop you off at Bromley nick. I'd like you to gather together everything you've got so far and bring it with you to HQ – that includes all statements, interview notes and CCTV images, if any. And tell your boss that you've been seconded to MIT. If he has a problem with that refer him to DCS Nash.'

Anna asked Officer Moore to obtain DNA swabs from Mr and Mrs Rossi so they could be separated out from any traces found on the boy's clothes.

'Have them sent to the lab as soon as possible,' she added.

Moore then went back into the house and Anna and Benning climbed into the car. Before switching on the ignition, Anna phoned DI Walker to check on how he was doing with the task she'd left him with of taking photos of the properties surrounding The Falconer's Arms pub.

He was now on his way back to Wandsworth from Camberwell, having left DC Sweeny at the crime scene to coordinate the door-to-door inquiries.

'I've been told that things have quietened down outside headquarters,' he said. 'Most of the mob who'd gathered there have moved on to other areas, including Balham and Clapham.'

'Do you know if things are still bad in Vauxhall?'

'Apparently so, and not just on and around the Marwell Estate. A two-storey restaurant close to Cobalt Square is on fire and a police chopper came under attack from rioters who stopped it landing in a car park. It was going to the aid of a young girl who was being attacked by two men.'

'So what happened to her?'

'They don't know. She got lost in the crowd.'

'Bloody hell. Well at least Tom got Chloe away from there. I can imagine how scary it must be even for all the people who are safely inside their homes.'

Anna quickly filled Walker in on the conversation with Jacob's parents and said she would now be making her way to Wandsworth too.

'Find out what the state of play is with the number of officers we can have,' she said. 'And make sure everyone knows they'll be working through the night. It's eight o'clock now so we should try to get everyone together for a briefing about nine.'

Anna hung up and turned on the engine. But before pulling off the driveway, she said, 'I've just had an idea. Now might be a good time to drop in on Neville Quinlan, the nonce who was spotted outside Jacob's school last week. I assume he lives fairly close to here since he was hanging around outside Jacob's school.'

'He does,' Benning said. 'His flat is about a mile away.'

'Well if he was involved in the boy's abduction then it's possible he doesn't yet know that Jacob is dead. But if he does know then I expect he'll be in a bit of a state.'

'Good thinking.'

Anna shoved the gearstick into first. 'Then point me in the right direction and on the way you can tell me what you know about him.'

CHAPTER NINETEEN

It had got to the point where all Chloe could do was put one foot in front of the other. It felt like she had no control over anything else. The fear had numbed her senses and her throat was raw from crying.

She walked as fast as she could, hands in the pockets of her puffer jacket. She focused on avoiding bumping into people and tripping over the debris that was scattered all over the place.

Her lungs were aching and her eyes were stinging because of all the smoke in the air. The pain in her head was still there and had spread to her neck and shoulders.

Around her the orgy of violence and destruction continued, yet there was no sign of any police. She could still see and hear the helicopter that had tried to rescue her, though. It was circling above the buildings ahead of her, well out of reach of the rioters and any objects they might throw at it.

The city was even more frightening now because it was dark. The fires were brighter and more dramatic. Shops, cars and piles of rubbish were ablaze. Those people who weren't causing damage were marching along with banners and chanting slogans that Chloe didn't really understand.

Time to take control

All coppers are cunts

Enough is enough

No justice, no peace, fuck the police

It shocked Chloe that some of the rioters didn't look much older than she was. She saw a boy who appeared to be in his early teens throw a flaming bottle onto an abandoned double decker bus. Another was walking across the road between two adults and in his arms was a laptop computer that Chloe guessed had been stolen from a store.

She was on a main shopping street, but even the smaller roads branching off from it were not free from trouble: down one a mass brawl was taking place between two groups of youths, and on another she spotted three men in balaclavas smashing their way into someone's house while four other men stood on the pavement watching them.

It was all so scary and upsetting. She felt vulnerable, helpless, and totally defenceless. Everywhere she looked something bad was happening, and her young mind did not know how to process it. She wasn't old enough or wise enough to get herself out of trouble and she knew it. She needed help, guidance, a grown-up to tell her what to do and where to go.

She was also discovering how much more complicated life

was without her mobile phone. Her mum's number was on it along with their address. But she hadn't bothered to memorise either of them.

The panic was building up inside her again; she was beginning to think that the rioters had taken over the whole of London and that nowhere was safe. She couldn't carry on walking all through the night. She was already exhausted and unsure how long she could keep going without a rest. And it was probably only a matter of time before she was attacked again or had another accident.

She passed a man who was begging a group of youths not to enter his shop. But he was pushed aside and they stormed in through the door. Seconds later she had to jump clear of a car that mounted the pavement and smashed into the front of a bank, setting off the alarm.

She quickened her pace, her eyes scanning the street in front of her, and every breath she took made her chest hurt.

She was on her own, and this horrible truth reminded her of something her father told her just before they left Spain and came to England.

'I will always be there to protect you, Alice,' he said. 'Just you remember that. It won't matter how old you are or where in the world you find yourself. I will never let you down.'

But he had. Big time. She was utterly confused about how she should feel about him now. She remembered how fiercely he had loved her. How he had given her so many cherished memories of their time together in Spain. She had loved and worshipped him in return. But now she found it impossible not to resent him for telling her so many lies. If it wasn't for what he'd done she would never have ended up in this perilous situation. And her beloved Sophie would still be alive.

CHAPTER TWENTY

Even before they got to Neville Quinlan's place, Anna knew that she was going to hate the man. Paedos were on her list of people who deserved never to be forgiven for the crimes they'd committed.

According to DI Benning, Quinlan was a fifty-five-year-old ex-teacher who was now on benefits as well as the sex offenders' register. He was released on licence two years ago after serving five years in prison for sexually abusing two boys aged thirteen and fifteen. They were both pupils at the school where he taught physical education.

He was also convicted of possessing no less than eight thousand indecent images of children, some as young as three. He'd downloaded them onto his computer and shared many of them with other paedophiles in a group to which he belonged.

'His name came up when we asked staff at Jacob's school if they'd received reports of anyone acting suspiciously,' Benning said. 'One of the teachers mentioned seeing a man sitting in a parked car across the road from the main gate on Friday afternoon of last week. She became suspicious because he was so obviously watching the kids in the playground. After about half an hour she crossed the road to confront him but he drove away. She got the car's registration number and it was reported. Unfortunately, it was considered a low priority and we failed to follow it up over the weekend. On Tuesday we identified Quinlan as the car's owner and a red flag came up against his name.'

'What was his excuse for sitting outside the school?' Anna asked.

'He told us he was driving home from the town centre when he suddenly felt unwell. He said he didn't pick that spot deliberately. He just happened to be passing the school when he thought he was going to faint so pulled over to the side of the road to rest for a bit.'

Anna gave a scornful grunt. 'So did the same car show up on any CCTV or number plate recognition cameras on Monday?'

'Well that's the thing. It didn't appear on those that we checked, but then the process got stalled because the riots led to a manpower shortage. We still need to view the footage from a number of cameras out there.'

'Did you search his car and flat?'

Benning nodded. 'Quinlan gave us access to both late on Tuesday after I told him that if he didn't we'd obtain warrants. Me and two of my team went through them but found nothing.'

'Did you bring in forensics?'

'I tried, but all the CSIs have been busy elsewhere. I've never known things to be as bad as they are in respect of people and resources.'

'Did you check Quinlan's phone and computer?'

'Of course, but there was nothing on them pertaining to Jacob and the school. And there was no porn.'

Quinlan lived on the ground floor of a shabby block of flats three storeys high, which was sandwiched between an MOT centre and a small Methodist church.

Anna parked at the kerb in front of the block and Benning pointed to a flat to the left of the entrance. It had a balcony and three front-facing windows. All the curtains were closed but they could see lights inside.

As Anna went to cut the engine, she paused; the news from the radio snagged her attention. She left the engine on idle and they listened to the tail-end of an interview with the Mayor of London, who described the riots as disgusting and shocking.

'It's clear to us now that criminal gangs are exploiting an unprecedented opportunity to settle scores, plunder shops and businesses, and cause as much damage as they can,' he said. 'This has gone way beyond a protest about the police. People have already been seriously injured and scores of buildings destroyed. For all our sakes this has to stop now.'

But the news roundup that followed his plea offered no hope of an imminent end to the unrest. As the rioting entered its fourth night it was obviously spreading and becoming more violent.

The boroughs now experiencing trouble included Tower Hamlets, Westminster, Hackney and Islington. Mobs had even descended on the West End and shops along Oxford Street, Regent Street and Tottenham Court Road had been torched.

Some police stations and magistrate courts had been under sustained attack since late afternoon and the homes of at least four police officers and three Members of Parliament had been vandalised. In some cases windows had been smashed and in others front doors had been sprayed with paint.

The worst trouble spots continued to be south of the river, and police had seemingly lost control of large parts of Peckham, Brixton, Vauxhall, Rotherhithe and Lewisham.

An increasing number of firearm incidents were being reported, and ambulances and fire engines responding to emergencies had been stoned and rammed with stolen vehicles.

'We understand that the army is now on standby,' the newsreader said. 'If the Prime Minster deems it necessary they'll be drafted in to assist an overstretched and overwhelmed force.'

Anna shook her head in dismay and blew out her cheeks. Then she reached for her phone and said, 'Before we talk to the paedo, do you mind if I put in a quick call to my daughter? I just want to make sure that she's all right.'

'Of course not,' Benning said.

But before she could even type in her passcode, the door leading into the flats opened up and a man stepped out.

'That's him,' Benning said. 'That's Quinlan.'

Anna left her phone in her pocket and they both stepped quickly out of the car.

*

'I was hoping I'd seen the last of you lot,' Quinlan said as they approached him. 'But I should have known better than to expect you to leave me alone.'

Benning did the talking while Anna fished out her warrant card and held it up.

'We need to have a word with you, Mr Quinlan. It's about the missing boy, Jacob Rossi. My colleague here is Detective Chief Inspector Tate.'

'Well it'll have to wait,' Quinlan said, arrogance coating his words. 'I've made a dinner reservation at a local restaurant, and I'd rather not turn up late. They might give my table to someone else.'

Anna was pretty sure she would have taken an instant dislike to the man even if she hadn't known that he was a child-molesting scumbag.

He was of average height, but on the plump side, with grey hair and a broad, stubble-covered face. He wore baggy jeans and a crew-neck sweater under a crumpled black overcoat.

'I couldn't give a toss about your reservation,' Anna said, unwilling to conceal her anger. 'You either talk to us in your flat or I'll arrest you and take you in to be formally questioned.'

Quinlan heaved his shoulders. 'There's nothing I can add to what I've already told the police. I didn't abduct that boy and I haven't the faintest idea who did. I went for a walk by myself on Monday afternoon about three. It's what I usually do and I can't remember exactly where I went. But I didn't see anyone and I didn't speak to anyone. I was back home by four. This is nothing more than harassment.'

'We've got a few more questions for you,' Anna said. 'So what's it to be? Here or at the nick?'

Quinlan made a noise of exasperation and turned on his heels. The two detectives followed him back inside the building.

His flat was poky and sparsely furnished, with worn carpets and damp patches on the walls. The living room stank of stale cigarette smoke and something else that Anna couldn't identify.

Quinlan invited them to sit on an ancient-looking sofa while he sat opposite and made a show of looking at his watch.

'So what's so important that you're prepared to waste time with me while your fellow plods are trying to stop London from being wrecked by thousands of marauding youths?' he said, a smirk tugging at the corners of his mouth.

Anna took out her notebook and pen and wrote the name Neville Quinlan at the top of the first page.

'We'll start with you telling us the name of the restaurant you're going to,' she said.

He raised an eyebrow. 'What's that got to do with anything?'

'Just answer the question, Mr Quinlan.'

He let out a sigh. 'It's called Milo's Bistro.'

'And is it within walking distance or were you intending to drive there?'

'It's a ten-minute walk. No way am I taking the car out tonight, not with all the stuff that's going on out there. It'd be madness.'

Anna made a note of the restaurant name and added a question mark.

'I'll be checking to see if you're telling the truth about the reservation,' she said.

'Feel free to. Why would I be lying about it?'

'Perhaps because we caught you off guard and it just popped into your head.'

His eyes flashed with anger. 'This is out of order. I'm sick of having to say over and over that I had nothing to do with that boy's disappearance. I can understand why I was questioned initially, but you've got no evidence to suggest I'm guilty of anything except stopping outside his ruddy school.

111

I promise you I'm not the man I once was. I'm older and wiser and able to control my urges. And it wouldn't even enter my head to kidnap a child.'

Anna pressed out a grin. 'And that's exactly what I'd expect you to say. But we both know that people like you can never change. It's who you are, and if an opportunity presents itself you're not likely to pass it up. Which I reckon is what happened when you learned that Jacob Rossi walked home from school most days along a stretch of road with no traffic cameras.'

'That's not the case and you know it.'

'All I know is that you like little boys, Mr Quinlan, and it strikes me as too much of a coincidence that Jacob went missing a few days after you were loitering outside his school.'

He flicked his head towards Benning. 'I've already told him why I was there.'

'And you really expect us to believe that?'

'It's the truth.'

Anna shook her head. 'We think it far more likely that you abducted him and now you're holding him captive some-where.'

'Don't be ridiculous.'

There was sweat on his brow now and Anna was pleased that she'd succeeded in unsettling him. That had been her aim because it made it more likely that he'd slip up and say something he'd regret.

'How often do you visit Camberwell, Mr Quinlan?' she asked him, then studied him carefully to assess his reaction. But if he was surprised by the question he didn't show it.

'I don't understand why you're asking that,' he said, his voice quietly controlled. 'But for what it's worth I've driven through it plenty of times, but never had a reason to stop there.'

'So you wouldn't be familiar with a pub known as The Falconer's Arms?'

He pulled a face. 'Never heard of it. Pubs are not my thing . . . I'm not a big drinker.'

'That particular pub hasn't been serving drinks for some years,' Benning chipped in. 'It's now a derelict building, and it's a good place to hide something – or someone – that you don't want to be found.'

It dawned on Quinlan then what they were getting at, and his eyes grew wide.

'Is this a convoluted way of telling me that the Rossi boy has turned up?' he said. 'Because if it is why don't you just come right out with it?'

Benning, unsure how much to reveal, looked at Anna, who said, 'I can confirm that Jacob was found in the cellar of the pub earlier today. He's given us a full description of the man who put him there, and the cellar happens to be bursting with forensic evidence, including fingerprints and DNA of the perpetrator. It won't be long before we have his name and address.'

It wasn't the first time that Anna had lied to a suspect in an attempt to extract a confession. It didn't always work, and it was of course unethical, but when it did pay off it often saved the investigating team a lot of time and effort.

The guy's face did register surprise at what he'd been told. Or was it shock? Anna couldn't tell because he quickly regained his composure and shook his head. 'There's something you're not telling me isn't there?' he said. 'If you had me bang to rights then you would have stormed in here mob-handed and carted me away. So something doesn't stack up. And since I know from experience that you people often don't play by the rules I'm guessing that what you've told me isn't strictly true. You're taking a punt that I'll fall for it and make a confession.'

Anna swore under her breath. It had been worth a try, but Quinlan was sharper than she'd given him credit for.

'Well at least I now know that you're a man who is not easily fooled,' she said.

Quinlan smirked again. 'Good. So now tell me the fucking truth.'

CHAPTER TWENTY-ONE

Chloe stood and watched as a brutal beating took place right in front of her.

The victim was a teenage black boy who refused to hand over his mobile phone to two much older white boys. One of the boys reacted by punching him in the face before pushing him roughly to the ground. The other boy then kicked him in the back of the head as he curled up on the pavement.

It happened outside a Chinese takeaway just yards from where Chloe was cowering in the doorway of a boarded-up shop.

She stared, numb with fear, as the attackers searched his pockets and stole his wallet along with his phone, before casually sauntering away, triumphant smiles on their faces.

Chloe was so shocked and horrified that she stopped breathing and couldn't move. She just continued to stare at the boy on the ground as he began to cry. Hundreds of people rushed past him as though he wasn't there. It reminded Chloe of the battles she'd seen in war films, where casualties, both dead and alive, are ignored by those who are determined to fight on to the bitter end.

Chloe had stepped into the shop doorway about fifteen minutes ago to rest her tired legs and get her breath back. But she couldn't stay there any longer. She had to move on.

What had happened to the boy stayed in her mind as she took to her heels again. She knew how lucky she was that the same thing hadn't happened to her. She was sure that it would eventually if she didn't get off the streets. But that wasn't easy because most of the doors she passed were locked, boarded up or burning down.

For a while her mind blanked out the chaos that raged around her. She found herself thinking about her father again, wishing he was there with her, holding her hand and leading her to safety. But he wasn't, because he had made the fatal mistake of bringing her back to London. And that was why he was dead along with Sophie. And why she was trapped in this terrifying situation with no idea if she would survive the night.

She wondered if he was looking down on her from Heaven and regretting what he did. And if so she just hoped he didn't find it so easy to forgive himself.

Suddenly the screaming and shouting wrenched her back to the present. It had got much louder, and so had the wail of sirens.

Moments later Chloe saw why when she followed the road as it curved sharply to the left. About fifty yards ahead of her a fierce battle raged between police and what seemed like hundreds of rioters.

Through gaps in the crowd she could see the police lined up across the road in front of two white vans parked sideways.

It looked to Chloe as though they were trying to stop the mob from getting past them.

Some carried shields and wore dark helmets that also covered their faces. Others had on the more familiar yellow coats.

But they were vastly outnumbered and struggling to hold their ground as bottles, stones and petrol bombs were hurled at them.

The air locked in Chloe's chest as she came to a stop. She couldn't move or breathe, but she could feel the heat from the fires on her face and the fumes in her throat.

For what seemed like an eternity she just stood there in the middle of the road, rooted to the spot by fear and indecision.

Then she heard a blast that sounded like a gun going off. It was followed by three more in quick succession. Suddenly the crowd of rioters started to disperse, and Chloe caught a glimpse of a figure lying in the road. It looked for all the world like a policeman.

But she didn't have time to make sense of it because most of the panic-stricken rioters were running towards her. It was like a stampede, and her only option was to turn around and run as fast as she could in the same direction.

CHAPTER TWENTY-TWO

Anna was fired up when she left Neville Quinlan's flat. She needed a cigarette to help calm her nerves and slow her pulse, but it was going to have to wait until after she'd dropped Benning off. It wouldn't be fair to smoke with him in the car, and there was no time for a fag break.

Quinlan had failed to convince her that he was as innocent as he claimed to be. When she'd told him how Jacob Rossi had died in the pub cellar he had shaken his head and said, 'That's really bad and I feel sorry for his parents, but I swear I didn't know he was there.'

As a cop, Anna was used to reading people, and she was in no doubt that Quinlan was hiding something. It was there in his voice and body language, the way he avoided looking at her when he spoke.

'We need to chase up forensics and get them to go through his flat and his car,' she said as they drove towards Bromley town centre.

Benning nodded. 'I'll make the call as soon as I'm back in

the office. Hopefully I'll have a response before I leave for Wandsworth with the case file.'

'So what did you make of him this time round?' she asked. 'Did you detect anything different in the way he responded to questions?'

'Not really. He seemed genuinely shocked when you told him that Jacob had died in the fire, but you'd expect that reaction even if he wasn't responsible for putting the boy in the cellar.'

'That was the impression I got. Sex offenders are in a league of their own when it comes to the art of misdirection, so he remains squarely in the frame. I've got a feeling he's involved somehow. We need to complete the trawl of CCTV footage and find out as much as we can about the guy. Did you check up on known associates? Paedophiles often operate in pairs so he might have an accomplice.'

'It's on our to-do list,' Benning said, somewhat sheepishly. 'I'm afraid it's one of the avenues of inquiry that's been held up because of the riots.'

Anna wasn't sure whether to take him at his word. She was beginning to wonder if the DI was using the riots as an excuse for not having found Jacob Rossi before today. If so then was it driven by guilt – or had he been less than thorough with his missing person's investigation?

Anna didn't understand why Quinlan, the prime suspect, hadn't already been put through the ringer. Every aspect of his life should have been looked into by now. And she was curious to know if Benning had pushed hard enough to bring in a forensics team to search for evidence in Quinlan's flat and car.

But it was far too early to voice these concerns since it was quite possible that she was misreading the situation. After all, Benning struck her as a seasoned, no-nonsense detective who was understandably shaken by what he'd seen in the pub cellar. She didn't want to needle him by casting doubt on his abilities at the outset. For the sake of the investigation she needed him and his team on her side. At least for now.

*

Anna dropped Benning off at Bromley police station. He said it wouldn't take him long to gather together the case notes and have a brief conversation with his commanding officer.

The plan was for him to arrange for anything not in hard copy form to be emailed to Anna's work address. Then he would make his way to MIT headquarters to present what he had at the team briefing.

As soon as she was on her way again, Anna fired up a cigarette. She hoped it would help subdue the anxiety that was making it hard for her to concentrate. Too many things were stressing her out – the thought of how poor little Jacob Rossi must have suffered before he died, the fact that she might never find those responsible, and, of course, the riots that were tearing London apart.

But at least she knew Chloe was safe and well thanks to Tom. It had been good thinking on his part to take her to his flat in Nine Elms. She tried calling him again, but as before there was no answer; but, given the time, she imagined they had gone to bed.

There were constant updates about the riots on the radio, including a list of the areas where disturbances were taking place. Anna was relieved that Nine Elms was not among them.

But it disturbed her to hear that the situation in and around Vauxhall was getting worse by the minute. Reports were now coming in that a police officer had been shot during a violent clash with over a hundred rioters. It wasn't yet known if his wounds were life-threatening because paramedics were struggling to get to the scene.

The sheer magnitude of what they were dealing with was terrifying. And unprecedented. It was no longer a case of grievances being addressed. This was now about looting and criminal damage on an industrial scale.

The police were at an enormous disadvantage because there were so few of them. Plus, they had to act within the law, whereas the rioters had no restrictions or concerns. And from the sound of it the mobs were making the most of things by becoming increasingly brazen.

Throughout the capital they were using stolen cars to create burning barricades across roads. As soon as police descended on one scene of violence, the rioters either engaged with them or moved swiftly on to another location. And it was difficult for officers to make arrests while dealing with disturbances.

'As was feared many more people are taking to the streets this evening,' the newsreader said. 'We're hearing that a Tesco superstore in Tottenham is on fire and in Balham police have been forced to abandon two armoured vehicles after they came under attack. Meanwhile, hospital casualty departments are being overwhelmed and callers are struggling to get through to emergency services by phone.'

Anna shook her head as a wave of impotent rage swept through her. It galled her to think that the threat of civil unrest had been hanging over the capital for years, but had not been taken as seriously as it should have been.

The politicians had been told time and again that they needed to prepare for the day when the shit hit the fan again. But time and again they had chosen to do nothing except put in place contingency plans that were proving strikingly ineffective.

Anna suspected that those same politicians would now refuse to accept any responsibility for what was happening – and deny, along with many of the rioters, that they too had the blood of innocent people on their hands.

*

Anna managed to steer clear of the active trouble spots on the drive to Wandsworth. She went via Beckenham, Penge and Streatham, and did not encounter any violence. But throughout the journey she saw evidence that rioting had taken place earlier.

She passed dozens of shops that had been looted and scores of cars that had been reduced to burnt-out shells. The streets were a mess, and in some of them clean-up operations were well underway.

The urgent screams of police sirens continued unabated, and she drove past gangs of feral youths who were clearly fired up and intent on misbehaving.

She even witnessed several acts of gratuitous vandalism against buildings and vehicles. In normal circumstances she would have felt obliged to intervene. But these were not normal circumstances, and no way was she going to get involved by herself when she almost certainly wouldn't be provided with back-up.

There was a heavy uniformed presence in front of head-quarters, but thankfully the rioters had moved on, leaving a road covered with shards of glass and the foul odour of oily smoke in their wake.

It was the first time Anna had been back to HQ since the start of her compassionate leave, and it felt strange entering the building.

DI Walker was waiting for her upstairs in the open-plan operations room used exclusively by the Major Investigation Team. He handed her a black coffee in a Styrofoam cup, and said, 'If you feel anything like I do then you're probably going to need this.'

She managed a smile. 'Thanks, Max. You're a star – I've been gagging for a caffeine fix. Let me dump my stuff and you can bring me up to date.'

Walker followed her into her tiny office and waited while she removed her coat and took her notebook from her bag.

'How are Jacob's parents?' he asked her.

'Just as you would expect,' she answered, with an echo of sadness in her voice. 'They're shocked and utterly devastated. I had to tell them everything about how he died and it felt like I was sticking needles into their eyes.'

'What we saw in that cellar is still jarring with me,' Walker said. 'I would really like to get my hands on the bastard who put him in there.'

'Or bastards,' Anna said. 'We still don't know if there was more than one of them.'

Walker nodded. 'That's true enough, guv. But if I was a betting man I'd put my money on it being the work of a single perp. It's just a gut feeling I have.'

Anna wouldn't have bet against him. She knew from having worked with him for so long that his instincts usually turned out to be spot on; he was one of the sharpest and most perceptive coppers she knew, which was why she regarded him as her number two.

She sat down behind her desk, and said, 'Now before I tell you about my trip to Bromley, I want to know how we're fixed in terms of numbers.'

Walker remained standing and gestured through the window into the ops room.

'Well you can see for yourself there aren't many bodies out there. As you know we've got DS Prescott and DC Niven, plus Sweeny who's still in Camberwell. We've also got DS Khan and DC Mortimer, along with four admin staff who'll be working through the night. Six detectives have been instructed to stay at home and get some sleep so that not everyone is bled dry by exhaustion tomorrow.

'The rest, along with most of the uniforms, have been assigned to duties elsewhere. These bloody riots are putting a real strain on resources all across London, and not just on the front line. Core services are under pressure, including the firearms command, forensics units, custody staff and body recovery teams.'

Anna told Walker what DI Benning had said about how the riots had impacted on the investigation into Jacob Rossi's disappearance.

'They hadn't got as far with it as I was hoping they had,' she said. 'CCTV footage still needs to be rounded up in and around the area where it's believed Jacob was snatched. And only two suspects have emerged. One is a convicted paedophile, but forensics have yet to examine his car and flat.'

Anna briefed Walker on what DI Benning had told her and about their conversation with Neville Quinlan.

'I've jotted down a list of action points,' she said. 'I'll go through them with the team when Benning gets here. Meanwhile show me what you've got set up out there.'

The officers and civilian staff acknowledged Anna as she walked across the ops room to where two large whiteboards had been positioned. She saw immediately that Walker had done a fast and thorough job.

Pinned to one of the boards were photographs taken at the crime scene. They showed the cellar from various angles and Jacob's body on the mattress. There were also photos that Walker had taken of the pub's exterior and the properties that overlooked it.

On the other whiteboard were photos of Jacob when he was alive, plus pictures of his parents, his school, and the road where it was believed he'd been abducted. There was still plenty of room for more pictures. They would include shots of the two suspects: Neville Quinlan and Gavin Pope.

'Can you put a map up showing the location of Jacob's school and home?' Anna said. 'And include the distance and routes between Camberwell and Bromley.'

'No problem,' Walker responded. 'I'll get right on it.'

Anna called her small team together and told them that the briefing would get underway as soon as DI Benning arrived.

'We need his input because he's been heading up the search for Jacob since Monday,' she said. 'He's bringing the case file with him. In the meantime, I suggest you spend the next few minutes checking out the Rossi family online – especially Jacob's dad, Mark. It's possible, given his high profile, that he's the reason his son was targeted. So the more you all know about him the better.'

Anna was heading back to her office to do that herself when her phone rang. It was DCS Nash.

'Hello, sir. I was going to ring you after the briefing.'

'Are you back at HQ?' he said.

'I am. I've just been put in the picture regarding the size of my team.'

'Good. I'm still at the Yard and will be here throughout the night so I'll keep checking in. I take it you've spoken to the boy's parents?'

She told him that she had and went on to provide him with a full update.

'DI Benning is on his way here now for the meeting,' she said. 'I'll then assign tasks and we'll get cracking.'

'I talked to a Detective Chief Inspector Mason at Bromley,' Nash said. 'He's got no problem with Benning working with us for the foreseeable future, but they can't spare any other detectives. Those who've been working on the misper case will be reassigned.'

'I'm not surprised, sir. At least we've got an extra pair of hands. And he can tell us stuff we won't have to find out for ourselves.'

'Precisely. However, I want it made clear to him that you're in charge of this investigation and if he doesn't toe the line or pull his weight you have my blessing to send him back to Bromley.'

'I've got no reason to believe that he'll be anything other than an asset to the team, sir.'

She heard Nash inhale a sharp breath before he spoke again.

'Well then it's only fair that you're made aware of something DCI Mason told me about Benning,' he said. 'It was in the strictest confidence so I don't want you passing it on to anyone else. Is that understood, Anna?'

Anna frowned into the phone. 'Of course it is, sir. I'm all ears, so fire away.'

CHAPTER TWENTY-THREE

Anna decided she would crack on with the briefing at ten p.m. sharp even if DI Benning hadn't arrived by then. It gave her forty minutes to go online to read and view the news stories relating to Jacob Rossi's disappearance.

They didn't add much to what she already knew, but it was interesting to hear his teachers paying tribute to him, and the interviews with some of his school friends. He came across as a pleasant, level-headed boy who was well liked. He had a passion for football and was described as mature for his age.

Anna also watched footage of police searching woodland between the school and Jacob's home, and a press conference fronted by Benning late on Tuesday morning when the story dominated the news agenda – before the riots began.

Anna then googled Jacob's father's name and got thousands of hits, which included photographs and video clips of the TV programmes he'd presented.

He had his own page on Wikipedia, detailing his private

life and career, and Facebook and Twitter accounts on which he had large followings.

Anna learned that Mark Rossi was aged forty-five and had been married to Clare for fourteen years. He was born in Dulwich, South London, the son of Nigel and Emily Kennedy. But his father died when he was just ten, and his mother married again four years later to Isaac Rossi, who was at the time a backroom journalist in television.

Emily took on the Rossi name and so did Mark. His stepfather then became a big influence in his life, and encouraged him to follow in his own footsteps and embark on a career in journalism. It started with a media studies course at university, and then a job as a reporter/presenter on a local TV news programme.

At the age of twenty-six, Mark was picked up by an agent who found him work on other types of programmes. About then his stepdad moved into documentary film making and gained an impressive reputation as a director/producer before setting up his own production company a decade ago.

The company made a string of programmes and Mark was one of their main on-screen assets. But the company, Glory Entertainment, folded three years ago, a year before Isaac Rossi died. It left behind significant debts and a bunch of very disgruntled former employees.

However, for Mark Rossi it proved to be only a minor setback since he did not have any money tied up in the business and had separate lucrative contracts with the BBC, ITV and Channel Four.

Both before and since his stepfather's death, Mark had led a charmed life. The family had homes in Cornwall and Spain, as well as Bromley. Mark was forever posting photos on

Facebook of family holidays around the world and events he attended where he met film stars, pop stars and other famous people.

Only three months ago he posted a dozen photos of Jacob's tenth birthday party, which took place on a friend's yacht moored in a marina near their Spanish villa.

Anna wasn't at all surprised that by sharing the images of his privileged lifestyle online he had attracted a fair amount of criticism and abuse. He was called a show-off, a flash bastard, and a man who liked to make other people jealous.

But for every negative comment there were twenty positive remarks. He had an army of fans who adored him and enjoyed being invited to see what he got up to off camera.

*

DI Benning arrived at ten minutes to ten, so Anna was able to have a quick word with him before she started the briefing. She got him to tell her what he'd brought with him and asked if he was prepared to work through the night, which he was.

She decided not to let him know that his boss had passed on confidential information about him to DCS Nash. She feared it would undermine his ability to do a good job, especially if he learned that she had also been made aware of it.

As she listened to him talk about the contents of the case file, it struck her that he didn't sound or act like a man who was keeping a shocking secret. His demeanour was self-assured and business-like, and there was no hint of the weight he was carrying on his shoulders.

He handed Anna photos of the suspects, Neville Quinlan and Gavin Pope, and said, 'These can go up on the evidence board, ma'am. I've got a hard copy of Quinlan's criminal record, but Pope doesn't have one. The threats he made against Mark Rossi only got him a caution. Plus, there are statements made by the people who saw Jacob before he walked out of school on Monday afternoon.'

Minutes later Anna introduced Benning to the others and noted that she had never seen her team looking so tense and sombre.

'Let me begin by stating what must be pretty obvious to you all,' she said. 'This investigation is going to present us with a real challenge. We're working with far fewer people than we normally have, and we've got to do our jobs while out there London is literally burning.

'In addition, you'll know by now that this is no longer a misper case. Jacob Rossi died from smoke inhalation while chained to a wall in the cellar of a derelict pub that used to be called The Falconer's Arms. We have not one, but two objectives: we need to find who put him in that place, and who set fire to the building, causing him to die.

'To start with we'll concentrate our efforts on who abducted Jacob and held him captive between Monday afternoon and today. The only way we'll get to the rioter who threw the petrol bomb into the pub is if someone comes forward with a name or names. Unfortunately we don't have CCTV of the incident and all that local witnesses saw was a mob of mostly masked youths descending on the building. It's also worth pointing out that whoever did start the fire almost certainly doesn't know that someone died in it because it hasn't yet been made public. And the same goes for whoever left him down there. They might not yet know about the blaze.'

'So there's a chance they'll return to the building at some point to check on the boy,' DC Niven said from a seat at the front.

Anna gestured for Walker to respond and he pointed out that DC Sweeny and a uniformed officer would be spending the night in an unmarked car across the road from the building.

'Tomorrow we'll see if we can set up a surveillance operation in one of the houses opposite the entrance,' Walker said. 'But it won't be of any use if those responsible turned up earlier today and saw the fire for themselves, or if they learn about it once the news breaks about how and where Jacob died.'

Anna then described the scene inside the pub cellar, using a pen to point to the photos on the whiteboard.

'Evidence recovery will be problematic because of fire and water damage,' she said. 'But forensics have Jacob's clothes and shoes in their possession, along with the chain and manacles used to secure him to the wall. We should know soon if they've found any prints or DNA traces on them. When Jacob disappeared he had his mobile and wallet with him, but they haven't yet been recovered. The phone's signal was lost soon after he vanished.'

She relayed the observations of the forensic pathologist who attended the scene and then handed over to Benning to present the details of the missing person's investigation. He drew attention to the photos of Neville Quinlan and Gavin Pope and explained why they were suspects.

'Quinlan is still our prime suspect,' he said. 'Since his release from prison two years ago he's been living in a flat just over a mile away from Jacob's school. DCI Tate and I were there

131

a short time ago and he's still insisting that he knows nothing about the abduction. We're not convinced he's telling the truth, though. As you'll hear shortly the riots hampered our investigation, so we need to catch up on inquiries that haven't yet been made, including having a closer look at his alibi, finding out who he mixes with, and arranging for CSIs to sweep his flat and car. Before leaving my office to come here I put in another call to forensics, but they need chasing.'

Benning then told the team that Gavin Pope had been questioned about Jacob's disappearance because Mark Rossi had brought his name up. 'Pope used to work for a TV production company run by Rossi's stepdad,' Benning said. 'But it went belly-up and his colleagues lost their jobs and their pensions. They resented the fact that Mark's career continued to thrive while they struggled. Pope also reckoned that Rossi didn't do enough to help them even though he was in a position to do so, and confronted Rossi about it at an awards event two months ago. He was drunk and told Rossi that he and the others would eventually get their own back on him.

'Pope denies involvement in the abduction, but there's nobody to corroborate his alibi that he was at home by himself on Monday. He's given us the names of the other eleven people who he claims have it in for Rossi. I'm afraid we didn't get around to talking to them.'

'But they aren't the only ones who Mark Rossi has upset,' Anna said. 'It seems he's pissed off a lot of people by boasting online about his luxury life. I had a quick look at his Facebook and Twitter pages and he's been bombarded with abusive comments. These will have to be looked at and a view taken as to whether any of them constitute a serious threat to him and his family. We can't rule out the possibility that a complete stranger developed a hatred for Rossi online and decided to punish him by kidnapping his only son. And since the boy was held captive for so long it might be that a ransom demand was going to follow.'

Anna ran through the various scenarios in respect of the possible motives and opened it all up for discussion. Once she was convinced that all the officers were briefed and ready to go, she assigned tasks, starting with detectives Khan and Mortimer, who she sent to Camberwell to assist with the door-to-door inquiries.

'Try to find out if anyone saw activity on the premises during the past few weeks,' she said. 'The perp's car or van must have been parked round the back of the building where there's a high wall between the pub car park and the side of a block of flats. And there's only one open gate in and out of the forecourt, so the chances are a vehicle would have been seen arriving and leaving.'

She asked DS Prescott to check the names on the list that Rossi had provided and to find out where each of them was on Monday, then decide who needed to be questioned.

'While you do that, DI Benning and I will visit Pope. He lives in Richmond so hopefully we won't have to drive through any riot areas.'

The rest of the team were given jobs to do that included chasing down CCTV footage in Camberwell, digging up more information on Neville Quinlan, and finding out when forensics would be able to visit his flat.

'I'm mindful of the fact that the riots are placing an unbearable burden on the Met's resources,' she said. 'There's a limit to what can be done and I'm sure we've gone way beyond that already. So we can expect every step of the way to be a struggle. And, be warned, the pressure will only build once the media gets wind of it. The story ties into the riots so they'll be all over it, and us.'

Anna then looked at her watch before inviting more questions, of which there were many. After another fifteen minutes she drew the meeting to a close and asked one of the admin staff to type up a list of the action points for circulation.

She then told Benning they would drive to Richmond in a pool car.

'There's something I have to do first,' she said, and went to her office to get her coat and thumb out a text to Tom.

Things are really hectic, hon, so I won't call in case you're both in bed. I hope all is well and thank you again for taking care of my baby. It's so good to know that I don't have to worry about her.

CHAPTER TWENTY-FOUR

'Are you fucking deaf or what? I asked you a question.'

'Leave her be, Wesley. Can't you see she's in shock?'

'So what? I still don't understand why you had to stop and pick her up.'

'I told you. If I'd left her in the road she would have been trampled on, and probably killed. And I couldn't let that happen. I've got a sister about her age.'

'So now you can tell your little sis that her brother Ryan is a superhero. That's pathetic, man.'

'Oh, come off it. You're acting like it's a big deal. And you're forgetting she's not the enemy. The coppers are. This kid was out there with the rest of us. I'm guessing she got separated from her mates or family. All we have to do is leave her here.'

Chloe could hear every word because they were standing right in front of her. She could also see their faces through the tears that clouded her vision.

She was sitting on the floor with her back against a wall inside a small gift shop that had been wrecked. There was enough light coming from somewhere to show up the stuff scattered across the floor and all the damage to the display cases and shelving units. The front door had been smashed in, along with most of the glass in the window. Through it she could see that a fire was raging close by, but she couldn't tell if it was a car that had been set alight or another shop across the road. People were running past in both directions and there was still a lot of noise outside.

She remembered clearly how she'd ended up here and why she was hurting all over. Every time she closed her eyes she felt as though she were back in the stampede. In the chaos she had twisted her ankle and fallen onto her face, which was why her chin was so painful. Someone stamped on her outstretched right arm and whoever it was swore at her, but didn't stop.

That was when the sound of her own screams filled her head and she began to feel weird and dizzy. She remembered being lifted off the ground suddenly by a man who kept telling her to stop crying. She could only just hear his voice above the shouting, the sirens, and the crackling roar of a helicopter.

As he carried her into the shop, she realised that he wasn't by himself. There were two of them and she heard them saying how much they hated the police and how great it was to have seen a copper get shot.

That was why she wasn't responding to their questions about who she was and why she was by herself. She was scared they would hurt her if she let slip that her mum was a detective.

Both were young black men wearing dark coats and hoods. The one named Wesley had a mean face and a loud, angry voice. Ryan was the one with the sister who had stopped to help her. He had a kinder face and a softer voice, and his compassion reminded her of the woman who had helped her earlier after she was hit by the motorbike.

Ryan knelt down beside her now and touched her arm.

'I can't help you any more if you won't speak to me,' he said. 'But I get it because I can see that you're scared of us, and I don't blame you. You're far too young to be out by yourself on a night like this.'

Chloe was sobbing and shaking, but she was also hoping that this man Ryan would tell her that he would take her to a safe place even though he was one of the people causing all the trouble.

Instead, he stood up, and said, 'You'll be safe here at the back of the shop until things quieten down. Then go out and find your way home. And try not to fall over again.'

His pal gave him a pat on the back. 'Well that's your good deed for the day, bro. Now let's get back out there before we miss all the fun.'

A rush of panic propelled Chloe to her feet and helped her find her voice.

'Please don't leave me,' she screamed. 'I can't . . .'

But she never got to finish the sentence because at that moment a bottle with a flame coming out of it flew through the shop window. It hit the floor just in front of the two men and exploded on impact. Flames shot up, and it was Ryan who couldn't move away quickly enough.

Chloe screamed, a shrill wail of terror, and then pushed herself back against the wall from where she watched as first his trousers caught alight and then his coat. Within seconds his whole body was engulfed in flames and he was screaming as he threw himself onto the floor and rolled around in an effort to put them out.

Wesley tried to help him, but he couldn't get close enough, and when he realised his own sleeve was alight, he jumped back so that he could struggle out of his coat.

By this time the flames had spread quickly through the shop, thanks to the mess on the floor and all the gifts that were made of wood, paper and cardboard.

Chloe started to gag and cough as smoke and intense heat consumed her. She tried to cry out but it proved impossible because of the fumes that clogged up her lungs.

She saw that Ryan was no longer moving, and his body was being devoured by the flames. She could see no way out for herself and she thought that she was going to die too.

And she almost certainly would have if Wesley hadn't suddenly grabbed her arm and pulled her away from the wall.

'Come with me,' he shouted above the fierce crackling of the flames. 'There must be another way out.'

And he was right.

There was a door behind the counter that she hadn't spotted and it led to a short corridor. At the end of the corridor there was another door. It was locked, so Wesley had to let go of her arm in order to kick it open.

Moments later the two of them stumbled out into the night, leaving behind a man whose name would later appear on the list of those who died in the riots.

CHAPTER TWENTY-FIVE

Presenter: *'This is the BBC news at eleven o'clock . . . and sadly we have to report that three people are now known to have died in the riots. One was a police officer who has passed away in hospital after he was shot during street clashes in Vauxhall. And a shopkeeper was killed when he was struck on the head by a brick as he confronted looters in Greenwich.*

'According to as yet unconfirmed reports the latest victim is a boy who perished in a fire that swept through a dere-lict pub in Camberwell. Scotland Yard say the blaze was caused by a petrol bomb that was thrown into the building by rioters. We hope to have more on that story later.

'Meanwhile, there are ugly scenes elsewhere in the capital tonight. Our reporter Anthony Desmond is in Oxford Street.'

Reporter: *'The rioters have been targeting shops and stores here in London's West End since much earlier this* *evening. They've caused extensive damage and a number of arrests have been made. Just half an hour ago I witnessed an attack on a police car as it pulled up outside a shop that was being ransacked. Fortunately, the two officers inside escaped without injury. But in nearby Regent Street a man was stabbed in the arm when he was set on by a group of youths. More from me later.'*

Presenter: *'We have reporters at various locations around London and we'll be bringing you updates throughout the night. But first we've been given a dedicated hotline number for those worried about friends and relatives who they fear have been caught up in the riots . . .'*

CHAPTER TWENTY-SIX

Anna's hopes of a trouble-free journey to Richmond were dashed within minutes of leaving MIT headquarters.

She made the mistake of taking the obvious route through Putney, and discovered too late that part of it had been turned into a raging inferno of cars and vans.

Mounted police were being deployed to beat back a mob of manic youths wearing military-style balaclavas.

So for the second time that evening Anna was forced to make a detour to avoid getting caught up in it.

'Surely it's time the army was brought in to help,' Benning said. 'At this rate the whole fucking city will be flattened by morning.'

Anna too was becoming increasingly alarmed. She was no longer confident that the Met would be able to bring the disturbances under control without help. Too many people were jumping on the bandwagon. There were those with an axe to grind who saw it as a way to vent their anger and frustration. Those who viewed it as a bit of fun. And those who were getting off on the sense of power they were able to wield.

It was clear to Anna now that what was happening was a seismic event that was going to be costly in terms of both lives and money. It would also have serious implications for the future of law enforcement, community relations and crisis management in the capital, and beyond.

The pool car was equipped with a police radio, and the number of 'urgent assistance' calls they were hearing was staggering. Officers all over the city were being threatened and attacked, and there were now reports that rioters had even turned their attention to Buckingham Palace.

'It's like a blinking war zone,' Benning said, which was exactly how DCS Nash had described it when he called Anna at home earlier.

Was that really only a matter of hours ago? she wondered. So much had happened since then. She'd stood over a dead boy chained to a wall in a cellar. She'd interviewed a vile paedophile. And she'd encountered scenes of carnage that had made her blood run cold.

It was frightening to think that the night was still so young.

*

The streets of Richmond were busy but calm, which came as an immense relief to the two detectives.

Benning directed Anna to Gavin Pope's house, a mid-terrace property close to the famous Royal Park.

'When I interviewed him he didn't try to hide his sheer contempt for Mark Rossi,' Benning said. 'He described the guy as being very different to the clean-cut family man image that he likes to project of himself.'

'Did you ask him to explain what he meant by that?'

'Of course, but his response was vague, like he didn't want to be drawn on it. He just said he'd worked on various programmes with the man over five years and the more he got to know him the less he liked him.'

'There are two sides to every story,' Anna said, as she parked the car in front of the house. 'So maybe Rossi wasn't too fond of him either.'

It was a woman who answered the door. Fiftyish, with unruly blonde hair that dropped onto her shoulders, and a slightly bloated face that was at odds with her trim figure. She was wearing a tight button-up white blouse, denim shorts and fluffy pink carpet slippers.

'Hello again, Mrs Pope,' Benning said. 'I know it's late, but we need to speak to your husband again. Is he in?'

Her eyes flashed with annoyance. 'Well I hope you're going to say sorry for accusing him of kidnapping that young boy. He's been in a dreadful state since then.'

'I did not accuse him of anything, Mrs Pope. I asked him some questions pertaining to his relationship with the boy's father.'

'You mean his dad told you that Gavin probably did it.'

'That's not what I mean, Mrs Pope.'

Anna was about to intervene when a man stepped into the hallway behind her, and said, 'What's going on, love?'

Anna recognised him at once from the photo that was now pinned to the whiteboard in the ops room. Gavin Pope was of medium height with short brown hair liberally streaked with grey, a designer beard, and sharp features. He was ruggedly good-looking and it appeared to Anna as though he kept himself in shape.

'Oh Christ, what is it now?' he said. 'I've got nothing to add to what I've already told you.'

'There's been a development in the Jacob Rossi case, sir,' Anna said. 'As a result I am now the senior investigating officer and there are some questions I need to ask you. My name is DCI Anna Tate. I'm a detective chief inspector with the Major Investigation Team.'

Pope cocked his head to one side and frowned.

'So what is this development? Has the kid been found?'

'I'm not prepared to have this conversation on the doorstep, Mr Pope. May we come in?'

Pope rolled his eyes and clucked his tongue.

'I suppose you'll have to. Let's get it over with. My wife and I were just about to go to bed.'

They were shown into the living room where the couple had been watching the television. It didn't surprise Anna that the screen was showing news footage of the riots. She turned her back on it so that it wouldn't be a distraction.

Pope sat on an armchair and his wife, whose first name was Laura, stood behind him, fidgeting nervously with the top button of her blouse. Anna and Benning lowered themselves onto the sofa.

'I'll start by answering the question you just asked, Mr Pope,' Anna said. 'Jacob Rossi has indeed been found, but not alive, I'm sad to say. His body was discovered earlier today.'

Pope's jaw dropped and the breath whistled out of him. His wife's hand flew to her mouth and she spoke though her fingers.

'That's awful. Please don't tell us that the boy suffered in any way,' she said.

'All we know for certain is that Jacob was abducted on Monday and has been held captive since then,' Anna said. 'But the derelict building he was in was set light to by rioters and he died in the fire because he couldn't escape. So our job is to find out who put him there.'

Mrs Pope shook her head as a sob rose in her throat.

'That is so terrible,' she said.

She placed a hand on her husband's shoulder and squeezed it as the colour drained from his face.

'I swear I had nothing to do with it,' he said, his eyes locked on Anna's. 'There's bad blood between Rossi and me – I admit that. But I'm not some nutcase who would snatch a child. You have to believe that.'

'Right now I don't know what to believe,' Anna said. 'All I know for sure is that you're a man with a serious grudge against Mark Rossi. You want him to take responsibility for the impact the closure of his stepfather's company had on your life. And because he won't you've tried to make life unpleasant for him with threats of legal action and menacing phone calls and emails. Then two months ago you confronted him at an event and threatened him.'

'I was drunk that night,' Pope said. 'I got carried away. But it was hardly a serious threat. He's exaggerating if he says it was. Just like he's exaggerating when he says I've pestered him with calls and emails. I phoned him a few times and fired off a couple of emails, but that's all. You can check my phone record and see for yourself.'

'When was the last time you had any contact with him?' Anna asked.

'It was at the do. I didn't even know he was going to be there.'

'I was with Gavin that night,' his wife said. 'Mark was prancing around as though he was the most important person there and even I felt like giving him a slap. He's always had that effect on people, especially those who've worked with him.'

'So were you also on the payroll of Glory Entertainment, Mrs Pope?' Anna asked.

'No I wasn't. I work for a recruitment agency. But I met Mark on several social occasions.'

Anna turned back to Pope. 'And where are you working at the moment, Mr Pope?'

'I'm between jobs,' he said. 'As a freelance producer-director I go through dry spells.'

'Is that why you were at home by yourself on Monday when Jacob disappeared?'

He licked his lips and swallowed hard. 'That's right. I didn't go out all day.'

'And what about since then? Have you been out at all?'

'Of course, but only to the shops and the pub. I've spent most of the time working on some programme ideas and watching the news.'

'But I take it that you've been alone so there's no one who can verify that.'

'During the day my wife works at the agency in Bromley,' he said. 'But we've been together every evening.'

Anna turned to Pope's wife. 'And is it just the two of you who live here?'

The woman nodded. 'We don't have any children. We gave up trying years ago.'

'But that's none of your business anyway,' Pope said. 'This is absurd. I can't believe I'm a suspect.' He switched his gaze to Benning. 'When you were here the first time I answered all of your questions and let you search the house. What more do I have to do to convince you that I'm not in any way involved in this awful business?'

It was Anna who responded. 'You can start by being totally honest with us, Mr Pope. When you last spoke to DI Benning you told him that Mark Rossi is not the clean-cut family man that his fans think he is, and your wife has also been less than complimentary about him here tonight. So if there's something you're not telling us about the man – or why you dislike him so much – then you need to open up because it might well have a bearing on what's happened to his son.'

Pope ran a hand through his hair and started to say something, but then thought better of it. This prompted his wife to step out from behind the chair and crouch down on her knees in front of him. A look passed between them and Anna felt her pulse accelerate.

'This is an informal interview, Mr Pope,' she said. 'So you are not obliged to answer our questions. But if you don't we will have no choice but to assume that you're withholding information and that's an offence. And I can assure you that whatever it is we will eventually get to the bottom of it.'

There was a long, pregnant pause, which ended when Pope said to his wife, 'I'll leave it to you to tell them.'

Mrs Pope stroked the back of her husband's hand and slowly stood up. Then she turned to face Anna and breathed in deeply through her nose before speaking.

'The reason my husband hates Mark Rossi so much is that I had a brief affair with the man some years ago,' she said. 'Gavin has managed to forgive me and for my sake he hasn't told anyone else. He can't forgive Mark, though, and for that

I don't blame him. But before you jump to the conclusion that Gavin has even more reason for wanting to punish Mark, you need to know that I'm not the only woman the bastard has played away with. And Gavin is not the only husband who found out.'

It was certainly a turn-up for the books as far as Anna was concerned. For no particular reason she had assumed that Mark Rossi was a happily married man. But she should have known better than to take anyone at face value. Her own husband, Matthew, had made her and everyone else believe that he was content with the life they shared while behind her back he was shagging a work colleague.

'OK. Tell me about this affair,' Anna said.

Mrs Pope looked at her husband for approval and he nodded.

'It lasted for three months and it's something I bitterly regret,' she said. 'Gavin and I were going through a bad patch after I'd learned that I couldn't conceive. Mark flirted with me at a company Christmas bash and I stupidly gave him my mobile number. I didn't expect him to ring, but he did and, well, you can probably guess the rest.'

Anna looked at Pope, who was chewing on his bottom lip.

'And when did you find out about this, Mr Pope?' she asked him.

His voice was a hoarse whisper. 'It wasn't until a year after it had ended. My wife went to work one day and left her phone behind. Out of curiosity I picked it up and scrolled through her messages. There were two from Rossi that she hadn't deleted.'

'And what happened then?'

'I confronted her and we had a big row. But she convinced

me it was a one-off and only happened because of the problems in our marriage at the time. I threatened to punch Rossi's face in but she talked me out of it and begged me not to let on to him or anyone else that I knew. She wanted us to stay together and for me to forgive her. So I did. My love for her proved stronger than my hatred for him. That's why I used the excuse of the company liquidation to get at him. I couldn't stand the thought that he could just get away with it like that.'

Anna turned back to Pope's wife. 'So to your knowledge how many other extramarital affairs has Mark Rossi had?'

Mrs Pope shrugged. 'We only know for certain about one because both the woman and her husband worked for a short time at Glory Entertainment with Gavin. His name is Roy Slater and he left the company just before it went bust because his wife Ruth had a fling with Rossi. Roy found out about it on the same day she announced that she was leaving him. Days later she packed in her job and moved to France to live with her parents who'd retired there. Roy took it really hard and fell into a depression.'

'So why did this never attract press coverage given Rossi's high profile?' Benning asked. 'Surely it would have been fodder for the tabloids. And yet I haven't come across any mention of it.'

'That's because Rossi's stepdad paid him off to leave the company and not to tell anyone,' Pope said. 'His friends and colleagues were told about his wife's affair with some man, but not who he was. I was the only person Roy confided in about Rossi and that wasn't until a few months later when we met for a drink.'

'Was this before or after you saw the message on your own wife's phone?' Anna asked.

'This was sometime after.'

'And did you tell him about your own experience?'

'I chose not to because I had always made him and others believe that my own marriage was rock solid . . . I didn't want him to know the truth.'

Anna mulled this over for a few moments, then said, 'So when was the last time you saw Roy Slater?'

'I haven't seen him in months.'

'We will obviously want to talk to him. Do you have his address?'

'I've got it written down somewhere. I haven't spoken to him for a while, though, either.'

'Is there anything else you can tell me about him? Do you know where he works, for instance?'

'He was unemployed when we last got together. And he said he was struggling to make ends meet, partly because he had fallen back into his old ways.'

'And what do you mean by that?'

'He was betting again. Roy was a compulsive gambler all the time I knew him. I reckon it was one of the reasons his wife strayed. He used to spend most of his time in betting shops, casinos, and on gaming machines, but more often than not he was unlucky.'

Anna thought about this and it occurred to her that Roy Slater might have been desperately searching for a way to hit the jackpot.

CHAPTER TWENTY-SEVEN

'Please don't leave me here,' Chloe screamed, as her mind raged in all directions.

Wesley turned back towards her, his face screwed up as though in pain.

'I got you out of there, but it don't mean you're now my responsibility,' he yelled.

But Chloe was desperate. She reached out, grabbed the sleeve of his jumper.

'Take me with you. Please. I don't know what to do.'

Wesley stared at her for a few seconds, and then looked up at the burning building in which his friend Ryan lay dead. Tears flowed from his eyes and ran down his cheeks. In any other circumstance, Chloe would feel sorry for him, but right now she was preoccupied with getting somewhere safe.

They hadn't moved from this spot since escaping the fire. They had watched the flames spread from the gift shop to the shops either side of it. Wesley had cried like a baby while calling out Ryan's name. And Chloe had struggled to stay on her feet as her head spun and a wave of nausea washed over her.

The fire brigade still hadn't turned up, but the street they were on behind the shops was beginning to fill up with rioters. Some were already pushing over wheelie bins and throwing things at the row of offices that ran parallel with the rear of the shops.

'I'm going to my flat,' Wesley said, turning back to her. 'The one I shared with Ryan. You don't want to come with me. You should go and get help.'

Chloe moved so that she was standing directly in front of him. He was several feet taller than she was.

'Please take me with you,' she begged him. 'I'll be safe there. I can try to contact my mum. She'll come and get me.'

He looked down at her, the flames from the fire reflected in his eyes, and she could see his mind working.

She knew she was taking a risk. After all, she didn't know him and he had not been happy that his friend had rescued her from the street. Plus, how would he react if and when he found out who her mum was? It was a risk she had to take, though. After all, it was thanks to him that she was alive. He could have left her to die in the shop, but he hadn't. For that reason she felt she could trust him.

He flicked his head in the direction he'd been about to walk off in.

'I live in the block you can see over there,' he said. 'It'll take us about ten minutes to get there so stay the fuck close to me.'

Chloe saw the block of flats towering above all the other buildings. Most of the lights were on and the sight of it filled her with hope.

She held on to Wesley's sleeve as he started walking and she had to almost run to keep up with him. Her breath was thumping in her ears and it seemed like every bone in her body was hurting. At the same time her eyes stung and watered, and her stomach lurched with dread.

But she kept going because she felt safer than she had since those men had taken Tom away. She was no longer alone. At last someone had taken her under his wing.

And she didn't even care that he was one of them. A rioter. A man whose hatred for the police had caused him to behave so badly. And so violently.

Up close the block was huge and imposing. It stood at the end of a street that was strewn with debris, including bottles, bricks and household rubbish.

There were groups of youths hanging around, but they weren't rioting. They were talking, smoking, looking at their mobile phones. Perhaps waiting to be told where to go next to cause trouble.

Some of them watched as Wesley strode towards the flats with Chloe clinging to his sleeve. But if he noticed them he didn't bother to show it. He just stared ahead, his face set in stone.

They entered the block, which was grim and dark. Graffiti covered the walls and the air was thick with the stench of urine.

Neither of them spoke as they went up in the lift, but Chloe continued to grasp Wesley's sleeve. She wasn't sure he even noticed she was still holding on to him. It was as though he was lost within himself while struggling to deal with what had happened to his friend.

Chloe was trying not to be sick, but her stomach felt like

it was being repeatedly hit with a hammer. She closed her eyes and a picture of her mum flashed in her mind. She desperately wanted to get in contact with her, and not only for her own sake. She wanted to know that she was safe and hadn't fallen victim to the violence like so many other people including Tom. She was, after all, a target for men like Wesley. He and Ryan had made it clear that they hated the police. It was why they were running riot and trying to destroy everything in their path.

Chloe had started to fear that her mother might already be dead. It was an unbearable thought and she kept telling herself that God wouldn't let her suffer such a terrible loss all over again. She wanted to believe that the worst had already happened to her, and that she would soon be out of danger and reunited with her mum. But for that to happen she needed Wesley's help.

When the lift door opened Wesley stepped out and Chloe walked with him along the landing to his flat. He unlocked his front door with a key and left her to close it behind them.

He went straight through to a small, untidy kitchen where he poured himself a glass of tap water before lighting a cigarette.

Chloe stood in the doorway and tried to think of something to say to him, but her throat felt so tight that she couldn't get the words out.

Wesley then brushed past her and she followed him through the living room and out onto a balcony. They were six floors up and the view across London made her heart jump. There were fires everywhere – some big, some small – and it looked as though dozens of bombs had dropped onto the capital.

'That's where we just came from,' Wesley said, pointing. 'I can't get my head around the fact that I'll never see Ryan again.'

They could see that the fire had spread further, claiming more shops and reaching higher into the sky.

Chloe coughed to clear her throat and said, 'Was he your best friend?'

He dragged on his cigarette before replying. 'We've been mates since primary school,' he said. 'A year ago we moved in here. He was like a bruv to me and he shouldn't be dead. And to think it was one of our own who lobbed the bottle.'

'Did Ryan have a family?' Chloe asked.

He gave a short, sharp nod. 'Parents and a younger sister he thought the world of. They live in Catford. I need to tell them, but I'm not sure I can.'

He stared out over London as he wrestled with his emotions. Chloe wondered if he was regretting taking part in the riots. Ryan would still be alive if the pair of them had stayed out of trouble. It was something that was bound to stay with him for the rest of his life.

For several minutes he didn't speak and neither did she. Eventually, he turned to her and said, 'So what's your name?'

'It used to be Alice Miller,' she replied. 'But now it's Chloe. Chloe Tate.'

He looked puzzled, but didn't bother to ask for an explanation. 'How old are you?'

'Twelve. Nearly thirteen.'

'And where do you live?'

'Somewhere near here. But I don't know the address.'

'Have you got a phone?'

'I left it at home.'

'So how are we supposed to contact your parents?'

'It's just my mum. My dad's dead.'

'OK then, so where is your mum now?'

'She went to work. Her boyfriend came to pick me up to take me to his flat. But he was attacked by a group of men who carried him off. I couldn't get back into my house so I started to run because I couldn't think what else to do.'

He was frowning now and shaking his head. 'Bloody hell,' he said. 'You've had a rough time of it.'

Chloe felt tears spike in her eyes. 'Please help me find my mum,' she said, her voice thick with emotion. 'Please.'

'I'm going to,' he said. 'It's why I let you come up here. Give me her phone number.'

'I don't know it.'

'Then where does she work?'

'A place called Wandsworth.'

'Oh, come on, kid. I need more than that. Where in Wandsworth does she work?'

Chloe hesitated a moment before blurting it out. 'She works at the police station.'

Wesley's expression changed in an instant and she didn't like what she saw.

'Are you telling me your mum is a fucking copper?'

Chloe nodded, and felt a cold panic tighten in her throat.

'I don't fucking believe it,' he seethed. 'My best mate is dead because he took pity on a copper's daughter.'

'It wasn't my fault he died,' Chloe sobbed. 'I didn't start the fire.'

He leaned towards her, his face inches from hers. 'But it was because of you that we went into that shop. If we hadn't, he would still be alive.'

She chose not to respond this time and took a step back from him. She thought he was going to carry on yelling at her, so it came as a relief when he suddenly straightened up and stormed back into the flat, muttering angrily to himself.

Chloe remained on the balcony because she was too afraid to follow him inside. Her skin was clammy with dread and she no longer believed that Wesley was going to help her.

She now feared that he might decide to hurt her instead.

CHAPTER TWENTY-EIGHT

The questions were piling up inside Anna's head as she and Benning walked out of Gavin Pope's house.

Was Mark Rossi really a womaniser? How many affairs had he actually had? And was it possible that a wronged husband had kidnapped Rossi's son as a form of retribution?

It was a well-documented fact that husbands who found out their wives had cheated on them were notoriously unpredictable. The annals of crime were full of cases where heartbroken spouses had punished their unfaithful wives or the men they had got involved with.

Anna herself had brought to justice two men who had gone down that road. One had stabbed his wife to death in a fit of rage. The other had exacted revenge on his wife's lover by first killing his pet dog, and then subjecting him to seven months of extreme harassment during which he ransacked the man's home while he was away and threatened to harm his children.

It was therefore something that Anna would have to

consider with both Gavin Pope and Roy Slater. Had either man thought it was a good idea to snatch Jacob Rossi so that his father would suffer?

She mentioned this to Benning when they were back in the car and his response surprised her.

'I feel bad because I didn't extract this information from Pope and his wife when I first interviewed them,' he said. 'I obviously didn't push them hard enough, and I should have.'

'The situation is very different now,' Anna pointed out. 'Jacob had only just gone missing. Now he's dead and they're having to answer some tough questions.'

'Even so time has been wasted. And there's another suspect in the frame.'

'And the sooner we can speak to him the better,' Anna said.

She took out her mobile and called DI Walker on speakerphone. Pope had given them Slater's address in Rotherhithe and she had passed it on to Walker with instructions to send someone straight to his home.

She then briefed Walker on what Pope and his wife had told them. 'Let's not mess about,' she said. 'Just have Slater brought in to be questioned and find out whatever you can about the guy in the meantime. Pope claimed he's a compulsive gambler and if that's true then maybe he thought that kidnapping Jacob would be a way to solve any money worries he might have. That would be plenty motive.'

She went on to say that Pope had provided them with a DNA cell swab, which would be compared with any forensic evidence found in the cellar and on Jacob.

'On the subject of forensics we managed to pull some strings,' Walker said. 'The team have finished up at the pub in Camberwell and a couple of the CSIs are going straight over to Neville Quinlan's flat. DS Prescott will arrive ahead of them with a warrant so it shouldn't be a problem.'

'That's great, Max. Anything else that I should know?'

'Well we have come up with one other person of interest,' Walker said. 'It's a woman by the name of Michelle Gerrard who has been particularly savage about Mark Rossi on social media. She posts more abuse on platforms than anyone else and seems to really have it in for him.'

'We need to check her out then,' Anna said.

'The wheels are in motion, guv. We're trying to get an address. The only thing we know about her right now is her name. But she does stand out from the other trolls who regularly slag Rossi off. I'll let you know when we've got more.'

'Good. We'll have another case conference when I'm back. I'm guessing that by then the media will be chasing the story so we'll have to think of drafting a press release and maybe even organise a presser. It might be a way to generate some leads.'

'That's assuming we can get more than a snippet of airtime on the news,' Walker said. 'The coverage of the riots is like nothing I've ever seen and the death toll is rising by the minute. And you should see the stuff that's appearing on social media. There are dozens of gruesome videos shot on phones, and all manner of hashtags are trending. I've seen *riots2019*, *taketothestreets*, *clobberthecops* and *letslootlondon*. It's fucking unbelievable.'

With the call on speaker, Benning heard every word, and as Anna hung up he was already checking online through his phone.

'I see what he means,' Benning said. 'Take a look at this.'

It was footage from a mobile phone that had been

uploaded to YouTube. It showed a group of masked youths pulling a police officer from a squad car and beating him up in the road.

Anna's eyes filled with a dark fury as she watched it and she felt her chest contract with every breath.

'There are lots more clips like that,' Benning said.

Anna couldn't resist checking some of them out before heading back to Wandsworth. The images were uncensored and shocking in the extreme.

The inside of a department store where rioters were stuffing goods such as jewellery and boxes of perfume into carrier bags.

A residential street where it appeared that every car parked outside the homes was on fire.

Two men in hoodies dancing on the roof of an abandoned ambulance.

A young black woman kicking and screaming as three white youths dragged her into an alley while a crowd looked on and cheered.

The moment a petrol bomb landed on the ground beneath a police horse and engulfed the animal in flames. The officer dismounted and tried to put the fire out with his hands, but was forced back as the horse went wild.

The last clip ended abruptly before Anna learned the fate of the officer and his horse.

She handed the phone back to Benning. 'That's enough. If I watch any more I'll probably be sick.'

Her hands were shaking as she switched on the engine and engaged first gear.

'This is worse than I imagined it could ever get,' Benning said. 'Those people are like packs of wild animals.'

'All London needed to explode was a spark,' Anna said as

she started driving. 'That spark was the fatal shooting of a pregnant woman during a police raid. It's exposed just how much bitterness and resentment has been bubbling away beneath the surface. Hatred of the police in deprived areas, friction between whites and blacks, a growing distrust of those in authority, and a belief that the future is looking increasingly bleak. Seems to me that as a society we fucked up big time by not learning the lessons from 2011.'

'But even before then we had the mass riots in Brixton during 1981 and 1995,' Benning said. 'And yet nothing has really changed since then and now. That's the shame of it.'

Yet again Anna had to force herself to stop thinking about the riots. She was reminded of how hard she struggled to focus on the job during all those years Chloe was missing. Her daughter never really left her thoughts, and as a consequence her performance during investigations was often below par.

This was different, of course. It was less about the pain of emotional involvement and more about trying to ignore, and avoid, the shocking events that were taking place all around her. But she had to. She owed it to Jacob Rossi's parents to stay focused so that she could bring to justice those responsible for his death.

'I've not had time to go through your case notes,' she said to Benning. 'You told me there was nothing suspicious on Neville Quinlan's phone and computer. What about Pope? Did you check his phone and digital footprint?'

'I'm sure I asked one of the team to sort it,' Benning said.

Anna threw him a glance. 'Are you saying you're not certain?'

He looked embarrassed. 'I'm saying that I haven't been able

162

to keep track of things since coming over to Camberwell. And when I went back to Bromley I didn't hang around long enough to get updates on all the action points.'

'What about Mark Rossi's phone?'

'What about it?'

'Did you examine his call list?'

'I didn't see the point. We didn't suspect him of kidnapping his own son.'

If it had been anyone else Anna would have given them a mouthful. But because of what she knew about Benning she chose not to pursue what she regarded as shortcomings in the investigation. Instead, she reached over and switched on the radio.

But Benning immediately switched it off again.

'Look, I don't want you to think that I'm a shit detective, ma'am,' he said. 'But there's a reason I'm not firing on all cylinders and perhaps that's why we weren't as far forward with the case as we should have been.'

'You've already told me that the riots caused logistical problems,' she said. 'And I know that to be true because those problems are still with us.'

'Well actually there's more to it than that.'

When Anna failed to respond after several seconds, Benning said, 'The fact that you seem to be showing a remarkable lack of curiosity leads me to believe that you already know about my situation. Am I right, ma'am?'

Anna saw no point in lying. 'Your boss thought we should know,' she said.

'Did he call you?'

'He spoke to Nash, and Nash told me on the understanding that I didn't mention it to anyone, and I haven't.'

'So what exactly did he tell you?'

Anna kept her eyes on the road, and said, 'That you were recently diagnosed with early onset dementia and that this could well be your last case.'

Benning expelled a long breath. 'Well I suppose it's only right that you're across it. But I want you to know that I'm a long way from losing my marbles so you don't have to worry about me not being up to the job. I've been told that the decline of cognitive functions will be gradual.'

'I'm not worried about that,' Anna said. 'I know these things can be slow to progress.'

'Exactly. And please don't offer me your sympathy or treat me any different to anyone else on the team.'

Anna allowed herself a slight smile. 'Message received loud and clear, Detective Benning. I see no reason why your unfortunate situation should be an issue during the investigation. Or why anybody else should become privy to it. Agreed?'

'Agreed. Thank you, ma'am.'

CHAPTER TWENTY-NINE

Chloe finally found the courage to come in off the balcony. This was after several minutes of crying and shivering in the cold.

Wesley had closed the door behind him, but to her relief he hadn't locked it. She stepped inside and cast her eyes uneasily around the living room.

There was no sign of Wesley, but as she shut the door behind her she heard what sounded like a voice coming from the kitchen.

Chloe drew in a deep, shuddering breath and fought to hold down the panic. Wesley's angry words were still ringing in her ears. He blamed her for what had happened to Ryan.

My best mate is dead because he took pity on a copper's daughter.

She had told him that it wasn't her fault, but in a way it was and she felt bad about that.

But what to do? That was the question she faced as she stood in the living room and stared through the doorway into the hall.

The kitchen was just to the left. She had a choice. Let herself out of the flat – if she could – and go back out onto the streets to fend for herself. Or try to talk to Wesley. Let him know how sorry she was over Ryan and plead with him to help her.

She was in no condition physically and mentally to go it alone. She was gasping for a drink and desperately needed to pee. She was also freezing cold as well as in pain.

Without coming to a decision, she started taking tentative steps towards the doorway. When she reached it, she poked her head out into the hall and looked towards the kitchen.

She saw Wesley straight away and realised that he wasn't talking to anyone. He was sitting at the table sobbing loudly into his hands.

But he must have sensed her watching him because his head shot up and their eyes met.

'You don't have to be afraid, kid,' he said. 'I'm not going to harm you. I promise. Ryan would never forgive me if I did.'

She ventured nervously into the hall, and as she approached the kitchen, Wesley wiped his eyes with a sleeve and stood up.

'The front door is unlocked if you want to let yourself out,' he said. 'I won't try to stop you. But if you do the sensible thing and stay I'll make you a cup of tea.'

'Will you help me to get in touch with my mum?' she asked him.

He nodded. 'It might not happen for a while. I've been trying to get through to the emergency services, but it just keeps ringing. I want the fire brigade to go to the gift shop before Ryan is nothing more than a pile of ash.'

Chloe entered the kitchen while Wesley crossed the room and started to fill the kettle.

'You might as well take your coat off,' he said. 'The heating's on so you'll soon get warm. And by the way I know it's not your fault that your mum's a copper. We don't get to choose our parents. My old lady was a prossy before she OD'd on H.'

Chloe didn't understand what he meant, but she didn't see the point in saying so.

She removed her coat, placed it over one of the chairs, and said, 'I need to go to the toilet.'

'Back down the hall,' he said. 'Last door on the right.'

Chloe felt better after she had emptied her bladder and rinsed the taste of smoke out of her mouth. But the sight of herself in the mirror sent her heartbeat rocketing again.

Dried blood covered a nasty gash on her chin and there was a bruised lump in the middle of her forehead. The rest of her face was smeared with dark red blotches. The skin around her eyes was swollen and her blonde hair had streaks of black running through it.

She would have had to undress to check what damage had been done to her elbows and knees so she didn't bother.

Instead, she gulped down a sob and told herself that she had to be brave. She looked a mess and she was scared out of her wits. But at least she was alive.

There was a mug of tea on the table when she returned to the kitchen.

'I put milk and sugar in it,' Wesley said. 'Is that OK?'

She nodded and sat down. The tea was hot and sweet and the best thing she had ever tasted.

Wesley watched her drink it as he sipped from a bottle of beer.

Even though they were high up and all the doors and windows were closed, they could still hear the sirens outside.

After about a minute Wesley spoke, his voice wavering with emotion.

'The truth is I'm to blame for what happened to Ryan,' he said. 'I persuaded him to hit the streets again today. He wasn't keen after we nearly got collared yesterday by the filth.'

Chloe said nothing. She could tell he wanted to get it off his chest.

'I reckon you're too young to know why this is happening,' he went on. 'You probably think we're all a bunch of nutters high on drugs. But it's not that simple. People like me have had enough of taking shit. The police pick on us because we're black. They treat us like scum and they think they can get away with shooting innocent women. Well we're showing them now that they can't. Not any more.'

'My mum's not like that,' Chloe said. 'She's nice, and she's kind. And her boyfriend is black.'

'Is that right? Well what kind of copper is she?'

'A detective.'

'So what happened to your dad?'

'He was murdered.'

Wesley raised his brow and shook his head. 'Fuck me, you're full of surprises for a twelve-year-old. Is that why your name changed? You said it used to be Alice.'

'No, Alice is what my dad changed it to after he abducted me ten years ago and took me to Spain.'

Wesley jolted upright and his eyes went wide. It was as though a light had been switched on inside his head.

'Holy shit, you're that girl who's been all over the news and in the papers,' he said. 'Everyone's been talking about what happened to you.'

'That's why I know that my mum is a good person,' Chloe said. 'She never stopped looking for me all that time. And I don't want her to lose me again.' Chloe dissolved into tears.

'Jesus, kid, you're as pathetic as I am,' Wesley said, and the next thing Chloe knew he was patting her back in an effort to comfort her.

But it made her cry even more.

CHAPTER THIRTY

Anna learned a good deal more about DI Joe Benning on the drive back to Wandsworth. And the more she learned, the more sympathy she felt for the man. It seemed that life had been terribly cruel to him.

He got married in his late twenties and his wife gave birth to a daughter, but she was tragically killed when she was hit by a car as she ran into the road at the tender age of six. Three years later his wife left him for another man and they divorced. And then, three months ago, he was diagnosed with early onset vascular dementia, aged just forty-six.

'It was the last thing I expected to be told,' he said. 'I went to the doctor because I started forgetting things, and I just didn't feel myself. They put it down to stress at first, but eventually I had an MRI scan, which showed that not enough oxygen was getting to the top of my brain, which is a tell-tale sign of the condition. But they told me it can take years to have a serious impact on my life and my work.

'Fortunately, the force has been incredibly understanding

and I'm being monitored by a specialist, even though the symptoms haven't progressed and most days it doesn't feel like there's anything wrong with me. However, on her advice it's been agreed that I'll soon step back from frontline investigative work and take a desk job. That's why I was so determined to find Jacob Rossi alive. I didn't want what might possibly be my last case to end in disaster. But now . . .'

Anna hadn't expected him to be so forthcoming, but she was glad he had been. It didn't mean she would make allowances, but she would keep a close eye on his performance. And she'd be sure not to overload him with work. After all, the riots meant that her team was seriously depleted, and she was confident that even a detective who was no longer at the top of his game would still be able to make a useful contribution.

*

When she got back to the office she checked her phone to see if Tom had responded to the text she had sent earlier. But he hadn't, and since it was well after midnight, she saw no point in ringing him. He would have let her know if there was a problem.

She was hoping that Chloe would appreciate what he'd done by taking her to his flat. With luck it might even change her daughter's opinion of him. She really hoped so because she loved both of them, and in the not too distant future she wanted them to be a family.

DI Walker had been holding the fort and told Anna that the team were still working flat out. However, the riots were causing problems at every turn.

'I sent DC Niven with a uniform to Roy Slater's home in Rotherhithe,' Walker said. 'But they ran into a disturbance while driving through Bermondsey. They were forced to take a detour along a road littered with broken glass and got a puncture. They're trying to fix it, but if they can't we'll have to send someone along who can do it for them.'

Other difficulties they were having included getting people to respond to phone calls and collecting CCTV footage.

'Give me twenty minutes or so to get my thoughts in order and we'll have another briefing,' Anna said. 'I want to make sure we're in a position to steam ahead when daylight comes. Hopefully things will settle down a bit then and we can make more progress.'

Benning said he wanted to make some calls so Anna told him to take his pick of all the empty desks. She also gave him directions to the vending machines and toilets.

Then she went to her office, switched on the telly, and settled down to pore over her notes.

But they didn't amount to much, and the reason Jacob Rossi was abducted and chained up in a pub cellar remained a mystery. It did not appear as though he'd been sexually abused, although they wouldn't know for certain until they'd heard back from Gayle Western.

So why was he held captive for so long? Was the kidnapper intending to demand a ransom at some point? Or was the aim simply to cause the family, especially his father, a lot of pain and anguish?

There were four potential suspects, but the frontrunner at this stage had to be Neville Quinlan. He was a convicted paedophile who claimed he was out walking when Jacob went missing. And he claimed not to remember where he'd walked.

Anna found that hard to believe because he struck her as someone who was careful about his movements.

Three days prior to the boy going missing, he'd parked his car opposite the entrance to Jacob's school and his unconvincing excuse was that he had stopped driving because he was feeling too unwell to carry on. Another lie, Anna reckoned, but one that would be even more difficult to disprove. It didn't mean they wouldn't try, though.

She felt that with their limited resources Quinlan was the one they needed to focus on. Gavin Pope was in the frame, of course, and they needed to find out if he had visited The Falconer's Arms since Monday while his wife was at work. Was he the person who had dropped by at least once with food and drink?

Of course, it was also possible that Pope or Quinlan had an accomplice who visited Jacob. If so then it struck Anna that it could be just about anyone.

It was too early for Anna to form an opinion of Roy Slater. But if what Pope and his wife had said was true then Slater might conceivably have decided to seek revenge against the man who effectively wrecked his marriage and caused him to have a breakdown.

And then finally there was Michelle Gerrard, the woman who'd been posting vicious comments online about Jacob's dad. According to Walker, the techies were still trying to find an address for her. Her social media accounts contained hardly any details so it was proving difficult.

They needed to establish whether there was a connection between her and Rossi. Or was she just a nutter with nothing better to do than offend celebrities she had never met?

It occurred to Anna that the worst-case scenario would be

that there was no link at all between the kidnapper and the Rossi family. That Jacob was taken by a complete stranger. Someone who planned it well in advance or else seized an opportunity. It would make their job more difficult, especially in the absence of solid forensic evidence and incriminating CCTV footage.

She rubbed at her eyes, which were dry and gritty. She had an uncomfortable feeling that this investigation was going to be one of the most difficult she had ever taken on.

The news coverage on the TV served only to fuel her pessimism. The riots had now claimed at least four lives, and it was believed that the bodies of more victims were waiting to be recovered from wrecked buildings and fires that were still raging.

There was also startling footage from a helicopter of a blaze that was tearing through buildings close to Vauxhall tube station. The newsreader revealed that it was started by a firebomb thrown through the window of a gift shop. This was known because one of the people who had witnessed it had just minutes ago posted a clip of the incident online from his or her mobile phone. It ran for only five seconds, but you could clearly see the front of the shop as a hooded youth hurled a blazing bottle at it.

The coverage then switched to the live scene outside Buckingham Palace where police had formed a line to stop rioters throwing objects over the railings into the grounds.

'The number of violent incidents outside London has also increased dramatically tonight,' the newsreader said over more footage of clashes between youths and police. 'This was the scene in the centre of Manchester an hour ago. It's not on the scale of London but it is putting an enormous strain on the city's emergency services. Reports are also coming in of disturbances elsewhere, including Birmingham, Leeds and Bradford.'

The roundup ended with a review of the newspaper front pages, which perfectly summed up the dire situation facing the country.

THE ANARCHY SPREADS

DESCENT INTO HELL

RULE OF THE MOB

THE BATTLE FOR LONDON

FLAMING MORONS

THUGS AND THIEVES TAKE OVER THE STREETS

Anna sat back in her chair as the blood hummed in her ears. She experienced a sudden urge to get in her car and drive over to Tom's flat so that she could put a protective arm around her daughter and tell her yet again how much she loved her.

The motherly instinct had resurfaced the moment Chloe had come back into her life. And it was stronger now than ever because it was obvious that at this moment in time nobody in London was safe.

CHAPTER THIRTY-ONE

Her tears had dried up but inside she was still crying. It was causing her body to shake and her heart to beat so hard that she thought she could actually hear it thumping against her ribs.

She was still at the kitchen table and Wesley was sitting opposite her again. She couldn't believe he was being so kind. He was like a different person now, and even his features were softer and less threatening.

She wasn't sure if it was because he now knew that she was the girl who had been on the news, the one who had been missing for ten years. But she didn't care anyway. He was making her feel safe, and she no longer thought that he was such a bad person.

'Do you want another cup of tea?' he asked her.

She nodded. She'd finished the first one and it had made her stomach gurgle. But it had also quenched her thirst and she felt better for it.

Wesley got up to reheat the water in the kettle and to get himself another beer from the fridge.

He had already tried to call Wandsworth police station to contact her mother but hadn't been able to get through. He didn't even get an answer when he dialled 999 again, and she could tell that it was making him anxious.

There was a clock on the worktop next to the toaster. It told Chloe that it was almost one a.m. on Saturday morning, which meant it'd be dark for at least another six hours. It made her wonder what state London would be in when the sun finally rose.

'Are you hungry?' Wesley asked as he placed a large round tin of biscuits on the table in front of her.

She shook her head. She didn't think she would be able to keep anything down, not even a biscuit.

'We'll just have to sit it out for a while,' he said. 'I'll keep trying to reach your mum, though. Try not to worry.'

But she couldn't help worrying, or being scared. She had seen so many bad things in such a short time. First there was the attack on the old man who lived across the road from their house. Then Tom was dragged off by those men. Not long after that she almost fell victim to a pair of rapists. And she could still hear Ryan's screams in her head as he fought against the flames that killed him.

Despite what Wesley had told her, Chloe was confused as well as fearful. She still did not understand why people like him thought that their actions were justified and that it was all right to turn on one another. And they were wrong to accuse the police of being the enemy. They were the ones who caught the murderers and thieves and gangsters and put them in prison. Without people like her mum nobody would be safe.

Wesley handed her another mug of tea and sat down opposite her again. His dark cheeks were damp, his eyes puffy.

'This is really fucked up,' he said. 'I can't remember the last time I cried. It must have been when I was about your age.'

'I've cried every day for weeks,' Chloe said, and the distress in her voice was evident. 'Ever since that man pulled me into his van.'

'I remember seeing it on the news,' Wesley said. 'Me and Ryan stayed in that night because we were babysitting his kid sister, Phoebe. They showed a picture of you and there was film of that warehouse. At least the sicko who took you there is dead. Shame about the woman, though. She didn't deserve that.'

Chloe could feel the tears gathering in her eyes again so she picked up the mug and sipped at the tea.

'You remind me of Phoebe,' Wesley said. 'You're both very mature for your age. She's taller and more streetwise, but I'm sure she'd find it just as hard to cope if she was in your shoes right now.'

Chloe put down the mug and said, 'Will you try to get through to the police station again please?'

Wesley nodded and stood up to retrieve his phone from on top of the worktop. But just as he picked it up, it started to ring.

Chloe watched him check the caller ID and noticed how his nostrils flared suddenly.

'This is what I've been dreading,' he said. 'It's Ryan's mum. She'll be wanting to know why she can't get through to him.'

'Are you going to tell her?' Chloe asked.

He shook his head. 'I can't. I'm not ready for that.'

He placed the phone back on the worktop and they both stared at it until the ringing stopped.

Wesley then turned back to Chloe. 'You must think I'm a coward.'

Chloe wasn't sure what to say so she didn't reply. Instead, she swallowed some more tea and winced as it burned a track down the back of her throat.

'I'll go over to their place as soon as I get the chance,' he said. 'It's best that the family hears it from me in person rather than over the phone.'

He remained standing with his eyes closed and his body stiff. Neither of them spoke for at least a minute.

Then Wesley opened his eyes, picked up the phone, and tried to get through to Wandsworth police station. But the line was still busy. He dialled 999 and got the same response.

This time it really got to him and he reacted angrily by throwing the phone across the kitchen. It smashed against the wall and dropped onto the floor.

Wesley rushed over to pick it up, but the phone was in pieces.

'I don't believe this,' he said, his voice a low growl. 'It's the only phone I've got. How could I be so fucking stupid?'

Chloe felt her spirits plummet because she knew it meant that she wouldn't be speaking to her mum any time soon.

CHAPTER THIRTY-TWO

Emotions were running high in Anna's head as she walked out of her office into the ops room. She knew that the only way to take her mind off Chloe was to get on with the job.

DI Walker had already set things up for another briefing. He'd scrawled some more notes on one of the whiteboards, adding updates he'd got from the detectives who were out and about, and he'd gathered the team together. Anna took up her usual position between the two whiteboards and inhaled deeply, filling her lungs with a calming breath. She kicked off with a word of thanks to everyone for working through the night. And she acknowledged how difficult and frustrating the investigation was proving to be.

'These are exceptional circumstances,' she said, and her voice shook a little. 'In all my years on the force I have never known anything like it. When any of you leave here to follow up a lead or simply to go home I want you to be extra careful, especially after dark. And do not take any risks. Is that clear?'

There were a few murmurs and nods of heads. The faces

that stared back at her were tight with tension. She knew that each one of her officers was just as anxious as she was about what they were up against.

Anna then launched into an account of their conversation with Gavin Pope and his wife.

'Pope repeated what he told DI Benning about having nothing to do with Jacob's abduction. He continues to claim that he was at home by himself on Monday afternoon.'

She then told the team about Mrs Pope's affair with Mark Rossi and it prompted more than a few surprised looks.

'This came as a bolt from the blue and opens up a whole new line of inquiry,' she said. 'Mrs Pope claims that Rossi is a bit of a player and she gave us the name of another bloke whose wife apparently fell for his charms.'

Anna ran through what they were told about Roy Slater, including the fact that he was paid off to leave Glory Entertainment and that he allegedly has – or had – a gambling problem.

'DC Niven and a uniform were on their way to his house in Rotherhithe,' she said. 'But the last I heard their car suffered a puncture and they were stuck somewhere along the way.'

She asked Walker if their situation had changed in the last half an hour.

'Niven just called in to update me,' Walker answered. 'They've managed to change the wheel themselves and are back on the road. But Christ only knows how long it will take them to reach their destination. Some of the streets in Rotherhithe are closed, and a mob has stormed the Surrey Quays shopping centre. Latest reports indicate that more than ten stores have been looted and two set on fire.'

Anna shook her head and a hot flush of rage burned across

her cheeks. She was appalled to think that so many people could behave so outrageously in what was supposed to be a civilised society.

'Let's hope that DC Niven can steer clear of the worst of it,' she said. 'Now what about Neville Quinlan's house? Are forensics there yet?'

Walker nodded. 'They arrived twenty minutes ago. DS Prescott was there before them and got Quinlan out of bed to serve him with the search warrant. Prescott will call if and when they find something.'

Walker then said that the forensic evidence from the pub, including Jacob's bag and clothes, were waiting to be examined at the lab.

'The forensics guys have finished up there now and will be moving on to another crime scene. They're going to board up the entrance before they leave.'

Anna asked Walker for an update on Michelle Gerrard.

'We've finally got some details, including an address,' he said. 'She's a single lady in her late fifties and it turns out she lives in Beckenham, which is only a couple of miles from the Rossi home. I've asked the locals to send someone round. Meanwhile, a techie is going through her social media posts. The last time she wrote anything offensive about Rossi was two weeks ago. She remarked on Twitter that he was getting too much media exposure and that she was fed up with him going on about how lucky he was to have such a great family.'

'Do we know if Rossi is acquainted with her?'

'I got the FLO to ask him and he says he's never met her. But he has seen the posts and they do piss him off.'

'Then we need to bring her in for a serious chat as quickly as possible.' Anna then summed up where they were with the investigation, and pointed out that although they had four potential suspects, there could be more who had yet to be identified.

'I don't anticipate we'll make much headway until the night is over,' she said. 'So we should make use of this time to view as much CCTV footage as possible and to prepare profiles on all the main characters so far involved in this sorry saga. I would urge you all to read through the missing person's case notes supplied by DI Benning. Meanwhile, I'll liaise with DCS Nash about getting a press release sorted and I'll talk to the pathologist to arrange for the family to formally ID Jacob's body before the post-mortem. I'll also circulate a list of action points for Saturday.'

Anna invited questions, and when none were forthcoming, she ended the briefing.

Before going back into her office, she asked DI Benning if he was still prepared to work on through the night.

'You couldn't drag me away from here, ma'am,' he said. 'I need to stay with this to the bitter end. That boy died on my watch so I feel the least I should do is help track down the bastard who put him in that cellar.'

CHAPTER THIRTY-THREE

It was almost two o'clock in the morning and at Wesley's suggestion Chloe had moved from the kitchen to the front room. He'd told her that he wouldn't be leaving the flat until it was light outside so she might as well make herself comfortable.

She was sitting on the sofa and he was slouched on the armchair opposite. They both had a view of the television, and Wesley kept switching between the news channels. He was no longer reacting to the pictures by shouting and swearing at the screen. Chloe thought that was probably because he had drunk too much alcohol. There were four empty beer bottles on the floor next to his chair and he was now drinking large amounts of vodka while smoking one cigarette after another.

He'd told Chloe to help herself to the cans of Coke in the fridge and she was on her second one. She was tired and uncomfortable, and even though Wesley had made her take a couple of painkillers, her head was still hurting. But she wasn't complaining because what she saw on the telly made her realise how lucky she was not to be on the streets still.

More buildings were being set on fire and the lady reading the news was saying that four people had so far died in the riots. Chloe wondered if the figure included Ryan.

On screen a man in uniform, described as the Commissioner of the Metropolitan Police, stood in front of a Scotland Yard sign and said a decision had been taken to deploy the army in parts of London. Chloe assumed that he was the big boss of all the police and she wondered if her mum knew him.

The man also said that hundreds of people had been arrested and would face the full force of the law. Chloe took that to mean that they would be sent to prison, but Wesley didn't appear to take it seriously.

'That motherfucker is a prick,' he said, slurring his words. 'Most of them will be back on the streets by this time tomorrow.'

It worried Chloe that Wesley was getting so drunk. She was old enough to know that drink caused people to do silly things. And sometimes it made them violent.

'This has got to be the biggest fucking wake-up call ever,' he said. 'From now on things will be different in this city, and that means Ryan won't have died for nothing.'

Chloe wanted to tell him that he was wrong, but she didn't dare because she feared it would provoke a nasty reaction.

If he hadn't been drinking, she might have been brave enough. She would have told him that it wasn't right that people had been killed, that buildings had been destroyed, and that her mum's boyfriend had been treated like an animal.

She couldn't stop thinking about Tom and what had happened to him. She was desperate to know if he was still alive. If not, then her mum was going to be heartbroken. If he was then she just hoped that he wasn't lying seriously injured somewhere with nobody taking care of him.

It was one of the many tortured thoughts tearing through her mind, along with so many distressing images. It felt like she was trapped in a never-ending nightmare.

For the past month she'd been struggling with Sophie's tragic death and the revelation that her real mum was still alive. Now she was struggling just to survive. And if she did, she had no idea what her life would be like in the future.

Her mind flashed on a long-forgotten memory from the years she spent growing up in Spain with Sophie and her dad.

The three of them were playing ball in the sea. The sun was shining and the white sandy beach was deserted. She recalled how much fun life was back then. Everything was so simple. And safe. But since moving to England it had been anything but. First her dad was murdered. Then Sophie sacrificed her own life to save her. And now she was sitting in the flat of a violent hooligan, knowing that he could turn on her at any minute.

'. . . and it's now been confirmed that a boy of ten died in the fire that swept through a derelict pub in Camberwell, South London, this afternoon. The blaze was started by a rioter who threw a petrol bomb.'

The words of the newsreader jolted Chloe out of her thoughts suddenly. There was an urgency in the woman's voice that grabbed her attention.

'The boy hasn't been formally identified, but a police source has told us that the body found in the building is that of Jacob Rossi who's been missing since Monday when it's believed he was abducted.' The newsreader continued speaking

186

over a photo of the boy. 'Jacob is the son of TV entertainer Mark Rossi. We understand that the Major Investigation Team has launched an inquiry led by Detective Chief Inspector Anna Tate.

'Detective Tate is one of London's most prominent police officers following several high-profile cases, including the kidnapping of nine children from a nursery school last month. She's also been in the news because she was recently reunited with her own daughter who was missing for ten years after being taken away by her father.'

Chloe gasped as the photo of Jacob was replaced by one of her mother. She sat bolt upright and thrust a rigid finger at the screen.

'There she is,' she blurted out. 'There's my mum.'

But Wesley wasn't listening or watching the TV. He was slumped back in the chair, his eyes closed and his mouth wide open.

The glass he'd been drinking from was resting on his stomach, and the vodka had spilled onto his jeans, making it look as though he had wet himself.

Chloe looked back at the screen. Her mum's photo had gone, but it was still there in her mind, instilling her with renewed confidence. Knowing that she was OK and doing her job came as such a relief. But suddenly a thought made her wince: *She obviously still doesn't know what's happened to Tom.*

Chloe felt an unfamiliar sensation stir inside her and she realised, perhaps for the first time, just how much her mother meant to her. Since the truth about her real identity came out a month ago, Chloe had struggled with her feelings. It had been hard to accept that Anna had taken Sophie's place.

After all, Chloe was only two when her dad whisked her off to Spain and she couldn't remember anything before then. Even the photos her father had kept of Anna hadn't brought back any memories.

But now Chloe couldn't bear the thought of losing her. And she didn't want to see her suffer in any way. But if Tom was no longer alive, she was going to be devastated. And the thought of that made Chloe feel sick and brought on a flood of tears.

And she didn't stop crying until she fell asleep.

CHAPTER THIRTY-FOUR

Anna was busy typing up the list of action points when the BBC ran the story about the boy found dead inside the derelict pub in Camberwell.

Surprise quickly turned to anger when they identified him as Jacob Rossi.

Quoting an unnamed source was their way of saying that there had been a leak. Anna was pretty sure it hadn't come from a member of her own team. She trusted them all implicitly. More likely someone at the Yard or within the fire brigade had let it out either accidentally or on purpose.

The press office would now have to release a statement pointing out that the body hadn't been formally identified. But they would also be obliged to say that it was believed to be that of the missing boy.

DI Walker came rushing into her office to tell her what she already knew.

'I'd stake my life on it not being one of our lot who leaked it,' he said.

Anna nodded. 'I agree with you, Max. So make it known that I'm not about to cast aspersions. It's bloody annoying, but not entirely unexpected. I'll talk to Nash about a response.'

The DCS had just emerged from a meeting of senior Met officers when Anna reached him on the phone. He'd been told about the BBC story but hadn't seen it for himself. And he didn't sound too fazed by it, probably because he had so many other things on his plate.

'I'll talk to media liaison right away and get them to issue a press release,' he said. 'To be honest I'm a little surprised it's taken this long for the hacks to get wind of it. You know yourself that the Met is like a sieve these days. Leaks are all too common.'

'Do you think we should make it known that Jacob was chained to a wall in the cellar, sir?' Anna asked him.

'I don't see why not. The more impact it has the more chance we've got of it generating some useful leads.'

He asked her how the case was progressing, but she sensed that he was only half-listening to what she told him.

'I won't be coming back to Wandsworth for a while,' he said. 'There's too much going on here and everyone is in a right panic. Have you heard about the army being deployed in some areas?'

'Yes, I have . . . I just hope that it doesn't make a bad situation even worse,' Anna said.

'I agree, but the truth is we're not coping. This is now a crisis of epic proportions.'

They agreed to talk again in a few hours, and Anna hung up. She then put in a call to Phillipa Moore, the family liaison officer with Jacob's parents. Unsurprisingly, Moore was awake because the couple had already received several calls from reporters following up the BBC story.

'On my advice, Mr Rossi has declined to speak to them,' Moore said. 'But he and his wife are really struggling. They still can't accept that it was Jacob who was found in the cellar.'

'I'd like one or both of them to carry out a formal identification as soon as possible,' Anna said. 'I'll talk to the pathologist and get back to you with a time.'

Gayle Western was also working through the night. When she answered the phone to Anna she was on her way back to the mortuary from Brixton where a man had died from a knife wound outside a superstore.

'We really need to get back control of the streets,' Gayle said, her voice shrill with anxiety. 'If this carries on we'll soon run out of body bags.'

Gayle said she would arrange for Jacob to be identified by his parents at ten a.m., and after that she would aim to proceed with the post-mortem.

Anna passed this information on to Phillipa Moore, then went back to typing up the list of action points. She printed off hard copies and attached it to a group email she sent to every member of the team, plus Nash.

The night passed quickly after that, and Anna spent it flitting between her office and the ops room. The questions continued to tumble through her mind at a rate of knots.

But the answers didn't start coming through until after five a.m.

*

The first update of any significance came from DC Niven who was in Rotherhithe. He had eventually arrived at Roy Slater's home only to find that he wasn't in.

'He's living in a terraced house that's a bit run-down,' Niven said. 'There was a light on next door so I rang the bell and spoke to the neighbour. She said he's a single guy, and keeps very much to himself. He works as a packer in a warehouse off the Old Kent Road. The neighbour saw him go out in his car yesterday afternoon, but he hasn't returned and his car isn't parked in its usual place out front.

'I went to the warehouse and it has a night shift. The supervisor told me Slater has been on leave for over a week and isn't due back until next Thursday. I was given his mobile phone number and I've tried ringing it, but it's switched off.'

'Did the supervisor tell you anything about the guy?' Anna asked.

'He's worked for the company for about five months,' Niven said. 'He's moody and quiet apparently, and not very popular with his colleagues who don't appear to know much about his personal life. He doesn't socialise with any of them. But it's no secret that he likes a bet. He's always moaning about losing money on the horses and fruit machines. And he confided in one workmate that he's been struggling to pay off a bunch of payday loans.'

'OK, if you haven't already got his car registration then go and get it so we can run it through the system,' Anna said. 'With luck it will turn up on an ANPR camera, which will hopefully give us a clue as to where he is. I'll see if I can get a warrant to search his house so go back there and wait for me to call. If by chance he turns up then let me know. It could be he's just gone away for a couple of days.'

DI Walker had already established that Slater, who was fifty-four, was on the police database. He'd been convicted and fined two years ago on three counts of shoplifting. Walker took it upon himself to pursue the search warrant and work up Slater's profile.

Meanwhile, the question of whether the forensics team would find anything significant in Neville Quinlan's flat was answered by DS Prescott.

'It looks clean,' he said. 'They've taken a few things away to be checked for Jacob's DNA and clothes fibres. But there was nothing to link him to the boy.'

'And how was Quinlan?' Anna asked.

'He was cooperative even though he wasn't happy about being hauled out of bed. I got the impression that he was expecting us to turn up at some point and was resigned to it.'

'Well I'm tasking you with staying on his case. Bring him in for further questioning if you think it's necessary. As I've already made clear, I just don't buy his story about parking outside Jacob's school because he felt too unwell to drive. The guy's a convicted paedophile, for heaven's sake. I'm convinced there's more to it than that.'

'I hear you, guv,' Prescott said. 'There's no point bringing him in yet, though. I need to carry out more checks and round up some more CCTV footage.'

'I'll leave it to you then,' Anna told him. 'Meanwhile, I've circulated a list of action points. It'll keep you abreast of what else is happening.'

Anna then called forensics to see if any of the exhibits taken from the pub had been processed yet. She spoke to a crime scene investigator named Kenny Fallon, who she knew quite well. He said they were under huge pressure so were making slow progress.

'What I can tell you is that we've carried out an initial

assessment of the boy's clothes, the mattress he was on, the quilt and the holdall that was next to the bed,' he said. 'No bloodstains are visible to the naked eye, but there are various hairs and fibres that will need to be examined under the scope. The problem we face is that most of the stuff has been contaminated by water, soot and dust. And as you know the cellar itself offered up very little in the way of potential evidence.'

Fallon said he would send over a preliminary report as soon as he was able to.

Walker then provided a further update on Michelle Gerrard, the woman who had been hounding Mark Rossi on social media platforms.

'She wasn't at home when an officer called round,' he said. 'But neighbours told him they don't see much of her and they don't know where she is. Apparently she often disappears for days at a time.'

'Well let's keep trying to find her, if only to eliminate her.'

During the next half hour Anna discussed the updates with the rest of the team while they all monitored the TV news channels. Stories relating to the riots were the only ones being covered, and included the boy who had died while chained to the wall in the pub cellar.

The press release from the Yard was enough to convince the media that it was indeed Jacob Rossi, even though a spokesperson stressed that the body hadn't been formally identified. The story was expanded to include information about Jacob's father, his school, and the search that had been underway for him since Monday.

At six a.m. Detective Khan returned from Camberwell, leaving detectives Sweeny and Mortimer behind to keep an eye on the crime scene and be on hand if a likely suspect turned up.

Khan had two nuggets of information to report from the house-to-house inquiries he'd been helping to carry out. A couple of the neighbours had told them that a homeless man named George usually slept rough in the doorway of the derelict pub, and sometimes inside it.

'Apparently he's a familiar face in the area, but since the riots began, he hasn't appeared,' Khan said. 'I'm guessing he's found a safe place to kip. Sweeny and Mortimer are on the lookout for him. Also, one of the home owners living opposite the pub had noticed a dark car drive onto the forecourt several times during the past few weeks and park around the back of the building. He assumed at the time that it belonged to someone working for the estate agents. According to this bloke, and several others we spoke to, there used to be a rope across the entrance along with a no trespass sign. But it disappeared months ago and was never replaced.'

'Do you have the make of the car or, better still, the plate number?' Anna asked.

'I'm afraid not. The guy said he didn't pay much attention to it. But he thinks it was a saloon rather than a hatchback. And it was dark blue or black.'

'Plug away at it then,' Anna said. 'We've got some officers starting afresh later having had a night's sleep. Arrange for them to take over from Sweeny and Mortimer. And put the word out on the homeless guy. If he was bedding down next to the pub it's possible he saw something. And speak to the estate agents to find out if the car does belong to one of their staff.'

Another hour came and went, then Anna took a call from Phillipa Moore. The FLO sounded breathless and distressed.

'You need to get over here right away, ma'am,' she said in a high-pitched voice. 'There's been a development.'

'Calm down and tell me what you're on about, Officer,' Anna said.

Moore took a breath before continuing. 'The postman just arrived with a letter for Mr Rossi,' she said. 'He explained that there's been a delay in delivering mail because of the riots, and that the letter was posted with first-class stamps on Tuesday, the day after Jacob disappeared. Inside was a note that appears to be from whoever abducted him. And with it is a photo of the boy chained to the cellar wall.'

'My God.'

'I've made sure that nobody has touched any of it apart from Mr Rossi. I've put each item into an evidence bag, including the padded envelope.'

'That's good, Phillipa. Now what I'd like you to do is take photos of the items and send them to me. I want to know what we're dealing with before I head over. And then you need to tell Mr and Mrs Rossi that I've arranged for them to visit the mortuary at ten o'clock this morning.'

Anna rushed into the ops room to alert the team. Seconds later pictures of the letter, the photo, and the envelope arrived on her phone. As she opened them up and viewed them, a cold weight settled in her chest and she was suddenly unable to speak.

The added pain that must have suddenly been inflicted on the poor parents just didn't bear thinking about.

CHAPTER THIRTY-FIVE

By seven forty-five, after another quick meeting with the team, Anna was heading back to Bromley.

At last dawn was breaking over London and the streets were quieter. But not all the rioters had decided to take a break. Major disturbances were still happening in parts of the city, and the morning rush hour was adding to the traffic chaos in places.

DI Benning was in the passenger seat of the pool car and the pair were discussing the contents of the letter that had been sent to Mark Rossi.

There was no question that it had come from his son's kidnapper. The colour photo showed Jacob sitting on the inflatable mattress in the cellar with his back against the wall. He was staring at the camera, eyes wide, a look of abject terror on his face. The leather manacles on his wrists were clearly visible, as was the chain that snaked off to the left and out of shot.

Jacob was wearing his blue shirt and trousers, but his shoes had been removed. There was no way of knowing if the photo had been taken on Monday after he was snatched or at some point on Tuesday before the letter was posted.

Anna could only imagine how awful it was for Jacob's parents to see for themselves how their son had spent the last few days of his young life. It was a truly horrific image of a boy who was scared, vulnerable and at the mercy of a sadistic monster.

It gave no clue as to the identity of the kidnapper, but it was further evidence of just how cruel that person was.

The short, printed note that accompanied it was just as chilling:

> *I'm sick of seeing you boast about your perfect life on social media, Rossi. You've had it too good for too long and that's not fair. You act as though you're special and more deserving than the rest of us. So I've taken your son because I want to see you suffer. And I'm sure you will when you're sitting at home wondering what I'm doing to him. Pleasant dreams, Mr big shot TV man.*

Anna had left the team with instructions to dissect the note and to solicit the opinion of one of the Met's criminal behavioural analysts. The message was stark and venomous, and it raised a number of questions that needed to be considered. She was curious to know, for instance, why there was no ransom demand. And also if the kidnapper was one of Rossi's followers on Twitter, Facebook or Instagram.

When she started reading it, she immediately leapt to the conclusion that it was written by someone with no link to Mark Rossi other than through social media. A complete stranger in other words, someone such as Michelle Gerrard, the mystery woman who'd been posting disparaging remarks about him.

Back at headquarters, DI Walker had pointed out that people often created an illusion of intimacy with celebrities through social media.

'I read a report recently that dealt with this very subject,' he said. 'It was commissioned by some behavioural science unit in the States following a big increase in the number of attacks on public figures, especially actors and pop stars.

'It coined some interesting phrases that have stuck in my mind. It said that for a lot of people a so-called digital relationship feels like a personal connection. By following their idols on sites like Facebook, Twitter and Instagram they somehow convince themselves that they're involved in a two-way conversation, which in turn amplifies infatuation. But it can also lead to problems when they blame those same idols for their own troubled lives and seek revenge against them.'

Anna had asked Walker to dig out the report and have it circulated. It was certainly something she would make a point of reading.

DI Benning had a different take on the kidnapper's note, though, and reckoned they should be cautious about reading too much into it.

'We can't ignore the possibility that the note might have been sent with two objectives in mind,' he said. 'One was clearly to upset Mark Rossi. But what if the aim was also to cause an element of confusion, to make us shift our attention away from the obvious suspects?'

Anna had to agree that it was certainly a consideration given that those suspects included a local paedophile and two men who found out their wives had slept with Rossi. If one of them was indeed the perp, then he might have anticipated being placed in the frame by the police and decided to pen the note as a diversionary tactic.

'One conclusion I think we can safely draw from the wording is that the kidnapper is acting alone,' Benning said. 'It's written in the first person – *I've* taken your son – *I* want to see you suffer – *I'm* doing to him.'

'And that's useful to know,' Anna said. 'It should mean we can rule out anyone who can provide a cast-iron alibi for when Jacob was abducted on Monday.'

Anna's mind spun with so many questions that it was beginning to make her head ache.

Would the perp have made the mistake of leaving a print or DNA trace on the note, the photo, or on the envelope they were put into?

Did the note suggest that the kidnapper had been planning to keep Jacob alive in order to taunt his father with more photos of him in the cellar?

Or had the intention been to eventually demand a ransom?

Anna also wondered if the kidnapper had known that the parcel hadn't been delivered on Wednesday. Having been posted first class on the Tuesday, it should have arrived the following day. But there'd been a delay because of the riots.

So had the perp spent Wednesday, Thursday and Friday wondering why there had been no reaction from the police and the family through the media?

If so, then would this have made him or her angry since the stated objective had been to see Mark Rossi suffer?

CHAPTER THIRTY-SIX

Presenter: *'This is the BBC news at eight o'clock . . . and another person has died as a result of the rioting, bringing the total number to five. Dozens more have been taken to hospital with serious injuries.*

'Most of the violence is still taking place in London. In Peckham rioters clashed with a group of soldiers who had been drafted in and there are reports of shots being fired. A petrol bomb was thrown through the window of a car showroom in Greenwich, causing a massive explosion. And a mob of youths has now descended on the Brent Cross Shopping Centre in Hendon where stores are being ransacked and vandalised.

'The Mayor of London has been speaking to reporters in front of City Hall.'

London Mayor: *'The level of violence and destruction that's being inflicted on our city is horrific. The police and other emergency services are coping as best they can and*

I am hopeful that the situation will soon be brought under control.

'A great many people are suffering, and so we're setting up a number of crisis centres to help those people who have lost their homes and businesses. Details will be available shortly.'

Presenter: *'The mayor went on to say that extra funding is being made available to help kick-start clean-up operations across the capital.*

'Outside London trouble has now spread to other cities . . .'

CHAPTER THIRTY-SEVEN

As expected, the vultures had descended on the Rossi house. A Sky News satellite truck was parked in the street and a group of about ten reporters and photographers were gathered on the pavement.

Camera flashes erupted and Anna and Benning faced a barrage of questions as they pulled into the kerb and got out of the car.

'Can you confirm that the dead boy is Jacob Rossi?'

'Was the boy killed before the fire started?'

'Had he been chained up in the cellar since he was abducted?'

'Do you have any suspects?'

'Is an arrest imminent?'

Anna decided to seize the opportunity to appeal for help from the public. She told Benning to go up to the house while she stood with her back to the driveway and gestured for the hacks, photographers and the one TV camera crew to gather round.

She introduced herself, which was unnecessary since they all knew who she was.

'I would ask you all to appreciate that this is a difficult time for the family,' she said. 'It's true that the body found in the derelict pub has not been formally identified, but all the evidence indicates that it's Jacob Rossi, who went missing on Monday. His death is believed to have been due to smoke inhalation. Jacob was trapped in the cellar of the building when it was set on fire and he was unable to escape because he was chained to a wall. There are therefore two strands to our investigation. We want to know who was holding Jacob captive in the building, and who carried out the arson attack.

'It's obvious to us that we're looking for two different people. The fire was started by a rioter who threw a petrol bomb, but we don't think that person knew there was a boy in the building. Nevertheless, he or she committed a serious crime, and we would like to hear from anyone who witnessed it.

'We believe that Jacob was taken to the building after he was abducted on Monday, and it's possible that someone has information that can help us with our inquiries.'

Anna provided more details, including the exact location of the old Falconer's Arms pub, and the road in Bromley where it was thought Jacob had been picked up.

She said that her team were still trying to establish the motive for the kidnapping, but decided not to mention the letter that had been sent to Jacob's father.

More questions were fired at her, but she politely declined to answer them and walked up to the house. Officer Moore was holding the front door open, and as Anna stepped over the threshold, she said, 'Mark's mother is here. Her name's Emily. And be warned, ma'am, they're all in a bad way.'

The three of them were in the spacious kitchen/diner. Rossi stood with his back to the sink, his arms folded, his face grey and pallid. His wife and mother were sitting at the table in the dining area, hunched over mugs of hot drinks. Benning was hovering next to the breakfast bar in the centre of the room. On top of it rested three evidence bags containing the letter from the kidnapper, the photo of Jacob and the envelope they arrived in.

A palpable sense of shock and despair hung heavily in the air. It was obvious to Anna that a lot of tears had been shed since the postman's visit. But Jacob's grandmother was the only one still sobbing. She was a small, frail-looking woman with wrinkled features and a crown of curly white hair.

Anna walked over to her and placed a hand lightly on her shoulder.

'I'm Detective Chief Inspector Tate,' she said. 'You must be Emily.'

The woman looked up at her through liquid eyes and spoke in a voice that was throbbing with sadness.

'Whoever did this to our darling boy should be made to suffer for all eternity,' she said. 'They can't be allowed to get away with it. They just can't.'

'And I will do everything in my power to ensure that they don't,' Anna said. 'I promise you that my team won't rest until those responsible are behind bars.'

Emily shook her head. 'Jail is too good for them. A slow, painful death would be the only acceptable form of justice.'

'My mother is right,' Mark Rossi said sharply. 'That photo of my son was taken by someone who has no right to go on living.'

Anna turned towards him and noticed how his good looks had all but disappeared. His face was tense and haggard, and there were tired shadows beneath his eyes.

'I just don't understand why a person would be so cruel,' he continued. 'I know that there are people out there who don't like me. But that's the same for anyone who spends his or her life in the spotlight. I can't imagine what I might have done to make someone hate me so much.'

If the circumstances had been different, Anna would have pointed out there and then that he was being disingenuous, and that sleeping with other men's wives was a sure way to incur their wrath. But the man was grief-stricken, so she would have to broach the subject delicately and preferably when she managed to get him by himself.

She crossed to the breakfast bar and picked up the clear evidence bag with the note inside.

'We've deduced from what's written on here that the perpetrator, who we strongly believe to be a man, is probably acting alone,' she said. 'And it's possible that you haven't actually met him, Mr Rossi, or given him any reason to hate you.'

His wife spoke up at this point, her voice weak, strained.

'Then why is he blaming my husband for what he did to Jacob? It makes no sense.'

'Our job is to try to make sense of it, Mrs Rossi,' Anna said. 'We've some way to go, I'm afraid. I'm hoping that the photograph and the letter will help us to get there.'

'So what progress have you made?' This from her husband.

Anna looked at her watch. 'We've got plenty of time before we need to leave for the mortuary, Mr Rossi. So I'll bring you up to speed, and if it's OK I'd like to ask you both some more questions.'

Anna tried to put a positive spin on what she told them. She said that Gavin Pope and the man who was seen loitering outside Jacob's school had both been re-interviewed and further checks were being carried out on them.

'We're also looking into the backgrounds and alibis of the other former employees of your stepfather's company who were left out of pocket when it collapsed,' she said.

Anna mentioned that other leads were being pursued, including the sighting of a dark-coloured car on the forecourt of the derelict pub.

'In addition, we're trawling social media sites for trolls who have uploaded posts which were either abusive or threatening against you, Mr Rossi,' she said. 'And I've issued a public appeal in which I've said I want to hear from anyone who thinks they might have information.'

Anna could tell that the family were not impressed, which was hardly surprising since she wasn't offering up anything concrete.

'I can't even begin to imagine what you're all going through,' she said. 'But I need to know if there is anyone else you think we should be talking to. Perhaps someone in the past who you had concerns about. Or did Jacob mention having an unusual encounter with anyone in particular? Maybe a teacher at his school?'

Rossi shook his head. 'We've been over this already. Jacob never mentioned anything like that, and we can't think of anyone who would want to do this to us.'

'So what about The Falconer's Arms pub? Had you ever heard of it before yesterday?'

'No we hadn't,' Rossi said.

'What about Camberwell then? To your knowledge do you have – or have you had – any friends, relatives or acquaintances who live or work in that part of London?'

The question prompted an unexpected reaction from Emily, who said, 'I've never heard of that pub, but I do know that my late husband's ex-partner was living in Camberwell when she died. That was five years or so ago.'

Anna's ears pricked up, but Rossi responded before she did.

'You never told me that, Mum. How do you know?'

'Your stepfather found out by chance,' she said. 'He bumped into a man they both knew while they were together, and he told Isaac that she was in the last stages of terminal lung cancer and was being looked after by her son who had moved in with her.'

'So why didn't you tell me?'

Emily looked at him. 'Because your stepfather asked me not to. You see, he managed to find out their address in Camberwell and out of guilt he went there to see if there was anything he could do to help. But there was nobody at home. A neighbour told him she was in Guy's Hospital. When he got there her son – who as you know, Mark, is also Isaac's son – was at her bedside. He was furious apparently because they hadn't heard from Isaac since he walked out on them and married me. He told Isaac to bugger off. When Isaac came home, he was really upset and didn't want to talk about it afterwards. He did tell me a week later that she died in hospital, though.'

Anna was intrigued. She shot a look at Benning, who arched his brow and gave a little shrug. She took it to mean that this was news to him as well.

Taking out her notebook, she said to Emily, 'Can you please tell me the names of your husband's ex-partner and their son?'

'Hilary and Joseph. Their surname was Metcalfe, but I believe it changed when she got married some years ago. Isaac never told me what her married name was.'

Anna made a note. 'I didn't realise that your late husband had a son of his own. And since his mother lived in Camberwell he'll need to be eliminated from our inquiries. Do you have any idea how we might be able to contact him?'

'None at all,' Emily said. 'Isaac never stayed in touch with them.'

'In that case I'd like you to think back and tell me everything you know about your husband's first family. We can't ignore the fact that there's a chance, albeit a slim one, that it could have a bearing on this case.'

CHAPTER THIRTY-EIGHT

Isaac Rossi's story was a familiar one. He met and fell in love with a woman named Hilary Metcalfe. After a year they moved in together and eighteen months later she became pregnant.

They often talked about marrying, but never got around to it, partly because they believed like millions of other couples that they could maintain a deep and loving relationship without having to get hitched.

Hilary gave birth to Joseph and the family lived in a rented house in Eltham for the next thirteen years.

But then Isaac decided that what he had wasn't enough. He started an affair with a woman he met through his job in television. Her name was Emily Kennedy, a widower with a son named Mark who was only a year younger than Joseph.

The affair continued for another six months before Isaac decided to leave Hilary and embark on a new life with Emily. But like many fathers who adopt another family, he decided to cut all ties with the old one.

'I bear some responsibility for the fact that Isaac didn't stay in touch with his son,' Emily said to Anna. 'Back then I was insecure and jealous, and I knew that Hilary was trying desperately to win him back, so I discouraged him from talking to her. She reacted by making it impossible for him to remain in contact with his son. She even moved up north for a couple of years.

'It suited me because Isaac then focused all his attention on Mark and became a devoted stepdad. I won't apologise for what I did because if I hadn't done it our relationship wouldn't have been so strong and we wouldn't have spent so many glorious years together.' She turned from Anna and looked at her son, who seemed shocked and confused. 'You had already lost your father, Mark, and I wasn't prepared to see it happen a second time. And before you or anyone else seeks to judge me, I'd like to make it clear that Isaac didn't need much persuading since he had never had a close relationship with Joseph anyway. In fact he told me once that he wasn't even sure he was the father because the boy looked so very different to him.'

Anna half expected Rossi to admonish his mother for what she did all those years ago. Instead he rushed across the room to embrace her and they both broke down.

It was an awkward, yet touching scene, and Anna let it play out as she tried to decide how to move things forward. Emily's impromptu confession had added to the cluster of emotions that had consumed the family.

And it had thrown another suspect into the mix – Mark Rossi's stepbrother, Joseph.

Anna needed to find out if he was still living in Camberwell, and if he harboured any kind of grudge against his father's adopted family.

It all got too much for Emily and her sobs turned into a raging coughing fit.

Her daughter-in-law seized control of the situation and offered to take her upstairs so that she could lie down.

'Can you bring my bag?' Emily spluttered between coughs as her son helped her up from the chair. 'I haven't taken my blood pressure tablet yet.'

'Are you sure you're going to be all right here by yourself when we go to see Jacob?' Rossi asked her.

'Of course. I'll be fine. There's no need for you to worry.'

Anna felt sorry for Emily, but nevertheless she was glad the two women were leaving the room. It gave her the chance to raise with Rossi the subject of his alleged affairs, and to ask him about Roy Slater.

She gestured for Officer Moore to follow them out, and after the kitchen door was closed behind them, Rossi sat on the chair at the dining table vacated by his wife. His eyes were swollen from crying and there was a light sheen of sweat on his forehead. He leaned forward, took a long, quivering breath, and balled his hands into fists on the table.

'How much of what your mother just said did you already know?' Anna asked as she went and sat opposite him.

'I was told at an early age that I had a stepbrother,' he said. 'But I was led to believe that his mum didn't want him to have anything to do with Isaac. As a teenager I was curious, but because it was never talked about, I eventually lost interest.'

Anna then told Rossi that she wanted to talk about the conversation they'd had with Gavin Pope.

'Well I still can't believe that it was him who took Jacob in order to punish me for not bailing him out after he lost his job,' Rossi said.

'Well actually that's not the only reason he has it in for you,' Anna said.

'Oh?'

Anna was still holding her notebook. She rested it on the table and opened it up.

'We also spoke to Mr Pope's wife, Laura,' she said. 'And she told us about the brief affair you had with her.'

A flash of anger crossed his features. 'Why the fuck would she mention that? It was a long time ago and when it ended we promised each other we would keep it between ourselves.'

'That's what she tried to do,' Anna said. 'But her husband found out about the affair a year later when he stumbled on messages on her phone between the two of you that hadn't been deleted. She persuaded him that it would serve no useful purpose to let you or anyone else know about it, so he kept quiet. But that didn't mean he wasn't going to give you grief.'

'Shit. So that's why he created such a fuss over the bankruptcy.'

'So it would appear.'

'And you think that because he wasn't able to screw me for money, he might have decided to punish me by taking Jacob.'

'It's one possible scenario,' Anna said. 'But there's another involving another former employee of Glory Entertainment named Roy Slater. I gather you had a fling with his wife as well.'

Rossi's breath faltered and his eyebrows climbed up his forehead.

'Jesus, I'd completely forgotten about that slime ball.'

'So it's true then,' Anna said. 'About the affair, I mean.'

'I'm ashamed to say that it is, but all that stuff is behind me,' Rossi said. 'It was a stupid phase and Clare knows nothing about either of them. Clare was aware that Slater and his wife worked for Glory and she met them a couple of times. But she was never told why they both suddenly left and if she finds out now it will kill her.'

'Well let's hope it doesn't come to that,' Anna said. 'But can you confirm that your father paid Slater to leave the company and keep quiet about it?'

He nodded. 'It got messy after Ruth, his wife, decided to leave him because she didn't love him any more. She knew I'd never leave Clare so she planned to start a new life in France where her parents were living. But Slater overheard her talking to me on the phone. The next day he confronted me as I left the Glory Entertainment offices with Isaac. He was ranting and raving but when he finally accepted that Ruth wasn't running off with me, he calmed down. Isaac gave him a choice – he could make a fuss and get the sack with no pay-off. Or be paid ten thousand quid to accept that I wasn't to blame for the marriage breakdown and go quietly. He went for option two.'

'And was that the last you saw of him?' Anna asked.

He shook his head. 'No, it wasn't. About five months ago he phoned me out of the blue and asked for more money. He said that the ten grand we'd given him hadn't been enough to get him back on his feet. I knew all about his gambling addiction so I told him it was out of the question. I thought he'd threaten to go to the papers or get in touch with my wife, but instead he just hung up and I never heard from him again.'

'We haven't been able to talk to him yet, but do you think he would have it in him to do something like this?'

By now Rossi's face was drenched in sweat and his eyes

were glazed and haunted. His breath was coming in short gasps, and he looked to be on the verge of crying again.

'I don't really know much about him,' he said. 'But Ruth reckoned he could be a nasty piece of work when he was down on his luck. And that was much of the time because of the gambling.'

There was a box of tissues on the table. Anna reached across, pulled a couple out and handed them to Rossi.

'You've been really helpful, Mr Rossi,' she said. 'Now you need to push Roy Slater, Gavin Pope and Joseph Metcalfe from your mind and let us worry about them. Focus on supporting your wife through what is going to be a tough ordeal for both of you.'

Rossi wiped his eyes with the tissues and nodded.

'I'd better go and get ready then,' he said.

After he had stepped out of the room, and the door was closed behind him, Anna asked Benning what he'd made of what they'd been told.

'Well we've been given a lot to think about,' the DI said. 'If you like I'll follow up the stepbrother angle. It shouldn't be that hard to track him down, especially if he's still living in Camberwell. We've got his name and we know his mother died in Guy's Hospital.'

'OK, but bear in mind that it might not be as easy as you think. Metcalfe was the mother's maiden name. We don't know what it changed to when she got married.'

'Leave it with me, ma'am. I'll crack on with it as soon as we're finished at the mortuary.'

'And what about Roy Slater?' Anna asked.

Benning shrugged. 'Well he's got to be a serious contender. If he's desperate for money again, then one plausible scenario is that he was planning to demand a ransom for Jacob and never intended to actually hurt him.'

'So why send the photo and note?'

Benning pursed his lips and thought about it. Then: 'That's a good question, ma'am. It could be that his aim was to ratchet up the fear factor before delivering the punchline. That picture of Jacob chained to the wall would surely have prompted his father to stump up any amount of cash to get him back.'

Anna was about to ask another question when the kitchen door opened and Officer Moore reappeared. She was clutching her phone in one hand and looked a little flustered.

'I've just taken a call from Detective Inspector Walker at MIT headquarters,' she said. 'He's been trying to ring you, guv.'

'My phone's on silent,' Anna replied.

'Well he wants you to contact him right away. He says it's urgent.'

'And did he tell you what it's about?'

Moore hesitated before answering. 'He did, guv. It's your partner, Tom Bannerman. Something has happened to him.'

CHAPTER THIRTY-NINE

Chloe was back on the streets, running for her life. There was chaos all around her. Buildings and cars were on fire, shops were being looted, angry men in masks and hoods were throwing projectiles at each other.

She could see a mass of emergency vehicles up ahead, their lights strobing in the gloom. And she could hear the loud growl of a helicopter as it circled overhead.

Just as before she had no idea where she was going, but she told herself that she had to keep moving. She couldn't believe that all of London had been taken over by the rioters. That surely wasn't possible. There were simply too many streets and too many buildings. So if she ploughed on she was bound to reach a safe place eventually.

The trouble was she felt so weak and tired. Her legs were aching and every breath she took filled her lungs with more smoke and dust from the fires.

She ran past a man who was lying in the road with half his face missing. Then she watched a woman jump from a window above a blazing shop and impale herself on spiked railings.

Rather than stop to look, Chloe swallowed down her terror and picked up her desperate pace. But just as she was approaching the roadblock of emergency vehicles, a bottle landed on the ground in front of her.

Flames shot up as the glass shattered and Chloe was going too fast to stop herself running into them.

She came to a juddering halt and stood there as the fire grabbed hold of her dungarees and climbed swiftly up both legs. She didn't move even though the pain was unbearable.

All she could do was let out a loud, high-pitched scream that drowned out all the other sounds around her.

*

It was the scream that woke Chloe up from the nightmare. Her eyes snapped open and it felt like a bolt of electricity was surging through her veins.

Several seconds passed before she realised what was happening and where she was. It took a few more seconds to get her breathing under control and force herself into a sitting position on the sofa.

She could see the night had ended because the sun was shining through the balcony window. The last thing she remembered was sitting there watching the television and thinking about her mother after Wesley had fallen asleep in the armchair. The telly was still on, but Wesley was no longer in the room.

She wondered where he was and if he had heard her screaming. Perhaps he was in the kitchen making tea or in the bathroom having a shower.

She needed a good wash herself. Her hands, face and clothes were still stained with grime and she smelled awful. And her head, knees and elbows were still sore.

She flinched suddenly as the last part of the nightmare replayed itself in her head. It made her think of Ryan and how he had burned to death in the gift shop. It was so sad, so tragic. She would never forget it as long as she lived. Just as she would never forget how she had watched her adoptive mother plunge to her death from the roof of the warehouse.

Death and destruction continued to dominate the TV news programmes. It seemed to Chloe as though her nightmare was being projected onto the screen. A female voice spoke over video footage of burning buildings and ugly confrontations between mobs of young people and the police.

'It was another night of mayhem across London,' the woman was saying. 'The confirmed death toll has now risen to seven. The Prime Minister has declared a state of emergency and more soldiers are being drafted into the capital. Elsewhere the violence has become more intense, with major outbreaks in five other cities and several coastal resort towns.'

The newsreader then mentioned the areas of London that had been worst hit, including Vauxhall where no fewer than thirty buildings had been set on fire and scores of shops had been ransacked.

'Police are now convinced that missing schoolboy Jacob Rossi was among those who have died in the riots,' she said, and the photo of Jacob that Chloe had already seen was shown again. 'Further details relating to his death were revealed this morning by the detective leading the investigation.'

This time instead of showing a photo of her mother they cut to her speaking to reporters outside Jacob Rossi's home.

Chloe stared, mouth agape, and her mum's words made her go cold.

'His death is believed to have been due to smoke inhalation. Jacob was trapped in the cellar of the building when it was set on fire and he was unable to escape because he was chained to a wall.'

Tears welled in Chloe's eyes in response not only to hearing her mum's voice, but also to what had happened to that poor boy. Why would someone do that to him? How could anyone be that evil?

She refused to allow herself to conjure up an image of Jacob Rossi in that cellar. Instead, she focused on the fact that her mum was OK. It was a relief to know that she had come to no harm. She was out there doing her job and probably still didn't know what had happened to Tom.

It was enough to force Chloe to her feet. She went looking for Wesley so that he could take her to Wandsworth police station.

But to her dismay she discovered that he wasn't there in the flat. Not in the kitchen, the bathroom or the bedrooms. And he wasn't on the balcony either.

A twist of panic wrenched through her gut. She was alone again, and it sent her sprits crashing to the floor. She didn't understand why Wesley had left her in the flat. Had he gone back out onto the streets to join the riots? Or had he . . .

The sudden chime of the doorbell broke her chain of thought and made her jump. She froze, unsure what to do. When she did nothing it rang again and this time she rushed into the hall, thinking it must be Wesley who'd gone out and forgotten to take his key with him.

But it wasn't Wesley who was standing there when she

opened the door. It was a man and a woman, and they were both clearly shocked to see her.

'Who the hell are you?' the woman said. 'Where's Ryan? Where's our son?'

CHAPTER FORTY

Anna's mind was thumping out of control as she steered a course from Bromley to Camberwell in the pool car. This time her destination was not The Falconer's Arms. It was King's College Hospital, which was less than half a mile away from the derelict pub.

Her beloved Tom had been rushed there five hours ago in an ambulance, having been found badly beaten and unconscious in the street.

After regaining consciousness, he had given them Anna's number, but the A and E department hadn't been able to get through to her so they'd contacted MIT.

Walker said that whoever he spoke to at the hospital had told him that Tom was in a bad way. His condition was serious, but thankfully not critical. He hadn't yet been interviewed by the police and he hadn't managed to describe what had happened to him.

According to the hospital, he was alone when the ambulance arrived to pick him up, but since waking he had been asking the same question over and over: 'Where's Chloe?'

Anna had tried ringing her daughter's mobile but it kept going to voicemail. She'd got the same response from her home phone and Tom's too. An icy fear was therefore flooding through her body and her heart fluttered in panic.

'Please let my baby be all right,' she kept saying out loud to herself. She couldn't lose her daughter again.

Before leaving the Rossi house, Anna had instructed Benning and Moore to take Jacob's parents to the mortuary. And she had asked Walker to pass on Chloe's description to all units so that they could look out for her.

Now as she drove with the blue light flashing, she tried to rein in her terror and not to assume the worst. But that was easier said than done without knowing the answers to the many questions that were prodding at her brain.

If Chloe wasn't with Tom, then where was she? And why wasn't she answering her phone? Had she been by herself all night? Was she also lying injured somewhere?

With her mind in such turmoil, Anna was finding it hard to concentrate on the road, but she needed to because although the night was over there were ongoing disturbances across London. Many streets remained blocked to traffic, while others were made treacherous by broken glass and other debris.

She was forced to avoid East Dulwich because rioters were on the rampage along the busy Lordship Lane. A Co-op convenience store had been looted before being set on fire and a police officer had been repeatedly beaten after he was dragged from his patrol car.

Anna prayed that her daughter hadn't been caught up in the carnage, and that she was somewhere safe. She was only twelve, after all. Far too young and immature to be by herself at a time like this.

Anna wanted to believe that Tom was asking where Chloe was because he was dazed and confused, not because he didn't know. Hopefully he'd be more coherent when she got to talk to him and would remember what had happened after he'd picked Chloe up from the house.

If he still didn't have a clue as to her whereabouts, then Anna's only option would be to embark on another anxious search for her daughter.

CHAPTER FORTY-ONE

'Now stop crying, young lady, and calm yourself down. You need to tell me and my husband who you are and what's going on.'

Ryan's mum had a loud, stern voice and a face like thunder. As she spoke, the folds of fat beneath her tight red blouse wobbled, and foam formed at the corners of her mouth.

Chloe was terrified. The woman towered above her, big brown eyes blazing with anger.

'So tell me your name and why you're here,' she said. 'We want to know where Ryan is. And Wesley. Why aren't they answering their phones?'

But Chloe was too upset to respond, so just stood in the middle of the living room, shaking and sobbing and wishing that this was another nightmare that she would wake up from.

She hadn't uttered a word since opening the front door to the couple, which could only have been a minute or so ago. The shock had rendered her speechless, and when she'd failed to tell them who she was, they had pushed past her and entered the flat, slamming the front door behind them.

Having discovered that Chloe was alone, Ryan's mum had grabbed her by the arm and ushered her roughly into the living room. Her husband, who was taller and thinner than she was, now hovered behind her with a deep frown on his forehead.

'Please just answer the questions,' the woman was saying in a softer, gentler voice. 'We want to know that our son is all right. And we don't understand why you're here and he isn't.'

Chloe's chest continued to heave with every sob, and she was struggling to gulp air into her lungs.

The woman reached out suddenly and placed a hand on her shoulder, which made her flinch.

'Look, we're not going to hurt you. We've got no reason to. But surely you can see how worried we are. It's obvious to us that something has happened and we want to know what it is.'

Chloe closed her eyes, swallowed hard, started to fight back against the tears. The woman's words gave her a crumb of comfort and made her feel less threatened, less scared.

Even so it took a while for her to stop crying, and when she did, the woman leaned forward and dabbed at her cheeks with a pink hanky from her pocket.

'That's better,' she said, and managed a weak smile. 'Now come and sit down and tell us what's going on.'

Chloe allowed herself to be led to the sofa where the woman sat next to her while her husband stayed where he was, his back to the balcony window.

'So let's start with your name and how old you are.'

Chloe drew in a breath and told her.

'You're younger than I thought you were,' the woman said. 'And that makes me even more curious to know what you're doing in our son's flat.'

Chloe was still trying to decide what to tell her when a sound came from out in the hall. They both turned towards it.

A moment later Wesley appeared in the open doorway, and his mouth fell open when he saw Ryan's parents. He was still wearing the clothes he'd had on last night and it looked to Chloe as though he'd been crying again.

'Oh fuck, I didn't expect you to be here,' he said. 'I was gonna come and see you later.'

'Well we've saved you the trouble, haven't we?' Ryan's dad said, speaking for the first time. 'So now tell us where our son is and what this slip of a girl is doing here.'

*

Chloe watched Wesley's face crease up as he told the couple that their son was dead.

Ryan's mother let out a cry of pain and then burst into tears. His father started moving towards Wesley, and Chloe thought for a moment that he was going to hit him. But the man stopped just in front of Wesley, and said, 'When? Where did it happen? Why didn't you tell us?'

Wesley struggled to get the words out, and the more he said, the more distressed Ryan's parents became. He told them that he and Ryan had taken part in the riots, and how they had ended up in the gift shop.

'It was Ryan's idea,' he said, pointing at Chloe. 'He wanted to save the girl because she reminded him of Phoebe. We planned to leave her in the shop where we thought it'd be safe. But just as we were about to leave a petrol bomb was thrown through the window.'

227

Wesley choked up as he described what had happened to his pal and how he had then led Chloe to safety.

'But how can you be so sure that our son didn't manage to get out of the shop as well?' Ryan's father said.

Wesley's eyes flitted nervously between the two parents, and then he glanced briefly at Chloe before responding.

'When I woke up earlier, I saw from the balcony that the fire brigade had finally put the blaze out,' he said. 'So I went down there to tell them about Ryan. But they already knew because they'd found a body at the back of the gift shop.'

Now it was the father's turn to break down, but through his tears he was still able to ask Wesley if his son's body had been moved.

'They were still waiting to do that when I left there about ten minutes ago,' Wesley said.

'Then take me to him,' the father said. To his wife, he added, 'I think you should stay here, my love.'

The woman nodded without speaking. But when the two men stepped out of the room she turned to Chloe, and said, 'As soon as these riots kicked off, I phoned my son and told him not to join in because I suspected he'd be tempted. But deep down I also knew he'd ignore me. That's why I panicked when I couldn't get in touch with him.'

'I'm so sorry he died because of me,' Chloe said tearfully.

The woman put a hand on Chloe's knee. 'Don't be silly, young lady. Ryan was no saint, and he did a lot of awful things in his short life that brought shame on his family. So I'm glad that the last thing he did before he died was to help save someone's life. That makes me so proud of him.'

She pulled Chloe into her arms and for the next few minutes they cried into each other's shoulders.

CHAPTER FORTY-TWO

As Anna approached King's College Hospital, her mind was fogged by fatigue and adrenalin. She had a pulsing ache in her head, and the feeling of dread sat like a brick in her stomach.

Her fears for Chloe's safety had spiralled during the drive from Bromley because of the sheer amount of damage that had been inflicted on London by the rioters. Virtually every district she'd passed through had suffered in some way. Buildings had burned down, shops were boarded up, and wrecked cars, vans and even lorries and buses were everywhere.

Last night had been the worst so far and the thought that her twelve-year-old daughter might have been in the thick of it chilled her to the bone.

The streets around the hospital were crammed with parked vehicles, including ambulances and police cars.

King's was one of the busiest hospitals in the capital, and many of those injured in the riots would have been brought here.

She found a space to park a couple of hundred yards away

and hurried on foot towards the entrance. The sun that had shone first thing had now disappeared behind clouds that were low and heavy. It would be good if it rained for the rest of the day and into the night, she thought. Perhaps it would deter a lot of people from taking to the streets again.

There were several police officers on duty outside the main entrance, and Anna assumed their job was to spot anyone who looked as though they were up to no good. They paid her no attention as she rushed inside.

Because it was so busy, it took her a while to find out where Tom was. She made her way along corridors that were filled with patients because there was not enough space for them on the wards.

Anna discovered that Tom had a recovery room to himself. Before going in there, she spoke to the doctor who had treated him in the emergency department when he was brought in.

He explained that Tom had mild concussion, a broken arm, two fractured ribs, and a mass of cuts and bruises. But no damage had been done to any of his vital organs.

'Thank God for that,' Anna said. 'At least his injuries aren't life-threatening. I've been so worried.'

'He took a severe beating,' the doctor told her. 'It seems to have been a racist attack carried out by a group of white men, or youths. After attacking him, they threw him onto the bonnet of his own car and drove along the road before crashing into a wall. Mr Bannerman rolled onto the pavement where he stayed for quite a while before an ambulance got to him. He's very lucky in that his injuries aren't as serious as they might have been considering what happened to him. And at least he wasn't stabbed like many of the other people who turned up here during the night.'

The doctor's words sent an icy shiver down Anna's spine. She hadn't realised that the attack on him had been so vicious. Sure, he was lucky to be alive, but it was going to take him a long time to recover, both physically and mentally.

'I gather he's been asking about Chloe,' she said.

The doctor nodded. 'That's right. He says the girl, who's twelve, was with him when the assault took place, but he doesn't know what happened to her.'

'Oh God. Chloe is my daughter and I haven't been able to get in touch with her. Tom was taking care of her for me.'

The doctor grimaced. 'Well I hope he can be of help, Miss Tate. But be warned, he's still feeling quite dizzy and disoriented, and the drugs we've given him are making it hard for him to concentrate.'

'Is he awake?'

'He was about five minutes ago when I last saw him.'

Anna's nerves were jangling as she walked into the recovery room. When she saw Tom, a hard lump expanded in her throat and her heart took a leap.

Her boyfriend was propped up against raised pillows, and even from a distance she could see several lumps on his forehead, and a graze on his left cheek.

There were more marks on his bare chest and his right arm was in plaster. He was also linked up to a saline drip and what looked like a blood pressure monitor.

His eyes were closed, but he opened them as Anna stepped up to the bed.

'I got here as soon as I could, Tom,' she said, fighting back tears. 'I should have suspected that something was wrong when you didn't respond to my last text message.'

She leaned over the bed and kissed him gently on the mouth, noting his bloodshot eyes and smoky breath.

'I do hope you're not in too much pain,' she said, her voice cracking like splintered wood.

He swallowed, which seemed to cause him some discomfort. 'Not any more,' he said, his voice low and croaky. 'The medication they gave me has kicked in. I'll be fine . . . it's Chloe I'm worried about. Have you heard from her?'

Anna straightened up, shook her head. 'No I haven't. I was hoping that you'd be able to tell me where she is. She's not answering her mobile, and the landline at your flat is also ringing out.'

'We didn't make it to my flat,' he said. 'I was attacked outside your house.'

Anna tried to still the fear that was gathering inside her. She reached for one of his hands and gently squeezed it.

'Tell me what happened.'

He shut his eyes, no doubt thinking back. 'The street was filled with rioters heading for the estate and a group of men pulled us both out of the car,' he said. 'Just before I was set upon I saw that they'd let Chloe go. I shouted for her to go back indoors, and when they were laying into me in the road, I heard her screaming at them to leave me alone. But then I was picked up and thrown onto the car . . . I think that's when I lost consciousness. The next thing I was aware of was waking up in the back of the ambulance.'

'Chloe probably went back into the house then,' Anna said.

Tom opened his eyes. 'I don't think so, Anna. You see, I was the one who locked the front door and then I put the spare key in my jacket pocket.'

A look of horror swept across Anna's face. 'Oh Christ. That

means she could be anywhere . . . Or maybe those men didn't let her go after all.'

'No, I really can't imagine that they would have hurt her. They were baying for black blood. I'm hoping that a neighbour took her in.'

'But if that is what happened then surely I would have heard from them by now,' Anna said, her voice a thin wheeze. 'Chloe would have got them to contact me.'

Anna didn't know what to think, which encouraged dark thoughts to swirl around inside her mind. It wasn't as though she could raise the alarm and spark a citywide search for her daughter. In the chaos caused by the riots there were probably dozens of people unaccounted for. And that, combined with everything else the force had to deal with, meant that Chloe would be low down on any list of priorities.

'You have to go and find her,' Tom said. 'She's been missing now for over fifteen hours.'

'I will,' Anna said. 'Are you going to be all right?'

'Of course. I'm really sorry about this, Anna. If I hadn't suddenly decided to take her to my place this wouldn't have happened. I just thought she'd be safer there. I didn't know that . . .' He lost it then and began to weep.

'And she would have been, Tom,' Anna said, stroking his face. 'You did what you thought was best and you've got nothing to apologise for. So don't even go there.'

She kissed him again on the mouth and told him that she loved him.

'Go and find her, Anna,' he said between sobs. 'She needs you now more than ever.'

'I'll be in touch as soon as I have news,' she said.

Then she hurried out of the recovery room.

CHAPTER FORTY-THREE

Anna wasn't prepared for the sights that greeted her as she approached Vauxhall.

It looked as though the area had been hit by a meteorite shower. Familiar streets were almost unrecognisable because fire had destroyed so many buildings, while others had been torn apart by looters.

Riot police were still involved in clashes with youths along parts of South Lambeth Road and around Vauxhall station. Fire crews who'd been working through the night were dealing with fresh arson attacks while struggling to ensure that damaged structures were made safe.

Anna heard on the radio that many residents had left their homes during the past forty-eight hours, distressed by events and fearful for their own safety.

She realised that last night this must have been one of the most dangerous places in London. At least three people, including a police officer, were known to have been killed here, and God only knew how many had been injured.

Blood was pounding in Anna's ears as she turned into her own street. It came as a pleasant surprise when she saw that it hadn't suffered too much damage. There was a lot of rubbish on the ground, but the houses appeared to be intact and there was no police presence. Several of the residents were out sweeping the pavements and picking up litter, while others were surveying the scene from their front gardens.

As she pulled onto her short driveway, she noticed the words that had been scrawled in red paint on her front door. They ignited a blast of anger inside her.

POLICE BITCH LIVES HERE

In addition to the graffiti on the door an upstairs window had been smashed and the bins had been emptied over the garden.

She remembered what DCS Nash had said about the homes of some police officers and politicians being targeted by the rioters. Whoever had done this must have known that it was the address of a Met detective, but around here it was no secret. She was on first-name terms with some of the neighbours, and those she wasn't acquainted with had probably been told that she was the woman whose daughter was abducted ten years ago. In fact the media had turned up here in force just a month ago after she and Chloe were reunited.

It seemed inconceivable to Anna that they'd been separated again, this time by the riots. She could only hope and pray that it wouldn't be for long.

She quickly let herself in and called out Chloe's name as she rushed from room to room. But her daughter wasn't there and every room was empty.

In Chloe's bedroom she found her daughter's mobile phone, which she had obviously forgotten to take with her when Tom came to pick her up. She checked it and saw all the missed calls.

She told herself to stay calm, to act like a police officer rather than a distraught mother.

She tried to put herself in Chloe's shoes. How would a twelve-year-old have acted in the situation she found herself in? The man who had come to take care of her was beaten up and carted off in front of her eyes. That would have been terrifying enough. But she would have realised then that she didn't have a key to get back inside her home. And all this while the street she was on was teeming with gangs of violent rioters.

The first logical step was to check with the closest neighbours. Being a Saturday most of them were in, but none of them had any knowledge of Chloe's whereabouts. And they hadn't witnessed the incident the previous evening when Tom was attacked.

Back in the house, Anna tried to control her thoughts, which had begun to run amok. Panic seized her chest, making it hard for her to breathe.

She knew well enough that her options were limited. There was no one to help her find Chloe. London was in the grip of a crisis and those officers who weren't trying to restore order were investigating an unprecedented spate of serious crimes, including the death of Jacob Rossi in the pub cellar.

Anna was alone. Again. She had not the slightest idea where to begin the search for her daughter. She was tempted to take to the streets with a photo of Chloe. But would that be a waste of time? What if her daughter had been abducted?

Or what if she'd wandered into one of the buildings that had been set on fire?

Anna's mind was raging in all directions now and taking her to ever darker places. She dropped onto a chair in the kitchen and her fingers drummed a nervous beat on the table.

Before long tears were pushing at her eyes, and she felt a scream building at the back of her throat.

Then suddenly her phone rang and she whipped it out of her pocket. The caller ID said Max Walker, and Anna gave a frustrated growl before answering.

'Ma'am—' DI Walker began.

'I'm sorry, Max. I don't have time for any case updates right now,' Anna interrupted abruptly. 'Chloe is still missing, and I don't have any idea where she could be.' Normally she would never be so short with one of her officers, but this was no ordinary situation.

'Actually, ma'am, Chloe is the reason I'm calling. I have news.'

CHAPTER FORTY-FOUR

It was the first time Chloe had set foot in her mother's office, and she was surprised how small it was. There was just a desk, three chairs, and a couple of tall metal filing cabinets. On the other side of the only window there was a big room with lots more desks and people who looked as though they were really busy.

'That's what we call the operations room,' said the uniformed policewoman who had been told to look after her. 'It's where all the detectives work on the investigations.'

Chloe's eyes were focused on one detective in particular. He had a bald head and was talking into his phone while looking back at her through the window.

He had introduced himself as Max, but others were calling him DI Walker. He was the one who had come rushing down to the reception area after Ryan's parents had dropped her off here. He seemed really nice and she liked him. Her mum was his boss apparently and Chloe remembered now that she'd heard her talking to him on the phone plenty of times during the past month.

When he ended the call, he smiled at her and walked straight back into the office.

'That was your mum,' he said. 'She now knows that you're here and she's told me to tell you that she loves you. She's been out looking for you and now she's on her way back. She wants you to know that Tom is in hospital, but he's going to be OK.'

Chloe caught her breath and felt her stomach go tight. She was so happy and relieved that Tom was still alive. She was looking forward to seeing him, almost as much as she was looking forward to seeing her mum.

'Sit on your mum's chair behind the desk,' Max said. 'It's the most comfortable. Constable Bryant here will fetch you something to eat and drink. I know you've had a bad experience, but you're safe now so try to relax.'

He had asked her where she'd been all night and she'd told him about running away from the house after Tom was taken and getting lost in the streets before ending up in Wesley's flat. He hadn't pressed her for details and she was glad because she was in no mood to say a lot.

Officer Bryant asked her what she wanted to eat, and until that moment she hadn't realised how hungry she was. She opted for a bacon sandwich and a Coke, and then settled down in her mum's chair.

She was glad now that she had washed her face and hands before leaving Wesley's flat. But she'd been too distressed to eat, especially after Ryan's dad came back from visiting the fire-ravaged gift shop.

He was crying uncontrollably, and so was Wesley, because they had seen Ryan's charred body being recovered. Chloe had wept to, and despite what Ryan's mother had said to her she hadn't been able to stop feeling guilty. If she hadn't fallen over in the road their son wouldn't have stopped to pick her up and he'd still be alive.

Ryan's mum, whose name was Dominique Claymore, had told Chloe that they would take her to Wandsworth police station. Her husband had given their contact details to the police, and the pair were anxious to get home and away from Wesley, who they held partly responsible for what had happened.

But Chloe viewed him in a different light because he had saved her life. So before leaving the flat she got him to write his name and number on a piece of paper and gave him a hug.

'Thank you for what you did,' she told him. 'I won't forget it. Or you.'

'And I won't forget you,' he said. 'For the record do you want me to call you Chloe or Alice?'

Chloe thought about it for a few beats and then smiled. 'From now on I'm Chloe. Chloe Tate.'

CHAPTER FORTY-FIVE

Anna did not know whether to laugh, cry or scream when she saw Chloe sitting behind her desk nibbling on a sandwich. So she followed her instinct and just rushed into the office.

'Oh, sweetheart, you had me so worried,' she said excitedly. 'Thank goodness you're all right.'

It was an emotional reunion for both of them with tears, hugs and loud sighs of relief.

Anna was brimming with joy. She'd got her daughter back for a second time, but was still reeling inside from the fright she'd had.

Chloe looked awful. There were wounds on her face and her clothes were badly stained. Her hair was a dirty mess and there were dark crescents under her eyes.

'I rang the hospital and told them to tell Tom that you're no longer missing,' she said. 'He was so worried about you. He was unconscious for most of the night and so he couldn't tell anyone what had happened until he woke up.'

'It was horrible what they did to him, Mum,' Chloe said. 'There was nothing I could do when they drove away with him on top of the car. I've been so scared that they killed him.'

'He's got some broken bones and a sore head, but he's already on the mend.' Anna gestured at the wounds on Chloe's face – the gash on her chin and the bruised lump on her forehead. 'You also look as though you've had a rough time of it. You told Max that you haven't been physically assaulted. Is that true, sweetheart?'

Chloe nodded. 'I fell over a couple of times while running, but I'm not hurting as much as I was last night.'

'Well I want to know exactly what happened to you. And you need to tell me about the couple who brought you here. Max said they didn't come inside the building.'

'They went straight home,' Chloe said. 'They'd only just found out that their son was dead.'

Anna told Chloe to sit back down while she closed the office door behind her. Walker was standing outside and she gave him the thumbs-up sign.

Then Anna pulled up one of the other chairs so that she could sit next to Chloe.

'You have to tell me everything,' she said. 'I want to know exactly what happened to you after you left the house with Tom yesterday. Then we'll go home, you can have a long, hot bath and we can spend the evening together.'

'Can you take me to see Tom first?' Chloe asked.

Anna smiled. 'Of course. The hospital isn't far from here and I know it will cheer him up no end.'

Chloe leaned back in the chair and her face crumpled in thought.

'So in your own time, sweetheart,' Anna said. 'What happened?'

*

Chloe's eyes were bright with tears as she spoke about her ordeal. As Anna listened, the blood seemed to clot in her veins and she felt an ache swell in her chest.

The events Chloe described were horrendous, and Anna was amazed that her daughter managed to hold it together so well.

It began with the attack on Tom and how she watched the rioters beat him up and then drive off with him on the bonnet of his car.

'I screamed at them to leave him alone,' Chloe said. 'But they ignored me.'

Then she saw a man spraying words on their front door while another man was urinating against the wall next to it.

'That was when I started running, but was I hit by a motorbike, which knocked me out,' she said, her voice shaking.

She explained how she almost fell victim to two creatures who wanted to rape her, and how she witnessed a boy being beaten up. And then a shadow flickered across her eyes as she spoke about how she was trampled on by a mob of rioters before being carried into a shop.

'That was why Ryan was killed,' she said, sobbing now. 'It was really, really terrible.' She struggled to describe the scene in the shop and Anna only just managed to hold back her own tears.

It shocked her that she herself had actually heard about some of the incidents on the news and she'd even seen the clip posted online of a hooded youth hurling a petrol bomb into the gift shop, killing the man named Ryan who had rescued Chloe from the street.

Anna made a mental note to get in touch with Ryan's mother and with the lad's friend Wesley who had saved Chloe from the fire. She would thank them both personally, let them know how grateful she was.

There was a faraway look in Chloe's eyes as she stopped speaking. Anna could see that she was physically weak, drained of energy, traumatised. And she knew that the full weight of shock had yet to kick in.

Anna reached out and stroked her daughter's cheek.

'You've had a terrible experience, sweetheart,' she said. 'You got through it because you're a sensible and mature girl, and I'm proud of you. Now I want you to wait here for a few minutes while I have a quick word with Max and the others. Then we'll head off to the hospital. OK?'

Chloe nodded and indicated her can of Coke on the desk. 'Can you ask the lady to get me another one of these please?' she said.

Anna grinned and told her she would.

Back in the ops room she asked Constable Bryant to get Chloe another drink and then filled DI Walker in on what Chloe had told her.

'I'll have to take her home,' she said. 'It's bad timing, I know, but I don't have a choice. She needs me right now.'

'Of course she does, guv,' Walker said. 'And it's not a problem. We've got everything under control. I've spoken to Nash and he knows what's happened. He says he'll be in later and he accepts that we won't be making much progress today because those of us who've been working through the night need to get some shuteye. Meanwhile, the powers that be are bracing themselves for another hellish night on the streets, and that will slow things down as well.'

'I won't be back tomorrow unless I can find someone to stay with Chloe. I don't want to leave her alone.'

'I don't blame you. Just let me know.'

'Have you heard from DI Benning? He was going to the mortuary for the formal ID.'

'He came straight back here afterwards and he told me the parents confirmed the dead boy is indeed their son, Jacob,' Walker said. 'He then said he was going to follow up on what you were told about Mark Rossi having a stepbrother he doesn't know who might be living in Camberwell.'

'That's right. He's another potential suspect, but an outsider at best. So where is Benning? I don't see him here.'

'He's one of those I've already sent home to get some rest,' Walker said. 'I thought he was looking pretty rough as well as tired. I get the impression he's taking the boy's death really hard.'

'He told me he blames himself for not finding Jacob,' Anna said, and felt a tad guilty for not making Walker aware of his fellow DI's health problem. 'But I think we would all feel the same in his shoes.'

Walker nodded. 'I know I would.'

He then informed Anna that they still hadn't managed to trace Michelle Gerrard and Roy Slater, but would hopefully be gaining access to both their homes later in the day or tomorrow.

'Forensics are still sifting through the stuff from the cellar,' Walker continued. 'And they've now got the letter and photo that was sent to Mark Rossi. We've just got to wait for the results to come through. But nothing's moving at its usual pace because of the riots.'

'And that will continue to be a problem for us and everyone else,' Anna said. 'Those nutters out there seem determined to drag this out as long as they can.'

CHAPTER FORTY-SIX

Tom was still in the recovery room when they got to the hospital. He was wide awake and smiled broadly when he saw Chloe. But within seconds they were both overcome by emotion and began to cry.

Anna struggled to suppress her own tears as she watched Chloe trying to articulate her feelings.

'I'm sorry I couldn't save you from those men,' she was saying. 'I tried but they wouldn't listen to me. And then . . . and then they took you away and I didn't know what else to do but start running.'

Tom put his good arm around her as she leaned over the bed and told her that he thought she was the bravest girl he knew.

He then asked Chloe what had happened to her. This time she seemed to find it a little easier to talk about, and her voice was clearer and more measured.

Tom was left clearly shaken by what she had been through. He squeezed her hand and shook his head.

'You've had far too many bad experiences for someone so young,' he said. 'Let's hope that from now on life will be much kinder to you.'

'I'll second that,' Anna said.

Tom then asked Anna how serious things were on the streets. Indicating the small TV on a stand in the corner, he said, 'I've seen bits on the news and it seems like the police have lost control of the situation.'

'We're having a hard time coping,' Anna said. 'These are so much worse than the riots of 2011. The amount of damage being done is off the scale.'

'What about the case you're working on?' Tom said. 'The boy in the cellar.'

'It's progressing, but slowly,' Anna replied.

'So will you be back on the job tomorrow?'

Anna shrugged. 'That depends on whether I can find someone to be with Chloe. I've got a couple of friends who will hopefully let her stay with them while I'm working. If they can't for any reason then the team will have to manage without me.'

'But I don't want to stay with any strangers,' Chloe moaned. 'Please don't make me.'

'Why not let her stay here with me?' Tom said. 'We can keep each other company and she'll be perfectly safe.'

'I can bring my tablet and some books,' Chloe said, smiling. 'And some games as well.'

Anna didn't bother to argue, mainly because she thought it was the perfect solution to her problem. She also hoped it would prove to be a good opportunity for them to bond.

'It's a deal then,' she said. 'I'll drop her off in the morning and pick her up when I've finished for the day.'

When they got home the first thing Anna did was grab a tin of wood stain from the garden shed. She used it to brush over the words sprayed on the front door. She then ran a bath for Chloe and had a quick shower herself.

She caught sight of the time as she was pulling on her dressing gown, and was surprised to see that it was already four p.m. The time had flown by, and it was no wonder that she felt sleep-deprived and hungry. She'd managed to fortify herself with cups of coffee during the day but she hadn't eaten a thing.

'What would you like for dinner?' she asked Chloe when the pair of them got together in the kitchen.

'I'd love a pizza,' Chloe said.

'Then a pizza it is, plus chips and some baked beans.'

She was glad to see that Chloe was looking so much better now that she had washed her hair and exchanged her dirty dungarees for her bright yellow pyjamas.

Anna stopped what she was doing and stared at her. She'd only had her back for a month and she hadn't let her out of her sight in all that time. But only now did it occur to her just how grown up she appeared to be. Rather than a twelve-year-old she looked more like a girl in her mid-teens. Was that because so many terrible things had happened to her? Anna wondered.

'I've put some Sudocrem on these,' Chloe said, and showed Anna the grazes on her knees and elbows from where she had fallen over. 'They still hurt but only a bit now.'

Anna was suddenly reminded of when Chloe fell over in a playpark and landed on a jagged rock. She was two and it was just before her father abducted her and took her to Spain.

That was the last time Anna got to nurse any of her daughter's many minor injuries, and she remembered it now as though it had happened yesterday rather than ten years ago.

Once again the tears threatened and so Anna busied herself with making the dinner.

After they'd eaten, they sat on the sofa in the living room and Anna put on the television. Chloe surprised her by asking if they could watch the news.

'Are you sure you don't want to watch a movie or something?' Anna asked.

'I'm sure, Mum.'

Sure enough, there was wall-to-wall coverage of the riots.

'I saw you earlier talking to reporters,' Chloe said, looking at her mum. 'Will you be on again tonight?'

'I'm not sure,' Anna replied. 'But it's possible, I suppose.'

'Well promise me that you'll catch whoever put that boy in the cellar.'

'I'll do my best, sweetheart.'

'Did you have to tell his mum and dad what happened to him?'

Anna nodded. 'I'm afraid I did. It wasn't easy – naturally they were very upset.'

'When that man Perez abducted me, I was really scared,' Chloe said. 'But I was lucky because at least I wasn't put in chains.'

Anna was so moved that she leaned over and put her arm around her daughter.

'I could never love anyone more than I love you, sweetheart,' she said.

Chloe looked up at her and for a fleeting moment Anna thought that she was going to say that she loved her back. But instead, she said, 'You don't have to keep saying sweetheart to me, Mum. I've got used to Chloe now so that's who I am. I think it's a nicer name than Alice anyway.'

Anna's heart jolted into her throat and suddenly she couldn't speak. Chloe, for her part, seemed totally oblivious to the impact her words had had on her mother. Her gaze returned to the TV and she carried on watching the news.

CHAPTER FORTY-SEVEN

Chloe woke up screaming twice during the night. She had insisted on sleeping in her own bed, so Anna had had to dash into her room to comfort her.

It wasn't unexpected, of course. Nightmares were inevitable after such a terrible ordeal. And Anna knew that they might well continue for weeks or even months to come.

The child counsellor who was already on Chloe's case would have to be informed at the earliest opportunity. Anna would just have to pray that what had happened to her daughter would not cause any lasting psychological damage. But coming so soon after the heart-breaking incident on the warehouse roof that had to be a possibility.

Despite the nightmares, they each managed to sleep for between six and seven hours. When Sunday morning arrived, they were both too hyped up to stay in bed. Anna was pleased to see that Chloe's facial injuries did not look any worse, and she wasn't in pain.

They had breakfast together, and Anna asked Chloe if she was still happy to spend the day at the hospital with Tom.

'Yes, I am,' Chloe insisted. 'I don't want him to be by himself, and I don't want to be left with someone I don't know.'

'But I could stay at home,' Anna said. 'I've told you that won't be a problem.'

Chloe shook her head. 'If you do that then you won't be looking for the person who put that boy in the cellar. And that wouldn't be fair.'

Her daughter's response caused Anna's heart to swell with pride. For Chloe to be so concerned about someone else after the hell she'd been through was commendable, and it said a lot about her resolve and strength of character.

While Chloe packed her rucksack with her phone, tablet, snacks and books, Anna switched her attention to the television.

It had been another shocking night on the streets of London, and Anna was surprised she had managed to sleep through most of it. Mob violence had broken out in Lewisham, Brixton, Stratford, Battersea, Islington, Holloway and Fulham. Two more people had died and three police officers and a soldier had been hospitalised.

Scenes captured on video included more battles between rioters and police, an Asda superstore engulfed in flames, vandals smashing up vehicles, and looters running out of high street shops with large bags of swag.

More politicians were taking to the airways to appeal for calm, but on social media activists and extremist groups were stirring things up and encouraging violence with inflammatory rhetoric.

Luckily Anna and Chloe had an incident-free journey from Vauxhall to King's College Hospital in Camberwell. Anna went inside with her daughter to see Tom and to clear with the staff that it was all right for Chloe to stay with him. They said it wasn't a problem even though he'd been moved to a ward.

After a brief chat, during which Tom assured her that he was recovering well, Anna gave Chloe a kiss and a cuddle and left the pair of them to get to know each other.

It was time for her to refocus on the job she'd been given, which was to find the cruel bastard who had abducted and imprisoned Jacob Rossi.

*

Anna arrived at MIT HQ at eight a.m. She had phoned ahead to say that she wanted the morning briefing to kick off at eight-thirty. The rest of the team had already reported for duty, having snatched at most a few hours' sleep.

The night shift officers had handed over the reins, and DI Walker was ready to present the updates. But first everyone was eager to hear what had happened to Chloe and Tom. There were murmurs of shock and disbelief as Anna told them.

'Thankfully they both survived what were dreadful experiences,' Anna said. 'But it seems that they were among the lucky ones.'

This was Walker's cue to provide a few headline points relating to the riots, including the appalling death and injury statistics.

'I've spoken to DCS Nash,' he said. 'He's back at the Yard with other senior officers and will feed us information throughout the day on what's happening. But as we all know things are still extremely serious out there. Our colleagues on the front line are all knackered, and every custody suite in the city is full with those who've been arrested. More officers are being drafted in from other forces today, but not nearly as many as we need because of disturbances elsewhere in the country. Things have been particularly bad here in London since this time yesterday, but despite that we have managed to make at least some progress with our own investigation.'

He pointed to a photograph that had been added to one of the evidence boards. It was a mugshot of a shaven-headed man with a wide, flat face and protruding ears.

'This is Roy Slater, the man whose wife had an affair with Mark Rossi,' Walker said. 'We're keen to question him about Jacob's abduction, but we still haven't been able to trace him. He's been on leave from his job as a warehouse packer and a neighbour said that he drove away from his house in Rotherhithe on Friday afternoon. This would have been shortly after Jacob's body was discovered in the pub cellar. So far the guy hasn't returned home, and his mobile phone is switched off and isn't transmitting a signal. But we've obtained his bank and credit card details from his employers and landlord, and they show that he's made a series of contactless payments using his Visa card. All purchases have been under thirty pounds so he hasn't had to use a PIN. They include petrol, booze and cigarettes. The last purchase was last night at a pub in Bermondsey, only about a mile from his home.'

'Well that suggests to me that he hasn't gone away somewhere on holiday,' Anna said. 'But it also strikes me as pretty odd that he hasn't been back home since Friday.'

'I did wonder if someone else is using his card without his knowledge,' Walker said. 'It could be that he lost it and doesn't realise it yet so hasn't phoned his bank.'

'Or it could also mean that something's happened to him and the card has been stolen.'

'Hopefully we'll find out soon enough.'

Anna mulled this over for a few moments, then said, 'So what else do we know about the guy?'

Walker shrugged. 'Not much, except that he lives alone and has a gambling addiction. A PNC check revealed a conviction for shoplifting, and as we know he went to Rossi a few months ago asking for money but was knocked back. So it's feasible he could have snatched Jacob because he planned to demand a ransom. As you know I've applied for a warrant to gain access to his house, but I'm still waiting for it to be authorised. Meanwhile, his car registration has been circulated, but there's been no sign of it. However, it's worth noting that a great many CCTV and APNR cameras have been vandalised by the rioters.'

'What about his ex-wife?' Anna said. 'Have we contacted her?'

Walker nodded. 'Indeed we have, guv. Her name is Ruth and she now lives just outside Rouen in France. She claims she doesn't know his whereabouts and hasn't spoken to him in over a year.'

Walker moved on to forensics and the news was just as disappointing. The only prints on the items recovered from the cellar belonged to Jacob. There were none on the note that accompanied it or on the envelope itself. And no DNA traces either, which suggested that whoever had sent them took great care not to leave any evidence.

Walker then reminded the team that Roy Slater was one of five people who were so far in the frame. The others were Neville Quinlan, the convicted paedo; Gavin Pope, whose wife also had a fling with Mark Rossi; Michelle Gerrard, the internet troll; and Joseph Metcalfe, Rossi's stepbrother.

DI Benning had been tasked with running down Metcalfe. He stood up to read from his notes, and it looked to Anna as though he'd had a rough night. He was sallow-faced and unshaven, and he kept having to clear his throat between sentences. It made Anna wonder if fatigue aggravated the symptoms of his early onset dementia.

He began by reminding everyone what Mark Rossi's mother, Emily, had told them.

'We asked the family if anyone had a connection to The Falconer's Arms pub in Camberwell,' he said. 'Emily told us that her late husband Isaac had an ex-partner named Hilary Metcalfe, who was living in Camberwell when she died about five years ago. She was the mother of Isaac's estranged son, Joseph, and therefore Mark's stepbrother.

'Isaac abandoned the boy, along with his long-term partner, when he married Emily. And he didn't bother to stay in touch with his son. But then five years ago Isaac discovered by chance that Hilary had terminal cancer. He went to the hospital to see if there was anything he could do to help, but his son Joseph was there and apparently told him to piss off.

'Emily knew that Hilary had got married some years ago, but Isaac never told her what the woman's married name was. However, it hasn't taken me long to find out. I rang the hospital and got them to check their records. Sure enough a woman named Hilary Walsh died there five years and three months ago. Her next of kin was a son named Joseph, whose stepdad, Brian Walsh, had died some years earlier. The address given at the time was a house in Camberwell just three streets away from The Falconer's Arms pub. Using the names I did a quick search of births, deaths and marriages, which provided confirmation that Hilary Walsh's maiden name was indeed Metcalfe.

'First thing this morning I went to the Camberwell address and found out that Joseph Walsh sold the house four years ago. The current occupants say he moved to Australia. They've given me the name of the estate agents who handled the sale and I intend to call them after this meeting to see if they have contact details for him.'

'Well it doesn't sound very promising,' Anna said. 'But I still reckon it's a bit of a strange coincidence that Mark Rossi's stepbrother used to live so close to The Falconer's Arms pub.'

'My thoughts exactly, ma'am,' Benning said. 'I'll try to find out if Joseph is actually living down under and if so whether or not he returned to the UK in recent weeks.'

'Stick with it then.' Anna turned back to Walker. 'Now what about Neville Quinlan? Anything new to report on him?'

Walker pointed across the room to where DS Prescott was sitting behind a desk with a phone clamped to his ear.

'I'm waiting for Doug to update me on that,' he said. 'Something interesting turned up on CCTV apparently and he's checking it out. Meanwhile the pathologist emailed over a preliminary post-mortem report. There are no surprises, though. The boy almost certainly wasn't beaten or sexually assaulted. There's no trace of semen in or on his body and cause of death was smoke inhalation for sure.'

'Well that's a relief,' Anna said. 'We need to let his parents know that he didn't suffer in that way. Now what about the house-to-house in Camberwell? Did it bear fruit?'

'Negative, guv,' Walker said. 'We've spoken to the estate agent about the dark-coloured car that one of the neighbours spotted on the pub forecourt several times during the past few weeks. But they say it doesn't belong to any of their staff.'

'And what about the homeless guy who was usually seen sleeping outside the pub?' Anna said.

Walker asked Detective Khan for an update.

'As I mentioned yesterday, the guy goes by the name of George,' Khan said. 'Before the riots started, he was usually seen kipping in the pub doorway. But the last reported sighting of him was well over a week ago when he was seen begging across the road from a local café. He hasn't been spotted since then, and we haven't got the manpower to trawl the streets looking for him.'

'That's a shame,' Anna said. 'It's yet another coincidence that gives me cause for concern. Homeless people tend to be creatures of habit so we need to find out why he stopped bedding down there.'

'We've asked people living around the pub to call us right away if they see him,' Khan said.

'Good. As far as I'm concerned tracking him down is a priority.'

Anna was about to ask for suggestions on where to go next with the investigation when DS Prescott shot to his feet and raised a hand to attract her attention. He was off the phone now and the look on his face sparked a surge of optimism.

'We need to bring Neville Quinlan in for questioning, guv,' he said. 'It turns out the bastard lied to us.'

'About what?' Anna asked.

'Well he claimed he went for a walk by himself on Monday afternoon between three and four, which was when Jacob was abducted. He said he didn't meet or speak to anyone. Well we've finally come across several clips of CCTV footage that shoot a hole in his alibi. It appears he did go out for a walk, but he didn't return to his home at four. Instead he met a man in a pub about a mile from his flat and after one drink they drove off in the other guy's car.'

'About bloody time we got a break,' Anna said.

Prescott held his notebook aloft. 'That's not all, guv. It gets better. The call I just made was to check who the car belongs to. And I've been given the name of a character who is more than a little interesting.'

CHAPTER FORTY-EIGHT

Ninety minutes later Anna and Walker entered Interview Room Two where Neville Quinlan and the duty solicitor appointed to him were waiting.

Detective Prescott and a couple of uniforms had arrested him at his flat and he'd been read his rights.

While that was happening, Anna and the rest of the team had viewed the CCTV footage that proved Quinlan had lied about what he did and where he went on Monday afternoon. They had also begun to gather more information on the man he'd met in the pub and driven off with.

Anna was carrying a small laptop that she placed on the table between them, along with a documents folder. She flicked the switch to turn on the wall-mounted video camera that would record the interview.

'For the benefit of the tape those present are DCI Tate, DI Walker, duty solicitor Kenneth Bloom, and his client, Mr Neville Quinlan,' she said.

Bloom was a familiar face at MIT HQ, and Anna rated

him highly. He wasn't a time waster, and he always gave his clients sound advice, even if they were low-life scum like Quinlan.

Bloom was smartly dressed in a light grey suit, but Quinlan looked as though he'd got ready in a hurry. His sparse grey hair clearly hadn't been brushed, and his dark shirt was badly creased, with some of the buttons left undone.

'Before you start asking your questions, I would like to make a statement for the record on Mr Quinlan's behalf,' Bloom said. When Anna nodded, he continued. 'My client would like it to be known that he regards what is happening as an extreme and unwarranted form of police harassment. He has already been interviewed twice and has continued to deny any involvement in the abduction and death of the ten-year-old Jacob Rossi. His flat has also been subjected to a thorough search and he's been led to believe that nothing incriminating was discovered.

'His only mistake was to park outside Jacob's school on one occasion last week and he's explained that he did that because he felt unwell while driving. He most certainly did not have a sinister motive. He has also given an account of his movements on Monday afternoon when Jacob went missing. So I'm . . .'

Anna felt a stab of irritation, which prompted her to cut him off.

'Let me stop you there, Mr Bloom,' she said. 'We are not harassing your client. He's a convicted paedophile who went to prison for sexually abusing two teenage boys. He was first interviewed after Jacob Rossi went missing. When the boy was found dead in the pub cellar, we felt it necessary to talk to him a second time. And now he's here again because new evidence has come to light, which proves that he lied to us about what he was doing on Monday afternoon.'

Bloom's face fisted into a frown and he turned to his client who was shaking his head.

'You're trying it on again,' Quinlan said to Anna. 'It's what you did when you pretended that the boy was found alive. You claimed that he'd told you I was the person who'd snatched him. Well I didn't fall for it then and I'm not falling for it now.'

Anna flipped open the laptop, brought it to life, and turned it towards Quinlan.

'You told us that you went out for your usual walk on Monday afternoon at about three o'clock,' Anna said. 'You insisted that you did not meet or talk to anyone, and that you returned home an hour later.'

'That's exactly what I did,' Quinlan said.

Anna shook her head. 'But that isn't true is it? The CCTV clips you're about to see prove that.'

Anna pressed a key on the laptop and the first clip started to play.

'This footage was captured on a camera opposite the Bell Inn pub which is just over a mile away from your flat,' she said. 'As you can see it shows you entering the saloon bar at three-fifteen that day.'

Quinlan shifted uncomfortably on the chair as he watched himself on the screen, and Anna noticed how his lower lip began to tremble.

'And this second clip is from a security camera inside the pub,' she said.

It showed a busy bar and at the far end of the room Quinlan could be seen sitting at a table opposite a large man in his mid-thirties, who had on a black leather jacket and a baseball cap.

'You stayed with this individual for forty minutes and you each had a pint of beer,' Anna said. 'From the look of it you had a lot to talk about and were clearly enjoying each other's company.' The clip ended and she moved straight on to another one. 'This third clip shows you eventually leaving the pub through the rear door and getting into the man's BMW in the car park. You can then be seen driving off together.'

Anna let the video play through before ending it and closing the laptop.

'So there you have it, Mr Quinlan,' she said. 'I can only assume that you must have had a good reason to lie to us. So I'll now give you an opportunity to put the record straight. Tell us why you met up with that man and where he took you after leaving the pub.'

Quinlan stared at her across the desk, his eyes filled with panic.

'I think we should suspend the interview while I consult with my client,' the solicitor said.

'And I think your client should stop pissing us around and come clean,' Anna said.

Quinlan's tongue flicked across his lips and the breath rushed out of him.

'It's none of your fucking business who I meet up with,' he said. 'So I don't see why I should tell you who he is.'

'Well for your information we already know who he is,' Anna said, and was unable to suppress a grin. 'He's the registered owner of the BMW. His name is Craig Sullivan and he lives in Norwood. He has previous convictions for drug dealing and theft. He's also the younger brother of one Tony

Sullivan, who was jailed three years ago on charges of child sex trafficking. It's strongly believed that he's now part of the same trafficking network that his brother ran, but so far he's managed to dodge getting collared.'

Quinlan clenched his jaw and hissed an obscenity at Anna. Then he leaned forward on the table and buried his face in his hands.

'I want to know where the pair of you went,' Anna said.

Without looking up, Quinlan responded with a 'no comment.'

Anna turned to Bloom. 'I suggest you explain to your client that he won't be leaving here until he's told us the truth.'

She then announced that she was suspending the interview and switched off the video camera. She got to her feet and picked up the laptop and documents folder.

Before leaving the room, she said to Quinlan, 'My officers are now on their way to Craig Sullivan's home so it won't be long before he's sitting in the room next door. It'll be interesting to see if he's just as reluctant as you are to tell us what the pair of you got up to on Monday afternoon.'

CHAPTER FORTY-NINE

'We'll let Quinlan stew for a while,' Anna said to Walker when they were back in the ops room. 'Meanwhile, get someone to go back over his phone records and online history. Let's find out how often he's been in contact with Craig Sullivan.'

DS Prescott had already been digging up info on Sullivan and the sex trafficking gang his brother had run. He'd spoken to the Yard's anti-trafficking unit who had told him that the gang stayed in business after Sullivan was banged up.

'They bring kids into the UK from all over Europe and Africa,' Prescott said. 'Most of the children have been kidnapped, but in a number of cases they've been sold by their parents. The children – some as young as five – are then sold on or rented out to paedophiles. It could be that Jacob Rossi was one of their victims.'

'But if that's the case then why send the note to his father?' Anna said. 'Surely they'd just be content with having the boy so they could put him to work.'

'Well perhaps they wanted us to think that it was an act

of revenge by a grudge-holding individual,' Prescott said. 'That way the spotlight wouldn't fall on them.'

'So where does Neville Quinlan come into it?' Walker said. 'Are we thinking he could be part of the gang?'

Anna shrugged. 'We shouldn't rule anything out, but I think it more likely that he's connected to them by way of being a customer. And one possible scenario is that he's spent months perving over kids at schools near to where he lives. And while doing so he noticed how Jacob walked home alone along a stretch of road with no cameras. So he flagged it up to Sullivan who realised they could grab the boy fairly easily. Quinlan might have been paid cash or given some free time with kids.'

Just talking about it was making Anna's spine tingle. But she knew that such things were going on every day on a huge scale. Human trafficking and sexual exploitation of children was big business across the world. Hundreds of thousands of kids were seized by crime gangs every year and then farmed out for sex. It was therefore quite conceivable that Jacob Rossi had been snared for that purpose. But if so then why had he been held captive in the cellar of a derelict pub in Camberwell? Surely a well-resourced and experienced gang would have taken him straight to a more secure place.

Anna went into her office and called DCS Nash to brief him on the new lead. The Sullivan name rang a bell with him and he remembered the case from three years ago when a total of four men were jailed for their parts in the multi-million-pound sex trafficking network.

'I've cautioned the team not to build their hopes up,' she said. 'We're still lacking solid evidence linking Quinlan or anyone else to the abduction. Plus, forensics have produced sod all. So I'm afraid we'll just have to hope we get lucky at some point.'

Nash explained that he would be spending yet another day at the Yard helping to coordinate the Met's response to the riots.

'I've been told what happened to Tom and your daughter,' he said. 'Thank God they're OK. When this crisis is over, I'll be insisting that you take some more compassionate leave so that you can spend some time with both of them.'

'And I'll be sure to hold you to that, sir.'

Walker entered her office just as she came off the phone and handed her a mug of coffee.

'I made it myself because the machine is on the blink,' he said.

'Thank you, Max. So what's the situation with Craig Sullivan?'

'DC Sweeny just called in, guv. She and DC Mortimer have arrived at his house in Norwood, but he's not there. They want to know what they should do.'

Anna gave it some thought. 'Tell them to park up a discreet distance away and keep the place under surveillance. If he turns up they're to call me for further instructions.'

Walker's phone rang so he stepped back out of the office to answer it, and Anna took the opportunity to call Chloe to check that all was well with her.

She sounded in good spirits and told Anna that Tom was napping and she was eating crisps while watching television.

'A doctor came to see him and he's doing well,' she said. 'We've been talking and playing games and he's been telling me a lot about you that I didn't know.'

'I'm not sure I like the sound of that,' Anna said.

267

Chloe laughed. 'Don't panic, Mum. It's all good stuff, mostly about what you did to try to find me over the years and how you never gave up.'

Anna was reminded that her daughter and Tom hadn't spent more than a few minutes alone together since Chloe's return a month ago. So this was the first time Tom had been able to give her his take on what it had been like for Anna during the ten years that Chloe was missing from her life.

'I probably won't be able to pick you up until quite late,' Anna said. 'Are you OK with that?'

'Of course, I am. Have you caught the man who kidnapped that boy?'

'Not yet, sweetheart – I mean Chloe. But we are getting close. I'm sure of it.'

Anna hung up after telling Chloe not to hesitate to call her if any problems arose. Then she called the team together so that she could update them. There were only nine in total, including four admin staff. She told them about the Quinlan interview and reminded them that they should soon receive the warrant allowing them to force their way into Roy Slater's home.

'As soon as we get the warrant we'll go to Rotherhithe,' she said. 'And we'll also need to be ready to shoot off to Norwood if DC Sweeny tells us Sullivan has turned up. It could be a long wait.'

But it wasn't. After just half an hour Sweeny reported in to say that Sullivan had arrived back home.

'Stay in position and continue watching the house,' Anna told her. 'Don't move in or do anything to alert him until we get there.'

CHAPTER FIFTY

So another suspect had been lobbed into the mix, and in terms of plausibility, Craig Sullivan certainly ticked the boxes. He was thought to be part of a child sex trafficking gang that used to be run by his brother, Tony. And he met up with the paedo Neville Quinlan the very afternoon that Jacob Rossi was abducted. It was therefore either a big coincidence or else the man was in it up to his neck.

Anna took the decision to hit the road with DI Walker. She instructed DS Prescott to stay in HQ and have another go at getting Quinlan to open up.

It had become a fast-moving situation suddenly, and even before they set off there was another development. DC Sweeny called in to say that Sullivan had re-emerged from his house after only a few minutes and was back in his car.

'We're tailing him, guv,' she said. 'But the roads are chaotic and there are diversions everywhere. So I don't know how long we can keep him in sight.'

'Where is he heading?' Anna asked.

269

'North along Norwood Road towards Tulse Hill.'

'Stay with him if you can, Megan. We'll head that way and I'll try to get some back-up.'

But it took Anna only minutes to discover that they were on their own. There were no patrols available to join the pursuit. Units were already responding to emergencies all across the city as a fresh wave of disturbances kicked off. The rioters were on a roll again, emboldened no doubt by the belief that they were on the winning side. They had the police against the ropes, and soldiers were taking to the streets to help quell the unrest.

As Anna and Walker embarked on the four-mile journey from Wandsworth to Tulse Hill, they soon saw for themselves that London faced another grim day of violent disorder.

Passing through Clapham, they witnessed skirmishes between police and mobs of young men on the Common, and then they were directed away from the High Street because rioters had erected a barricade across the road.

They were rerouted through Balham, the neighbourhood where the accidental shooting of a pregnant woman during a police raid on Tuesday had triggered the riots. Damage to homes, shops and vehicles was considerable. Some buildings had burned down, while others were still smouldering. The pavements were packed with restless youths of both sexes who seemed to be having the time of their lives. They were winding each other up, intimidating local residents and shop-keepers, brazenly committing acts of vandalism.

'What I find really scary about all this is how the emotions have changed from anger to euphoria,' Walker said. 'They're really fucking lapping it up, aren't they? The more people they hurt, the more buildings they trash, the more clobber they nick, the happier they are. And the icing on the cake is seeing us struggling to subdue them. It's as though Christmas has come early for everyone who has a grudge against authority and feels the need to do something about it.'

Anna was about to make a point of her own when a news-flash on the radio broke into her thoughts, and caused them both to wince.

'Video footage has emerged which shows two police officers beating a teenage girl with batons during street clashes in Brixton,' the newsreader said. 'The girl, who's black, was forced to the ground where one of the officers then kicked her twice in the head before other protesters managed to drag her away. It's understood she's now being treated in hospital. In the last few minutes a Scotland Yard spokesperson has said the incident will be the subject of an investigation. Meanwhile, a prominent community leader in Brixton has described it as a vicious example of the type of police brutality that has encouraged many people to take part in the riots.'

Anna slammed her palms against the steering wheel and gritted her teeth.

'That's all we need,' she said. 'It's like throwing gallons of petrol onto a fire that's already raging out of control.'

*

DC Sweeny called with another update as they were passing by Tooting Bec Common.

'Sullivan just stopped to pick someone up, ma'am,' she said excitedly. 'They're now heading west towards Dulwich.'

'So who did he pick up?' Anna asked her.

'A man in a grey overcoat who looked to be in his fifties.

He was waiting on the corner of Norwood Road and Leigham Vale. As soon as Sullivan's car pulled up he got straight into the front passenger seat.'

'So where exactly are you now, Megan?'

'We're on Thurlow Park Road. Fortunately, it's pretty quiet here.'

'That's good. We're actually not far behind you.'

'Do you want us to pull them over?'

'Absolutely not. I want to see where they go. This is looking increasingly iffy to me.'

Anna was very familiar with this part of London so she stuck to the back streets once they had passed Tooting. They encountered fewer problems because the rioters were focusing on the high streets, shopping malls and council estates. Just beyond Tulse Hill Sweeny came back on to say that they had followed Sullivan to a detached house on the edge of Dulwich Village.

'He parked on the driveway and both he and his passenger got out,' she told Anna. 'We managed to pull into the kerb about twenty yards back and saw them approach the front door. It was opened by a young woman who let them in.'

'So you're now parked up with a view of the house.'

'That's correct, ma'am.'

'Then give us your exact location. We'll be there in minutes.'

Walker tapped the address into the sat nav and they were on their way.

'So how do we play this, guv, bearing in mind that we have no idea what the hell is going on here?'

'Craig Sullivan is a person of interest in the abduction and imprisonment of Jacob Rossi,' Anna replied. 'We know he's an acquaintance of another suspect, namely Neville Quinlan, who happens to be a convicted paedophile. We therefore need to question him ASAP.'

'So what do we do if we go knocking on this house and he won't come to the door?'

'We execute a forced entry. And before you remind me that we're without a warrant, as far as I'm concerned we don't need one. We're in pursuit of someone who we believe has committed a serious crime.'

Walker laughed. 'That's why I like working with you, Boss. We're always on the same wavelength.'

Seven minutes later they turned into a short residential street. There were terraced homes on one side and detached houses on the other. Most of the cars were parked in front of the terraced properties, including the familiar black Vauxhall Corsa from the MIT pool.

There was a space directly behind it, which Anna pulled into. Seconds later she and Walker were in the back seat of the Vauxhall behind detectives Sweeny and Mortimer.

Sweeny pointed through the windscreen. 'It's the house on the right over there. You can see Sullivan's BMW on the driveway. No one has appeared since he and the guy he picked up went inside.'

The house was smaller and less well maintained than those either side of it. The white exterior was in dire need of a fresh coat of paint and the tiny front garden to the right of the driveway had weeds sprouting up through the gravel.

'So what we know is that there are at least three people inside,' Anna said. 'One of them is a man who we believe to be involved in the trafficking of children for sex, which is why we want to question him about Jacob Rossi. However, we don't know the identities of the guy he brought here or the woman who answered the door to them. And we don't know if there's anyone else inside. For that reason we need to tread carefully.'

'It might be sensible to wait for back-up,' Sweeny said. 'Or even an armed response team.'

'If we do that we could be waiting all day,' Anna said. 'And my gut's telling me that we need to move quickly. Something bad could be happening inside that house and it might well involve children.'

They all knew it was a justifiable concern, which far outweighed the risks they faced by forging ahead unarmed and without back-up.

'Max and I will go to the front door and I want you two to see if you can make your way around the back,' Anna said. 'Be prepared to stop anyone fleeing the scene, but don't confront them if you think they might have a weapon.'

Anna's brain was in overdrive as she approached the house and her stomach was in tight knots. Her suspicions were further aroused when she saw that the curtains were closed across all the windows despite the fact that it was a bright day.

A gate to the side turned out to be unlocked so Sweeny and Mortimer were able to access the back garden while Anna rang the front doorbell. When there was no response she pressed it again and left her finger on it. Eventually a woman's voice came from inside.

'Who are you and what do you want?' she said in a gruff voice.

Anna suspected the woman was watching her through the peephole so she held up her warrant card.

'I'm a detective with the Metropolitan Police,' she said. 'I'm here with my colleagues to speak to Mr Craig Sullivan.'

'Nobody by that name lives here,' the woman said.

'That may well be so. But we know that Mr Sullivan is here at the moment because we saw him enter the property. And that's his car on the driveway.'

The woman didn't reply, so Anna continued. 'You might as well open the door because we won't be leaving here until we've spoken to Mr Sullivan. And if that means forcing our way in then so be it.'

'Have you got a warrant?' the woman asked.

'We don't need one since we're acting on information that Mr Sullivan may have committed a serious crime.'

The woman fell silent, and for about twenty seconds nothing happened. Then suddenly they heard shouting coming from the rear of the house.

Anna told Walker to stay put as she dashed over to the side gate, fearful that her two colleagues were in trouble. She pushed the gate open and ran along a path to the back garden.

She arrived in time to see her two detectives grappling with Sullivan in the middle of a large paved patio. He was lashing out with his fists as they tried to pull him to the ground so that they could cuff him.

As Anna approached them, a woman in jeans and a T-shirt stepped out through an open back door. She was brandishing a baseball bat in both hands and began screaming at the detectives to let Sullivan go.

Anna threw herself forward and lunged at the woman just as she was about to strike Sweeny from behind. The woman was taken by surprise as Anna rammed into her, shoulder first. She lost her balance and tumbled sideways onto the patio, dropping the bat as she did so.

Anna didn't give her a chance to recover. She leaned over,

grabbed the woman's T-shirt, and rolled her onto her back before pinning her down with both knees. She then pulled her arms up her back, whipped out the cuffs she always carried in her jacket pocket, and slipped them on the woman's wrists.

Behind her Sweeny and Mortimer were managing to do the same to Sullivan.

Anna stood up and hauled the woman to her feet. She was somewhere in her twenties with short black hair and a freckled face.

'You have no right to do this,' the woman cried out. 'I haven't done anything wrong.'

'Then why wouldn't you let us in?'

'We thought . . .'

'Shut the fuck up, you stupid bitch,' Sullivan yelled at her as he was being pulled up off the patio floor. 'Don't say another bloody word.'

Anna looked at him and saw that his nose was bleeding and there was a swelling on his forehead above his left eye.

'So what is your problem, Mr Sullivan?' she said. 'Do you have an aversion to talking to the police or have you got something to hide?'

He glared at her, baring his teeth.

'Go get fucked, copper,' he fumed. 'I'm saying nothing until I talk to my lawyer.'

Just then Walker appeared in the doorway that Anna now saw led into a kitchen. He was holding on to the arm of a man in a grey overcoat, who Anna realised must be the guy Sullivan had picked up in Tulse Hill. He too had been placed in cuffs.

'I caught this fellah trying to do a runner out the front door,' Walker said. 'I've checked all the downstairs rooms and they're empty. But I think I heard a noise upstairs.'

Anna turned back to Sullivan. 'So who else is in the house, Mr Sullivan?'

He swallowed, and Anna saw the anger in his eyes turn to fear. He opened his mouth to speak, but then decided not to and clamped his lips together.

'We'll find out for ourselves then,' Anna said.

She told Sweeny to hold on to the woman while she and DC Mortimer took Sullivan back inside. Mortimer was a big, beefy lad with more muscle than fat under his suit, and he had no difficulty forcing Sullivan through the kitchen and along the hall.

Anna followed closely behind, dread pooling in her stomach. She had an awful feeling she knew what she was going to find.

As they mounted the stairs, Sullivan started muttering curses and trying to free himself, but he was no match for Mortimer.

When they reached the landing, they encountered five doors, all closed. Anna moved ahead of Mortimer and opened the first door. It led to a bathroom that was empty. But when she opened the next door and saw what was inside her heart exploded in her chest.

Two boys wearing pyjamas were sitting on top of a made-up double bed, their faces pale and fearful. Anna asked them if they were all right and they both nodded.

'I'll be right back,' she said and hurried along the corridor to check on the other three rooms.

They were all bedrooms, but only one of them was occupied by a girl who was no older than twelve. Chloe's age. She was curled up in the foetal position on a king-size bed and sobbing quietly into a pillow.

And she was completely naked.

CHAPTER FIFTY-ONE

After helping the girl to get dressed, Anna called it in. As she expected, the case was immediately granted priority status and officers were going to be pulled off other duties – including the riots – to attend.

Central control also said they would arrange for an ambulance to be sent to the house, along with a team from social services.

'I want forensics here too,' Anna said. 'Along with local CID.'

She phoned Nash to update him and to ask him to make sure that she got what she wanted in terms of resources. He promised to do what he could and said he hoped to be back at MIT HQ later in the day.

Anna then confronted Sullivan, who was being held by Mortimer on the landing at the top of the stairs.

'You've been using this place as a child brothel, haven't you?' she said, prodding him hard in the chest with her finger. 'You sick, vile bastard.'

He just stared back at her, saying nothing, his eyes flat and empty of all emotion.

'Tell me why you didn't bring Jacob Rossi straight here,' she said. 'Why did you leave him for so long in the pub cellar?'

His eyebrows snapped together. 'Are you talking about the kid who went missing in Bromley? The son of that TV bloke?'

'You know I am.'

'That had nothing to do with me. I only know about it because I saw it on the news.'

'I don't believe you.'

'And I don't give a fuck.'

Anna had to resist the urge to punch him in the face.

'Take him downstairs before I do something I'll regret,' she said to Mortimer. 'Send Megan up here to help me with the kids and tell Max the cavalry will be here soon.'

Anna then got the three children together in one of the bedrooms where she quickly discovered that only the girl was English. The two boys were from Romania.

It wouldn't be Anna's job to delve into their backgrounds or to launch an investigation into the gang that had preyed on them. That would be the job of specialists working for the National Crime Agency. Her job was to find out if they had information that would help bring to justice whoever had been behind Jacob Rossi's abduction.

She found it hard to contain her emotions as she stood looking down on the three youngsters who were sat on the edge of the bed. They seemed confused rather than scared. Their eyes were wide but vacant, and the thought of how much they must have suffered tugged at Anna's heartstrings.

The boys were wearing T-shirts and Anna noticed some bruises on their arms. The girl, who was no longer crying, was now wearing shorts and a crew-neck jumper. She had short black hair and delicate features. Anna hadn't spotted any bruises or marks on her body when she'd helped her to get dressed.

Anna began by asking them whether they were related to each other or to the people who had been in the house with them. They all shook their heads.

She then asked them their names and ages. The girl said she was Vicky Woods and she was eleven, almost twelve. The boys were Christian Orban and Darius Anca. They were both thirteen and spoke pretty good English.

Anna explained who she was and told them that they were now safe and would be properly looked after. But their reaction was muted. Even when she said that efforts would be made to contact their families, the only response was a weak smile from Vicky. It made her wonder if they had been given drugs to control their behaviour.

When DC Sweeny entered the room, Anna introduced them to her and said that there were other police officers downstairs.

'More will be arriving shortly and you'll be taken to a place of safety,' she said.

'What will happen to Lorna?' Vicky asked, her voice low, wary.

'Is she the woman who's been here in the house with you?'

The girl nodded. 'She's the one who feeds us and tells us what we have to do when the men come. She says she'll kill us if we tell anyone what happens here.'

Anna balled her fists involuntarily and felt her entire body tense.

'Well you won't have to worry about Lorna any more,' she

said. 'She'll be going to prison for a long time. And the man too. What do you call him?'

'Lorna calls him Craig,' Vicky said. 'We're not allowed to talk to him.'

'And what about the other man who arrived here a little while ago? Do you know who he is?'

Vicky lowered her eyes and clasped her hands together in her lap.

'He paid them so that he could do things to me,' she said, and it shocked Anna that she was so matter-of-fact about it. 'He was getting undressed when Lorna shouted that the police were here. So he ran out of the room.'

Anna got Sweeny to take notes while she asked the questions. And the more she heard about how they had suffered the angrier she became.

All three had met for the first time about four months ago when they were brought together at another house, which Vicky believed was somewhere in London. Before that Vicky had been living with her stepfather in Norwich. By the sound of it he was a brutal drug addict. Her mother was dead and she said she had no other relatives. The stepfather didn't like having her around and sold her to two men he met in a pub. She had been abused by lots of different men ever since.

The boys had been abducted from an orphanage just outside Bucharest in Romania and trafficked to the UK in the back of a lorry with five other children. The three had been moved to this house around two months ago and that was when they met Lorna. Since then they had been sexually abused and raped almost daily by a succession of men who had paid for the privilege.

Anna learned that the woman, Lorna, resided in the house

and the abusers were brought there by Craig Sullivan and sometimes other men.

'They don't let us go out except into the back garden, and if we cry Lorna hits us,' Vicky said.

It was a set-up that had become all too familiar in recent years in the UK and across Europe. Nobody knew for sure how many children were being cruelly exploited in this way, but unofficial estimates put the figure in the thousands.

Anna continued to ask questions even as she heard reinforcements arrive at the house. Walker popped into the room to tell her that Sullivan and the other two had been arrested and cautioned and were about to be transferred to Wandsworth.

'A forensics team is on its way,' he said. 'Meantime, I'll organise a search of the house.'

Anna sensed the children were becoming anxious and she wanted to get some more questions in before the social workers arrived.

She took out her phone and showed them a photo of Jacob Rossi. All three said they had never seen him before. They also said they had never spent any time in a pub cellar.

But both boys did recognise a photo of Neville Quinlan.

'He's been here many times,' Darius said. 'The last time was about a week ago. He told me I was his favourite, and when he was finished, he gave me some sweets.'

CHAPTER FIFTY-TWO

During the next hour no less than twenty more people converged on the house in Dulwich. They included patrol officers, local CID detectives, paramedics, a forensics team, and three social workers.

The paramedics examined the children before whisking them away from the scene. Arrangements would be made for NCA officers to question the children further.

The three perps were also taken away in separate vehicles. Craig Sullivan was seen as a real catch. The fact that he'd been collared purely by chance wouldn't stop the Major Investigation Team taking full credit for it; Anna knew that Nash would see to that.

Unfortunately Sullivan's arrest, and the discovery of the child brothel, probably wouldn't move them any closer to solving the Jacob Rossi case. They knew that Neville Quinlan had met up with Sullivan last Monday afternoon. But it now appeared that the pair hadn't set off together to abduct Jacob on his way home from school. Instead, Sullivan had brought

Quinlan to the house so that he could satisfy his lust for young male flesh.

Both of them would be questioned further, of course, along with Sullivan's accomplice, Lorna Fitzgerald. She hadn't spoken since Anna had stopped her clobbering Sweeny with the baseball bat. But she'd been easily identified from the driving licence and credit cards in her purse. And a PNC check had revealed that, like her paymaster, she had form for dealing drugs.

The perv who was about to have his way with Vicky Woods also had a criminal record. Samuel Broderick was a fifty-four-year-old accountant who had served time for molesting three underage girls some years ago. His profile was similar to that of Quinlan, and Anna guessed they were part of the same paedo network that made use of the services provided by human traffickers like Craig Sullivan.

It was a lot for Anna to get her head around, even before the search of the house uncovered some disturbing pieces of evidence.

Walker found a drawer full of medications that had clearly been used to control the children. There were sleeping pills, tablets that were known to cause listlessness, and batches of the notorious date rape drugs – Rohypnol and Ketamine.

Far more incriminating evidence was found on Lorna Fitzpatrick's laptop, which she had obviously been using when Anna and the team arrived. In her panic she'd neglected to switch it off.

When a forensic technician fired it up, a shot of the bedroom that Vicky Woods had occupied filled the screen. It transpired that there were hidden cameras in all the bedrooms. This led to the discovery of a folder on the laptop containing fifteen video clips of 'punters' having sex with the children, presumably used for blackmailing the men or selling the clips to online paedophile sites.

Among those caught on camera was Neville Quinlan, and the time and date stamp on the recording showed that he was abusing Darius when Jacob was snatched off the street.

So on the one hand it seemed to clear him of direct involvement in the abduction. But on the other it was proof positive that he had been up to his old tricks.

*

Eventually everyone except the forensics officers moved outside the house in order to protect the integrity of what was now a crime scene.

Anna welcomed the opportunity to light up a cigarette. She desperately needed a nicotine fix and the first drag went down a treat.

She was anxious now to get back to Wandsworth so that she could put Quinlan on the spot and conduct a formal interview with Sullivan before handing him over to the NCA.

She also wanted to get the team together for another status review. Quinlan had been their prime suspect in the Rossi case, and if he was no longer in the frame then it was a serious setback.

She said as much to the group that was gathered around her on the driveway. Walker, Mortimer and Sweeny had been joined by two detectives from the local CID and three uniforms.

They all compared notes, and Anna passed on what Vicky Woods had told her. Walker mentioned the drugs, the cameras

285

in the bedrooms and the video clips on the laptop. One of the local detectives said that he had spoken to several neighbours who'd had no idea what was going on in the house.

'It's owned by a bloke who lives in Spain with his wife,' the detective said. 'He lets it out fully furnished through an estate agent. We've found documents showing that the current tenant is one Lorna Fitzgerald and she's leasing it for six months. The rent comes from a bank account that was set up in her name only three months ago.'

'It's an MO that's often deployed by sex trafficking gangs,' Walker pointed out. 'They move between various rented properties so they don't arouse suspicion by staying for too long in any one place. And they market the kids on the Dark Web or through personal contact with paedos like Quinlan who are known to them.'

'It's a sick fucking business,' Sweeny said, and they all nodded in agreement.

Anna then handed over responsibility for the crime scene to the locals and they said they would liaise with the NCA team.

'We'll question Sullivan and Fitzgerald first just to satisfy ourselves that they weren't involved in Jacob's kidnapping,' she said. 'But I don't think they were. Then it'll be over to you guys and the crime agency. With any luck this could be the beginning of the end for at least one of the child trafficking gangs who for too long have been operating in this city with impunity.'

Minutes later they were heading back to Wandsworth and this time Walker was driving. Sweeny and Mortimer were following on behind.

Anna stared out of the window, her mind stuck on what

she had seen and heard in the house. The children's stories had been upsetting enough, but those vile video clips had been burned onto her retinas. They would always be there, a gruesome reminder of the depths of depravity to which some men can sink.

'Cheer up, guv,' Walker said. 'You should be buzzing with a sense of satisfaction. Those kids are out of harm's way thanks to us.'

Anna looked at him, shook her head. 'You and I both know that they'll suffer for the rest of their lives because of what's happened to them.'

'That doesn't mean that we shouldn't be pleased with ourselves. It was a result. And a good one.'

Anna sighed. 'I suppose so. But what we do just doesn't seem to be enough when it comes to this sort of thing.'

'We can only do our best, guv. You know that.'

She did, but it didn't make her feel any better.

'We might well have earned brownie points for closing down a child brothel, Max,' she said. 'But we've been dealt a blow with the loss of our prime suspect in the Rossi case. We now know that Quinlan was busy elsewhere when Jacob was abducted. That's why he lied to us about his movements.'

'But we do know for sure that he was parked outside the lad's school a few days earlier.'

'I'm inclined to believe that it was just a coincidence. He probably went there to have a wank in the car while ogling the kids.'

'Or he was scouting for talent on Sullivan's behalf.'

Anna shrugged. 'We can push him on that. And Sullivan too. But I don't think that is what happened.'

'So if you're right we're now down to four persons of interest

– Roy Slater, Gavin Pope, Michelle Gerrard and Mark Rossi's long-lost stepbrother Joseph Walsh, or whatever his name is now.'

Anna nodded. 'That's correct, but three of them we still haven't managed to trace, which is so bloody frustrating.'

But as luck would have it there was an encouraging development on that front before they got back to Wandsworth. A message came through from HQ that Michelle Gerrard had turned up at her house and was being brought in for questioning. So at last they would be able to find out why the sick troll had been targeting Mark Rossi with vile and offensive remarks. And if she had anything to do with Jacob's abduction.

CHAPTER FIFTY-THREE

Presenter: *'This is the BBC news at three o'clock . . . and we're now hearing that a sixth person has died in the riots. Police say a man in his early twenties suffered a heart attack when he was crushed by a mob of youths as they tried to gain access to a supermarket in Birmingham.*

'The Home Secretary has described the fatalities as tragic and senseless. And he's condemned all those involved in the disturbances.'

Home Secretary: *'Those causing trouble are not legitimate protesters. They're criminals who are intent on causing as much harm as possible. They should be ashamed of themselves.'*

Presenter: *'The Home Secretary's remarks prompted one community leader to say that the police and politicians* *should share responsibility for what is happening. Lionel Robson was speaking an hour ago while standing outside a blazing restaurant near his home in Tottenham.'*

Community Leader: 'We've been warning the authorities for years that this was going to happen. But they did sod all about it. Too many people have been treated like dirt for far too long, especially ethnic minorities here in London. Most of those who've taken to the streets are not causing wilful damage. They're just trying to make a point.'

Presenter: 'The first of our live reports now from Lewis Forbes in Stratford . . .'

CHAPTER FIFTY-FOUR

Chloe checked the time on her phone and saw that it was three-thirty in the afternoon. It surprised her because she hadn't realised that she'd been at the hospital for over seven hours.

The time had passed so quickly and even now she was in no hurry to go home. She had enjoyed being with Tom. They'd talked and played games and when he'd slept – which had been for much of the time – she had wandered around the hospital. She'd bought drinks and snack bars in the canteen and watched television in the visitors' room.

Tom had just dropped off again after they'd had a long chat about her mother.

'I want you to know that I love her very much, Chloe,' he'd said. 'My feelings for her haven't changed as a result of you coming back into her life. If anything, they're stronger now because she's much happier and more optimistic about the future. And so am I.'

Chloe had hung on to his every word, and she knew he meant it when he'd said that he wanted them to be a family.

'Your mum and I were planning to move in together soon,' he'd told her. 'But it's only right and sensible that it gets put on hold so that she can spend time with you first. You both have a lot of catching up to do, and you must believe me when I say that I really don't have a problem with that.'

She did believe him because she was sure now that he was an honest man. Unlike her father who had told her so many lies. And she was glad that she had agreed to stay with him in the hospital because it had allowed her to get to know him.

He had a broken body because he'd tried to help her, and it was such a relief that he wasn't more seriously injured or even dead. She wanted to be nice to him, to show him that she was so very grateful. It was important to her, partly because she wasn't able to thank Sophie and Ryan for saving her life. She wouldn't be here if it wasn't for them. It made her feel sad, and guilty, and she swore to herself that from now on she would include them in her prayers.

A nurse came up to the bed to check on Tom. She was the one with the nice smile and the uniform that was too tight for her.

Chloe had been watching her talking to the other patients on the ward. Every bed was occupied, so it took her a long time to get from one end to the other.

'You look very tired, Chloe,' she said. 'Would you like me to get you a cup of tea?'

'No thank you. I was about to go for a walk.'

'Well just be sure to take care of yourself. We don't want to see you ending up as one of the patients.'

But all the doctors and nurses *were* treating her like she was a patient, and she suspected that it wasn't just because they felt sorry for her. They knew who she was and what she'd been through. The doctor treating Tom had said that he had followed her story from the day she was abducted by her dad ten years ago, because he had a daughter of his own who was the same age as Chloe.

'My wife was actually moved to tears when you were reunited with your real mother last month,' he'd told her. 'She even opened a bottle of bubbly so that we could celebrate.'

It was a strange feeling to be recognised and talked about by people she didn't know. People who seemed to regard her as some kind of celebrity. She realised now that one of the reasons her mum had kept her indoors during the past four weeks was to shield her from all the attention. And she was glad that she had because the curious stares and the questions made her feel uncomfortable.

She got up from the chair and looked at Tom. He was snoring and she reckoned he would be out cold for a while. Time then for a wee and a walk.

She couldn't believe how busy the hospital was. There were so many people and so much noise. It was a wonder that any of the patients could get any sleep.

The canteen was packed so she didn't hang around in there. Instead, she got a Coke and a chocolate bar from a vending machine and went up to the visitors' room next to Tom's ward. There were five people in there watching the news on the television. Chloe joined them, and within minutes of seeing what was going on across London her stomach was cramping with nerves.

The rioting had got much worse apparently because two police officers had been filmed beating a young woman with batons. It had further inflamed the situation and caused many more outbreaks of violence.

'Police stations have come under attack in Brixton, Stoke Newington, Fulham and Peckham,' the newsreader said. 'Rioters are also targeting magistrate courts as well as high street stores and shopping malls. In the last hour the official death toll has risen to nine, and the number of arrests in London alone to over four hundred.'

The newsreader then read out the names of several of those who had died. Photographs were also shown of some of them, including the boy who had lost his life while chained up in a cellar. Another was a middle-aged shopkeeper who was stabbed in the heart as he fought against youths who stormed into his convenience store.

Chloe felt a flash of heat in her chest as a familiar face filled the screen.

'Ryan Claymore was killed on Friday night,' the newsreader said. 'He was trapped in a gift shop in Vauxhall that was set on fire by rioters. It's believed that two people who were with him managed to escape the blaze. His mother today described him as the perfect son and said he died while in the act of saving the life of a young girl he didn't know.'

Chloe let out a strangled sob as a great torrent of sadness welled up inside her. A flood of hot tears followed, blurring everything around her.

Suddenly she was no longer in the visitors' room. She was back in the gift shop watching Ryan screaming as he was consumed by the flames. Her own blood felt like it was on fire, and although she could hear people talking to her, she had no idea what they were saying.

CHAPTER FIFTY-FIVE

Michelle Gerrard did not fit Anna's preconceived notion of an internet troll. She was tall and slender, with full lips, sharp cheekbones, and grey hair that was gathered up and pinned. And she looked smart in a black trouser suit over a cream blouse.

Anna had been told that she lived by herself and worked as a librarian. Apparently she hadn't been at home when the police first called at her house because she had been staying with her ageing mother in Maidstone, Kent.

She certainly didn't come across as the sort of person who would kidnap a small boy and hold him captive in a cellar.

But then Anna knew that appearances could be deceiving. Before entering the interview room she'd read some of the offensive remarks that Gerrard had posted online about Mark Rossi. Based on those it was clear that for whatever reason she had it in for him.

One of the remarks that stuck out had been posted to Facebook below photos Rossi had uploaded showing Jacob's tenth birthday on board a yacht in Spain.

It's time you stopped showing off your wealth, Rossi. I can't wait to see your privileged world come crashing down around you. And mark my words it will.

The woman was clearly nervous as Anna sat down at the table and took out her notebook.

'Before we start, are you sure you don't want to be represented by the duty solicitor?' she asked her.

Gerrard shook her head. 'There's no need. I've been told what this is about and I can't come up with any legitimate excuses for my behaviour. But I can assure you that Mark Rossi has heard the last from me. I won't be posting any more remarks about him online.'

'Why stop now?' Anna said.

Gerrard turned down the corners of her mouth. 'Isn't that blindingly obvious? I've seen the news so I know what's happened to his son. I wouldn't wish that on anyone, not even Rossi. It's only right and fair to let him and his wife grieve in peace. And it's made me realise that I was wrong to do what I did. I took it too far and I'm sorry.'

Anna opened up her notebook and tapped her finger on the first page.

'This is a short brief that's been prepared for me, Miss Gerrard. And it makes for disturbing reading. You've been trolling Mr Rossi for months. But it seems that you've never made it clear why. So would you please tell me what made you hate him so much?'

Gerrard ignored a tear that started sliding down her left cheek. She tightened her jaw and said, 'It was because he was so rude to me when our paths crossed. Afterwards I couldn't forgive him for the way he acted even though I'd been a big fan of his up until then. I wanted desperately to get back at him and the only way I could do it was through social media. I didn't mean for it to carry on, but once I started, I couldn't stop. I felt he deserved it.'

Anna frowned. 'But Mr Rossi says he's never met you.'

'Well he has. It was a few months ago in Bromley.'

Anna's frown deepened. 'I'm afraid you need to be more specific about that.'

Gerrard finally wiped away the tear from her cheek. 'Rossi was opening a new store in the town centre. I went along because I'd seen the posters and I'd set my heart on getting a selfie with him to show my mum.' She paused there and stiffened her jaw.

'So what happened exactly?' Anna pressed.

Gerrard raised her eyes to the ceiling. 'Well first off I arrived late because I got held up in traffic. The event was over but there were still around twenty people outside the store and Rossi was signing autographs. I joined the crowd, but as I was fishing my phone out of my bag he announced he had to leave and started walking away. I instinctively rushed forward, grabbed his jacket sleeve, and asked him if I could snap a picture. His reaction took me completely by surprise.'

'What did he do?' Anna asked.

'He snatched his hand away which made it look as though I'd attacked him. Then he turned towards me and yelled abuse. His actual words were: *for pity's sake act your age woman and get a fucking life.*" I was really shocked and upset, but he didn't care. He just hurried off. I was left standing there in the street trying not to cry. It was made worse because everyone around me heard him and a couple of teenage girls even started laughing.

'Then a young man came up to me and said that Rossi was one of those celebrities who don't like having their photos taken with fans. It was no consolation, though. I felt angry and humiliated, and in the days that followed I couldn't stop myself checking him out online. That wound me up even more because of the way he kept harping on about his great life. Before I knew it, I was having digs at him and if I'm honest it filled me with a cruel sense of satisfaction.'

The woman's story would be an easy one to check out. All they had to do was ask Mark Rossi. Her reaction to what had supposedly happened outside the store was shocking, but not terribly unusual. People often went OTT when they felt they'd been unjustly treated. And social media was the perfect vehicle through which they could sound off.

Gerrard was sobbing now, but quickly became far more upset when Anna's follow-up questions made her realise what she'd been suspected of.

'Are you out of your bloody mind?' she yelled. 'How can you possibly believe I would do something like that? I could never hurt a child.'

By the time Anna finished asking questions she believed the woman's story. Gerrard said she was at work when Jacob disappeared, that she'd never been to Camberwell, and she didn't know Roy Slater or Gavin Pope. She also agreed to let officers into her house to have a look around.

'I'll arrange for you to be taken home,' Anna told her. 'And once we've confirmed that you've been truthful with me, I see no reason to bother you again.'

Anna returned to the ops room and told the team she was satisfied that Michelle Gerrard could be ruled out.

'I really can't imagine that the woman was involved,' she

said. 'So once we've checked out what she told me let's not waste any more time on her.'

Anna was disappointed but not altogether surprised. There had only ever been an outside chance that Gerrard was anything other than an offensive internet troll.

She was eager now to refocus on the other suspects, and it so happened that while she'd been conducting the interview DS Khan had come up with a possible lead.

'It might be nothing, guv, but I've been running checks on Gavin Pope and his wife,' he said. 'Mrs Pope told us she works for a recruitment agency and that's true. Her base is in Bromley and she's an assistant manager. But the firm is part of a chain and three weeks ago they opened a new branch in Camberwell, and it's just a short walk from The Falconer's Arms pub.'

'Well it's a tentative link at best,' Anna said.

'That was my initial reaction until I made inquiries and found out that Mrs Pope spent the first two weeks there helping to set it up.'

Anna grinned. 'That's most definitely something we can't ignore. But before you ask her about it, go to Camberwell and find out from her colleagues if she mentioned the pub while she was there and acted in any way suspiciously.'

'I'll get right on it,' Khan said.

Anna decided it was time to sit down in her office and carefully go over everything they had. At last the pace of the investigation was picking up and things were happening. She wanted to make sure that she was across every last detail and that her notes were up to date.

But as soon as she sat down behind her desk DS Prescott

appeared in the doorway with a concerned expression on his face.

'I've got some news about Roy Slater, ma'am,' he said, a tremor in his voice.

'Has he turned up?'

'Indeed he has, but he won't be telling us if he's the bastard who put Jacob Rossi in the cellar.'

Anna felt her heart sink. 'And why is that?'

'Because he's dead. It seems he was murdered early on Friday evening just hours after Jacob Rossi died.'

CHAPTER FIFTY-SIX

The scene of crime was a narrow alley off Southwark Park Road in Bermondsey. It was wedged between two boarded-up shops and crammed with half a dozen large wheelie bins.

Anna and Walker arrived just before six p.m., having driven through the parts of South London that had suffered the most damage at the hands of the rioters. Sweeny and Mortimer had been instructed to go back to HQ and brief the rest of the team on what had happened at the house in Dulwich.

The focus of Anna's attention now switched from Neville Quinlan and Craig Sullivan to Roy Slater, the man whose wife had an affair with Jacob Rossi's dad, Mark. She'd been told that DI Benning and DS Prescott were already on their way to his home in Rotherhithe with a couple of uniforms to force their way inside.

'The body was found two hours ago by a shopkeeper dumping some rubbish in one of the bins,' said Detective Inspector David Bolt, of Bermondsey CID. 'The poor sod was stabbed in the neck and beaten about the face and head. We were able to identify him as Roy Slater from the driving licence in his wallet, which was lying on the ground next to him. His name was flagged up as soon as I called it in and I was told that he was a suspect in the Jacob Rossi investigation. So I made sure that your people were informed straight away.'

Bolt had been told they were on their way and had been waiting at the mouth of the alley to greet them. He was a large man in a crumpled grey suit and he had a belly that flopped over his belt. He and his colleagues had already sealed off the scene and begun talking to people living and working nearby.

'The body is still in situ because we're waiting for forensics and the pathologist to get here,' Bolt said. 'But I've been told we're likely to have a long wait because of all the aggro that's going on elsewhere. I just hope we can clear off from here before it gets dark and the rioters come back, as I expect they will.'

'The officer you spoke to at our office told me that you suspect Mr Slater was killed by a bunch of them,' Anna said.

Bolt nodded. 'That's correct. It was mayhem here late on Friday afternoon and well into the evening. A mob about a hundred strong stormed along Southwark Park Road smashing their way into shops, starting fires, and mugging people they didn't like the look of. It wouldn't be a stretch to assume Mr Slater was one of those people. From the look of the body, I think it's fair to say that it's been here since then. But because of the disturbances many of the shops around here were closed for business yesterday so these bins didn't get used much, if at all.'

Anna looked along the alley, which ran for about thirty yards before arriving at a brick wall.

'You can tell us what else we need to know while we take a look for ourselves,' she said.

Bolt raised the crime scene tape and Anna and Walker ducked under it.

'As you can see we've pulled the last bin on the right away from the wall,' Bolt said. 'The body was stuffed behind it and was barely visible.'

Roy Slater was lying on his back. His eyes were closed but his mouth was open. He was wearing a black quilted jacket and denim jeans.

The stab wound was on the right side of his neck and the blood that had spilled from it had left a big stain on the ground. His face was badly bruised and there was a nasty gash in the centre of his forehead.

'Are there any wounds that we can't see?' Walker asked.

Bolt shook his head. 'We lifted him off the ground slightly so that we could have a look at his back, but it seems he was stabbed only the once in the neck, and probably died pretty quickly.'

Anna hunkered down next to the body, careful not to disturb anything around it. She was in no doubt that his was the face she had seen in the photo on the evidence board that morning.

'So it appears that Mr Slater was the victim of a random act of violence,' she said. 'That would mean his death was not linked to Jacob Rossi's abduction.'

'But it doesn't mean he wasn't involved,' Walker said.

Anna stood back up and asked Bolt if Slater's pockets had been searched.

He nodded. 'We found a set of car keys and a couple of betting slips that were issued on Friday by a bookies' just down the road from here. I reckon he must have been attacked shortly after leaving there. He'd placed four bets and laid out a total of two hundred pounds on horses that were running yesterday. There was no cash in his wallet so I'm guessing that the guys who did this made off with it. There were no credit cards either.'

'We know that his Visa card has been used since then on contactless machines, but only up to thirty quid a time,' Anna said. 'If you access the details you might be able to track down whoever has it.'

'We'll get straight onto that,' Bolt said.

'Have you found his mobile phone?' Anna asked.

'Not yet. It wasn't in his pockets and it's not in the alley. It could be in one of the bins. We'll go through them once forensics are here.'

'Now what about his car?' Anna said. 'Do you know where it is?'

'We do. He had a Renault key ring, so I got one of the uniforms to have a look around and he spotted it in a small car park behind the shops. We've had a look inside and didn't see anything suspicious.'

'We'll need to take a look ourselves,' Anna said. 'And I'll want forensics to examine it as well.'

They then walked back to the pavement and Anna felt a shivering unease when she saw that a group of youths had gathered on the other side of the road. They were shouting and making abusive gestures at the uniforms who were standing around the entrance to the alley and the two marked patrol cars at the kerb.

'That's all we need,' Bolt said. 'I guarantee there'll be a lot more of them soon and they'll start taking liberties.'

'You need to request more support,' Anna told him. 'I'll do the same from my end and stress that we need to protect the crime scene.'

'Thank you, ma'am,' Bolt said.

'Have you sussed out CCTV?' Walker asked him. 'There must be plenty of cameras around here.'

'It's in hand,' Bolt said. 'If we get a result I'll let you know, but there's a big backlog of tapes from all over the city that haven't yet been viewed.'

Bolt then asked Anna why Slater had been in the frame for the Jacob Rossi abduction.

'His wife had an affair with Jacob's father,' she explained. 'He was then paid not to go public with it, but he had a gambling addiction and not long ago he went back to Rossi to ask for more money and was turned away. So we were working on the basis that he could have taken Jacob out of revenge or to squeeze more money out of the dad.'

'I get the picture,' Bolt said. 'Have you guys been to his house?'

'We went there last night,' Anna said. 'When there was no answer, we applied for a warrant that we won't need any more. MIT officers are on their way there now. I'll get them to tell you what they find. We will obviously have to liaise closely on this one. If we rule Slater out as a suspect in the Rossi case we'll step back and leave it to you.'

Anna then got Bolt to take them to Slater's car, a light blue Renault Clio. She donned rubber gloves to check inside the boot and glove compartment, hoping to find something that would link its owner to Jacob Rossi or The Falconer's Arms pub in Camberwell. But there was nothing.

After that she saw no point in hanging around.

'We'll head back to Wandsworth,' she said to Bolt. 'Please call me later with an update. Meanwhile, I'll do what I can to get you more support down here just in case things turn ugly.'

CHAPTER FIFTY-SEVEN

The ball of anxiety in Anna's chest continued to grow during the drive from Bermondsey to Wandsworth.

She was concerned about the lack of progress she was making with the investigation. And she was worried that another night of savagery was about to descend on London.

Darkness was encroaching fast, and already sirens were ringing out and riot police were on the move.

Anna called central control and said it was imperative that DI Bolt was provided with more back-up at the crime scene in Southwark Park Road. Then she phoned DS Prescott to see if he had arrived at Roy Slater's house in Rotherhithe.

'I'm here now with DI Benning, guv,' he told her. 'We had to force the door open and we're just starting the search. The place is empty, and so far we haven't come across anything of interest.'

Anna was finding it increasingly difficult to get her thoughts together. It didn't help that she felt it necessary to have the radio on. The news was a constant and alarming distraction.

A battle between police and an angry mob was taking place outside the Westfield Shopping Centre in Stratford. There were reports that a supermarket was on fire in Putney. Shops were being looted in Kentish Town. And two petrol bombs had been thrown at the Crown Court building in Southwark, causing serious damage to the entrance.

Five hundred more coppers had been drafted in from southern counties to support the Met. And there were now a thousand soldiers helping to keep order.

But so far the impact appeared to be insignificant, which was no great surprise to Anna considering there were thirty-two boroughs in London and a population of almost nine million.

The pressure on law enforcement agencies was now unbearable, and some commentators were claiming that key services were at the point of collapse.

Hundreds of people who had been arrested still hadn't been processed, 999 calls were not being answered, there weren't enough forensic teams to attend ongoing crime scenes, or enough ambulances to respond to emergency call-outs. Plus, forty-two police vehicles were out of commission having been vandalised or set on fire, and public transport services – including buses, tubes and trains – were severely disrupted.

Anna felt a thud of dread in her stomach at the sheer scale of civil disobedience.

'I fear things will get much worse before they get any better,' she said. 'And God only knows how many more lives will be lost.'

*

Once back at HQ, Anna did things in order of priority. First off, she phoned Chloe to let her know that she wouldn't be able to pick her up from the hospital until much later. Her daughter's reaction came as a huge relief.

'Don't worry, Mum. I'm all right. And it's been fun here.'

'Are you sure, sweetheart?'

'Yep. Honest.'

'And how is Tom?'

'He sleeps a lot, and he's still in pain, but the doctor says he's slowly getting better.'

'Can you put him on the phone so that I can speak to him?'

'Not right now. I'm in the shop getting some sweets and a comic. And Tom wants a newspaper.'

'Oh, I see. Never mind then. But look, you are OK aren't you? I mean, it's not all too much for you being in the hospital all this time? I suspect it's pretty boring.'

Anna detected a slight hesitation before Chloe responded.

'There isn't much to do,' she said. 'And I did get a bit upset earlier in the television room. I was watching the news while Tom was sleeping and they put up a photo of Ryan and said what had happened to him. I didn't expect it.'

'You poor thing. I can imagine it was quite a shock.'

'I'm fine now, though. The nurses were really nice, and so was Tom.'

'Well we can talk about it when I pick you up. And I'm so sorry I can't get there any sooner.'

'And I told you not to worry.'

'Thanks for being so understanding. I love you very much.'

Anna held on for a beat, hoping her daughter would say

I love you back, but she didn't. So Anna told her she would call when she was on her way and hung up.

Speaking to Chloe, and knowing that she was coping well in what was an extraordinarily stressful situation, gave a much-needed boost to Anna's spirits. She no longer felt so tired and fractured when she addressed the troops in the ops room.

Detectives Sweeny and Mortimer had already briefed them on the dramatic events at the house in Dulwich. She was told that Craig Sullivan and Lorna Fitzpatrick were now in the custody suites and would be represented by the same lawyer who had turned up an hour ago.

'Quinlan is still spouting no comment,' DS Khan said. 'He doesn't yet know what we've got on him and the duty solicitor is on standby because I told him you'll be wanting to talk to his client.'

'I'm going to formally question all three of them,' Anna said. 'But only about a possible connection with our own investigation. If there isn't one, which I now suspect is the case, then we'll be handing the scumbags over to the National Crime Agency.'

Anna sent one of the civilian staff to inform the two legal reps that she would soon be along to interview their clients.

'Before I get stuck into that I'd like to know if we've made progress elsewhere,' she said.

She was told that what Michelle Gerrard had said about the incident in Bromley was true. Mark Rossi had been asked about it and recalled what had happened. But he apparently hadn't realised that she was the same woman who went on to abuse him online. DI Benning was still trying to get the lowdown on Mark Rossi's stepbrother, Joseph Walsh, who

309

had apparently moved to Australia after selling his mother's home in Camberwell. Before Benning set off for Roy Slater's house in Rotherhithe, he'd told the team that he was waiting to hear back from the Australian embassy. Someone there was trying to find out if Walsh was still in the country.

And they still hadn't managed to find the homeless man named George, who until recently was sleeping rough outside The Falconer's Arms pub in Camberwell. Anna was disappointed because she knew it was possible he had seen whoever had taken Jacob there to put him in the cellar.

After the briefing, Anna collected her notebook and asked Walker to sit in on the interviews with her.

They were on their way to the custody suites when her phone rang. It was DI Benning, calling from Roy Slater's house in Rotherhithe.

'I'm about to make your day, ma'am,' he said when she answered it. 'We've had a breakthrough.'

Anna stopped in the middle of the corridor and felt her stomach clench into a hard ball.

'Well spit it out, man,' she said. 'What is it?'

'We've found Jacob Rossi's mobile phone and wallet. As you know he had them with him when he went missing. They were in a drawer in Slater's bedroom.'

CHAPTER FIFTY-EIGHT

It was indeed a major breakthrough. According to Benning, the phone and wallet found in Slater's house had most definitely belonged to Jacob.

'The wallet is exactly how his parents described it to me,' he told Anna. 'It's a canvas trifold type with a Velcro fastener. It's personalised with the name Jacob embroidered on the front. Inside are his house key, about three quid in loose change, and a few boiled sweets.'

'And the mobile phone?'

'I found the phone next to the wallet in the drawer. It's a Samsung Galaxy. The battery has been removed which is why it hasn't been transmitting a signal.'

'And you're sure it belonged to Jacob.'

'Positive. It's in a leather case and his name is written on the inside.'

'I don't suppose Jacob's rucksack is also there is it?'

'Well if it is we haven't come across it,' he replied.

Every muscle in Anna's body was suddenly taut, her shoulders rigid. The phone and wallet provided an unambiguous link between Roy Slater and Jacob. For whatever reason the guy had decided to keep them in the house instead of getting rid of them. It was conclusive evidence that he was involved in the boy's abduction, either alone or in cahoots with someone else.

'It's a crying shame that the bastard is dead,' Anna said. 'Unless he had an accomplice who we can collar we may never know what he was planning to do with the boy.'

She told Benning to gather up Slater's personal stuff, including all his paperwork and digital media devices.

'Bring them back to base with the camera and wallet,' she said. 'I want to know what he's been doing and who he's been seeing. And we need forensics to sweep the property as soon as possible.'

Anna was flush with excitement as she broke the news to Walker.

'Let's go tell the team before we talk to Quinlan and the others,' she said. 'We need to rethink our approach to the interviews anyway in light of this development.'

Inevitably the team were delighted with the news and they responded enthusiastically when Anna dished out more tasks. These included going through Slater's phone records, drawing up a list of known associates, and talking to all his work colleagues.

'I don't want this getting out until Jacob's parents have been informed,' she said. 'That will have to wait until tomorrow. By then we will hopefully have established whether there's a link with Quinlan and the sex traffickers. And we should be in a better position to answer their questions in respect of circumstances and motive.'

She paused there as an unsettling thought wormed its way

into her brain. Then: 'I've just remembered what Mark Rossi said about his brief affair with Slater's wife, Ruth. He told me his own wife Clare knows nothing about it, and that it would kill her if she finds out. But it's hard to see how that can now be avoided.'

*

As soon as Anna walked back into Interview Room Two she sensed that Neville Quinlan was nearing the point where he was ready to cough up. The duty solicitor had no doubt marked his card about the police having fresh evidence against him.

He looked pale and drained, his eyes throbbing with fear and exhaustion.

After Walker switched on the recording equipment, Anna announced who was present and then got straight down to business.

'The last time we spoke you told us that you were out walking by yourself last Monday when Jacob Rossi was abducted,' she said. 'We then established with the help of CCTV footage that that was a lie. The truth is you met a man in a pub and then went off with him in his car. That man was Craig Sullivan, who is involved in the trafficking of children for sex.'

Quinlan's mouth dropped open and he started to breathe faster as he fought back the panic.

Anna's mind suddenly flooded with images from the video clip she'd seen of him raping the Romanian boy. She bit down hard on her lip, determined to keep her temper in check.

'I asked where the pair of you went when you left the pub

but you refused to tell me,' she said. 'And I understand that you've continued to say no comment in response to questions from my colleagues. Is that so, Mr Quinlan?'

'You know very well that that's the case, Detective Chief Inspector,' the duty solicitor said. 'Can you therefore get to the point? You've indicated to me that as a consequence of further information coming to light you would like to ask my client more questions. So what are they?'

Anna leaned forward, resting her elbows on the table, and fixed Quinlan with a hard stare.

'First you need to know, Mr Quinlan, that a few hours ago we arrested Craig Sullivan and his associate Lorna Fitzpatrick at a house in Dulwich where three children were being held against their will and used as sex slaves.'

Quinlan blinked as though he'd been caught off guard and a pulse started to throb in his left temple.

Anna continued. 'We spoke to the children and one of them, a young Romanian boy named Darius, described how you raped him when Sullivan took you to the house last week. He also told us that you were a regular visitor there.'

'He's lying,' Quinlan shot back. 'I've never been to any house in Dulwich and I've never met anyone named Darius.'

'You're the one who's lying again,' Anna said. 'You see unbeknown to you there are spy cams in the bedrooms at the house and you were filmed in the act. I've seen for myself what you did to that boy, and the video will be used as evidence when it comes to trial.'

Quinlan stopped blinking and clenched his eyes shut. Next to him the duty solicitor slumped back in his chair, shaking his head.

'The National Crime Agency will be responsible for the

investigation into what has been going on in that house and they'll charge you in relation to the offences you committed there,' Anna said. 'The questions I intend to ask relate to the boy who died while chained to the wall in the pub cellar in Camberwell. And let me tell you that you'll be digging an even deeper hole for yourself if you don't answer them truthfully.'

Quinlan sat there without responding, his eyes closed, his shoulders stiff with tension.

Anna cleared her throat, said, 'So tell me, Mr Quinlan, did you act as a talent scout for Craig Sullivan by telling him where and when his people could abduct Jacob Rossi? And what is your connection with a man named Roy Slater?'

Quinlan's eyes sprang open then and Anna saw that tears had breached the lower lids. Rather than meet her gaze, he raised his head and stared up at the ceiling. It was several seconds before he began to speak, and when he did the words came out in a tortured wail.

CHAPTER FIFTY-NINE

After her session with Neville Quinlan, Anna grilled Craig Sullivan and Lorna Fitzpatrick. In both cases it was like trying to squeeze blood out of a stone. On the advice of their lawyer they said as little as possible and only answered her questions when he gave them the nod.

It was eight o'clock when she decided she had got as much out of them as she was ever likely to get. She asked Walker to contact the National Crime Agency.

'Tell them they can come and collect all three of the scumbags,' she said. 'And make sure we pass on all the video recordings from the interviews.'

Anna planned to hold another briefing so that everyone was kept abreast of what was going on. Detectives Benning and Prescott were on their way back from Rotherhithe with Jacob Rossi's phone and wallet, plus some of Roy Slater's personal belongings. And DCS Nash was due to arrive at any minute, having spent another day at the Yard with the Met's senior management team.

Anna decided she needed a cigarette break before the meeting got underway. On the way out to the rear car park she grabbed a coffee from one of the vending machines.

The night had closed in and the cold air made her wish she had put her jacket on. As she lit up, she tried to tune out the wail of sirens that came from every direction. The riots were in full flow again and she had to force herself not to think about all the harm that was being done to people and property across London. Instead, she focused her mind on the events of the day. And what another extraordinary day it had been.

She'd begun it by dropping Chloe off at the hospital to be with Tom. Soon afterwards she had found herself racing across South London to a house where despicable things were being done to children. Then later she had rushed to the scene of a murder, where she had stood over the body of Roy Slater, the man who'd been in possession of Jacob Rossi's mobile phone and wallet.

It had been like a ride on a nerve-racking rollercoaster. Her emotions were still spinning and she felt limp with fatigue.

She consoled herself with the fact that the mystery of who had kidnapped Jacob appeared to have been solved. But there were still far too many unanswered questions for Anna's liking.

And for that reason she wasn't prepared to signal the winding down of the investigation just yet.

*

Anna was on her way back up to the ops room when she received a call from DI Bolt, who was still at the crime scene in Bermondsey.

'I've got a couple of updates for you, ma'am,' he said. 'Is it convenient to talk?'

'Of course. What's the situation there? Any problems?'

'Nothing we can't handle at present. We did get some more back-up so thanks for weighing in on our behalf. The scene's secure now, and as you're probably aware the action has moved away from this manor to the London Bridge area.'

'Actually, I haven't heard that,' Anna said.

'Well it's only just flared up. One mob descended on the tube station, caused a lot of damage there, and then moved on to the Shard building where there's now a battle with riot cops. Another bunch rampaged through Borough Market and a few shops are on fire.'

Anna pulled a quick breath and felt a chill race over her skin.

'I'll get across it when I'm back in the office,' she said. 'Meanwhile, tell me what you've got.'

'Well first we struck lucky with CCTV footage,' he said. 'There's a private security camera outside one of the shops close to the alley. We managed to retrieve it and confirm what we suspected. A group of five youths wearing hoods and masks can clearly be seen attacking Slater as he walked from the betting shop towards the car park. They dragged him into the alley, then reappeared five minutes later and scarpered. It'll be difficult, if not impossible, to identify them since their faces are covered.'

Well thankfully that's not my problem, Anna thought to herself.

'So Slater just happened to be in the wrong place at the wrong time,' she said.

'That's about the size of it. And from the CCTV we know that the time of the attack was twelve-thirty. As soon as I get the chance I'll email the CCTV clip to you.'

'Thanks.'

'I also contacted the betting shop manager,' Bolt said. 'He told me that Slater was a regular there and had been for a couple of years. It suited him apparently because he drank in a pub just along the road.'

Bolt then confirmed that forensics had swept the alley and Slater's body had been taken away, along with his car.

Before hanging up, Anna told him what her officers had found at Slater's house, and said the details would be sent on to him.

When Anna returned to her office, she found DCS Nash waiting for her. The boss was in his early fifties, tall and broad-shouldered, with a grey beard and a blunt, square face.

Anna had never seen him looking so tired. His eyes appeared heavy and dry, and his voice sounded like gravel in his throat.

'I hear we've identified the perp in the Rossi case,' he said. 'It makes a change to get some good news. It's been nothing but murder and mayhem these past few days, and still there's no end in sight to the bloody riots.'

'But it's not all good news,' Anna pointed out. 'Roy Slater is dead, and there's a lot we don't know about what he did and why he did it.'

Nash shook his head. 'Well you need to neutralise those negative thoughts, Anna. I want us to flag this up as a result for the MIT. And then I want us to pull back from the case until the riots are over. We need to reassign all but a couple of the team. I'll arrange for a press conference at which I'd like you to also mention how you uncovered the child brothel in Rotherhithe before the NCA takes the credit for it.'

'But there are still leads that have to be followed up, sir. And we haven't even informed the parents yet.'

'You can break the news to the parents before the presser, which probably won't be before tomorrow afternoon. And I'm not saying we should drop the investigation entirely. Just let it be known that Roy Slater kidnapped the boy and was subsequently knifed to death in an unconnected attack by a gang of youths. You can mention the note that was sent to the parents and which we now assume came from Slater. But there's no need to let on about Slater's wife having had an affair with Jacob's dad.'

Anna felt uncertainty beat in her heart. It was surely too soon to shout from the rooftops while easing back on the investigation.

Nash must have sensed her concern because he patted her on the shoulder, and said, 'These are unprecedented circumstances, Anna. The Commissioner has issued an instruction that all investigations not connected to the riots need to be either put on hold or run with a skeleton crew.'

'But this case *is* linked to the riots. It was a rioter who threw the petrol bomb into the pub, which led to Jacob's death.'

'I appreciate that. But you're not actually looking for the arsonist, are you? And I doubt we'll ever find whoever it is unless someone phones in with a name or turns up here with mobile phone footage of it taking place. And so I can't justify leaving you with a team of a dozen or more when the Rossi case is now all but solved thanks to what was uncovered in Slater's house.'

'Well at least let me keep the team together for one more day, sir. I need to satisfy myself that we've covered every angle and I can work out what to say to the media.'

Nash rubbed a hand over his face and nodded.

'That seems reasonable. I'll get back to you with the time and place for the press conference.'

'Thank you, sir. Will you be returning to the Yard?'

'I will first thing in the morning. The set-up over there is like a wartime command centre. You wouldn't believe how hard it is to know where and how to assign our limited manpower and resources when so much shit is happening.'

Anna nodded. 'I can imagine. I've just been told that the latest trouble spot is London Bridge.'

'That's one of many. There's a lot of bother again in Tottenham, Peckham and Stratford, and mobs are even heading towards the Yard from both ends of the Embankment. Riot police are in place to push them back, but it looks as though there's going to be one hell of a battle.'

'Sounds like it's being organised to me,' Anna said.

'Oh, much of it is. We understand that some of the targeting is being coordinated through social media, especially Facebook and Twitter. There are now dozens of hashtags relating to the riots and they're all trending. It's aimed at stretching our resources. We can't be everywhere, but the rioters can if they can mobilise enough support and so far that's not been a problem for the gangs and anarchists behind it. Some of the spooks at MI5 are even speculating that the Russians have got involved in order to make things worse. They believe they're behind some of the incendiary online posts and rants that are encouraging riotous behaviour.'

Nash said he would say something about the riots at the briefing, prompting Anna to glance through her office window into the ops room.

'I think we can get on with the meeting now, sir,' she said. 'It looks like everyone is here.'

CHAPTER SIXTY

Nash took the floor after Anna had called everyone together for the briefing. He had an audience of eleven, including DI Benning and DS Prescott, who had just arrived back from Roy Slater's house in Rotherhithe.

Nash told the team how pleased he was that the Jacob Rossi case had been resolved so quickly.

'I'm sorry I haven't been here to lend a hand,' he said. 'But myself and other senior officers have been coordinating the Met's response to the riots. It's been a mammoth struggle, and as you all know the situation on the streets has deteriorated since the video of those officers beating the girl was posted online.'

He went on to describe the current situation and made mention of the disturbances at London Bridge and the battle that was looming between police and rioters on the Embankment close to Scotland Yard.

'The strain this is putting on manpower is intolerable,' he said. 'Thankfully this latest development in the Rossi case means that we can scale back on the investigation so in the days ahead some of you will be reassigned to other duties.'

Nash then said that he was confident the forces of law and order would eventually prevail and normality would return to the capital.

'We have been here before, notably back in 2011, and it has never taken the city that long to recover,' he said. 'But until the streets are safe once again, I implore you all to be careful out there.'

He then handed over to Anna before slipping out of the room.

She could tell that what Nash had said about scaling back the investigation had taken them all by surprise. So the first thing she did was reassure them that they still had plenty of time to make sure they hadn't missed anything.

Referring to the notes she'd hastily drawn up, she started to work her way through all the points she wanted to raise.

'I'll start with the paedo, Neville Quinlan,' she said. 'A short time ago I confronted him with the evidence from the house in Dulwich, including the video clip from the hidden camera that recorded him raping the boy. He had no choice but to fess up to being a customer of the trafficking gang to which Craig Sullivan and Lorna Fitzpatrick belong. But he continued to deny any involvement in the Jacob Rossi abduction, and we know now that he was otherwise engaged when it took place.

'He also said that he did not tip the gang off about the boy's route from school to home. And he insisted that he didn't know and had never heard of Roy Slater. Both Sullivan and Fitzpatrick said the same, and I'm convinced now that they're telling the truth. I can't in all honesty believe that any of them sent that note to Jacob's dad. But I can believe it came from Slater. So unless evidence emerges that proves they're lying we forget them and hand them over to the NCA.'

Next Anna passed on the updates from DI Bolt, saying that the CCTV footage showed that the Slater murder was not linked to Jacob's kidnapping.

'He was another victim of mob madness,' she said. 'It seems he drove over to Bermondsey on Friday to visit his favourite bookmakers' about the same time The Falconer's Arms pub was hit by the petrol bomb. So Slater would not have been aware that the pub was on fire. We'll therefore never know if he would have attempted to rescue the boy if he'd been alerted.'

Anna explained that Slater's Renault car would be examined and that forensics would search inside it for traces of Jacob's DNA.

'For now the assumption has to be that he snatched Jacob by himself,' she said. 'He was probably waiting in his car for the lad to walk past him last Monday, then grabbed him and shoved him in the boot before taking him to the pub cellar. His motive is less clear. Either he was out to get revenge on Jacob's dad for screwing his wife. Or he was planning to extract a ransom payment to sort out whatever gambling debts he'd racked up. It could very well have been both.'

She invited detectives Benning and Prescott to talk to the team about the visit to Slater's house in Rotherhithe.

It was Benning who stood up and pointed to a cardboard box on the desk in front of him.

'We brought back most of his small stuff and paperwork,' he said. 'His laptop and clothes, along with Jacob's mobile phone and wallet, are with forensics.'

'What about the rucksack that Jacob had with him when he vanished?' Anna said. 'Was that in the house?'

Benning shook his head. 'Definitely not. We searched every room and the loft as well. It was obvious to us that he was a man of few possessions and my guess is he sold most of what he had to fund his gambling addiction. There are a couple of his bank statements in the box and they show a big overdraft in his current account.'

Benning pointed out that they didn't come across anything to suggest that Jacob had ever been in the house, and there were no photographs or newspaper clippings of him or his father.

Before Benning sat down, Anna asked him if he had heard back from the Australian embassy about Mark Rossi's step-brother, Joseph Walsh.

'Not yet, ma'am,' he replied. 'I'll call them again after the meeting.'

'Great. It's one of the loose ends I want tied up. Tomorrow we'll try to pull everything else together and go tell the parents. The boss is also keen to stage a press conference so before then we need to know everything there is to know about Roy Slater.'

Anna was then told that two officers would be on duty in the ops room overnight and she encouraged everyone else to go home to bed. She had her own notes to type up but decided to leave them until tomorrow.

As she was collecting her coat and bag from her office, DI Benning popped in. Seeing him up close gave her a bit of a shock. He looked really rough. His eyes were sunken and shadowed and his face was a ghostly pallor.

'Are you feeling OK?' she asked him.

'I'm just tired and gutted,' he said. 'It's all so fucking sad. To think that poor Jacob probably died in that hellhole of a cellar because his father played around with another man's wife.'

Anna nodded glumly. 'I know what you mean. And I dread the thought that Jacob's mum will now learn about it. Breaking the news about Slater tomorrow won't be easy.'

'That's why I'd like to be there with you, ma'am,' Benning said. 'Would that be possible? You see, I still feel that I let them down. I should have found their son before he died and I didn't. I failed.'

'I was intending to take you with me anyway,' she said. 'It will probably have to be in the morning first thing. Do you want me to pick you up?'

'No, I can either make my own way there or meet you here. Just let me know what time.'

'I will. Now try to get some rest, Detective. You look as though you really need it.'

When he was gone, Anna put on her coat, turned off her office light and headed for the car park. On the way she called Chloe to let her know that she would soon be picking her up from the hospital.

CHAPTER SIXTY-ONE

Anna drove the whole four miles from Wandsworth to Camberwell with her heart thumping in her chest.

Along the way she passed through areas that were eerily quiet, with few people and little traffic. But in others she bore witness to more shocking acts of vandalism and looting.

Whilst stuck in traffic outside one clothes store, she watched, open-mouthed, as a group in hoodies bundled inside. Most headed straight for the shelves while others pulled out cash registers and searched storage rooms.

The worst of the trouble was in Brixton. Two shops were ablaze in Coldharbour Lane and the fire brigade were not in attendance. Among the people gathered on the pavement were two uniformed police officers who were yelling into their radios.

Everywhere Anna looked there were groups of excitable yobs charging around in hoods and balaclavas, tipping over rubbish bins, screaming abuse, smashing windows. Fortunately, it being a Sunday evening, there weren't that many vehicles on the roads for them to hurl missiles at.

Anna had her closest shave with the rioters when she arrived in the centre of Brixton. Cops in full riot gear had formed a protective barrier in front of Lambeth Town Hall, which was under attack from an angry mob.

The officers were being bombarded with rocks, sticks and bottles, and they were struggling to hold their line. Nearby a currency exchange was being ransacked and across the road from it a police car was on fire outside the iconic Ritzy cinema.

It was all such a distraction for Anna that she came within a whisker of running down two hooded youths who stepped into the road in front of her.

She managed to slam on the brakes and bring the car to a screeching halt just a couple of feet away from them.

The taller of the pair stuck two fingers up at her even though she mouthed the word 'sorry' at him. The other one screamed 'fucking stupid bitch' and gobbed onto the bonnet. Then they both rushed towards the front doors, giving the distinct impression that they were intent on pulling her from the car.

Anna reacted instinctively by flicking on the locks, and as the pair reached for the door handles, she stamped on the accelerator and the car shot forward.

She heard one of them cry out and then saw the tall one in her rear-view mirror hopping about on one leg, his face creased up in pain.

She had obviously run over his foot, and at any other time she would have been mortified. But now she responded with a grin and a chuckle.

'Serves you fucking right,' she said aloud to herself as she steered the car on a course for King's College Hospital.

*

Tom gave her a big, beaming smile when she approached his bed.

She felt a tidal wave of relief because he looked so much better. The familiar glint had returned to his eyes, and the cuts and swellings on his face from the beating he took appeared less pronounced.

Chloe jumped up from the chair next to the bed and walked into her mother's arms.

'I've missed you, Mum,' she said.

Anna spotted straight away that her daughter looked worn out. Her features were white, brittle, her movements sluggish.

'And I've missed you too,' she said.

Anna let go of Chloe and gave Tom a kiss.

'And it goes without saying that I couldn't wait to see you again, Mr Bannerman,' she said. 'How are you?'

'I'm much better than I would be if this young lady hadn't been here to keep me company,' he said, looking at Chloe. 'She's made me laugh, she's been my gofer, and she's kept the boredom at bay.'

Anna grinned. 'I'm so glad.' Turning to Chloe, she added, 'Does that mean you'd like to come back tomorrow?'

Chloe hesitated and Tom responded for her. 'Actually, we've had a chat about that, Anna. We've really enjoyed each other's company but I don't think it's fair to expect her to hang around for another whole day. Most of the time I'm asleep, when I'm not I'm being poked and prodded by doctors and nurses. She'd be better off at home with all her stuff and where she's not surrounded by scores of unwell people.'

'Would that be all right, Mum?' Chloe asked.

Anna grimaced. 'Not really, my love. I've got to work so I won't be able to stay with you. And I don't want to leave you by yourself.'

'But I'll be fine,' Chloe said. 'I'm not a baby any more. So please let me.'

Anna gave it some thought and eventually gave a reluctant nod. 'Well I suppose it will be all right if you promise not to open the door to anyone or go outside. And I could get Peggy from next door to keep tabs on you.'

'That's settled then,' Tom said and gave Chloe a wink.

Tom then enquired about the Jacob Rossi case, and he and Chloe reacted with delight when Anna told them that they had identified the man responsible for abducting the boy. But this turned rapidly to disappointment when they learned that Roy Slater was dead.

'Well at least he won't be doing harm to any other kids,' Tom said.

Anna didn't stay long because she knew that the later it got the more dangerous it would be driving home. Tom understood and told her to be careful.

'Call the hospital to let me know that you got home safely,' he said.

Anna promised that she would and told him she'd come to see him tomorrow.

'Take care, my love,' she said. 'And if there's anything you need, then just let me know.'

Anna held on to Chloe's hand as she exited the hospital and walked to the car. She was dreading the two-mile journey to Vauxhall, and the thought that they might run into trouble was causing the blood to thunder through her veins.

Once behind the wheel she told Chloe to buckle up and cross her fingers. Then she started the engine, locked the doors and turned on the radio.

CHAPTER SIXTY-TWO

Presenter: *'This is the BBC news at ten o'clock . . . Rioting is continuing tonight in several cities across England. The most serious disorder is once again in London where police are advising people not to leave their homes unless it's absolutely necessary.*

'Violent clashes are taking place between riot police and mobs in Brixton, London Bridge, Tottenham and Peckham, and we're receiving reports of a major confrontation on the Embankment as hundreds of rioters try to reach the Scotland Yard building over-looking the Thames.

'It's now known that at least eleven people have died in the riots, and many more have been injured. The number of arrests is approaching five hundred, and it's estimated that over a hundred buildings have been destroyed by fire.

'The Prime Minister has just issued a statement to reporters in Downing Street, which began with a

commitment to restore order and reclaim the streets from the rioters.'

Prime Minster: *'These are indeed dark times for this country and I can assure you that we are doing everything we can to bring the riots to an end. Thousands of police officers are being deployed along with hundreds of army personnel, and I would like to pay tribute to their bravery. I would also like to send my condolences to the families of those police officers and members of the public who have been senselessly killed.*

'Nothing can excuse or justify what is happening, and those behind the violence and destruction of property will be dealt with harshly by the courts.

'At the same time this government will seek to remedy the serious social problems that have led to the disorder to ensure that it doesn't happen again. These problems include the gang culture that exists in our towns and cities, the fact that many young people feel alienated and disaffected, poor job prospects for those living in deprived areas, and a growing mistrust of politicians and the police by large numbers of people.'

Presenter: *'Meanwhile, only half of those people who've lost their lives in the riots have so far been named. Among them is Jacob Rossi, the ten-year-old boy who died while chained to a wall in the cellar of a derelict pub in Camberwell that was set on fire. Police are still searching for the person or persons who abducted Jacob last Monday while he was on his way home from school and then held him captive for four nights. They're also appealing for* *information on the rioter who threw the petrol bomb into the pub that started the blaze.*

'Jacob's father is the television presenter Mark Rossi, who lives in Bromley with his wife, Clare. In the last hour he spoke publicly for the first time since learning of his son's death.'

Mark Rossi: *'It's impossible for me to put into words how we feel about what has happened. All I can say is that his mother and I are devastated. Jacob was a wonderful, loving son and he meant everything to us. We still can't believe that we will never see him again. Whoever imprisoned our boy in that cellar doesn't deserve to live. It was beyond cruel and we just can't bear to think how he must have suffered during all those days and nights when he was alone in the dark with his wrists chained to the wall. The person who caused the fire in that building must also bear responsibility for Jacob's death. I appeal to anyone who has information to pass it on to the police.'*

Presenter: *'That was Mark Rossi, whose son Jacob died tragically on Friday. Now before we go I have to bring you some late breaking news. The Scotland Yard press office has just announced that the Metropolitan Police firearms officer who accidentally shot and killed a pregnant woman during a raid last Tuesday has been murdered.*

'It was the death of twenty-seven-year-old Grace Fuller that sparked the riots. She was the wife of alleged drug dealer Warren Fuller, and was in the bedroom of their

home in Balham, South London, when police burst in. The fatal shot was fired by officer Barry Noble, who has been on suspension while an internal investigation was carried out.

'Mr Noble, who was thirty-five and married with two children, was repeatedly stabbed by an unknown assailant when he answered the door to his home in Fulham earlier this evening. He was rushed to hospital after his wife rang for an ambulance, but there was a delay in it getting there and he died on the way.

'Scotland Yard did not release the identity of the officer who shot Mrs Fuller, but it's understood that Mr Noble's name was leaked and published on social media several hours before the attack. We'll bring you further details when we get them.'

CHAPTER SIXTY-THREE

The journey home thankfully passed without incident, but it was slow and unpleasant nonetheless.

Chloe seemed so nervous that she didn't speak, which allowed Anna to listen to the news bulletin uninterrupted. And what she heard shocked her. Eleven people dead. Five hundred arrests. A hundred buildings destroyed. Plus, the brutal murder of firearms officer Barry Noble.

Mark Rossi's heartfelt words added to the sense of despair that was growing inside her. Vivid images of the man's son chained to the wall in the cellar crashed back into her mind. She could picture Roy Slater standing over him, grinning maliciously as he took the photo that he sent to the family home.

Anna's shoulders were high with tension as she stepped through her front door behind Chloe. It was good to be home, but the house felt cold and weirdly claustrophobic.

'You go upstairs and put on your PJs,' she said to her daughter. 'I'll make us both a mug of hot chocolate, which should help us relax before we call it a night.'

Anna turned up the heating and put on the kettle. She was tempted to switch on the television to check on the latest situation with the riots, but decided to wait until Chloe was in bed. She knew that she was going to find it hard to get to sleep herself. She felt too uptight, and a dark unease had pushed its way into her mind.

The hot chocolates were poured and on the table by the time Chloe came down in her pyjamas and dressing gown.

'Do you want anything to eat?' Anna asked her.

Chloe shook her head. 'I'm not hungry. I ate lots of stuff at the hospital.'

'Then drink this and try to get a good night's sleep.'

Her daughter's face was gaunt and colourless, her eyes sagging with exhaustion. But was it any wonder? In just a single month the poor girl had experienced more pain and trauma than many people experience in an entire lifetime.

'Thank you again for staying at the hospital today,' Anna said. 'It was very grown up of you and it clearly meant a lot to Tom.'

Chloe shrugged. 'I didn't mind. Really. Will he be all right on his own tomorrow?'

'Of course. The doctors and nurses will look after him and I'll pop in to see him. Are you sure you want to be here by yourself?'

Chloe nodded. 'I'll stay in my bedroom for most of the time. I won't get bored and I promise not to leave the house.'

'Well before I go, I'll ask Peggy and Ron next door to keep an eye on you. There's no sign of trouble in this area now and hopefully the louts won't be coming back.'

Anna curled her hands around the warm mug and sipped at the chocolate.

After a beat, she said, 'Do you want to talk some more about when you got upset today?'

Chloe licked her lips and heaved a sigh. 'Not really. I just felt so sad when I saw that picture of Ryan. I can't stop thinking that he died because he helped me. If I talk about it now I'll cry.'

Anna put a hand on her shoulder. 'Don't worry then. I understand perfectly.'

Chloe drank all of her chocolate and said she was ready for bed. Anna stood nearby while she cleaned her teeth. Minutes later she tucked her beneath the duvet and kissed her goodnight.

'I'll have to leave early in the morning,' she said. 'I've got a lot to do.'

'Are you going to tell that boy's mum and dad that you've found out who put him in the cellar?' Chloe asked.

'I am indeed, sweetheart. And I'm really not looking forward to it.'

*

Back downstairs, Anna went straight into the living room. She switched on the television, opened a window, and lit a cigarette.

She only smoked indoors at times when she felt really stressed out. And this was one of those times. Her mind resolutely refused to switch off and kept grinding away at all the things that had happened over the past twenty-four hours. She had never known a time during her seventeen years on the job when so many wheels were frantically turning in her head at once. And it was striking how everything was linked in some way to the riots.

Jacob Rossi was killed because someone threw a petrol bomb into the pub where he was imprisoned.

Tom was in hospital because rampaging thugs had attacked him.

Chloe had spent hours on the riot-torn streets trying to stay alive.

Roy Slater was stabbed to death by one of the many gangs who were brazenly committing criminal acts.

And still the violence and disorder continued to rip London apart.

A pulse thundered in Anna's temple as she once again watched the coverage on the news. The Embankment had been turned into a battleground as police and rioters clashed close to Scotland Yard. Riot shields were being hammered by missiles, and in several shots officers could be seen lying injured on the ground.

There was trouble elsewhere too. Two buses were on fire at London Bridge while a mob was causing mayhem down in the tube station there. Meanwhile there was now widespread looting of the posh shops along Bond Street in the West End and Brompton Road in Knightsbridge.

Anna sat glued to the coverage for over twenty minutes. In order to steer her thoughts away from the riots she had to switch the TV off. She wanted to focus on her own investigation, which to all intents and purposes had been solved.

Or had it?

She couldn't put her finger on why she was nervous about closing the case down just yet. It wasn't solely because she didn't like to be rushed into it. It was more than that. She was troubled by a niggling doubt that it might not be as clear-cut as it appeared to be.

Roy Slater may well have gone to Bromley last Monday to abduct Jacob Rossi. But not having the answers to all the obvious questions that followed on from that made Anna nervous.

Did Slater have an accomplice?

Why did he bother to keep hold of Jacob's phone and wallet, but not his rucksack?

Why did he choose that particular pub in Camberwell to hide the boy?

And if he was planning to ask the father for money, why didn't he mention that in the note he sent?

This last question was the one she was really puzzling over. She didn't understand why Slater, having taken the boy, did not demand a ransom. After all, money must surely have been as important to him as revenge.

It felt to Anna as though her job was only half done. But because of the riots the pressure was on her to call it a day and move on to something else. And she was reluctant to do so.

She went into the kitchen and poured herself a glass of wine, then sat at the table and fired up her laptop. She decided that if she wasn't going to be able to sleep she might as well make use of the time by searching for at least some of the answers.

She began by going through the case notes, including those provided by DI Benning on the missing persons investigation following Jacob's disappearance. She reread all the statements, the forensic reports, newspaper cuttings.

She checked back through what Mark Rossi had told her and then the interview with Gavin Pope and his wife. Was it possible, she wondered, that Pope and Slater had colluded in the boy's abduction? After all, they both bore a grudge against Rossi because he slept with their wives. Pope claimed that he hadn't told Slater about his own wife's affair, but perhaps he was lying.

And then there was the fact that Pope's wife had been based for a couple of weeks in a recruitment agency office so close to The Falconer's Arms. Was it possible that she had earmarked the pub as a place to hide Jacob?

Anna then went online in the hope that she might come up with something of interest through Google.

She spent the next hour typing names into the search engine. Mark Rossi. His late father, Isaac Rossi. Roy Slater. Gavin Pope. The Glory Entertainment production company.

But she didn't stumble upon anything new or in any way interesting until she looked up The Falconer's Arms pub in Camberwell. It appeared on a list of London boozers that had closed down in recent years. And it was also the subject of an old newspaper feature that had appeared in a local rag to mark the pub's thirtieth anniversary.

There were lots of photographs, some of which showed how the building had changed both inside and out over the years. But one photo caught Anna's attention. It was of a group of bar and restaurant staff, and it had been taken on Christmas Day twenty-five years ago.

Among those smiling for the camera was a blonde woman in a black trouser suit who was identified in the caption as Hilary Metcalfe.

Anna immediately seized on the possibility that she might be the same Hilary Metcalfe who had been Isaac Rossi's partner before he left her and married Mark's mother, Emily.

It was Emily who had told Anna that Hilary had been

living in Camberwell at the time of the woman's death from cancer five years ago. But Emily had also said that she'd never heard of The Falconer's Arms pub.

So had Emily told the truth? Or was it just a coincidence that her grandson had died beneath that particular pub all these years after that photo was taken?

It was too late for Anna to check it out now, so she printed off the picture and added it to her to-do list for tomorrow.

She knew that it probably wouldn't turn out to be any kind of smoking gun. But it was certainly something that needed to be followed up at the earliest opportunity.

CHAPTER SIXTY-FOUR

Anna was awake at the crack of dawn, having managed only a few hours' sleep.

She switched on her bedroom TV to find out what had happened on the streets overnight.

And a lot had.

Riot police had beaten back the mobs on the Embankment before they were able to cause any damage to Scotland Yard, but eight officers were badly injured in the process.

No less than twenty premises along Bond Street and Brompton Road were invaded by rioters, among them the top designer stores of Burberry, Louis Vuitton and Tiffany & Co.

Meanwhile, at London Bridge a man was badly beaten when he tried to stop thugs entering his restaurant, and a woman was critically injured in hospital after she was hit on the head by a brick thrown by a rioter in Brixton.

All the news channels gave comprehensive coverage to the murder of firearms officer Barry Noble. There were photos of him and footage of his home where the crime took place.

The reports also mentioned the sickening social media posts from people who reacted by expressing 'delight' at the death and describing the killing as being 'fully justified'.

So even before she got showered, Anna could feel the blood fizzing in her ears.

After she was dressed, she made two phone calls. The first was to Phillipa Moore, the family liaison officer who was still on duty at the Rossi home. Anna told her she would be dropping by this morning with some news on the investigation.

'If possible I'd like Jacob's grandmother, Emily, to be there,' she said.

'I can go and pick her up,' Moore replied. 'She doesn't live far from here.'

Anna then phoned DI Benning on his mobile. He was still at home and agreed to meet her in Bromley.

'By the way, I came across something interesting last night,' she said, and then told him about the old photo of Hilary Metcalfe at The Falconer's Arms pub.

'Let me have the URL and I'll see what I can dig up,' he said. 'But why are you bothering to pursue it, ma'am? The case is solved isn't it?'

'Too many questions remain unanswered,' she said. 'But I'll talk it through with you when we meet up.'

Anna woke Chloe up with a cup of tea and some biscuits. Her daughter wasn't ready to get out of bed so Anna told her to lie in for as long as she wanted.

'I'll speak to Peggy and Ron next door on the way out,' she said. 'You've met them so you know they're a nice couple, and they'll be in here like a shot at the first sign of trouble. Now are you sure you'll be all right here by yourself?'

'I'm sure, Mum. Now let me go back to sleep.'

*

There were warnings on the radio that the start of the working week would bring chaos and gridlock to London because of the damage caused by the riots.

Some of the roads were closed, but most remained open and traffic flowed along the main arteries in and out of the city.

It helped that after another night of anarchy the rioters had dispersed, no doubt to rest up and decide what areas to target later in the day.

It was evident, too, that a great many commuters had opted to stay at home, having seen the startling images on the television.

So for Anna the drive to Bromley wasn't half as bad as she'd expected it to be. DI Benning was already there, parked up in his Audi in front of the Rossi house. He got out when she pulled into the kerb behind him.

Before going inside, Benning asked her about the old photo she had come across, which showed the staff at The Falconer's Arms pub.

'I messaged the link to you before I left,' she said.

'I know and I've seen it.'

'So what do you think?'

'Well it really wouldn't surprise me if the woman identified in the photo as Hilary Metcalfe is also Isaac Rossi's ex-partner. We've already established that the woman lived in Camberwell before she died so does it matter that she worked in that pub all those years ago? I thought we'd accepted that Roy Slater abducted Jacob.'

344

Anna shrugged, knowing that the rest of the team, along with DCS Nash, would probably ask the same question.

'I just think it's one hell of a coincidence,' she said. 'I also want to be sure that Hilary's son – Joseph Walsh – is definitely in Australia. So you need to keep chasing that up with the embassy.'

'I did put in another call last night but the bloke I've been dealing with had gone home.'

'Then try again today. The sooner we can rule him out the better. You see, I'm still not a hundred per cent convinced that Slater was working alone. That's why I also want us to have another go at Gavin Pope. He knew Slater and worked with him.'

'But of course that wasn't the only thing they had in common – both their wives had affairs with Jacob's dad.'

'Precisely. And he had no one to corroborate his alibi that he was at home by himself on Monday afternoon when Jacob disappeared.'

'But we've gone down that road, guv. We interviewed the couple and their phone records were checked.'

'I know that. But we'd be doing a lot more if we hadn't come up with the incriminating evidence against Slater. So all I'm saying is that before we wind up the investigation we ought to satisfy ourselves that we're not missing anything.'

Benning nodded. 'That's fair enough. I'll get back onto the Australian embassy as soon as we've wrapped up here. And I'll check to see if that old photo can lead us anywhere.'

CHAPTER SIXTY-FIVE

Jacob's parents and grandmother listened in stunned silence as Anna told them about Roy Slater, including the fact that the man had himself been killed. The depth of their pain was evident in their stricken expressions. And in Mark Rossi's eyes Anna saw the unmistakable glimmer of guilt.

'The fact that Jacob's phone and wallet were found in his house leaves us in no doubt that he was responsible for your son's abduction and incarceration,' she said. 'At this stage there is no evidence to suggest that anyone else was involved, but we are continuing to explore that possibility.'

Clare Rossi was the first to react, saying, 'Is this the same Roy Slater who used to work for Glory Entertainment?'

'It is, Mrs Rossi,' Anna said.

'But that was a long time ago. And as I recall he and his wife left before the company went bankrupt . . . He wasn't one of those who felt that Mark's father had let them down. So why would he have done this to our boy?'

Anna didn't want to ramp up the woman's suffering by

alluding to Mark's affair with Slater's wife, Ruth. So she said that the man's motive was something they had yet to determine.

'What we do know is that Slater had a serious gambling addiction and so he may have had a financial incentive for doing what he did,' she said.

Clare was about to say something else, but her husband got in first with his own question, which Anna guessed was aimed at deflecting the conversation away from Slater.

'What about the bastard who threw the petrol bomb into the building?' he said. 'Do you have any idea who it is?'

Anna shook her head. 'Not at this time, I'm afraid. But we won't stop looking.'

She then ran through the salient points of the inquiry and pointed out that the police were due to hold a press conference later in the day.

'After that I expect you'll be badgered by the media again,' she said. 'Officer Moore will stay with you as a point of contact and she'll make sure the hounds keep their distance.'

By this time Clare Rossi was an emotional wreck and the FLO stepped in and offered to take her upstairs. Mark's mother got up at the same time to go with them, but Anna asked her to stay for a few minutes.

Anna then showed Emily the old photo of the staff at The Falconer's Arms pub.

'It was taken twenty-five years ago and shows a group of people who were working there back then,' she said. She then pointed at the blonde woman in the black trouser suit. 'That lady is identified in the caption as Hilary Metcalfe. Do you happen to know if this is your late husband's former partner?'

Emily squinted at the picture for several seconds and then nodded.

'I never met the woman, but when Isaac died I found some old photos taken when they were together,' she said. 'And yes, I'm pretty sure that's her. I had no idea she worked at that pub, though.'

'Neither did we.'

'But is it relevant now?'

'Only if it enables us to shed some light on why Jacob was placed in that particular pub cellar,' Anna said. 'It's probably just a coincidence but I'd like to be sure. And to that end we're still trying to track down Hilary's son, Joseph, who we believe to be in Australia.'

'Well if you do would you be so kind as to tell him that I would like to get in touch with him?' Emily said. 'I've never spoken to him, but I'd like the opportunity now to tell him that his father wasn't the bad man he thought he was. Isaac always regretted not staying in touch with his son, and as I've already explained to you I was part of the reason that he didn't.'

Anna assured her that if they tracked Joseph Walsh down, she would pass on the message.

After Emily went upstairs, Anna again offered her condolences to Mark and said that if any other facts surrounding his son's abduction came to light, she would be in touch.

She left it to DI Benning to mention the big fat elephant in the room.

'It might be wise to come clean with your wife about your affair with Ruth Slater,' Benning said. 'There's a very good chance that it will come out now, and it might be better if she heard it from you first.'

They left the man to make up his own mind, and he didn't say a word as they walked out of the house.

CHAPTER SIXTY-SIX

The two detectives headed back to Wandsworth in their own cars. On the way Anna called King's College Hospital to check on Tom. She was told that he'd had a comfortable night and that his condition was continuing to improve.

That put a spring in her step as she walked into the ops room at MIT HQ.

The air in the room oscillated with tension as Anna got on with the briefing. She said that she and DI Benning had been to see Jacob Rossi's parents and that they'd be going public with Roy Slater's name at a press conference later.

'But as I made clear yesterday, I want us to spend today pulling together all the threads and loose ends,' she said. 'I'm concerned that there's still a lot we don't know, including whether Slater had an accomplice.'

DS Khan had provided the first update. He had followed up the fact that Gavin Pope's wife had spent two weeks at a recruitment agency in Camberwell.

'I went there and spoke to the manager,' he said. 'But he

349

never heard Mrs Pope mention The Falconer's Arms and he didn't think she acted suspiciously at all. Most days they all had lunch together and after work he assumed that she drove straight home.'

'So now go back and interview her and her husband,' Anna said. 'Her working in Camberwell was probably another co-incidence, but see what she has to say. And press Pope on his relationship with Slater after they left the Glory Entertainment production company where they worked together. Pope told us he hadn't spoken to the guy in months, but he may be lying.'

She told the team about the old photograph of Hilary Metcalfe at The Falconer's Arms pub.

'It's a tenuous link to Jacob's abduction, I know, but it's a link nonetheless. DI Benning will be looking into it. Those other members of staff in the picture are also named in the caption and they might still be living in the area. So we should see if we can talk to them. At the same time DI Benning will try to find out if Hilary's son, Joseph, is indeed in Australia. If he is then he's in the clear, but if he isn't it raises all kinds of questions. We know from what we've been told that he's harboured a grudge all these years because his father, Isaac, left him and his mother to take up with Emily and her son, Mark. What we don't know is if Joseph knew Roy Slater and got together to cook up the plan to abduct Jacob.'

Finally, Anna asked DI Walker and DS Prescott to wade through all the documents and personal belongings that were brought back from Roy Slater's house in Rotherhithe.

'See if you can find anything that tells us how and why he kidnapped Jacob,' she said.

CHAPTER SIXTY-SEVEN

Almost an hour passed before things started to happen. First DI Benning came to her with an update that was disappointing but not entirely surprising.

'Just got word back from the Australian embassy, ma'am,' he said. 'They've confirmed that Joseph Walsh, formerly Joseph Metcalfe, is indeed resident down under and hasn't left the country since he moved there four years ago. They're coming back to me with contact details for him.'

'Well at least that's one loose end we've tied up,' Anna said.

Ten minutes later DS Prescott came striding into her office waving a small piece of paper.

'You're not going to like this, guv,' he said. 'It's a receipt that was found in one of Roy Slater's jackets.'

He placed it on the desk in front of Anna. She looked at it and frowned. It was a cash receipt for drinks at a well-known casino in London's West End. But she couldn't see why it was significant.

'Look at the date and time of issue,' Prescott said.

'Three-twenty on Monday of last week. That was when Jacob Rossi was taken.'

Anna felt a tight spasm in her chest as she studied the details on the receipt.

'I just called the casino,' Prescott added. 'They still have security footage from that day on their server. I've arranged to go straight over there to look at it.'

'And if Slater makes an appearance, we'll know that he couldn't have snatched Jacob.'

Prescott nodded. 'So either he had nothing to do with it or you're right to suggest that he did it in collusion with someone else.'

Anna told Prescott to hurry over to the casino and report back ASAP. She then broke the news to the other members of the team before phoning Nash to tell him to postpone or cancel the press conference. He wasn't happy but agreed that they had no choice.

There were two further developments during the next hour. Anna heard back from the detectives who had gone to re-interview Gavin Pope. He wasn't at home, and according to a neighbour he and his wife had left their home in Richmond on Sunday morning and hadn't yet returned. And they weren't answering their phones, which set off an alarm bell in Anna's head.

She was still trying to get her mind around what was happening when DC Sweeny approached her with another update.

'The guy who runs a greasy spoon café near The Falconer's Arms pub just called me,' she said. 'He's one of the people who told us that a rough sleeper named George regularly bedded down outside the pub until just over a week ago.'

'Ah yes, any word on him?' Anna said.

'Precisely that, ma'am. He's back in the area apparently and he's pitched up at one of his usual spots across the road from the café. Do you still want to talk to him?'

'Too bloody right I do. He's the only potential witness we have. You and I will go and see him. Tell the café owner not to let him out of his sight before we get there. Or better still get him to offer the guy something to eat and drink and I'll reimburse him.'

Anna decided that she would make the most of the trip to Camberwell to drop in on Tom at the hospital.

She was stepping out of her office to brief the others on the developments when Prescott phoned her from the casino.

'I've seen the CCTV footage, guv,' he said. 'It shows that Roy Slater was here from two p.m. to ten p.m. last Monday. So there is no way he could have abducted Jacob Rossi while the boy was walking home from school.'

*

So I was right to be concerned about winding down the investigation too soon, Anna told herself. Now there were even more questions that needed to be answered.

But as various scenarios unfolded in her mind, she struggled to make sense of any of them.

From the start, the investigation had been less than straightforward, and it had been hampered by the riots at every stage. Somewhere along the line they must have missed something.

But what?

She updated the team before heading over to Camberwell

to talk to the rough sleeper. They were all just as confused as she was by the latest turn of events.

'We're trying to track down Gavin Pope to question him again about his relationship with Slater,' she said. 'But he's not at home or answering his phone. So I want us to throw everything at trying to find him. Meanwhile, the homeless man we've been looking for has finally turned up so DC Sweeny and I are going to Camberwell now to have a chat with him. He's back on one of his regular plots near The Falconer's Arms. It might well be a waste of time, but there's a chance he saw our kidnapper coming and going between Monday and Friday while Jacob was locked up in the pub cellar. If so, he may be able to provide us with a description.'

Anna then asked if a forensics team had visited Roy Slater's house yet and was told that they hadn't.

'I wouldn't bank on them finding anything else when they eventually do turn up,' DI Benning said. 'Me and Detective Prescott searched it thoroughly and the only things we came across were Jacob's phone and wallet.'

Anna nodded. 'In that case there are several questions we need to find the answers to. Was Slater looking after those objects for an accomplice? Or did someone who knew he was a suspect plant them there for us to find? And where the hell is Jacob's rucksack?'

CHAPTER SIXTY-EIGHT

Presenter: *'This is the BBC news at one o'clock . . . A man has been arrested in connection with the murder of police firearms officer Barry Noble. Officer Noble was stabbed to death last night when he answered the door to his house in Fulham.*

'The twenty-nine-year-old man being questioned has not been named, but it's believed he lives in the same area of London.

'Officer Noble shot and killed a woman during an armed raid in Balham six days ago, and it was this incident that sparked the riots. Scotland Yard has insisted that it was an accident but an internal inquiry was launched. Meanwhile, the Metropolitan Police Commissioner, Gary Trimble, condemned the killing during a press conference, which has just ended.'

Commissioner: *'This was a savage, unwarranted attack on a man who devoted his life to protecting the* *people of this great city. His wife and children have been left devastated and we will do everything we can to ensure that the person responsible for this heinous crime will not escape justice.'*

Presenter: *'Commissioner Trimble also responded to criticism that the force had been ill-prepared and ill-equipped to respond to the scale of the riots that have rocked the capital over the past week.'*

Commissioner: *'There are indeed lessons to be learned from what is happening. And I'm sure that our politicians now accept that in a city the size of London it is grossly irresponsible to continue cutting back on police numbers and resources. These riots clearly demonstrate that law and order can only be maintained if there is sufficient commitment and investment.'*

Presenter: *'The Commissioner also hit out at social media companies for allowing their platforms to be exploited by those who are trying to marshal support online for the riots.'*

Commissioner: *'There's mounting evidence that criminal gangs are brazenly encouraging people to descend on specific targets, which include shopping areas. One Twitter post that went viral this morning named a high street and said that it was full of shops waiting to be ransacked. And another Tweet pointed out that the riots offered a fantastic opportunity to those who wanted to make a lot of money just by turning up.'*

Presenter: *'As that press conference was taking place there were fresh outbreaks of violence in town centres across London, including Clapham, Eltham, Brixton, Notting Hill and Vauxhall. More from our reporters . . .'*

CHAPTER SIXTY-NINE

The mention of more trouble in Vauxhall caused Anna to panic.

DC Sweeny was driving so she took out her phone and speed-dialled Chloe's number.

She suddenly regretted her decision to leave her daughter at home alone. What the hell had she been thinking?

But when Chloe answered on the fourth ring, she quickly put her mother's mind at ease.

'It's quiet outside and the street is empty,' she said. 'I can hear sirens but they sound a long way off. And the people next door have already been in to check on me.'

'That's a relief,' Anna said. 'What are you doing?'

'Having something to eat. I haven't long been up. And I'm OK, so don't worry.'

'I'll try not to. Just don't forget what I said about staying indoors, and phone me if for any reason you get scared.'

As they approached Camberwell, it was strange seeing that things had almost returned to normal. Traffic was moving and there were pedestrians on the streets. A lot of the shops were boarded up either because they'd been vandalised or because the owners had decided not to open them.

The route to the café took them past The Falconer's Arms. The police and forensic officers were long gone and it was back to being a derelict building that nobody was paying any attention to.

The café was just around the corner from it, and as they pulled up outside there was no sign of any rough sleepers.

'I expect the owner did as we suggested and invited him inside,' Sweeny said.

Anna's phone rang as she was getting out of the car. It was DI Walker with some news about Gavin Pope and his wife.

'We've solved the mystery of why they're not at home and haven't been answering their phones,' he said. 'Turns out they've been to visit his parents who live down in the New Forest. The house is in an area with no mobile signal. They're heading back now and we've arranged to talk to them. Meanwhile, we haven't come up with anything concrete that implicates them in Jacob's abduction.'

'That doesn't mean they weren't involved, so let's pursue them until we're sure,' Anna said.

'Will do, guv. Have you arrived in Camberwell yet?'

'Just. The roads were pretty clear so we didn't have any problems.'

'And have you touched base with the homeless guy?' Walker asked.

'We're about to,' she said.

*

There were only four people inside the café and it was obvious to Anna right away who it was they had come to see.

He was sitting at a corner table tucking into a plate of egg, chips and baked beans.

Sweeny spoke to the café owner who told them the guy's name was George Rigby and he didn't know that the police wanted to speak to him.

'He's a pleasant enough bloke,' the owner said in a thick South London accent. 'He's been hanging around these streets for as long as I can remember. And this ain't the first time I've let him have a meal on the house.'

As Anna approached George Rigby it occurred to her that he appeared typical of the almost four thousand homeless people who were rough sleeping on the streets of London.

He was bundled into a dark overcoat and had lank, shoulder-length grey hair that clearly hadn't been washed in weeks.

When Anna reached the table he looked up at her and smiled, revealing a random scattering of yellow teeth.

'Do you mind if I join you, Mr Rigby?' she said, pulling out a chair. 'And before you answer, I should tell you that I've asked the owner over there to feed you until you're full and then to give you a goody bag when you leave.'

He stared at her for several beats, his eyes shot with blood. Then he spoke in a voice that was gravelly from too many fags and poor health.

'Suit yourself,' he said. 'Are you some kind of social worker then? Is that it?'

Anna took out her warrant card and showed it to him.

'I'm a police officer,' she said. 'Detective Chief Inspector Anna Tate.'

At that moment Sweeny joined them at the table.

'And this is my colleague Detective Constable Sweeny,' Anna said.

Rigby's eyes stretched wide as he looked from one to the other, clearly confused.

'So what am I supposed to have done then?' he asked, sitting back in the chair.

Anna smiled. 'Absolutely nothing as far as I know, Mr Rigby.'

'Then what's this about? Why are you being nice to me?'

An empty ache touched the pit of Anna's stomach suddenly. The man opposite her looked so pitiful, and she couldn't help feeling sorry for him. She guessed he was in his fifties or early sixties but she really couldn't be sure.

She watched him shove a chip into his mouth and wondered when he'd last eaten a proper meal.

The café owner came over with a tray of teas and placed three mugs on the table. Anna waited until he'd gone before answering Rigby's question.

'We want to ask you about The Falconer's Arms pub,' she said. 'As you probably know there was a serious fire there on Friday.'

He nodded. 'I heard that a lad was killed. The bloody estate agents or owners should have made sure nobody could get inside. But I didn't start it if that's what you think. I haven't been there for over a week now – I've been kipping in the doorway of an empty shop over near the leisure centre instead.'

'We know the fire had nothing to do with you,' Anna said. 'A mob of youths turned up there and one of them threw a petrol bomb.'

He gritted his teeth. 'Bloody animals. It's hard enough finding somewhere safe to bed down without them causing all this trouble. I've been living on the streets for four years and I've never known anything like this.'

'Neither have we, Mr Rigby,' Anna said.

She paused then while he ate another chip and washed it down with some tea.

'We've been told that you used to sleep in the doorway of The Falconer's Arms,' she said.

'That's right, and I'll be going back there soon I hope. It's set back from the road so I don't keep getting disturbed. And it feels like home as well because many years ago I worked there behind the bar.'

Anna was taken aback. 'We didn't know that, Mr Rigby.'

He shrugged. 'Well you do now. Best job I ever had. But then fifteen years ago me and my wife, who's now dead bless her, moved to the other side of London so I had to pack it in. Shame it closed down. I reckon it was the best boozer around here.'

Anna reached in her pocket for the old photo showing the group gathered in the pub.

'I downloaded this from the internet,' she said, handing it to him. 'It was taken twenty-five years ago and shows some of people who worked there then. Do you recognise any of the them?'

He examined it carefully through half-closed eyes.

'This was before my time,' he said. 'But yeah, I knew about half this lot.'

Anna pointed to the blonde woman. 'What about her?'

He nodded. 'Yeah, that's Hilary. Nice lady she was. In fact, I saw her son recently. He came up to me a little over a week ago and paid for me to stay in a hotel for a fortnight.'

Anna felt the air crash out of her lungs and it was Sweeny who responded first.

'Is that really true?' she asked him.

'I ain't got no reason to lie,' he said. 'He told me that the pub owners had made complaints about me but if I disappeared for a while it would blow over and I could then come back. He said he didn't think it was fair and he felt sorry for me. So on the Saturday before last he picked me up in his car and drove me to this little place in Blackfriars. He paid them in advance for bed and breakfast for two weeks and gave me some cash to keep for spending. Now don't get me wrong. The hotel is a pile of crap, but I wasn't complaining. I had a warm bed to sleep in and cooked breakfasts every day for a week.'

'I thought he paid for two weeks,' Sweeny said.

'That's right, he did. But the manager kicked me out because I spent the money I was given on booze, got drunk and chucked up in reception. So I found myself back on the streets sooner than I expected. I thought it best to steer clear of the pub so that's why I ended up near the leisure centre.'

Anna leaned over the table, ignored the awful smell that assaulted her nostrils, and said, 'I need to be clear about this, Mr Rigby. You're saying that Joseph Walsh, Hilary's son, paid for you to stay in a hotel so that you would move away from The Falconer's Arms.'

He frowned. 'I don't know anyone named Walsh.'

'We're led to believe it was Hilary's married name. Before that she was Hilary Metcalfe.'

Rigby stuck out his lower lip and Anna could see that he was becoming even more confused.

'We've found out that Hilary died five years ago from cancer,' she said. 'Joseph then sold the house they lived in near here and moved to Australia.'

Rigby shook his head. 'You've got this all very wrong, Detective. I may have lost a lot of things in recent years but not my memory. First of all, Hilary never married anyone named Walsh. I met her husband plenty of times when he came into the pub. It's where they first got together. And their son has always been known as Joe, not Joseph. I also know for sure that Joe didn't sell up and move away. He still lives around the corner in Devlin Road. In fact you might even know him.'

'What makes you think that?' Anna said.

'Well because he's a bleedin' copper.'

'Are you serious? What's his name?'

'Benning. Joe Benning.'

CHAPTER SEVENTY

It felt to Anna as though she had been punched in the stomach.

She exchanged a look with Sweeny, whose mouth hung open as though waiting to trap a fly. Neither of them could believe what Rigby had just told them about DI Benning. It was ridiculous, obscene, too far-fetched to be taken seriously.

Surely.

'Why are you looking at me like that?' he said to Anna. 'I'm telling you the truth. Ask Pete if you don't believe me.'

'Who's Pete?' Anna said.

He gestured towards the café owner. 'That's him. Joe is a regular in here. I know because when he sees me sitting across the road, he always makes a point of crossing over and giving me some change. He's a generous bloke.'

Anna sat still for a few moments as the blood beat in her ears. Then a thought occurred to her and she took out her phone while Sweeny got up to go and speak to the café owner.

Anna tapped *Jacob Rossi press conference* into the Google

search engine, having remembered seeing Benning stage a presser the morning after the boy went missing.

She found it in seconds and held her phone up for Rigby to see.

'Is this the man you're talking about?' she said.

He nodded without hesitation. 'That's him. That's Joe. He's always been pleasant to me – treated me like a proper human being, unlike most people.'

Anna's mind spun wildly as she tried to make sense of what she'd been told. But it didn't make sense. How could it? Benning was the detective who led the investigation into Jacob's disappearance. Anna recalled him being visibly shaken when he walked into the cellar and saw that the lad was dead. He was then desperate to stay with the case when MIT took it over. Anna just couldn't imagine that he had written the note that was sent to Jacob's dad. She was reminded now of those hateful words.

I'm sick of seeing you boast about your perfect life on social media, Rossi. You've had it too good for too long and that's not fair. You act as though you're special and more deserving than the rest of us. So I've taken your son because I want to see you suffer. And I'm sure you will when you're sitting at home wondering what I'm doing to him. Pleasant dreams, Mr big shot TV man—

Her mind screamed and her heart raced. And questions came crashing down on her.

Did it all start when Isaac Rossi abandoned Joe and his mother all those years ago?

Did Joe find it impossible to forgive his father?

366

How much damage did it do to him psychologically when his father married and Mark became Isaac's stepson?

And did he become insanely jealous when Mark's career took off, thanks in part to his stepfather's TV production company?

Was that why he hated Mark so much and wanted to see him suffer?

Anna was still deep in thought when Sweeny returned to the table with the café owner in tow.

'Mr Fowler has just confirmed what we've been told,' she said. 'He's met Joe Benning many times.'

'That's true,' the man said. 'He usually pops in once a week. It used to be a lot more often before he was transferred from Peckham police station to Bromley. I've always felt sorry for the poor bugger.'

'Why is that?' Anna asked.

'Well he's had a tough life. He's talked to me about it a few times. His daughter was killed by a reckless driver aged just six. Then his wife left him and since then he's not had much of a life outside his work. To top it all, a few months ago he was diagnosed with some kind of dementia.'

'Benning told you about that?'

'He came in here straight from the hospital because it was too early for the pubs, and he was really upset. I asked him what was wrong and he broke down, which I didn't expect. The place was empty so I sat with him and we talked about it.'

'See I told you both that I didn't make it up,' Rigby said as he continued to stuff his face, oblivious to the huge bomb he'd just dropped.

Anna thanked them both and signalled for Sweeny to follow her outside.

'Were you aware that Benning has dementia, guv?' Sweeny asked when they were stood out on the pavement.

'I was, but I was sworn to secrecy,' Anna said. 'It's early onset so he was carrying on working. But he was aware that this case was likely to be his last and I thought that was why he was so passionate about sticking with it.'

'Well he did a good job of hiding his condition from the rest of us. I would never have guessed, but then I suppose he hasn't been around us long enough for it to have become obvious.'

Anna reached for her phone and called DI Walker.

'Something's happened and I need you to run some checks for me,' she said when he answered. 'But first is DI Benning there with you in the ops room?'

'No he isn't,' Walker replied. 'He rushed out of here just after you left saying he had to go somewhere. I thought it was odd because it looked like he was in a panic. I left it a few minutes and went looking for him but the front desk told me he'd driven off in his car. He still isn't back.'

'Then we need to move quickly,' Anna said. 'I want you and the others to drop everything else and find out as much as you can about the guy. Get his home address and come straight back to me with it. Then get a team together and head there yourself. Also, Benning has been telling us that he's been liaising with the Australian embassy in respect of Joseph Walsh. Contact them and find out if it's true.'

'This all sounds pretty weird, guv,' Walker said. 'What in hell's name is going on?'

'It's more than weird, Max. Two people have just told us that Hilary Metcalfe's real married name was Benning, and not Walsh. And that DI Benning is her son and therefore Mark Rossi's estranged stepbrother. And one of them – George

Rigby, the homeless guy – says Benning paid for him to stay in some cheap hotel for a fortnight to keep him away from The Falconer's Arms.'

'Jesus Christ. Where are you now?'

'Not far from the pub. We've been told that Benning lives close by in Devlin Street. Sweeny and I will go there now, but I want you to confirm that is where he lives and get me the house number.'

'Have you phoned him?'

'I'll do that next. But ask the techies to trace his mobile signal because I don't expect him to answer.'

'Do you think he's doing a runner?'

'That's highly likely. When I told the team that the home-less guy had turned up, and that I was coming to see him, he must have realised that the game was up.'

'But this is crazy, guv. One of our own detectives is now our chief suspect. Do you really believe he could be the one who abducted Jacob and shut him in the cellar?'

'All I can say is that I don't think these guys are lying. And Benning was really keen to work with us after the body was found. That could be because he wanted to be on hand to muddy the waters and try to steer us in all kinds of directions and away from himself. Just think about it. Benning was the one who found Jacob's phone and wallet when he and Prescott went to Slater's house. So who's to say he didn't put them in that drawer as soon as he arrived? He might have been carrying them around with him while waiting for just such an opportunity. Or they could have been hidden in his car.'

'That didn't occur to me.'

'Or to any of us.'

'Well you need to be careful, guv. It could be he's heading home.'

'I'm aware of that. So get some back-up down here as quickly as you can.'

Anna hung up and called Benning's number. She wasn't at all surprised when it failed to go through.

CHAPTER SEVENTY-ONE

Sweeny knew the way to Devlin Street so they got in the car and headed there. By the time they reached it three minutes later, Walker had already sent her a text confirming that Benning lived there and giving her the house number.

Twelve.

'That's Benning's Audi parked outside,' she said as they drove up behind it. 'I saw it in Bromley this morning. So he must have arrived back here while we were in the café.'

'Shouldn't we wait for back-up?' Sweeny said.

Anna nodded. 'We probably should, but we don't have time.'

It was a Victorian terraced house with bay windows and a small front garden. Anna led the way along the path to the front door, her heart pumping like a turbine.

'Joe's not in,' someone shouted. 'You've just missed him.'

It was an elderly woman and she was in the garden next door. They hadn't spotted her because she was kneeling on the paving slabs behind the hedge while picking weeds out of a plant pot.

Anna asked her how she knew.

'He came home about ten minutes ago and then rushed straight out again,' the woman said. 'I tried to speak to him, but he was in such a hurry that he ignored me and walked off along the street.'

'Was he carrying a case or bag?' Anna said.

'No, but he was holding a bottle of what I think was whisky.'

'Do you have any idea where he was going?'

'None at all, but he didn't take his car so it's probably not far.'

Anna was now convinced that Benning was their man and it rattled her to the core.

'So what do we do, guv?' Sweeny asked her.

Anna made a quick decision and showed her warrant card to the neighbour.

'We need to get inside Mr Benning's house,' she said. 'I don't suppose you have a key.'

The woman shook her head. 'I'm afraid I don't.'

Anna turned back to Sweeny. 'In that case we'll force our way in.'

But in the event, they didn't have to. The door had been left ajar so all Anna had to do was push it open.

There was a large hallway with stairs and two rooms leading off it, one the lounge, the other the kitchen. And it was in the kitchen that Anna saw the note that Benning had left for her to find. It had been hastily scrawled on a sheet of white A4 paper.

Detective Tate
I've been preparing for this day since my diagnosis,
but it's come sooner than I thought it would because of

what's happened. I want you to know that Jacob wasn't
meant to die. So please tell his parents that I'm so very
sorry that he did. I just wanted to see his father suffer
like I have all these years. No one else was involved so
you can stop wasting precious police resources on the
case. I know that you'll be coming for me after you talk
to old George, so it's time for me to go.
   DI Benning

Anna's mind seized again on that memory of when Benning
entered the cellar and was told that the dead boy on the
mattress was Jacob. She remembered him blurting out: *'Oh
my God this wasn't supposed to happen.'*

He had then gone on to say that he had promised to bring
the boy home to his parents, which was why Anna hadn't
considered it to be a strange reaction.

Threads were now beginning to weave together in her mind
and hopefully there would soon be answers to the questions
that had been plaguing her. But at the same time she was
confronted now by two new questions. Where had Benning
gone? And was he planning to run away or top himself?

'Sounds to me like he's planning to take the easy way out,'
Sweeny said after reading the note. 'Or in his case the only
way out.'

They carried on looking around the house, and in the room
that Benning used as a study they came across a file folder
full of newspaper cuttings featuring Mark Rossi and going
back years. They also found the rucksack that Jacob had been
carrying when he was taken.

'Well that's another mystery solved,' Sweeny said.

Anna called Walker and got him to put out an alert for

Benning. However, she knew that with the riots kicking off again not much effort would be put in to trying to find him.

'I've spoken personally to the Australian embassy, guv,' he said. 'They're adamant that nobody there has been in contact with Benning or anyone else from the team. Seems he made it all up to make us think he was looking in to that angle.'

Anna told him about Benning's note.

'Well if he is planning to kill himself then he could have stayed at home and slit his wrists or taken an overdose,' Walker said. 'So maybe he wants to make more of a drama of it and is heading for a tall building or a bridge over a railway line.'

But Walker's words prompted another thought to pop into Anna's head.

'I actually think I know where he might be going,' she said.

CHAPTER SEVENTY-TWO

Anna told Sweeny to follow her as she broke into a run.

'Forget about the car,' she called out. 'It'll be just as quick on foot.'

'Where are we going, guv?'

'The Falconer's Arms,' Anna said.

The blood pulsed and hammered inside Anna's head as she raced along the street towards the pub. It was in the direction that the neighbour had said Benning had walked off in, and it was only a few minutes away from the café.

Anna's gut was telling her that Benning had gone there because the building obviously held a special place in his heart and mind. So if he intended to end his own life then it might well be where he'd decide to do it. If she was wrong then no doubt he'd be long dead before they found him.

Her breath was constricting every time she inhaled, and when she saw the pub up ahead she felt a hot flush in her veins.

A sign had been hung on a chain across the entrance warning people that the building was unsafe and not to trespass. Anna stepped over it and jogged across the forecourt to the double doors that had been put back in place with boards across them.

She hurried around to the back of the building with Sweeny close behind her. Straight away she saw that since the fire nothing much had been done to make the place more secure. The lock on one of the back doors was still broken, and the glass that had been missing from two of the ground-floor windows still hadn't been replaced. Anna and Sweeny gained access to the badly damaged interior within seconds.

It still stank of smoke and damp, and they had to take great care as they made their way across the debris-strewn floor.

There was no sign of life in the ravaged bar area, so Anna headed for the stairs that led down into the cellar.

Shafts of light seeped through gaps in the ceiling created by Friday's fire. So even before she reached the bottom of the stairs, Anna was able to see that once again she'd been right to follow her instincts.

Joe Benning was sitting on the floor, in the exact same position where Jacob Rossi had been lying on the inflatable mattress while chained to the wall by his wrists.

The detective watched Anna and Sweeny descend the stairs. In one hand he held a bottle of whisky, and in the other what looked like a 9mm semi-automatic pistol.

CHAPTER SEVENTY-THREE

'Well I reckon that what people say about you is spot on, DCI Tate,' he said as the two detectives reached the bottom of the stairs and stepped cautiously towards him.

'And what is it they say?' Anna asked him.

'That you're as sharp as a fucking razor blade. I imagined I'd be half way to hell before anyone thought to come looking for me here.'

'So I was right to jump to the conclusion that you're intending to top yourself?'

He held up the gun. 'What do you think this is for? And don't look so worried. I'm not going to use it on the pair of you. But if you've got questions for me then I suggest you don't do anything to make me blow my own brains out before I've answered them.'

He was sitting with his back against the wall, still in the suit he'd been wearing earlier. Beads of sweat clung to his forehead, and there was a dull, lacklustre expression in his eyes.

He looked calm rather than anxious, and Anna reckoned that was partly because he was resigned to his fate and partly because he'd downed a fair amount of whisky. The bottle was half empty, and the smell of it wafted across the cellar on his breath.

'The first thing I'd like you to tell me is where you got the revolver,' she said.

He gave a small shrug. 'As you know most hardcore perps in London carry around a knife or a gun these days. So as a copper such things are easy to acquire. I nabbed it off a drug dealer months ago when I started to seriously contemplate suicide. I knew it would come in handy when I decided the time had come.'

'And that time is now?' Anna asked him.

He nodded. 'Well I've got fuck all to live for. No way am I going to spend the rest of my days in a prison cell as the dementia eats away at my mind and my dignity.'

'So why haven't you already pulled the trigger?'

He swigged back some more whisky before responding.

'I came here for a reason. I wanted to speak to Jacob, and since this is where he died it seemed like the obvious place. I wanted to let him know how sorry I am for what happened to him. And I wanted to tell him what a shit his grandfather was for leaving me and my mum. He wasn't supposed to die. I was only going to hold him for a few days so that I could watch his old man suffer. Then I intended to drop him off somewhere with all his stuff. I told him that when I brought him here, and I like to think he believed me. I took steps to make him reasonably comfortable and he didn't go without food and drink. I was shocked and devastated when I heard that some bastard had set fire to the building.'

'I'm surprised you actually thought you'd get away with it,' Anna said. She wanted to keep him talking as long as possible while she tried to think of a way to make him pull back from the abyss.

'I would have if it hadn't been for the frigging riots,' he said. 'You see, after I grabbed the boy, I brought him straight here. Then I went to the office to wait for the alarm to be raised so I'd be the detective who'd be put in charge. That was important to me because I wanted to be on hand to watch his dad suffer, especially when he read the note I sent, which unfortunately got delayed, again by the riots.'

'But what I don't understand is why you hate Mark Rossi so much,' Anna said. 'It wasn't his fault that your father left you and married his mum.'

'That's true, and in the beginning I just resented him for taking my place. But as time went on, my own life became one long nightmare. My stepdad died of a stroke way before his time, which left my mother heartbroken. Then my daughter was killed by a reckless driver who took his bloody eyes off the road, and soon after that my wife ran off with another bloke. But at the same time Mark Rossi was living the dream. My father helped his TV career prosper and he had the perfect family. He didn't stop boasting about his great life on social media, which pissed me off big time. Like it did lots of other people, including Michelle Gerrard.

'The day of my daughter's funeral he posted photos on Facebook of himself, his wife and son enjoying a holiday in the Maldives. Then a week after my wife left me he decided to renew his marriage vows in a lavish ceremony in the South of France. And it was *my* dad who made a speech describing Rossi as a terrific stepson.

'Then a few years later a lot of publicity was given to Isaac's funeral and sure enough it was Rossi who took centre stage, saying what a wonderful stepdad he'd been blessed with. When Rossi then decided to set up home in Bromley it felt like he was deliberately trying to wind me up. And that was when I started to fantasise about ways to sink his boat. But it was only when I was diagnosed with dementia that my hatred for him soared to a new level. After all I'd been through it was just so fucking unfair. All the bad stuff was happening to me and never to him. I suddenly realised that I wouldn't be satisfied unless I did something that would shatter his perfect fucking life. And something that would make me feel good for the first time in years.'

He paused there and his eyes shifted from Anna to the gun he was holding. It was now resting against his chest, the muzzle pointing at his face.

Anna took a tentative step forward, telling herself that if she could get just a little closer she might be able to rush at him and grab the gun. But as a copper himself he obviously knew what was going through her mind.

He raised the gun, pressed it into the flesh below his chin, said, 'One more step and I'll pull the trigger. So get on with it. Anything else you want to know before I depart this world?'

The breath hissed out of Anna's throat as she asked the first two questions that sprang into her mind.

'How did you know where Jacob would be last Monday afternoon? And how did you go about snatching him?'

He raised his brow and left the gun where it was. 'After I'd decided that the best way to get at his dad was through his son, I monitored the lad's movements. To my mind Jacob was too young to be walking home by himself, but that made it easy for me. He strolled past my car on two occasions before that day, but I didn't make a move because there were either other people around or other vehicles passing. But on that Monday the street was clear so it required little effort to grab hold of him and bundle him into the boot. I was wearing a false beard and a hoody so he'd never be able to recognise me, and I'd set this place up well in advance so it was ready for him to move straight in.'

'And you weren't planning to kill him?'

'Of course not. I'm not a killer or a pervert. My objective was to take his father to hell and back. Then after a few days I was going to leave Jacob in a safe place and go on sick leave so I wouldn't be the one to interview him when he was safely back home.'

'But then he was killed.'

'And that was tragic. Afterwards I knew there was a chance that it would lead back to me so I had to stay close to the investigation to try to ensure that it didn't. I thought I'd be in the clear after Slater turned up dead and I was able to plant Jacob's phone and wallet in his house. As for George, I just assumed I'd done enough to keep him away from the pub. When he turned up again I knew he'd tell you who I was and what I'd done. So that was when I rushed home, picked up the gun, and came here.'

'Why did you bring Jacob here of all places? It's more or less on your doorstep.' This from Sweeny.

Another shrug. 'It was for that very reason. I knew about the cellar and that the building was easy to get into. I also wanted to be close enough so that I could come over to check on him at night and bring him what he needed.'

'But weren't you worried that he'd scream the place down and attract attention?' Sweeny asked.

'I warned him that if he did, I'd kill him. And the chances are he wouldn't have been heard anyway.'

Anna stood there without moving, her body drenched now in a cold sweat. She knew that if she made the wrong move then Benning might not be the only one to end up dead.

She watched him guzzle some more whisky. Then he placed the bottle on the floor and held the gun in both hands.

'That's enough talking, Detective. I've used the opportunity you gave me to get a load of stuff off my chest for Jacob's sake as well as my own. I just hope the boy has been listening. But now I'm ready to go, and I hope it's obvious to you that I'm not going to let you stop me.'

Anna gulped at the fetid air, struggling to get it into her lungs. She would have pleaded with him not to go through with it if she'd thought he would listen. But she knew he wouldn't.

'I'm going to count to ten and then squeeze the trigger,' he said. 'So unless you want to see my brains splattered all over the wall and ceiling I suggest you get out of here sharpish.'

As he started to count, Anna told Sweeny to go upstairs.

'But what about you, guv?' Sweeny said.

'Don't worry about me, Megan. Just go. Someone needs to bear witness to what's going to happen next.'

Benning finished counting just as Sweeny reached the top of the stairs.

'If I could go back and change things I would, Detective,' he said. 'But I can't, and I'm really sorry about that.'

They were his last words. Anna closed her eyes and the gun went off. It was so loud in the close confines of the cellar that she feared her eardrums might burst.

CHAPTER SEVENTY-FOUR

Four days later

Presenter: '*Welcome to the BBC news at nine o'clock . . . This is the second consecutive day of peace on the streets of London and other major towns and cities across the UK. The end of the disorder is being attributed to a number of factors, including battle fatigue among the rioters, the heavy, persistent rain that has been falling on most areas since Tuesday, and the tough prison sentences that are being handed out by the courts to those convicted of serious public order offences.*

'*Arrests in connection with the riots are still taking place, and in the last hour there's been a major development in the case of Jacob Rossi, the ten-year-old son of entertainer Mark Rossi. The boy was abducted and chained up in a derelict pub where he died of smoke inhalation after the building was set on fire.*

'*His kidnapper, Met Detective Joe Benning, committed*

suicide in the very same cellar on Monday. Scotland Yard has confirmed that an eighteen-year-old man has now been charged with throwing the petrol bomb that caused the blaze. It's understood he was identified after someone posted mobile phone footage online of the incident taking place.

'Meanwhile, according to the latest figures released by the government, a total of twelve people were killed during the riots. There were six hundred arrests and four hundred people face charges. In London alone the damage is put at more than a billion pounds. This afternoon the Prime Minister addressed reporters outside Ten Downing Street.'

Prime Minister: 'At last we have reclaimed our towns and cities from the criminals who sought to destroy them. It's not true to say that we completely lost control of the situation, but there were times when it appeared to be the case.

'Thanks to the self-sacrifice and bravery of our frontline teams order has at last been restored. This government will now take whatever action is necessary to ensure it never happens again.

'A cross-party group will spearhead an inquiry that will examine the root causes of the riots and how the emergency services responded to them. We will seek to find long-lasting solutions to the social and economic inequalities that blight so many communities, the high rates of youth unemployment, the shocking cycle of re-offending, the racial tensions that persist, the mistrust of law enforcement agencies, and the epidemic of gun and knife crime.

'The way forward will not be easy, but we have to pull

together and work hard to get to where we want to be. And we must succeed for the sake of our children and our children's children.'

EPILOGUE

It was the first time Anna had ever attended two funerals in one day. First thing, she joined scores of mourners in Bromley to pay her last respects to Jacob Rossi.

There was a media scrum at the gates to the cemetery that included two television crews who were filing live reports.

During the service a friend of the family read the eulogy and there wasn't a dry eye in the chapel. Afterwards, as the coffin was lowered into the ground, Mark Rossi let go of his wife's hand and dropped to his knees next to the grave.

'We will always love you, Jacob,' he cried out. 'I'm so sorry that we weren't there to protect you. Please forgive us.'

As Anna watched from a distance she thought about the moment two weeks ago when she broke the news to him that it was his estranged stepbrother who had abducted Jacob, and not Roy Slater. Thankfully he hadn't got around to telling his wife about his affair with Slater's wife, so at least she was spared the agony of knowing that her husband had cheated on her.

Later Anna stood with Chloe in the crematorium chapel as another coffin slid towards the furnace. Inside it was one of the young men who had saved Chloe's life.

Ryan Claymore.

This was a much smaller gathering, just a handful of people including the lad's mother and father, and his best friend Wesley.

After the service, Wesley gave Chloe a small framed photograph of himself and Ryan sitting side by side on a park bench.

'This is so that you won't forget us,' he said to her.

'As if I would,' she replied, but the words were barely out of her mouth before emotion overwhelmed her and she started to cry again.

Anna folded her arms around her and pulled her close.

'Let it all out, Chloe,' she said. 'I'm here for you and I want you to know that I love you so much.'

Chloe looked up at her mother, her eyes drenched. She then uttered the words that Anna had been desperate to hear.

'And I love you too, Mum,' she said.

ACKNOWLEDGEMENTS

Once again I would like to express my appreciation for all the help I got while writing this book from the team at Avon. A special thank you to my editor Molly Walker-Sharp who found so many ways to improve the first draft I submitted to her.

Love DCI Anna Tate?
Then why not read the first
book in the series to see where
it all began . . .

Nine missing children.
The hunt is on.
But has time run out?

IN SAFE
HANDS

A DCI ANNA TATE THRILLER

J. P. CARTER

A gripping thriller that will have you
on the edge of your seat.

What happens when the past comes back to kill you?

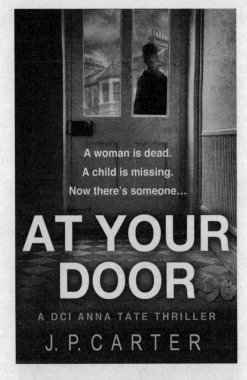

A woman is dead.
A child is missing.
Now there's someone...

AT YOUR DOOR

A DCI ANNA TATE THRILLER

J. P. CARTER

An addictive new thriller in the DCI Anna Tate series, for fans of Cara Hunter and M. J. Arlidge.